THE HANDYMAN

STEPHEN ROBERTSON

PINNACLE BOOKS
WINDSOR PUBLISHING CORP.

PINNACLE BOOKS

are published by

Windsor Publishing Corp.
475 Park Avenue South
New York, NY 10016

First printing: July, 1990

Printed in the United States of America

ACKNOWLEDGEMENTS

Organizations such as The Horror Writers of America, The Mystery Writers of America, The Writer's Guild; and such publications as THE WRITER, WRITER'S DI-GEST, and PUBLISHERS WEEKLY ultimately help in the creation of the magical illusion of fiction. Such a grand dreamer they made of me. . . .

Fiction, or dream magic, also happens when a writer and his editor connect on every level, and for this I must thank David Hirshfeld for his perception, insights and labor, as well as Roberta Grossman for being a fan.

PROLOGUE

He wasn't sure why he had cut off the other man's hands; wasn't sure of the perverse inner drive that had led him to carry through with the plan. He had rationalized much over the past hour, that he had done it to see if it were at all possible. Yes, maybe that was it after all: to test his own abilities and power over another human being. The hands were not necessarily the important thing after all. Of course, he couldn't very well have cut off the man's head; the brain must still be functioning for the experiment to work. Yet the hands were called the "visible" portion of the brain. Slicing them off like two large sausages, now that was a different story.

He liked hands.

He liked their comfortable shape and weight and size and function and all-around feel. He was, in the end, a feeling person. He liked the portability of the hands now that they were severed from the rest of the ponderous body. And he might carry them in his coat pocket if he liked, carry them to where he worked, to the café, down to the laundry room, over to the park, and take them out and gaze at the wondrous beauty in the creation of them. He could cart them about the city wherever he liked, and no one would be any wiser. Or he could do with them what he'd planned right along.

Felix would object at first, but he'd come to like the hands too, he was sure.

Felix could drive him insane at times. Sometimes, he thought Felix was insanely jealous of his hands, and this way . . . this way, Felix might have a pair of his own. The surprise might be shocking at first; Felix would call him names, tell him he was insane to do such a thing. But they both knew better.

He was not insane.

At least not in the usual sense.

What's more, he knew this.

He was super-normal, super-intelligent, too much for this world, other men, women. He'd tasted of this world long enough to feel as though he had tried everything, and he'd come away feeling short-changed.

Why did he do it? Why did he cut the hands off a man? It was too complex to analyze; and if he stopped to do so, it would all be spoiled. Yet he knew why.

Severed hands were interesting objects. They made great ashtrays, for instance.

Where he had stored them, they made interesting everyday things. His collection was not kept under glass, or behind walls or baseboards, or buried in shoe boxes or books. His collection was all round him. In fact, the bed he lay on presently had a mattress fashioned from the hands of once-living men and women. Well, not quite, but it was so in the dreams he had—daydreams too. Perhaps, one day, his dream would become a reality. For now, just learning he could do it, well, it was like other men climbing Mount Everest, or a champion swimmer conquering the English Channel. It gave him a thrill, a high, a kick like nothing he'd ever felt before.

Damn, he was good, he told himself.

He had spent his entire life perfecting his craft, and now look what he was capable of. He'd peeled away his outer clothing and had placed the two severed hands on the bed with him. They were the hands of a man who'd soon be dead; the hands of a man who'd soon be *allowed* to bleed to death, but whose bleeding, for the moment, was held in check: a kind of suspended animation.

He got up from the bed and bounced the two beauties with his movement. They spewed forth their own little reservoirs of blood onto the cover he'd placed over the mattress. He put on a robe, as the hour was growing late.

He had to dispose of the body, which for the moment was more zombie than body. He opened the door to the kitchen, where he'd left a mess in the basin where the hands had first fallen, spitting forth under the sudden pressure of the hand-held guillotine he'd used, an instrument he had fashioned and built in his workshop. For a long time he had dreamed and planned of this.

The body stood before the sink, still breathing rhythmically, still very much of this world, yet soon to be a corpse. The killer vaguely remembered that he'd first seen the man in the company of a blonde. They'd been drinking heavily, and he'd caught the man's attention when he tried to make overtures to the woman. He'd thought a woman's gentle hands would be infinitely preferable, but who was arguing now? Now that he had the hands?

There were two ugly stubs where the man's hands and part of each forearm had been; the bone was sheared clean and precise, no jagged edges. The weight on the guillotine was right after all. Despite the fact that the man's hands were missing, and his horrid wounds remained unbandaged, they remained clean of blood. When the guillotine had fallen, and his hands with it, there was no outcry. There had been no feeling.

He had accomplished the impossible. He had made real the unreal. His success ought to be applauded. He wanted to shout it to the world, but he knew the world wasn't ready. His abilities were manifold. Medicine could benefit suffering millions, anyone in pain or trauma, he had told himself, if he could perfect the "trick" of the mind. At least, that's how it had begun, years ago, when he first encountered the idea on the fringes of his own mind. It had crawled to the center of his consciousness lately, taking over everything, becoming his obsession. It had also changed, metamorphosed. It was no longer for the good of

9

mankind so much as it was for the fun.

If the human mind was powerful enough to control the flow of blood through the body, and ignore severed limbs, its power was truly enormous and great. Perhaps the human mind really was God.

He spoke to the man who would soon die. In a warm, glowing, and friendly voice he said, "Now, Oscar . . . if that is really your name"—he had reason to believe otherwise since he had rifled the other man's wallet before returning it—"we're going to go for a nice drive. I want you to put your hands now deep into your coat pockets. Don't want anyone seeing anything they shouldn't." He helped tuck the loose ends and torn coat sleeves into the coat pockets. It looked a bit awkward, yet it must do.

"What's the matter, Oscar? Don't you want to go for a ride?"

The tall, middle-aged, somewhat handsome man nodded dumbly, following him into the other room. There he shed his robe and dressed quickly. He told Mr. Rhodes-who-didn't-want-to-be-known-as-Rhodes all about his plans for him. "You've made your contribution to science, Mr. Rho—Oscar. I'll lead you now to a nice place to die so that you won't disturb anyone, too much."

"Yes," replied the handless man, "yes."

"Really very nice of you not to bleed all over my place, Oscar."

"Yes, sir . . . thank you."

"Come along now."

"Yes, sir . . ."

They went out into the lobby of the apartment complex and rode the elevator straight down into the underground parking lot and found the car. He had to open Oscar's side for him; the poor man couldn't manage the handle even if he could think to do so. "Inside, Oscar."

He looked around the lot, thinking he saw some movement at the far end, or heard a slight skittering noise. Spooky places, modern underground lots. He never felt quite comfortable in them. He always felt as if he were being watched. Funny thing. His whole life, he always felt as if someone was watching his every move. For a long time it was his father, and true enough, the old man watched him just as if he were a plant growing, and the old man wanted to see every millimeter that he grew. Even in an open lot with tall buildings all around, he had always believed someone up in some window somewhere was watching. He felt that way now in the parking lot; he had had the same feeling when he was alone with Oscar in the apartment.

Foolish feeling, and yet . . . *Oscar was there*, after all. Maybe deep down inside his frozen state he knew what was happening to him, despite his outward acceptance. Maybe if he'd had more willpower he might've resisted more and he'd still have his hands.

Still, he knew how terribly alluring his voice, his eyes, and his manner could be. He knew he was extremely good, the best. Poor Oscar/Rhodes didn't know what hit him; didn't know before, and didn't know now.

He started the engine and wheeled out of the space he was in, starting for the ramp. In his rearview mirror he saw someone had gotten out of another car and was walking toward the elevators. It was the Burroughs woman from 11C, next door to his apartment. His mind raced. How much had she seen? Had she noticed him and Oscar/Rhodes at all? Why'd she remain so long in her car? Why hadn't she popped out with that usual giddy, post-college giggle of hers and said something witty like, "Keeping late hours, or are you just going out?"

The hour was either extremely late or extremely early: three-fifty A.M. What was she doing getting in at this hour? What was he doing going out at this hour? Perhaps she was fearful he would see her; perhaps she had reason to keep her mouth shut about this, and that'd be to their mutual benefit. Meanwhile, Oscar's missing hands hadn't been seen. Hell, they were up in the apartment.

He drove out into the night. His search for a place to leave Oscar would have to be quick; yet he wanted some

11

distance between his place and where police would find the body. For as soon as Oscar's little ride came to an end, he would be a complete corpse. He would bleed to death from both severed limbs, if the hysteria didn't bring on a heart attack first. At the moment, Oscar had no idea of his condition.

ONE

The man in the misshapen, low-brimmed hat was a shock—an unexpected addition to the landscape of the dark hallway.

Willie Floyd said hello without meaning it—just wanted to get past; had much to do tonight; his mind was on his ladies. He sold a lot through his ladies. Along with a hot time, a man could make hot purchases of another kind with Willie's girls. He thought Mr. Loomis was good to him to allow him to operate his business as he saw fit, so long as Mr. Loomis got his. Willie smiled at the thought as he saw the bum crawl off the floor and start at him begging for a buck.

The corridor was narrow; the bannister rickety and creaky. Too much pressure and a guy could go right over, six stories to his death. The old-timer was white, and Willie was black, and like most whites—bum or not—the old sot thought he had the right of way. For no reason, out of his moth-eaten, drab gray coat the bum pulled the longest single-shot pistol Willie Floyd had ever seen, and suddenly his annoyance turned to fear. The stranger had taken on a whole new meaning; he seemed unreal: a Wyatt Earp stepping from out of time.

"You're gonna die, nigger," he said coldly.

The gunman smelled from two-week-old liquor, sweat, and filth. He looked wild-eyed, as if he might pull the trigger at any moment. Willie tried to back down the

13

hallway in the direction from which he had come.

He did so slowly, fearing any sudden move would set off an explosion, and his own death.

Another gunman stepped from out of nowhere. He was in Willie Floyd's face, pushing and shoving. The big, black Floyd didn't know where he'd come from; hadn't seen him until now, as he took another shove.

"I dunno who the hell you is."

"Angel-la-death, Willie. Just call me the Angel of Death. And that there's my partner, Satan." This one was black and taller than Willie. He pointed to his white friend. Both men looked as if they had just stepped from a soup kitchen or off a boxcar. The black man chewed and rolled an unlit cigar stub.

"Whatchu-talkin' 'bout? Don't jive me! What'd I ever do to you guys?"

"Took my girl, you black bastard, and this gonna take off your private parts!" The black one jabbed his Uzi into Willie's crotch; and Willie knew it had enough firepower to sever his upper and lower halves within seconds at this range.

Willie was sweating, shaking. "Hey, hey, man! You got the wrong dude, man!"

"You Willie Floyd, aint-chu?"

"Yeah, but no! I aint got nothin' b'longs to you! Never did!"

"You tell me den," shouted the thin black with the powerful weapon jammed into Willie's rib cage, "you tell me den 'bout dis sonofabitch named Tyrrell Loomis you been hangin' wid, because that sucker tol' me it was you!"

"Say what?"

He jammed the gun hard enough to make Willie double over in pain. "Blow yow brains out, mother! Now, tell me 'bout dis T-rell Loomis. Whataya know 'bout him?"

"Ok-Okk-Okkk!"

They were both dressed in the manner of bums with long coats which had effectively concealed their weapons, and had also allowed them to blend in with the shadows. One was hefty, the black one slight.

"Where's this creep you work for? What number in the building?" asked the white one.

"Aint nobody 'n dare now, brother," Willie said to the black one, his eyes imploring.

"Don't call me brother, pigshit!"

"Tell ya I don't know nothin' 'bout yow girl, man!"

"She got some bad stuff from you, Willie, and she was only fourteeeeeeen!"

Floyd suddenly grabbed the black stranger, twisted away the Uzi, forced it overhead, and pushed him into a wall and tore so hard he sent the "brother" back and over the bannister, which gave way with a ripping, crowbar sound. But the Uzi flew down eight flights; and the guy now hung onto a rail, his white pal trying to pull him up.

Willie Floyd took this opportunity to run in the opposite direction. He knew they were right behind him. Ahead of him was safety, and he shouted for Tyrell and the others to help him.

The door he was racing for suddenly burst open, and from it automatic gunfire ripped through the stairwell and corridor, splintering everything in sight, including Willie Floyd. All three men in the corridor screamed at once. Floyd's body came down on the white bum like a stone pillar, knocking the man nearly senseless. Still, Ryne Lanark, a cop in bum's clothes, felt that it was only by extreme luck that not a single bullet had passed through Floyd's body to his own, though he did feel the impact of several sucked into his police vest.

"Get back! They've got AK-47's!" Lanark shouted, firing off several rounds from his own 9-mm pistol, sending the narcotics people back behind the door. But the big black guy in ragged clothing grabbed onto Lanark, yanking, helping to free him from the trap Willie Floyd's inert form had become; this, moments before it was drilled with another peppering of bullets from yet another door that burst open.

For Ryne Lanark, it seemed like a nightmare concocted by one of those impossible computer simulations at the police academy in which a no-win situation was the norm.

Looking down into the long, gaping mouth of the corridor ahead of him—Jake Stokes, his new man on the undercover unit, breathing down his neck—Lanark watched the mesmerizing naked bulb waving wildly. Like Lanark, it had been near-missed enough times to be shaken up, yet the bulb remained intact. Lanark drew aim on it and exploded it in mid-air as it swept pendulumlike, the dark infinitely preferable to the crazy shadows.

"You okay, Lieutenant?" Stokes asked so many times that Lanark understood it was nerves. The man had almost fallen to his death moments before, and here he was, beside Lanark, facing death from another direction. Stokes had come on to replace Sergeant Maxwell Yoshikane, whose funeral was still fresh in Lanark's mind. It was a trial run for Jake Stokes, his first undercover action. He'd come up through patrol and had applied year after year for detective status with an undercover operation. He'd gone through all the paperwork, taken all the courses, had even done a long stint in fingerprints and as an evidence tech, and found himself labeled suddenly as a desk jockey. When he heard of Yoshikane's death, he'd gone directly to Lanark and made an impassioned plea for a chance to step into Yoshikane's shoes.

His timing stank, but his message was clear, and Lanark was giving him the chance he requested. And it had almost cost him his life. And it might still.

"I'm fine, Stokes."

"You telling me you're not leaking anywhere?"

"Not a drop . . . yet."

"I caught one."

"What? Where?"

"Not bad, just the ankle. Going to slow me if we have to chase. Damn," he cursed his own luck and himself.

"You did fine work back there. Had me convinced," Lanark told him.

Stokes was basketball lanky. Even in a crouch, he presented a big target. "Surprised me when he grabbed the gun. Coulda cut him in two with it, but—"

"You did fine."

"Almost-got-myself-killed-fine."

"Concentrate on the present."

"Yes, sir."

Stokes had convinced Ryne Lanark that he was an irate father about to blow Floyd away if he didn't cooperate. The man they really wanted was Floyd's supplier, Loomis, an ugly, pockmarked half-white Negro with gold in his teeth and a Satanic smile that turned his beet-colored eyes to blood. They'd studied his movements and photos taken of the man for days now. They had staked out this building for more days. They had bided their time, and had gotten information on Floyd and half a dozen others who did legwork for Loomis. Loomis was not as big an operator as many another drug dealer in Chicago, but his methods were messy; and if left unchecked, would soon result in a drug war the likes of which Chicago had never seen. No doubt, Loomis believed the men in the hallway after him were not cops, but rivals in the trade.

A shout of pain reported that one of Jake's shots had hit its target, and that the Uzi-wielding warrior at the doorway was giving second thoughts to hanging around.

But automatics gave men a false sense of invincibility and Ryne knew this. Something about the silence made Ryne feel uneasy, however. Had they bugged out on the fire escape? A set of back stairs? A dumbwaiter, or even a service elevator he knew nothing about? He hated the thought of losing Loomis.

Then Lanark heard skittering, mouselike noises, seeming to come from all around him. There were sounds from nowhere and sounds from everywhere, when suddenly a blaring tape on a ghetto blaster exploded into life with screeching electric guitars and rock music. *Poison*, Lanark thought. The rock tape was turned up to a deafening level. It smothered the sound of talking coming from ahead, the whispering through walls, and the mobilizing. It was meant to confuse Lanark and Stokes, and it was working. Stokes must have had good ears, however, for he, like Lanark, was hearing other sounds as well. Both men searched the darkness for movement.

17

"Whataya think?" Stokes shouted over the blaring sound of rock music.

"Poison!"

"What?"

"The music, it's *poison*."

"Poison on my ears."

Just then a noise, and Lanark wheeled, shouting, "Behind you!" Lanark fired six shots as the Uzi opened fire. Out of the corner of his eyes, he saw Stokes sail over the railing, unsure if he did so under his own power or if the bullets had sent him over. Two of Lanark's shots hit the assailant, one in the heart, instantly killing him.

"How'd the bastard get behind us?"

"Walls," shouted Stokes, poking his head above the landing.

"What?"

"Center walls on this floor must all be taken out. Loomis must own the whole damned floor!"

"Likely right."

"Think there're any more left behind?"

"Could be. This guy likes to feel secure."

"Wish I felt a little securer."

The firepower commanded by Loomis was too much to meet head-on. "They must have known something was afoot; Loomis was just waiting. Floyd was sent out as an expendable decoy."

"You think so?"

"What do you think?"

Stokes nodded. He was learning. Lanark, dressed in the ratty clothes of a beggar, and Stokes, disguised as a black beggar, had only fooled the now-dead Willie Floyd.

If it were a normal police raid, Lanark would have backup; he might at least call for backup. But this was no normal police maneuver, and at the moment he was not a policeman in charge of one of the most effective undercover units in Chicago. Rather, Lanark was a man bent on revenge and murder, attempting to finally put to rest the pain and anguish of his past. The only certain way to do that, he believed, was to put to rest a man called

Whitey, a former acquaintance of and friend to Loomis. Loomis might lead him to the other man. Stokes knew nothing about this "aspect" of the case they were working on.

Presently, however, it appeared Loomis had the upper hand. Tactically speaking, Lanark found himself in a bad position. A set of stairs deep in the bowels of a tenement he didn't know enough about, heavily armed men anxious to kill him, and him with his 9-mm pistol. He hadn't expected Loomis to turn on him so abruptly and with such precision.

Somewhere in the distance, Lanark heard police sirens. Stokes was heartened and encouraged by this, saying, "Cavalry's on the way, Lieutenant."

Lanark didn't want the cavalry; he wanted his hands on Loomis.

"All we got to do now is sit tight, let 'em circle the building. Get a SWAT team up here, and we can retreat. Hell, it's murder now, with big Willie lying there."

A few feet from them Floyd suddenly moaned. "Damn," said Stokes, "he's alive. How can that be?"

Suddenly, another volley of fire lit up at the end of the hallway, pumping more bullets into Floyd, silencing him completely, and sending Ryne racing for the opposite end of the corridor to where the other dead man lay. He snatched up the Uzi from the dead assailant. Stokes, from the stairs, made his way after Lanark, saying, "Oughtn't we to wait, Lieutenant? Lieutenant?"

Lanark didn't hear him. His ears were ringing from the impact of the gun blasts in the enclosed space. Besides, adrenaline had put him onto another plane of existence. He went into the room from which the back-shooter had come. He drove through this room straight through to the next, and the next, the Uzi readied and extended in front of him.

Each room was like another level in a computer game, and as he entered each, he fully expected to be fired on. He snatched open closet doors, fired through others, and kept going for the rear rooms from where the last shots had come. When he got there, he was met with an explosion of gunfire. Stokes had almost caught up when he heard battling Uzis. He saw Lanark jump back behind a doorway that was splintered and mutilated by someone on the inside firing repeatedly. Stokes saw Lanark dive into the line of fire, roll, and come up firing his own weapon, looking like a commando regardless of his shoddy attire. He blew away the assailant with a rapid blast on his Uzi, sending him crashing through a glass window to the street below, an eight-story drop. *If the bullets didn't kill him . . .*

Stokes rushed in, gun ready, but there were no more of them. Loomis had left the others as a delaying tactic, and it had worked. Stokes went to the boom box and clicked it off, the silence both welcome and startling at once.

Stokes relaxed, breathed deeply, staring at his new lieutenant in disbelief. Jake Stokes had been a policeman for six years, but never once had he believed he was going to die. He had believed it tonight no less than six times. Now he wanted to tell Lanark that what he'd done either took a lot of guts or a lot of stupidity. At best, Lanark's action was reckless, at worst, suicidal. Stokes had been warned about Lanark. He'd heard all the stories about how many of the man's partners wound up dead, and now he knew why.

Instead of saying a word about what was going through his mind, Jake simply asked, "You okay, Lieutenant?"

Lanark looked up at just the moment the double doors in the wall behind Stokes creaked almost imperceptibly. Ryne tackled Stokes, who fell with him below the rain of bullets that came showering through the thick, oak doors. Both Lanark and Stokes emptied their magazines at the wall where the doors had been blown open to display a Murphy bed that folded into the wall, now dripping with blood. The guns now silenced, the bed came careening down with a deadly thud. Behind the bed, the semi-nude form of a woman wrapped about yet another Uzi flopped to the floor with the impact.

Stokes went for her instinctively, but Lanark grabbed

20

him by the arm before he touched her. "Leave it for forensics. Don't touch a hair."

"But Lieutenant!"

"One of Loomis's old girlfriends," said Lanark. "Latasha Nadeer, unless I miss my guess."

"How can you tell?" Stokes wondered aloud, staring at the pulp of bleeding flesh they'd turned the woman into.

"Hey, partner, she almost got us both."

"This'll be fun to explain to Captain Wood and IAD."

Lanark knew Stokes was right; there'd be too damned many questions and—even if he did manage to answer them—no one would completely believe him. Internal Affairs would be on his behind like dog-crotch fleas. They'd pick it over three ways to Sunday, then they'd start over. A peck here, and a peck there. Picking, picking again, and picking some more. The Jewish word for a guy in IAD like Morris Fabia was a complete *nudge*, meaning a person who pecked and pecked at someone or some thing until it fell apart under the pressure of pecking.

"Stokes, just tell it like you saw it. We did everything by the book. We were pinned down by fire while on a drug raid. We got paper for the raid. It was all going fine when they opened up on us."

"We got paper?"

"We do."

"Then, sir, why'd we spend half the night on our butts out in that hallway, smelling like fishermen just off the damned—"

"Paper doesn't tell us how to go in; only says that we can."

"But why, Lieutenant?"

"'Cause that's how you get the ones at the top, Jake. With paper, coming in here on a routine search and seizure, we might've bagged Willie Floyd, but never Loomis."

"We still don't have Loomis, and Floyd's dead."

Stokes walked away from his lieutenant, shaking his head. Everybody said Ryne Lanark was impossible to understand and deadly to work with. Stokes was beginning to wonder about exactly how Yoshikane was killed, and he wondered why he hadn't stayed an evidence tech.

Still, hadn't the strong, handsome Lanark saved his life twice during the foray? Once at the bannister that'd given way, and just now when the woman had opened fire on them?

Other cops were now streaming into the building. Some commotion now surrounded the dead man who'd flown from the window to the sidewalk below. The first cops on the scene were pointing up to the window. Some of the cops outside had seen the man's body arch out of the window and sail down to the curb that had turned it into a kind of human curd that drained into the gutter. Lanark shouted from the window that it was over, calling out his name and rank, holding his shield up.

The police coming up the stairs saw the debris of the fight: Stokes's lost Uzi, the broken bannister, walls riddled with bullets, darkened corridors, people crying and yelling, Willie Floyd's body in their way. Stokes came out into the hallway with his shield held high, but one of the younger, white cops raised his gun to him and Stokes thought he was going to fire.

"I'm a cop, damnit!"

They reacted with distrust, rushing at him, one pushing him into a wall, turning him and about to cuff him when Lanark grabbed hold of the guy with the cuffs and threw him into the others. "Slow it down, you bunch of morons! Jake Stokes, and Lieutenant Ryne Lanark, Undercover Division, Thirteenth Precinct. Check us out! Meantime, we keep our hands and our weapons."

"Get IAD down here," ordered the sergeant who'd tried to cuff Stokes. "Lanark, sure, heard about you," he said. "You can understand where my boys might be a little jumpy. Come into a situation like this, walls blown out, see a . . . ahhh—"

"A nigger!" shouted Stokes.

"A man coming out claiming to be a cop . . . can't be too careful."

"Easy, Stokes."

"Easy?" He was emotionally fired up.

"I said, ease off, dammit!"

"This sonofa—"

"Back off, mister, that's an order!" Lanark shoved him away.

"Easy?" Stokes said into Lanark's face. "You 'bout get us both killed, and we do our level best to blow away anybody in the building, and then these honky cops rush in here like they're going to save the building from this black maniac—me!"

Lanark laughed. "Does sound bass-ackward, but you should've stayed inside the apartment where the shoot took place. Hell, they saw Willie's body out there and they freaked. No prejudice works so powerful as fear, my man!"

"Yeah, yeah, that's how it happened," said the sergeant, afraid of being called on charges of racial prejudice.

"Now, Sergeant, get one of your guys here to radio a Captain Paul Wood, Precinct Thirteen; get him down here. He'll vouch for us. We're not only cops, we're upstanding cops."

"Yeah . . . yeah," agreed the sergeant, a roly-poly man with quicksilver eyes that shifted with his thoughts. "I've heard about you, Lieutenant."

"All the best, I hope."

"You're the guy got that maniac on the subways, right?"

"No, no, that took a lot of guys, Sergeant, my entire unit, one of which is Officer Stokes here."

"I . . . I'm sorry 'bout that, ahhh, Stokes. Look like you two kicked some butt here, huh? Huh?"

"Hey, Sarge!" shouted one of his men who'd poked his head into the apartment. "They done killed a woman in here. Killed her twenty times over."

The sergeant's face and eyes shifted again, a look of horror flitting in and out of his consciousness when he asked, "She black, or white?"

"Black."

"Has to do with drugs, huh?" he asked Lanark.

"That's right."

"One helluva mess you boys made here."

Stokes laughed. It started simple enough, as a chuckle in response to the bigoted sergeant, but then it grew and grew, until it was as loud as the radio music that Loomis had left on earlier. The only one who joined him in his laughter was Lanark. Everyone else thought the two men grisly, and to be feared. Stokes had never had people react to him in quite this way before. He liked it. He kept up the laughter for this reason.

"Hands! I tell ya the sonofabitch had no hands!" a man was shouting for the world to hear as he burst past the sergeant's desk where O'Hurley had been unable to contain him. He rushed into the squad room shouting it so loud every cop in the place went instinctively for his weapon, including Ryne Lanark, who was passing from his unit upstairs to Captain Paul Wood's office here on the second floor where detectives operated in Precinct 13.

Ryne shouted for everyone to be calm, and something in his voice must have told the man coming at him that he was in charge. The man wore ratty clothes, cotton coat, felt hat. His eyes were wild with a rigid fear that had hold of him. He was not so dangerous as he was on the verge of a heart attack. "Man had no hands . . . all blood where his hands oughta've been!"

It took some coffee to steady the old man, whose several years on the street had hardened him to anything—he had thought. All this he calmly told Lanark, who wondered why he was bothering with the old guy. Most everyone in the precinct had gone back to their business, but Lanark had walked the old man into an interrogation room, called for coffee, and listened to what he had to say.

It all sounded like the old man had gotten some bad wine, or had gotten into some angel dust, maybe too much Thai stick—hard to tell. He claimed to have been approached in the predawn dark by a man who bled from both wrists and had no hands. Classic trip shit, Lanark thought. But the old man claimed it was real, and that the man was lying in an alley some ten blocks distant, very likely dead by now.

Stranger things had happened in Chicago just last week.

"What's your name, sir?" Lanark asked, preparing to jot it down on a form he'd snatched from a desk on his way into the interrogation room. As he watched the suspicion grow in the old man's eyes, he realized suddenly the man's manner and stature were not unlike his father's had been. Deep beneath the old clothes and the stubble and the dirt, the old man was of a type of Irishman who, if he held true to form, saw leprechauns when he drank, not banshees or headless creatures, or men with forearms dripping blood.

"I just need your name for the report, Mister *ahhhh*."

"Cocoran, Irskine Cocoran."

"Residence?"

The old man frowned. "Damn you, the poor man is dead by now!"

"Then it won't matter if we take our time and get this information. Or would you rather some clerk do it for you?"

He regarded Lanark again with the piercing eyes. "Blame fools! 1434 Armitage."

Lanark tried to picture such an address, and he knew there were no apartments or even flophouses on that block of Armitage. "I'll just put down: no permanent address. Any place where you can be reached, where a message can be got to you?"

"Oh, *ahhh*, that'd be the mission."

Lanark sighed, wishing he hadn't gotten involved. "Name of the mission? Address?"

"St. Luke's, back of the church over to Humbolt."

Lanark knew the location. "Fine, they know you there well, huh?"

"'Nough to know I'm no liar!"

"All right, we're going to check your story out." Lanark tried to calm him with an upraised palm. Lanark called upstairs and asked Shannon Keyes if she could get free.

"Excursion? Any time with you."

They'd only recently returned from a long, restful R & R together. The precinct was still buzzing about it. Some rumors even had them secretly married, which was far from true.

"Got a bizarre story I want to check out."

"Word came up about something to do with a wino and a headless horseman."

"Handless."

"Sure, I'll give you a hand."

Lanark frowned, and then said, "I'll meet you at the unit in the lot. I'll try to explain along the way."

With the street person in the back of the sports car Lanark used for undercover work, they sped to the scene. They arrived at the alley in question at 9:03 A.M. Another unit from a neighboring precinct was already there and they'd called in a "meat wagon."

Lanark went to the policemen standing about the inert form of a man in the alley amid a trash pile where he'd turned over cans onto himself as he fell. "Allen, Jim," said Lanark, who knew the two patrolmen. "Who called it in?"

"Anonymous, somebody up there," Jim Bledsoe, an experienced, hard cop, said with a blasé wave of a limp hand in the general direction of the windows on all sides.

Irskine Cocoran stared, pointing at the corpse. "He come at me from there." He indicated the west end of the alley. "Could hardly stand, blubbering some gibberish."

"You saw what happened to this man?" asked Jim Bledsoe suddenly in the old man's face.

Shannon came around quickly from the other side of the car and stood between Bledsoe and the old man, who cowerered away like a frightened hamster. "Back off!" shouted Shannon. Lanark watched her work. He had explained all he had gathered from Cocoran, and until now they both had reserved judgment.

"Allen, you and Bledsoe here touch the body? Find any ID on him?"

"No sir—"

"No, what?"

"No, we didn't touch nothing."

Bledsoe frowned and said, "We know our place, Lieutenant."

"Then you didn't see the hands?"

"Hands?"

Lanark went close to the body and pushed back paper and debris from around the dead man's hands to uncover the truth of Irskine Cocoran's statement: Both hands and much of the forearms were gone, sheared completely through, the ends of each shirt sleeve with them, the white sleeves purple with blood.

"God!" gasped Bledsoe. "Damn! This . . . oh, Lord."

Allen was trembling with the sight, unable to take his eyes off and getting sicker to his stomach by the moment.

Shannon shook Allen, saying firmly, "Get on the box and get the coroner down here. This guy's not moving until Dr. Black has a close look. Tell him to bring his best team."

Allen shakily responded while Lanark went to Cocoran and said, "Irskine? You mind if I call you Irskine?"

"No, no, not-ta'ttal," he stuttered. "Men go through a thing like this together, it kinda' makes 'em comrades, don't it?"

Lanark exchanged a quick glimpse with Shannon, with whom he had gone through so much. He then turned back to Cocoran. "Yeah, yeah, it does, Irskine. Now, tell us slow and easy, when did you first encounter this man? Take me to the exact location. Maybe we can find the . . . the hands."

"And the weapon," added Bledsoe.

"I don't know nothing about no weapon," said Cocoran. "I was tending my own business when it happened."

"What business is that, Mr. Cocoran?" asked Bledsoe in a threatening manner which made Cocoran wince.

"Bledsoe, I'll ask the questions," said Lanark sharply. "See if Allen needs your hat. He's looking rather green."

Bledsoe marched off, a big man who didn't step lightly. Lanark asked the old man to walk him through it. They went down the length of the alleyway, and Irskine

Cocoran, like some animated Rumplestiltskin, recreated the whole scene for Lanark and Shannon Keyes.

"I was napping, right about here . . . no, here!"

Lanark saw the Irish whiskey bottle lying near empty, much of its contents spilled. He lifted it on the end of a pencil, and what was left of the brown liquid trickled out. Cocoran watched it with a sad eye, but said nothing. "He come out of nowhere and was almost atop me, his bloody stubs reaching for me. I tell you, I very near had a heart attack."

"But you didn't."

"I was in the war, the big 'un, son, W-W-2 . . . seen plenty of nasty wounds in my time. I just got hold of myself and hauled myself out of there. Want to know if I was 'fraid, don't ya—well, I was! And am not 'bout to apologize for it. You have a bloody mess of a man come barreling down on you middle of the night and see how you react."

"He didn't come from nowhere, Irskine. Show me where he was when you first saw him, the very first instant you looked up and saw him. Think."

Cocoran did so, studying the lay of things. A garage to his left, another to his right; trash cans lining the way; telephone poles, fences. "By day it looks all different," he complained.

"Did you hear any car tires squeal? Before or after you saw him?"

"Pay no attention to such things."

"See any gates open or close? Windows? Any other witnesses?"

"Naw, nothing like that."

"Any of these garage doors open or close before, after, or during the time you saw the dead man?"

"I saw nothing except those bloody stubs coming for me. I . . . I ran. I'd been drinking. Thought at first it was, you know, like a mirage, what they call the DDTs? So at first, I sat there and it . . . he came closer and closer, until he got so close I felt the blood spurt onto my coat. Look at the spots it made on my pants too."

28

Lanark realized for the first time the heavy stains on the old man's clothes were those of blood. "When that evidence team gets here, I want this whole area, every backyard searched for the hands, and the weapon," Lanark told Shannon. He also knew he'd have to impound Irskine's clothes.

"I'll see to it."

"Now, Irskine," said Lanark with a smile more painted than genuine. "Tell me the whole story again."

"I jus' tol' ya'!"

"Again, Irskine, before anyone else arrives."

This time Irskine pointed out a different location the man had first appeared in. Lanark went to the spot.

"I didn't see him here, though," said Irskine of the dead man. "Just heard him banging into things. He couldn't hardly walk; couldn't speak. Was in shock, I reckon, when he come up on me. Kinda like a wounded animal."

"But you heard nothing else, nothing that might account for how he lost his hands? No explosion—"

"Mercy, no! Was kinda dozing, but I would've been woke up by an explosion, I reckon."

"Something did wake you, though."

"Him, gasping and knocking at trash cans," he said, pointing.

"No car sounds?"

"No, sir."

"No shop tools, high-pitched, whine?"

"No."

"You're sure?"

"Sure as I might be sure; what's sure when something like this happens to you?"

"Sorry."

"Sorry? What've you got to say sorry for? I'm the sorry one. Can't recall hardly much anymore. Booze, I guess, turned my head into a spongeful of air."

Black arrived, followed by the ET guys. It looked as if it was to be a long day. The body was identified as William Joseph Rhodes, Senator Sandra Rhodes's husband. What he was doing in this part of the city, alone and at night, would make for speculation for the remainder of the year, depending on the fickle interests of viewing audiences. Already, the TV camera crews were setting up; already cops and men in lab coats were being interviewed and asked inane questions. The horror show had begun, and at the center of it all, a dead man turned into a freak by virtue of having no ends to his arms. The body was now being meticulously and assiduously picked over for dust, fiber, and microscopic trace evidence. Dr. Howard Black would soon have some explanation of the mutilation to the limbs, but it would be no real explanation, rather a statement of the facts. Howard Black was the best forensics man the city had to offer, but not even he could explain why Senator Rhodes's husband had died in such hideous fashion.

When Black looked up from the corpse and saw Lanark looking back at him, he said, "Why is it you always bring me my worst cases, Lieutenant?"

Lanark knew what he meant, recalling the horror on the trains left by the Subway Killer only the month before. One killing had been particularly heinous.

"Looks on the surface as if it could be the work of a hired assassin, but no one with such a messy MO's in our computer. We sent out a request to Langley. The man's name is not unheard of in Washington circles."

"God, what was he doing down here?"

"Slumming, I suppose."

"Dig deep enough . . ."

"Scrape the surface . . ."

"Park on a doorstep long enough . . ."

"Some bull slingin' about the guy was gay. Another has it he was here for a buy—drugs."

"Might fit," said Shannon, who came closer, listening to the talk. "Drug 'enforcers' of the not-so-friendly kind would do just such a mutilation job to send a message to others who screwed with them."

"Good thinking," agreed Lanark. "Time to shake some

nown creeps out of the trees, see what kind of fleas we ind on 'em. You want to organize a sweep?"

"Not if you think it's pointless. You don't sound too nthused about the notion; so why're you bringing it up, nd why're you shunting it off to me?"

"Procedure, standard."

"Really?"

"Sure, stands to reason. Captain Wood'll get pressure rom the commissioner because he's getting the screws ightened by Senator Rhodes, who'll want results over-night. What better way to show that the department is working on it than to fill the holding cells with scum-buckets?"

"See your point."

"We'll spend thousands of man-hours filling out forms, booking people, only to turn them out in the A.M."

"What else do you propose?"

"No luck on finding the man's hands?"

"None."

"What about where he lost his hands?"

"Nothing. But there is a trail," she replied. "Come on, I'll show you."

Lanark was soon as confused as Shannon and the others. There was a clear blood trail, but no huge blood spills where the cuts to both forearms should have left unmistakable signs. "What, did the perp lay down a drop cloth? Did Mr. Rhodes stand about waiting for him to do so? Who held out the man's hands? Has to be more here."

"Infrared photo might show footprints even on the asphalt, if you all haven't distorted them completely," suggested Black. Then he sighed heavily. "Likely too late. Does smack of an execution, albeit a bizarre one. I'll have to look it up in the literature; see if it's peculiar to any particular place or nationality."

"Thanks, Doc. Anything else?"

"At the moment? No."

"Hope it was an execution," said Shannon, saying what was on all their minds. If it was an execution rite, it was

31

not likely to recur, and they wouldn't have a *repeat kille* on their hands. Grisly thought; one they didn't wish to g. away with. However, there appeared no ready answer t. the mystery of the handless corpse. The worst-cas. scenario was likely to be the gnawing image they'd a. climb into bed with tonight.

TWO

The neighborhood where the senator's husband was found was not an area for sightseeing or casual strolls. However, according to Forensics, it appeared that first impressions were right: Rhodes's mutilated hands had been chopped off elsewhere, and he'd been dumped there.

"But he was alive," Ryne protested when Coroner Black said this.

"No way to prove that by me, not in this alley this morning, anyway."

"This makes no sense whatsoever," Shannon said, running a hand through her long, blond hair.

"No sense, huh? You cops, always out to make sense of the world." Black sounded tired and despondent.

Ryne Lanark looked into Shannon's eyes, giving her a look that told her to leave Black to him. She stepped slightly away, just within earshot, as Ryne told the coroner, "Dr. Black, what Lieutenant Keyes means is that none of this makes sense if we're to believe Irskine over there." He pointed out the befuddled bum sitting on a wooden back porch some distance away. The woman living at the location had come out, offering coffee. Irskine was getting on with her well, telling her in detail what he had seen not fifty yards from her flat in the back alley.

The middle-aged woman's face was white and getting whiter as Irskine related his tale to her.

Coroner Black frowned when he looked in Irskine

Cocoran's direction. The man looked a bit like the famous author Elmore Leonard, save for the seedy clothing. "If you want to believe this guy was sober, and actually saw what he said he saw, Lieutenant, then be my guest. But the lab will show without a doubt that this man's wounds, as great as they are, do not show enough blood loss at this location to make me believe he was alive when he was dumped here. That's all I'm saying on it for the time being."

Lanark caught a caustic edge in Black's voice. The coroner had recently taken a bath on testimony he'd given in a homicide investigation. He'd stood by evidence his lab had produced, but there simply hadn't been enough, and there hadn't been any way to turn twelve jurors from a wrong decision, despite his certainties. Jurors were often in awe of scientific findings, but only when they could be made fully understandable. It helped too if a jury could see, in Dick-and-Jane fashion, the step-by-step procedure that linked a laboratory test to a man's perspiration, saliva, or semen. In this case, as in many, truth lost out to doubts. Lanark had followed the case closely as it had unfolded in the *Tribune*.

Lanark bit his lower lip and considered whether a jury would believe that Irskine Cocoran had seen a man walk up to him without his hands. He knew he must find firmer ground. He'd have to begin with the victim, Rhodes. He turned to Shannon and began asking aloud the questions that would haunt them until answers were forthcoming: "Who did Rhodes spend the evening with? Where did he eat his last meal? How did he come to this alley without his hands?"

"On his feet?" she said with a glibness that would be inappropriate if she weren't a cop.

There were so many macabre ways sick cop humor would deal with this grisly crime. Ryne Lanark knew the precincts in and about Chicago would be teeming with groaners and one-liners. Cops would be doing a lot of "hand-holding" and "hand-jobs" over this one. Detectives would be using hand language to decipher the case. Handy humor would be given a hand by the press; they'd be at hand, on hand, and have the sordid story in hand. A handle would be sought for the killer, and he'd likely be called The Handyman, his mutilation "handiwork," before it was over.

"I want Senator Rhodes interviewed. Maybe she knows something, maybe she doesn't, but—"

"She's flying in from Washington. I'm meeting her at O'Hare next."

"Not a bad idea. See if you can keep the press off her back. See if you can size her up, learn what you can about the relationship. What business did he have in Chicago? That sort of thing. And watch her for moves."

"Moves" was police jargon for body language. A good detective like Shannon could read a liar quite often by the movements of her hands, fidgeting with cigarettes, pens, clenched fists. Eyes spoke a lot too, as did the legs and mouth, and even the nose might decide to become uncooperative when the brain was in conflict—a kind of "body over mind" thing. Liars gave themselves away by using handkerchiefs to hide their lies. They sneezed and coughed a great deal through an interview, sometimes to the point of distraction.

Yet there were those liars who remained in complete control by virtue of willpower and practice, or absolute certainty they were truthful. A sociopath was but the end extreme on a continuum. Lanark had learned there was a full gamut of liars and practiced liars, many of whom lied in order to cover for a larger lie. The worst were those who'd begun to believe their own lies; such people had convinced themselves they were innocent of guilt through denial or insanity.

At some point soon, he hoped to see Dr. Richard Ames. Ames had been unable to promise Lanark that he'd get there before the body was carted off, but he'd said he would try. More and more the "blue shrink" was seen at the scene of grisly murders.

"You think the senator could have anything to do with her husband's death?" asked Shannon, breaking his concentration.

"This stage of the game, let's consider her the wife, not the senator."

"Yeah, right."

"*Most*-case scenario."

She nodded. In most cases the killer knew the victim. In most cases, the killer was related to the victim.

"I'll get out to the airport. She's coming in on a private jet." Shannon looked at her watch. "Gives me about forty minutes."

"Get going. We'll see you and the wife at the morgue for identification." Some rumor was already being spread about how the man wasn't dressed in a London Fog or Gucci shoes, and that maybe it wasn't Rhodes at all, maybe just some ordinary thief who'd stolen Rhodes's wallet for the Diners and Exxon cards and what cash he might find. An APB was issued for information on Rhodes and where he might have been staying. But before the information hounds back at Precinct 13 got back to Lanark with the answer, a friend in the press corps informed him that Rhodes was known for his preference for the Palmer House, one of downtown Chicago's finest, oldest, and most expensive.

"Spent the senator's money like it was water," said Jeff Sandler, Lanark's press friend. Sandler was a lanky man with a Jimmy Stewart calmness about him that seemed at odds with his profession as crime reporter. There was also an edge about him, something underneath that made him strong and vulnerable all at once. Maybe it was simply that he cared about people, despite what they did to one another, and despite what became grist for his paper mill. Sandler was a throwback in many ways, not unlike Lanark in that he despised injustice. Lanark had known him to squelch a story if he felt it would do someone a terrible wrong. Lanark could admire that in a man whose profession was printing the truth, the whole truth, and nothing but the truth. Admire it because so much of the truth in newsprint was distorted truth nowadays.

"You know what this character Rhodes looked like?"

Sandler, standing behind the police barrier with the other press men, shrugged. "Sure, I think so. I've seen pictures, I mean."

"Come with me. Let him through," Lanark told the uniformed officer keeping the newsmen at bay.

Sandler stepped easily over the sawhorse barrier in his way as the other newsmen grumbled, bitched, and complained at the injustice. Some cursed Sandler.

"Pull back the sheet," Lanark told one of the attendants who was readying the body for Black's downtown morgue.

Sandler stared, moved his head from side to side, and nodded before verbally committing himself. "That's him."

"Who him?"

"Rhodes, that's Senator Rhodes's husband, the guy they call Mr. Rhodes."

"You'd swear to it?"

"Sure, it's his hands that're mutilated, not his face."

"So how much do you know about this guy, Rhodes?"

"Just what I read in the papers."

"Tell me about him."

Sandler laughed.

"What's so funny?"

"The man's life reads like Howard Hughes, for Christ sake."

"Was he filthy rich?"

"Not really, but he was once, and he continued to live as if he were. Senator Rhodes has been trying to disengage herself from him for the past year. Divorce was finalized yesterday. Word was he was despondent."

"Over the divorce?"

"Over the loss, yeah, of his income from her."

"I see."

"Don't read the society pages, do you, Lanark?"

"Never appealed to me, no."

"Lot of motive for murder there. You should."

"Thanks, I'll keep it in mind."

"Nobody's happy."

"What? Sandler, I don't have time for goddamned word games."

"No one, not you or me, not the poor, and certainly not the rich—nobody's happy. You can surround yourself with every goddamned creature comfort on the planet, insulate yourself from the world, have everything paid for and brought in—say, the way Michael Jackson lives—and still you're unhappy. Rhodes was unhappy all his life. Senator Rhodes just learned that too late. Now she's trying to get into something more . . . *more happy than blue!*" He ended with a lilting song, then he changed the subject abruptly. "So any leads on The Handyman? Any ideas?"

"Nothing, not a clue, except the fact he used a very powerful, sharp instrument. Cuts were quick, brutal, and effective." Lanark had begun giving Sandler now what he'd give out to the others later. Sandler knew it. He returned to the other side of the barrier with a mild acceptance that made him appear most professional.

Lanark watched as Mark Robeson and Jake Stokes emerged from the surrounding crowd. Lanark had put his two black operatives in the crowd to mingle and ask questions and register anything of any value in their minds and report back to him. It was a racially mixed neighborhood with blacks predominating. They'd blended in for over an hour now. Lanark hoped something had come of their time and effort. But both men had negatives to report. No one had seen, heard, or even smelled anyone in the alley the night before. They hadn't even smelled Irskine Cocoran.

"Bullshit," Lanark replied.

Robeson, the more experienced of the two decoy agents under Lanark, nodded. He moved a toothpick from one side of his mouth to the other as he spoke. "Place like this has a thousand eyes at night."

"We could come back here at night, get the feel," said Stokes.

"Night, hell, we startin' in right now," Robeson

corrected his junior partner. "We start at the end of the alley and go door to door. Work most of the day that way. Later, after dark, and after we've fed ourselves and gotten into some raggedy clothes, we'll come back down here and wait around where Irskine said he was last night."

"Just reading my mind, Mark," said Lanark. "Go to it." He slapped them each on the back. "But go easy. People all over this neighborhood're scared six ways to Sunday over this. Show 'em your badge before you let them shoot you, okay?"

"Great comforting words, Lieutenant."

"Carry on."

Stokes stopped, however, and he raised his hands to Lanark and asked, "Why? Why'd someone cut off the man's hands? Is it true, to sit and watch him slowly bleed to death?"

"Where'd you hear that?" asked Lanark, feeling his wrists, his temper rising. "That's just more crap, Stokes."

"Saying it doesn't make it so," Mark replied.

The two detectives sauntered off to put in motion Mark's plan to canvass the immediate surrounding area. Every house, garage, and trash can, every backyard and laundry-room window held a potential eyewitness. If Aunt Millie or Sister Nell was doing laundry the night before, and was in the basement and looked out on the alleyway when she heard a car pull up, or Cocoran shout, she might have seen something useful. No stone must be left unturned. And in the back of everyone's mind was one question: Was it a lone mutilation, or the first of a series?

Lanark started away, knowing there was little else he could do there at the moment. But then he saw Dr. Ames's car pulling in behind some squad cars. Lanark instantly shouted to the ambulance attendants who'd already put the body away and were closing the rear door, telling them to hold on.

The attendants grumbled to one another, but one yanked it wide, and with the unnecessary and exaggerated gesture of a man welcoming a king inside, he opened his right arm to Lanark and bowed. Ames came to Lanark, and together they climbed into the back of the ambulance.

"Glad you could make it."

"Broke away as soon as I could."

Ames was too tall for the back of the ambulance, and his dark skin against all the white stood out in stark contrast. When he pulled back the sheet for a look at the dead man, his eyes went instantly to the hands. No one had told him about the condition of the body. The eyes simply sought the mutilation as if magnetized by it. The black man found a seat, gasping a bit at the sight. What remained of Rhodes's appendages looked like thick worms encrusted with mud, but the mud was dried blood over the ripped ends of his dinner coat and shirt. The gaping holes at the end of each forearm sent a chill through Lanark for the second time now as he experienced the sight anew with his friend Ames, a police psychologist.

Lanark had learned to trust Ames's insights and intuition. So uncanny was Ames's summation of an unknown killer that in fact some people in the department thought him a psychic. Ames himself shied very much away from the term. It got in the way, he'd once confided in Lanark. "It's about as welcome in the department as a black man who's smarter than the commissioner."

Lanark had laughed at this, but had added, "Who isn't smarter than Lawrence?"

At any rate, if Ames was psychic, his training in psychology and criminology certainly had nurtured his "gift."

"What do you think, Richard?"

Ames was still shaken. He seemed for a moment to be somewhere else, and Lanark watched him lift his own two large open palms to his eyes before turning them slowly round, peering at them and through them, seemingly studying each vein and groove and shade of skin. His fingers slowly extended and then curled inward. "I . . . I don't . . . know, Ryne. Have to get out of here. Too damned hot in here with this stinking body."

Lanark saw that Ames's forehead and face had become soaking wet with perspiration. He was more than simply shaken by Rhodes's condition; he was having some sort of response to it that Lanark could not have predicted, some sort of anxiety attack. Ames pushed past Lanark and raced for his car.

Lanark hesitated at the ambulance, hopping out. He didn't want to create a disturbance by chasing after Ames, nor did he wish to embarrass Ames. Yet he needed to help the man who'd done so much for him over the past several years. He wanted to shout to him, jump into his car with him, take him down the block for a drink at the first watering hole they came to, or take him back to Ryne's bar, the Lucky 13th, where they could hash this thing out. But if he did any of this, he'd have Sandler and every other reporter wondering what was going on. Let him go, he told himself.

The ambulance attendant who'd been exaggeratedly polite before, a tall, thin fellow, now was shouting in Lanark's ear.

"You fuckers all done? Can we get to our eff-in' job now? Or is that asking too friggin' much? Huh, Cap?"

The strain of the day and the evening before conspired with Lanark's infamous short fuse. As Ames tore off in his car, Lanark tore into the ambulance attendant. He rammed him into the door he was closing, brought the man's arm up and up until he squealed, "Hey! Hey! Please, I was just—oh, Jesus!"

"You've got to learn to treat the law with respect," said Lanark, just letting him go when the other attendant came around with a tire iron demanding that his partner be let alone.

"He's all yours," said Lanark, shoving him into the other man before turning and starting away.

"Lanark!" shouted Sandler from the crowd of onlookers just as the tire iron was hurled by the burly attendant.

Lanark ducked, the iron narrowly missing him, flying at the crowd, where one man was struck in the leg, and others shouted. Lanark instantly went for the hairy ape who'd hurled the iron, blocking a blow before bringing up an explosive right to the man's jaw that sent him staggering against the van. He brought up a leg to kick out at Lanark, but Lanark grabbed it with ferocious intent, yanking it straight up. This sent the ambulance attendant's entire weight down on his head against the pavement.

"Oh, *Jezzzzzz*, oh! Man! Look what you done!" shouted the other attendant, going to his friend.

He was hurt badly, bleeding from the head. His partner was throwing up his hands and shouting, "You've killed him!"

Lanark picked up the bleeding bull and threw him over his shoulder. He then took him to the back of the ambulance and dumped him beside the handless man without ceremony. Lanark turned to the other attendant and said, "Get your pal to the hospital, and get that body to Dr. Black's by eleven, and not a minute later!"

"Yes, sir . . . yes, sir," he said, rushing to lock up the back and race the ambulance out of there.

Sandler came to Lanark's side. "*Shhhhhheeeee,* you really know how to handle yourself."

"Boxing," he said simply. "That tub of lard was no match. Promised myself I wouldn't let idiots and small people get me angry so easily, so I guess, in a sense, he won."

Sandler had to think about this a moment.

"Something Dr. Ames taught me," said Lanark.

"Oh, yeah . . . I see, I think. Only thing is, that guy, the big one, he looked familiar to me."

"What?"

"Dead ringer for a guy works over in the Thirty-fourth Precinct."

"A cop?"

"Just said he looked like this guy, Vinny something or other."

"You're kidding." Lanark knew Sandler was not kidding, and he also knew it was quite within the realm of possibility that the ambulance attendant and some cop named Vinny from the 34th were one and the same. Not a few months before, the Feds had been trying to get their meat hooks into Lanark, to use him. They'd succeeded too, with the help of Morris Fabia, who had set him up. Could Fabia be up to something new already? Fabia was head of Internal Affairs, and he used his power like a mini-Hoover, amassing information on cops by using other cops to spy on them or entrap them. Lanark knew of two cases this year where good cops had been suckered into bad deals with other cops who were wired.

"Like fleas . . . bastards are everywhere," he muttered.

Sandler studied his features and said, "Ames didn't stay very long. Looked upset?"

"Lot on his mind."

"I'm sure. Lot on everybody's mind at the moment. Not every day we get a body with missing parts. What about the crime computers, Lieutenant?"

"What about 'em, Sandler?"

"Anything like this in the files?"

"Somewhere, sometime, I'm sure someone's done this to somebody."

"Seem to recall a case in California myself."

"Oh, you mean the rape victim. Rapist cut off her forearms, left her for dead."

"But she survived, got to a road, got help."

"And the sonofabitch made parole a few years ago."

"Right."

"And so maybe you think he's acting out this scene over and over in his head, and now he's doing it with men?"

Sandler frowned and shrugged at once, his thick, sandy hair falling in his eyes. Lanark laughed lightly.

"What?" asked Sandler.

"We've already checked on the guy's whereabouts. He's over six thousand miles away. Nice try."

Lanark dismissed everyone, and told Cocoran to check in on a daily basis, assuring him he would make it worth his while.

Sandler was persistent. "Blood relative of the California rapist maybe? Did the guy have a kid?"

"Sandler, stick to news."

"Lieutenant, pick up a paper! You are news!"

"What're you hanging about here for anyway?"

"I smell something, something big."

"Pulitzer, maybe?"

"I'd settle for a few answers."

"The hell you would. You reporters are all after one thing."

"What's that?"

"Try this for size, Sandler," said Lanark as they walked together toward the Jaguar he drove. "I don't need a hand from you."

Sandler watched Lanark disappear into the car ahead of him, but he shouted at the top of his lungs over the pulsating motor of the Jaguuar, "No, you don't need a hand from me! Not from anybody do you need *a* hand! Because you need *two*! Two missing hands!"

THREE

All the way back to Precinct 13, Ryne Lanark thought about the brutality of the killing, and he summed up in his own mind the facts as they were known: a senator's husband dead of horrendous wounds, each hand neatly cut off; the body dumped in another location, according to Black; yet the man was alive when Irskine Cocoran had seen him.

The hum of the Jaguar's engine helped Lanark think. He passed from the neighborhood where Rhodes's body had been found, crossing into another, the demarcation line being Division Street. On all sides of him the signs had changed, the businesses suddenly having Italian names. Somehow, in the face of inordinate change all around them, some few areas of Chicago had remained almost untouched.

Lanark had to file his report at the precinct, and rush from there to Black's offices downtown where he'd meet with Shannon and Senator Sandra Rhodes.

Perhaps the senator could fill in some gaps, but Lanark doubted she'd be of much help. Politicians knew best to keep tight rein on what they said. Still, he'd reserve judgment until he met the woman.

The conflicting information played over in Lanark's mind—Black's certainties against Cocoran's befuddled nightmare. For the time being, Black's judgment had to be accepted. Rhodes was killed elsewhere and died elsewhere, his body dumped in the alleyway.

As he drove, Lanark's mind went back into the past, to when his parents and his sister were killed while he was away in Los Angeles pursuing a blossoming acting career. They'd been savagely beaten and mutilated in his father's pub, which Ryne now operated. Lanark had rushed back to Chicago filled with guilt, self-doubt, horror, and rage. A period of *Death Wish* tactics had gotten him nowhere, because in real life "civilians" had no access to police records and computers; information on the case was withheld from him. He later learned that the primary reason information was withheld from a bereaved family member was not so much out of concern for the surviving members, but largely due to fear that the surviving member would do exactly what Lanark had proposed to do—go after the killers himself. The fact the file was so scant, once he did manage to pry it loose, also factored into the desire to withhold it.

That was when he got smart. He traded in his career as an actor to ply his trade as an actor-cop, an undercover operative with the CPD. It took time, of course, much more than Charles Bronson had in the movies, but he completed work at the Police Academy and rose in the ranks quickly, making lieutenant in under three years. His skill with makeup and disguise was little short of miraculous, and much of what his unit members knew of acting he had taught them.

In the meantime, he was privy to police computer files. He had also learned to use informants, and to decipher street-level dealings. Combining all of this with his badge, he had been able to locate and destroy two of the four men who had destroyed his family. And the search for the other two continued. When he got his hands on Loomis, he'd have his hands on the other two, he was certain.

This side of Lanark frightened people, he knew, even Shannon, who claimed to understand his rage. Internal Affairs had attempted to prove him a murderer with a badge on more than one occasion. The Feds had had the evidence to convict him on the charge of murder, but had chosen to blackmail him instead in order to trap a drug czar in Colombia with his help.

There had been assassination attempts on Lanark, presumably brought about by a street-price on his head, placed there by those he intended on cornering and killing for their actions against his sister, mother, and father. In the process he had endangered friends and fellow cops on occasion: Shannon Keyes, Mark Robeson, and now young Stokes.

He silently cursed himself for having done so.

Senator Sandra Rhodes strode into the morgue's viewing room in a calm born of either strength of character or several Quaaludes. Lanark was inclined to believe the latter, but reserved judgment when he saw Shannon give him a nearly imperceptible shake of the head to indicate she'd gotten nothing from the "Iron Woman of Capitol Hill" as she was called in some DC circles.

The senator was gray-haired, which made her appear older than her husband, which was not the case. Her premature graying, some said, was due to her difficult wars on Capitol Hill, while others said it was due to her personal life, which had fallen into a shambles.

"Where is he?" she asked as though certain the visit was a routine matter, that it was natural for her husband to be wheeled into the viewing area of a morgue.

"They're preparing him now," said Lanark, who also wondered at the delay. "I am Lieutenant Ryne Lanark, Precinct Thirteen, CPD, Senator."

"I'm not here for introductions, Lieutenant." Her eyes told the story of a stern woman who had been through many hardships, and they told Lanark she could handle this one. "Please, if you have any influence, perhaps you could hurry this along?"

"Senator Rhodes," said Shannon, "I'll see what I can do."

"Yes, dear, please do."

But just before Shannon got through the door, the door inside the viewing booth swung wide. An attendant pushed the corpse into the room. Lanark saw the senator's jaw quiver—just a flash—and it was gone. The corpse was covered in a sheet, making it look shrouded, ready for the grave. One of Black's assistants had been waiting in the viewing area with Lanark, and now he spoke through an intercom to the attendant behind the glass, telling him to please lower the sheet from the face for identification.

Rhodes's gloved hand went to the glass when the sheet was moved down, revealing the forehead, eyes, nose, chin. It was the only display of emotion from the woman, and she quickly caught herself, removing her hand from the window, placing it properly at her side. She looked into Lanark's eyes, then round to where Shannon stood behind her. Beside her was a man named Drummond, a lawyer and friend of the family. Lanark thought she might lean on him, but instead she said, "What about his hands?"

Lanark looked to Shannon. "You told her?"

"I insisted on knowing the cause of death."

"I see."

"I would like to see the . . . the extent of—"

"Senator, that's not necessary," Lanark said.

"I have every right, Lieutenant."

Lanark thought of a time when he had had to deal with the police in similar circumstances, and how they had wanted to protect him from the horrors of the crime.

"All right, if you're sure."

"I am."

Again, the attendant was hailed on the intercom and told to now uncover the body to the waist. The arms and what was left of the forearms were folded in over the chest but stuck upwards. The only consolation was the fact the wounds had been cleaned, presenting a less bloody aspect. Even so, Senator Rhodes swooned and Lanark grabbed for her. Drummond seemed to take offense that Lanark did not leave this chore to him. Lanark backed off. Shannon said, "Over here," pointing to a settee out of range of the viewing booth.

"That's enough," said Lanark to the man inside the booth, who flung the sheet back over the corpse and slowly wheeled it from view.

"ID complete," said Black's young assistant. "Thank you."

Shannon whispered, "I tried to tell her on the way up, but she was insistent. There's water and a more comfortable waiting area down the hall."

Lanark watched the senator regain herself in a matter of minutes. She'd accepted her husband's death, almost expected the ID to be completed without a hitch, but her reaction to the removal of his hands had been too much for her. Was it just the vulgar thought of the pain it must have caused him, or was there something deeper inside all who looked upon the mutilation of any appendage of the human form that made it too horrible to bear?

"Are you all right?"

"Can we get you anything?"

The others were being solicitous to the senator and she was angry at them for it. Lanark saw his chance to break through her armor. "I think it is high time you answered some questions, Senator Rhodes, now!" He almost shouted it, making both Shannon and Drummond look up at him.

Lanark continued to push. "Isn't that right, Senator?"

"Just a minute," Drummond began.

"Ryne!" said Shannon.

"The senator knew her husband better than anyone else. If she knows something that could help us find his killer, she must tell us."

"Yes, but at the moment," said Drummond, "the poor woman—"

"Out of my way, Arthur," she said, standing and pushing both Drummond and Shannon away, marching up to Lanark. "I'm no poor woman. If the lieutenant wants to ask me questions, he'd better do so quickly. We have a flight back to DC departing your Midway Airport in a little over an hour."

"Good, we can talk on the way," said Lanark.

"Then start firing away, Lieutenant. Believe me, I've dealt with worse than you before."

"You may think so."

"Indeed."

The sparring had begun, and Lanark could see she liked that; she liked confrontation and a good battle, thrived on it. His first question was, "Did you and Mr. Rhodes fight a lot?"

"Define a lot."

It was going to be a tough interrogation.

"Daily?"

"Does anyone fight daily?"

"If anyone does, I'd say you do."

"I fight for women's rights, women's causes daily, but marital squabbles are your concern, and if you think for one moment that I had him killed for . . . for our differences . . ."

Lanark thought she'd been about to say for his hands, but he let it go.

"We are, you realize, divorced."

"As of a couple of days ago, yes."

"Then what earthly reason would possess me to see him killed in this brutal fashion?"

"Did he have business dealings with anyone here in Chicago?"

"He had hundreds of schemes going about in his head his entire life, and the list of would-be contributors to those schemes is endless."

"One man, one company in the city he dealt with routinely, Senator."

They had walked the length of the hospital as they spoke, and were now in the underground lot where her limo awaited her. Lanark took Shannon aside, giving her the keys to the Jaguar, telling her to follow.

She was glad to be rid of the senator and took no offense. Lanark got into the limo with Arthur Drummond and Senator Rhodes. The driver knew the destination and did not wait to be told again, pulling the vehicle out slowly into the afternoon sun. Lanark continued his questioning as photojournalists began snapping pictures through the tinted windows! Some new film was capable of doing so, and they were taking full advantage of it.

"A name, Senator, anything to begin a search of where your husband—"

"Former husband, and I want that made clear in your local rags!"

"Former husband—where he might have dined last night. Who he might have seen."

"Entirely his business, and none of mine."

"But surely—"

"He sometimes saw a woman here."

Drummond put up a hand to stop her, saying, "You do not have to answer these questions, Sandra."

"Don't go obstructing the law, Counselor," said Lanark.

"Don't tell me how to—"

"Gentlemen, please!" Senator Rhodes shouted. "Arthur, I am prepared to help Lieutenant Lanark in any way possible, and if that means—"

"But you know what this kind of publicity can do to—"

"Damn the publicity!" She turned to Lanark. "Speak to a Muriel Green. She operates Green Garments, a business my husband bought for her to run. That's all I can tell you."

"What was his relationship with this woman?"

"Anything he wished to make it. Now please, I'll say no more."

Lanark sat back a moment in the plush of the limousine. "Nice way to travel," he muttered, reading over some of the labels on the bottles at the bar beside him. "If I weren't on duty."

"Oh, go right ahead," said Drummond.

"Sure, and you wouldn't make trouble for me, would you, Drummond?"

"You have a suspicious mind, Lieutenant," he said.

"That's how I stay alive, Counselor."

They remained silent all the way to Midway after this,

51

but on their arrival, with Drummond seeing to baggage and ordering porters about, Senator Rhodes said, "Lieutenant, my former husband likely lost his hands because he dipped them into the cookie jar once too often, and with the wrong woman. He was a whoring bastard. The world will not miss him. Don't trouble yourself over him. Good-bye."

Lanark looked up to see Shannon pulling in behind them. He rushed to join her, glad to be rid of the senator and her boyfriend, feeling strangely sure that he too would not have liked Mr. Rhodes, and certain that he did not like Mrs. Rhodes either.

The body had been found. It was headline news in the second edition of the *Times* and the *Tribune*. He'd killed the husband of a prominent senator, the senator from New Jersey. Most of the story centered around her, and the history of a nasty divorce settlement. The story made mere mention of the hands of the victim having been cut off, and the lost hands were presumably floating around Chicago's sewers. This lopsided view of the process enraged him, and he tore the paper to smithereens before the owner of the nightclub grabbed hold of him and shouted in his ear, "What's wrong, Sayer! Morgan!"

He realized where he was and what a foolish thing he'd done. "Sorry, sorry, Danny, it's just thoughts . . . bad things happen to good people and I read about 'em getting hurt in the papers and it drives me crazy."

"Crazy, huh? Well, maybe you ought not to read the damned papers. Be more like the rest of us. Ignore it. You live longer that way. *Sheeeeezzzzz,* kid. You got anything new for the act tonight?"

"Yeah, sure . . . always perfecting the act. You know me, Danny."

Blithering idiot, he thought of Danny, the nightclub owner. Danny was slow. Too much weight for one thing, and those cigars. He'd inhaled too damned many fumes in his day. Danny was a moron.

Danny ambled away to see to his books, no doubt thinking that Morgan Sayer was a creepy guy.

Morgan "The Soothsayer" Sayer returned to the stage and lifted a wooden-headed dummy from out of an ancient trunk. He had made the dummy himself. One night he had met a man who worked in toys in the audience, and the man had come backstage with a proposal to market the dummy along with books on how to do ventriloquism for kids. Morgan had liked the idea, but the man had taken it elsewhere for some reason, and Morgan now saw the book in bookstores wherever he went, with another name and another dummy on the cover.

"How's it going?" asked Felix, his dummy.

"Up and down, you know."

Felix's voice was a bit raspy and high-pitched. "How well I know of up and down, and up and down, and up and down, kiddo! And who's to blame? You! You, you stupid schmuck!"

"Don't have to talk that way, Felix."

"Hell, who else is going to tell you, the mirror?"

"Very funny."

"Funny? It's hilarious, pathetically hilarious, if you get my drift."

"Hey, what're you doing with your hands, Felix? Felix, get out of there!"

Felix's hands had roamed into Morgan's pants, running his fly down without his even having known it.

"It's not funny, Morgan! Kind of weird, but not funny." It was Danny again. He'd come back for a drink to go along with the agony of the books. He'd been listening.

"I know it's not funny, Danny, but it's the way I work. By tonight, it'll be funny. I have to explore the possibilities."

"With that dummy on your schlong, looks like you're exploring, all right—or he is!" Danny laughed uproariously at his own words, poured his drink, and was about to disappear when he came closer and said, "Hey, you change the dummy?"

"Whataya mean?"

"The hands . . . they look, Jesus, they look real."

"Yeah, I refashioned them, Danny. You like?"

"Look too real to go with his dumb face . . . in this light, they look like . . . I don't know . . . kinda large for the rest of him, don't you think?"

"Hey, audience has to see them, if I'm going to give them any hand jokes."

"Sure . . . I guess."

The lights were turned down in the place and the dummy's hands were creepy-looking, so far as Danny was concerned, but then part of Morgan's act was to be creepy. It brought in creeps who put down money for drinks.

When Danny had gone, Morgan Sayer lifted Felix's hands to his cheeks and rubbed them back and forth. They were hard and unfeeling now that he had used his taxidermist's skills on them. No one would think to look for William Joseph Rhodes's hands on Felix.

Soon the nightclub would be packed again, and he would go from jokes with Felix to his hypnotist's act, and this time his selection would include someone else who would gladly give of herself. Maybe Danny was right about the hands being too large for Felix. Maybe a woman's hands, smaller, more petite, would do just right.

Of course, neither the dummy nor the hypnotism act was important any longer. What was important was his discovery, and this time his discovery would not be stolen by anyone. He must carefully write it up, so as to leave out the exact recipe but gain a patent on the skill. Once it was secured, he could go into the business of healing enormous numbers of people who merely needed to train their minds. He would be rich, famous, and loved by all of humanity, and even Felix who knew him so well—even he would have to bow down before the great Morgan Sayer.

Sayer stood six feet tall, with eyes as blue as a pale, clear sky. His dark hair rippled in waves from the forehead back, and the thick beard he'd grown was equally sensuous. On stage, he wore a black cape with red velveteen inner lining. It was his father's cape before he had died; the cape he was wearing when he vowed to come back from the dead and get Morgan by reaching through the dimensions to take him by the throat with his bare hands in revenge for his murdering him.

Nightly, the old ghost tried to make good on his threat, but Morgan had stayed one step ahead of him for all these years.

FOUR

"Where to next, Ryne?" Shannon asked as they pulled from the Midway Airport traffic onto the Stevenson Expressway. "Back to HQ?"

He stared at his watch and shook his head. "Not much we can accomplish now. Shift's over in an hour. Gives us about enough time to make it back to my place."

"Exciting idea."

"I thought you'd like it."

"Certainly beats escorting the Queen Bee around. What a bitch."

"Just her style. Mostly a front, you know, bluster."

"Bluster or blunder? Blunderbust, maybe," she said, wheeling the car into the faster lane and opening her up. "She fires like a scatter-gun."

"Feel kinda sorry for her," he said.

She stared across at him. "What's this? You puttin' me on, or are you trying to impress me with your sensitivity?"

"Sweetheart, think about it. What does the woman have, besides her title, I mean?"

"She's got Drummond."

He laughed. "That's what I mean."

"What you're trying to say, Lanark, in your circuitous way, is that she reminds you of yourself, desperately lonely."

"The way I used to be," he corrected her, "before I met you."

"You get any more from her, or was it a wasted ride?"

"Hey, you saw the interior of that limo. No, it wasn't a waste. I got a bone she tossed, a girlfriend by the name of Muriel Green, operates a garment company. The husband set her up in business here. May have been seeing her last evening."

"Did the senator say all that?"

"Not in so many words."

"I can believe that. Hmmmmm, Green? Garments? Green Garments?"

"You know the company?"

"Jesus, who doesn't?"

"I don't," he confessed.

She shook her head, exasperated. "You always have your mind on business, Lanark. When do you have any fun? The billboards around Chicago are filled with half-dressed blondes in Green Garments—"

"Bathing suits?"

"Green bathing suits, and green underthings, expressly marketed for green-eyed blondes! Christ, Ryne!"

"That little thing you had on the other night?"

"Thick . . . all men are thick."

He chuckled lightly and replied, "Deep, all women are deep."

She replied with a lopsided smile and a shake of the head. "I need a drink."

"My place, all the drink you can drink, and it's on the house. Then we'll talk about green undergarments again—"

"The color of hope."

"What?"

"Green means hope in the parlance of colors."

"Is-sat right? And what is it you're hoping for, Shannon Keyes?"

She didn't readily answer, but bit her lip instead in a gesture he'd come to recognize as one of concern and worry.

"Hey, what is it?"

"Just thinking."

"Oh, about tonight?"

"About tonight, about tomorrow, about the future."

"Like I said, deep."

"Not funny, Ryne."

"Okay, sure . . . you're worried about our future, I know, but we've talked about the subject before, or have you forgotten?"

"No, no, I haven't forgotten."

Until Lanark's vengeance had been vented completely on the men he sought to destroy, until the ghosts of his family had been finally and absolutely put to rest, he could make no future with her.

"I'm sorry," she said, once again accepting the bad bargain she'd made with the man she loved. "No more talk of the future."

He knew enough to say nothing at this point.

They were pulling into the parking space behind the Lucky 13th Pub, owned by Lanark and operated by his Uncle Jack Tebo, who usually manned the bar. It had become a favorite cop hangout over the years, and Lanark's unit in particular frequented the 13th. Above the bar was Lanark's flat. Tebo and his wife, Maria, also lived in the building, also owned by Lanark. It had become the site of many parties, roasts, memories, wakes, and it was also the site of death. It had been in the bar on New Year's Eve several years before, at the close of business, that Lanark had lost his family to knife-wielding thugs.

His sparse, rugged flat was filled with mementos large and small from his sister and his mother, and the war memorabilia and gun collection belonging to his father. The floors were polished wood, no carpets. The bed was a large brass bed many years older than Ryne himself. The walls were cluttered with framed pictures of his family members and awards and citations he had garnered as a policeman and earlier as an actor.

They entered the building from the rear, and came through the kitchen, where Maria, a short, dark-skinned woman with tightly curled black hair and a continuous smile, waved to them and shouted, "Jack! Your boy is here with Shannon! Hello, hello! You are hungry? Maybe some chili? Fresh! Or a sandwich, Ryne?"

"That'd be great," replied Ryne.

"Which one?" she asked as Shannon was saying hello and they passed through into the darkened bar.

"Both," replied Lanark, "smells great."

Tebo came from around the bar and gave Shannon a big hug on seeing them. Lanark said, "Only time he ever gets to squeeze a blonde. Come on, Uncle Jack, let her up for air."

"What're you kids up to?"

"Damn, Tebo," said Lanark, "we aren't kids. Hell, I'm thirty-something."

"Speak for yourself!" protested Shannon. "Give me another hug, Uncle Tebo." She grabbed him this time and he winked over her shoulder. "Tol' ya she's falling for me! And if you don't lock her up with a wedding ring—"

"Jack!"

He threw up his hands. "Oops! Sorry, it just bubbled right out of me. So what're you drinking, your usual? Shan? Nephew?"

"Usual, yeah, in the back booth."

"Somebody's got it," said Jack.

"What?"

"Your cap'n showed up."

"Oh, shit."

"Doesn't say much, does he?" Tebo eyeballed Captain Paul Wood where he sat in Lanark's usual booth.

Wood curled a finger at Lanark and Shannon, saying, "Thought I might catch up to the whirlwind couple here. Got a minute for your goddamned captain, Lanark?"

"Sure, sure, Captain, what're you drinking?"

"Blatz."

"Hit him again, Tebo, and no charge to the captain."

"Buttering me up won't help, Lanark."

Lanark strode over to the table with Shannon and the captain's second beer. Tebo was back of the bar again, fixing a John Collins for Lanark and a Bloody Mary for Shannon. The two lieutenants sat down with their captain in what appeared to be an awkward social moment between them.

"You heard from Senator Rhodes?" asked Lanark.

"From some guy named Drummond."

"Figures."

"DC lawyer," said Shannon, "a real nobody."

Wood gave her a cool stare. "Seems Drummond is putting in a complaint."

"What the hell for? We did everything by the book, Captain," Lanark protested.

"Something to do with Shannon here; says she made a sexual slur against the senator within earshot of reporters, called her a dyke."

"What?"

"That's nonsense."

"You said nothing to that effect, Lieutenant Keyes?"

"What's this Lieutenant Keyes crap, Captain?" Lanark said, quickly objecting to the tone of Wood's voice.

"Hold it down, Lanark," Wood ordered him. "Any truth to the story, any at all, Lieutenant?"

Shannon swallowed hard. "I . . . I may have said something . . . to someone, but it was in strict confidence, and off the record, Captain, and it won't be printed, I can assure you."

"Oh, Christ," said Lanark. "When'd this happen?"

"She was so damned rude to me, Ryne. All apple pie with you, but toward me, the moment we met, she began to order me around along with her goddamned chauffeur. I reminded her several times of who I was, and my rank, but she just insisted on calling me honey, and sweety, and it . . . it just got to me. I made an offhand remark to Jeff."

"A reporter?"

"I kept the reporters away from her."

"Sure, you called her a dyke and they all ran for the phones."

"That's not the way it happened."

"Drummond characterized it as pretty serious," Wood said.

"Captain, can we cut the crap?" Lanark said. "Will you

60

just tell us what Drummond wants in return for a favor from you?"

"Drummond doesn't want any bad PR for Senator Rhodes. He doesn't want word one about her husband's affair with some woman here in the city—none of it—in the papers. For that, he'll let Shannon's head stay on her shoulders."

"Great. We have to investigate a murder but we can't do so openly and freely. We have to watch our backs at every turn and corner to be sure no one's watching us, and with the press, that's near impossible." Lanark was clearly disgusted once more by Drummond. His mind played over the question of Drummond's having perhaps played a part in the husband's death. Sure would be nice to pin the whole bloody matter on the bastard, but he had been in DC, hadn't he?

Tebo came with the drinks and tried to warm the chill air about the table with a few homey remarks, and by asking Captain Wood if he'd care for anything to eat.

"No, no, I won't be staying much longer."

Tebo frowned and disappeared.

"There's something else troubling me, Lanark. It's about this roust you and Stokes pulled in the wee hours last night. Just tell me one thing. Why'd you involve this green kid on a bust like that when you knew going in there was going to be so much gunplay? And why just the two of you?"

"It was all circumstantial, Captain. We did not go in. They came out after us when they caught on to us. It came as a surprise."

"Surprise? Really? Yet you had a warrant? Lanark, you go on burning both ends of the stick and someday—and I mean soon—the bright, burning light of IAD is going to focus down on my command again, and none of us, not you or me or most in my command, can long endure with that kind of intense heat beating down on us. Do you understand that, Lanark?"

"Yes, sir."

"No, I don't believe you do."

61

"But, sir—"

Maria stepped in with Lanark's chili and sandwiches. Wood stood up and almost knocked the food out of the little woman's hands. A bit of commotion followed him out the door.

"What was that all about?" Shannon asked Lanark while Maria smiled and hummed and hovered about them, setting their meals before them.

"No big deal, Shannon."

"You said you were working on something with Stokes, breaking him in, but what the captain described is not what you described. You were after *them*, weren't you?"

"No, a guy named Loomis. Drug bust, plain and simple," he lied outright, using his actor's guile to make her believe him. She wanted to believe him, and he simply helped her to do so. If Loomis led to *them*, then it would be a lie, but so far, Loomis had not done so, and therefore, in his own mind, he rationalized the lie. But in his heart he knew that he had indeed jeopardized young Stokes in his vendetta that had gotten others killed or wounded in the past.

"It's one thing to carry on with your vengeance, Ryne," she said icily, "but quite another to risk that boy's life."

"Stokes fingered Loomis. We staked him out. It got out of hand when Loomis made Stokes"—he jerked his head to one side—"and maybe me. We got careless, and all hell broke loose."

"And you never said a word."

"When the hell was there time? We've been flat out all day on this Rhodes thing, for Christ's sake."

She breathed in a deep whiff of the aroma of the food before them. "I'm sorry, it's just that . . . you make it hard to trust you, you know."

"Don't try. I've warned you before that you can't."

"Partners have to trust one another."

"Part of this partner you can trust. Another part of me . . . you can't. Leave it at that, Shan."

They ate for a time in silence as she absorbed all that had

happened, and swallowed all her suspicions. Soon, the food and drink had relaxed them both. For a time, they listened to old songs on the jukebox, and to tales of the great Northwest where Tebo had traveled and for a time had been a lumberjack! His stories never failed to entrance Shannon, who saw them unfolding in her mind as he spoke. All the difficulties, differences, drudgery, and horror of the day melted from her mind. She felt safe in the company of these two strong men, Lanark and his robust, tall Uncle Jack. As she was warmed by the drinks inside, a mellow feeling had reached out to her, and she wanted nothing more than to go upstairs with the man she loved, strip away the clothes, shower with him, and lie down in his arms.

But Lanark missed the signs at first, telling his own story in earnest to her and to Tebo, a story about Dr. Ames. Something about Richard Ames's behavior at the scene of the Rhodes crime today. Lanark was genuinely concerned about Ames, saying that it simply wasn't like Dr. Richard Ames to display as much uncontrolled emotion at a crime scene. He'd been on many crime scenes before and never a flicker of emotion, but something odd had occurred this time, something inside Ames.

She only half heard the talk.

Tebo said something about "different strokes for different folks." Or something to that effect, she could not be sure. She had become too tired and too vague to care. Her mind was on peace and tranquility and they were talking about disturbances and disorders and shrinks that went to other shrinks for help.

"But Ames is the smartest guy I've ever known, Jack," Lanark said, pounding the table.

"Smarter than me?" Tebo shot back, pounding the other side of the table.

"Hey, can we get some rest, Ryne?" she asked, but only half heard herself. She'd had one too many, and she seemed to be the only one who noticed.

They turned to her and Tebo chuckled, and Lanark

helped her to her feet and guided her toward his upstairs quarters. She was soon where she wanted to be: nude and under the spray of a warm shower with his arms around her. They washed one another down with soap and sponges, the action of it driving them each wild. They kissed passionately and long below the jet spray, until Lanark lifted her off her feet and carried her to his bed, where he threw down the covers and placed her inside them, treating her like a jewel to be encased in a protective sheath.

They made love.

It seemed half dream and half real. Both halves felt like the best of both worlds—dream and reality. She fell asleep believing she had experienced all that was important in life, and that she would experience it again, and that together, despite everything, and even despite him, they did have a long, luxuriant, bright future ahead.

She felt herself arching and aching in her dreams as she dozed off, imagining his touch was still inflicting its wondrous, flicking, darting stabs to her flesh.

Felix was misbehaving.

He would do that at times when Morgan Sayer was doubly occupied, both with his performance and with that partitioning of the mind with which he had learned to separate out his true self to oversee the performance. It was a strange part of him, a "third eye" of sorts that moved in from various angles of the stage, watching his own physical performance as if from a distance. Other great magicians, ventriloquists, and hypnotists had this ability, but his was very powerful and very real. He watched himself work, and yet it was also him to the right of center of the room, then down to the left, next out front, to the rear of the club—always watching, shadowlike, planning his other's next move and the next like a well-greased machine. And somehow it all came together and the audience loved it. A true mystery.

Then Felix would fuck his concentration by grabbing him in an impolite place for a cheap laugh.

They were laughing now, and Felix stared back at him with this frozen, dumb grin, winked, and said, "Just checking to see if you're all there, Morgan."

Felix was immature and silly, and prophetic at times, the way a child is when critical of its elders.

Felix was like a child to him, sometimes. A regular Pinnochio that sometimes came to life before Morgan and the crowd. It was good little Felix who first charmed the crowd, got them distracted, feeling loose and relaxed—pliant, as it were.

"Stop that, Felix," Morgan said sternly, poking a finger into Felix's face.

Audience laughter.

"That's bigger'n the other one, folks," Felix said in his high-pitched voice. "But no thanks."

Audience hysteria.

He was surprised at the reaction Felix's big hand going into his fly had created. But he didn't have time now to analyze why it was so.

"That's quite enough, Felix!" Morgan shouted. "Back to your books. He reads constantly, folks; sort of a hobby." Morgan said this as he stuffed the complaining, whining dummy into a suitcase.

"Ever try to iron out the wrinkles in your goddamned skin?" Felix shouted, which wasn't rehearsed.

More audience laughter.

Felix wouldn't shut up; from inside the box he shouted: "Hobby, hell, I hate reading, but I'm building a nuclear bomb, and it takes research. Up to three cereal boxes a day!"

The laughter subsided as Felix was no longer on stage. Morgan, now alone on stage, turned to his audience, watching his own movements and calibrating the timbre of his now-serious voice.

"Ladies and gentlemen, now if we may look deeply into the more serious realm of hypnotism, who among you is willing to be my subject for tonight? I guarantee you no harm. In fact, it was so pleasant for Felix there that he never wanted to leave me again."

A few chortles and mild laughter, as others pleasantly buzzed, some trying to get a friend up on stage.

The stage was cramped and couldn't accommodate too many, but all he needed was a few.

"Preferably a pretty face, something easy for the rest of us to look at after Felix, huh? Who's brave, courageous, and bold? Miss, miss, what about you?"

The other Morgan, watching from the back, had seen her first. She was entranced with Felix and the entire performance of Morgan Sayer. She didn't hesitate when his stage self stepped down and put a hand out to her. The other two choices were done almost blindly. It was the first one he was interested in. She had lovely, petite hands. Hands he liked. Hands Felix would like as well.

"Now, you will observe why I am called The Soothsayer. Everyone has a secret past that goes beyond the veil of mortal time, a past we cast off when we are reborn into the natural world, yet the spirit lives on deep within us. And tonight, The Soothsayer will make you a believer."

He asked their names and they answered in succession, ending with the least interesting of the lot.

"James Adams, car sales from Glencoe."

"Okay, Jim, may I call you Jim?"

"Call me anything, but don't call me late for dinner," the heavy man said, chuckling.

"Watch the hands, Jim . . . Jim, keep your eyes trained on my hands."

He hypnotized people by the movement of his hands and the soothing, reassuring tone of his voice alone. People placed themselves, their very lives, into his hands, and for all these years he had never betrayed that trust, but to test the boundaries and very limits of his power, he'd seen no other recourse with Rhodes. He was, he knew, obsessed with his recent discovery.

The stage routine had become boring for him, although

he continued performing, as he was currently doing. At the same time a part of his mind—quite apart from his stage presence—was plotting out tonight's plan.

Jim fell under his spell so quickly it appeared to be a hoax. Morgan had to calm the crowd.

The second volunteer, a middle-aged woman, introduced herself at his request. "Catherine Powell . . . I . . . I'm an accountant, and I don't know what I'm doing up here."

"Why, my dear," he consoled her, "you came to find your secret self."

"I don't think I . . . I really don't think—"

"*Shhhhh*, settle your mind and your eyes here on my palms. Watch them float above your eyes and round and round about. See how much strength is there in the hands? They are God's creation, Catherine, and they are the most supple and pliant of tools on the face of the earth. Watch them float like a pair of butterflies mating. You're growing weary and your eyes are heavy, so I want you to close them, but keep the image of the comforting hands before you. There now, Catherine, there . . ."

She finally relaxed totally and fell entranced under his power. He then went to his third volunteer of the evening, who had watched the movement of his hands from the beginning, and she stepped into it in a loving, wishful way, wanting to be guided by him, unafraid and unemotional.

"And your name?"

"Sarah . . ."

"Sarah? A pretty name." His hands wove an invisible web before her eyes. "You have no last name, Sarah?"

He forced the suggestion on her without either her or the audience being aware of it, and she agreed. "No . . . no last name."

"You had another name once, long ago, and it is buried in your soul and in time, is it not?"

"I . . . I don't know."

She was very pliant. He could control her. He felt the

surge of feelings that this created in him whenever he came across such a person as Sarah. Rhodes, in his way, was the same.

"Sarah, you're going to count for me," he said, his hand still in flight before her eyes, making the audience wonder if there was some sort of mechanical device in his palm that so captivated the young blond-to-sandy-haired woman's complete attention.

"Close your eyes now, Sarah, and count backwards beginning with one hundred."

She began chanting the numbers backwards until she reached 87, and he stopped her with a question "Where are you now, Sarah? Sarah?"

"My name is Heather, not Sarah."

"Where are you, Heather?"

"Far away, a place of silence and sadness, stones all around, a prison of sorts from which I have no escape."

Danny, the club owner, was making facial grimaces. He detested it when the show went from guffaws to this, and to lighten things up a bit, Felix shouted from inside his box at the rear of the stage, "Hey, Morgan the Morbid, you going to take this one through puberty or what? Let's get on with the show."

"Who are you, Heather, and why're you locked up?"

"My mistress found me abed with my master."

The audience perked up for this.

"And you were so cruelly punished because of a mere infraction of the moral code of your times?"

"My mistress is a duchess, and he a duke, and one loathes me, and the other fears me, for I am with child. Both the child and I are ill and dying, and are like to die here . . . both, before my dear child sees light of day from the womb!"

The house was silent and people sat in awkward poses, suddenly caught by the tragic moment in time in which a supposed spirit life from another era had come forth to speak with them, thanks to the power of Morgan Sayer to reach into the depths of Sarah's soul.

68

"Sleep now, Sarah, but we will want to speak again with Heather at another time." Again, it was not a normal suggestion, but an implanted suggestion. "Perhaps when midnight tolls, you'll come again to seek out Morgan Sayer to confide your whole story so that it might be recorded for all ages."

"Yes," agreed Sarah.

"Spare me, please," said Felix from the box, causing laughter all around, but Sayer kept his hand on Sarah's arm, holding her entranced in such a fashion that his other self saw his stage self as a battery from which she was drawing energy. She was feeding off him. A troubled psyche, he told himself.

He tried the same tack with Catherine, but twisted her up in her own words, placing her in a barnyard as a cow, and she went about the stage on all fours, mooing and asking to be milked. This drew whistles, catcalls, and laughter, as well as snide remarks from the inelegant Felix. Twice Morgan had to go to the box and plead with Felix to please keep silent, ending with a thundering. "This is science, and you . . . you dummy, you know nothing of science!"

He finished with the car salesman, whose past life was also turned into a fiasco when he suddenly began to bleat like a sheep. When the audience had been silenced by Morgan Sayer's outraged, upraised hands and burning eyes, his cape flowing with a sudden burst of wind from the direction of the floodlight panel, he said, "You all miss the point. Mr. Adams is not a sheep, or a goat. He was a Volkswagen in his former life!"

After a final burst of laughter, Morgan brought all three volunteers around with three pats of his hands before their eyes. Each awakened feeling refreshed and surprised and wondering when Morgan was going to hypnotize them. Catherine had to get up off the floor, amazed that she found herself on all fours. All this to the roar and clap of approval from the nightclub people, including Danny, whose smile meant that Morgan's risks had been worth it.

Later, at midnight, when his final show was finished, he fully expected to go out into the street and find that Sarah *Nobody* had returned to him. She'd come seeking *him;* not answers to her troubled spirit, but him. She knew in her secret inner soul that he had commanded it of her and she could not refuse.

FIVE

The aged woman tripped on her own tattered skirt when it drooped below her heels as she fought with the mainstay of her existence, the bag over her shoulder which was bulging and filled to capacity. She negotiated up one street and down another amid the pale orange glow of the modern "gaslights" of Chicago, the eerie vampire shadows of night all around her. She neither saw nor cared about the four-legged creatures scampering about. The occasional bat swooping overhead didn't perturb the big lady either. Yet something quickened her pulse. It began as a stone caught and tossed by a shoe somewhere behind her. Some *thing* on two legs was nearby—a much more dangerous proposition. Still, she'd existed for years on her own, on the street, journeying the length and breadth of the big city without ever once being killed. She'd been beaten up once or twice, but not before she'd busted a few heads herself.

She chewed on an unlit cigar. Her hands were in old cloth gloves, the fingers gone out of each. She wore her change of clothes over the others, and topped her wardrobe off with a floppy hat she'd found back of Fanny May's Candy Factory over toward Adams, or was it Jackson? She couldn't recall street names no more than she could recall the names of the Presidents.

She never thought of such things, or if she did, they were fleeting thoughts causing her pain and headaches.

71

She didn't know why it should make her sad, but it did, whenever she thought of the little girl she had been; of her school days which she'd never finished; of her home which she had abandoned; of her family and the bastard who had destroyed her mother's love for her. That was a million worlds away from her now, and she just never gave it more than a fleeting thought. Much more important at the moment was finding a piece of brass, because Sam Ollins, down at the dump, had said he'd give her a fair price for any brass she could find.

The neighborhood was a rough one, but one she'd been in before without incident. There were gangs roaming about, but most of the kids saw her as they saw the trash bins and lampposts. She didn't fear them.

But someone was nearby and had seen her, and seemed to be stalking her.

You couldn't be too careful.

She pretended to be deaf and dumb, going about her business as usual. She found a couple of interesting items in the dumpster behind a hardware store. She went down the row of little businesses—searching, lifting, poking items into her bag and from time to time feeling the cold, hard steel she intended using for protection should she need it. It was concealed within her bag, close at hand.

She was growing impatient with the stalker. He had either decided to stand still where he was all this time, or he had doubled around and would be waiting for her at the end of the alleyway. Damned street lamps were so bright she was an easy target. Damned things were supposed to keep down molestation and fear on the streets at night, but they only served the bad people. She had no place to hide even if she wanted to.

She got to the last of the pickings in the alley, and still no brass. Sam had said brass was hard to come by, and he hadn't lied.

Then she heard it again, footsteps, and from nowhere a large, young man stepped into the alleyway entrance, making a show of blocking her way. "Hey, Momma, what's y'got in the bag?" It was an Italian voice, but she could not make out the face. There was complete blackness where he stood looking like some hulking monster.

She felt for the cold steel in the bag. "You . . . you really want to know?" she croaked in a rough, manly voice.

"Hey, it is you, isn't it, Lanark? My man Lanark."

The old bag lady relaxed her grip on the gun in the bag, and beneath his makeup, Ryne Lanark's gritting teeth and facial muscles relaxed. "Where the hell've you been, Dinetto?"

"Hey, man, I got my own businesses to operate, you know. This is just a sideline. Know what I mean?"

"You get anything for me on Loomis?"

"Guy has gone underground, Lanark."

"Underground?" Lanark was sweating under the bag-lady outfit. "What do you mean, underground?"

"Protected, man. The higher-ups are covering him over. They got their own, whataya-ma-call-it? Relocation plan. They're hiding him out somewhere."

"Where?"

"I don't know. Nobody knows."

"Somebody knows."

"And they're moving him out, soon."

"Where to? When?"

"I'm working on it, Lieutenant, but you got to give me time and finances. Takes a lot of bread to learn about shit like that. People don't talk so easy if they know they might die for it, so you got to pay them better."

"Christ, you're like a leech; come here with nothing but you want to suck money out of my pockets. To hell with you. Not a dime more—"

"But Lanark—"

"—until I see some evidence you got something. Then I'll double the initial investment."

"All right, tomorrow night? The church?"

"See you in confession."

With that the bag lady and the street kid ambled away

from one another. People seeing them from windows or at any distance would have seen a punk harassing an old woman for pocket change. Lanark would have to walk a good two miles back to his car, drive back to his place, and try not to wake Shannon. She hadn't a clue he had left when he did.

SIX

Sarah-who-preferred-to-be-called-Heather returned just as Morgan knew she would; she was unable to do otherwise, unable to resist the suggestion he'd planted deep within her psyche. He had found her outside the club on leaving. She'd come back for the midnight performance and had stayed, entranced with him, or his power, or a combination thereof. She'd been standing in the shadows outside the rear door where he exited every evening after the final performance. He wasn't wearing the cape any longer and Felix was silent for the evening, but she remained enthralled with him anyway. She was young and very pretty in a fawnlike, innocent way, her eyes as egg-shaped as a forest doe's. Frail too . . . very frail.

"You came back," he said.

"Yes."

"I had hoped you would." He put down Felix and the case he was in and took her hands in his, massaging them, fondling each finger within his large grasp. She was lost the whole while in his eyes. "Will you come with me, Sarah?"

"Heather . . . my true name is Heather."

"Yes, I know."

"You possess . . . magic, don't you?" she asked.

"Solutions, perhaps, but magic . . . no, that is something we all possess in our hearts and minds, Heather. Would you like to end your eternal sadness, Heather?

Would you?"

"Yes, oh, yes."

"Then come with me."

"I knew you could help me."

"Place yourself completely in my hands, and it shall be done. You will never be hurt again, never feel fear or hatred again. You will find peace, Heather, at last."

"Thank you."

He picked up Felix and together the three of them went to his Victorian house on Devon instead of the apartment complex. It had been his father's house before him, and now it stood as a monument to the past, crushed between two more modern homes. It was closer to the club, and he had the uneasy feeling that someone was watching his apartment complex, waiting for him there. A neighbor might have identified Rhodes's body as the man that had left with him the night before, and the place could be secretly surrounded by the entire Chicago police force. The fear might be unfounded, but it was real. Even Felix knew enough to know that what Morgan had done could cost each of them their lives.

So they went to the house on Devon, with Felix in the backseat, deep in his trunk, a snore and a whine welling up from him now and again, but otherwise comfortably asleep (as he was when Rhodes's hands were dispatched—and yet the next morning, Felix knew everything). Sarah/Heather sat in the passenger seat alongside Morgan and asked a lot of questions of him, questions that were giving him a headache.

He drove and tried to answer her without sounding irritated. Any show of anger could frighten her off. Anything to upset her and the *trick* wouldn't work.

"Where're you from? Far away, I bet? Europe maybe, or the Scandinavian lands, or maybe Greece? I've never met anyone like you before. Bet you've been all over the world."

He couldn't tell her otherwise, and he *had* traveled the States extensively when he was young, but he had lived most of his life in Chicago in the house on Chase. "How

76

did you know?" he asked in reply to her volley of questions.

"Oh, you're so well mannered and—and smart."

"You are very bright too, Heather."

"Ohhhhh, no, I'm not."

"But you are. You just need someone to show you how much you have to offer the world, to offer a . . . a man."

She stared lovingly across at him in the darkened cab of the car. "Really? You really think so?"

"With a little hypnosis and self-confidence building, you could please any man, Heather. Your fears and self-doubts have been forged over many, many years, remember? Not since your soul was imprisoned have you released it. Have you? Have you?"

"No, no . . ."

"I thought not." A virgin, he thought. Incredible.

Later, turning on lights so as not to frighten her, he moved about the old house filled with bric-a-brac and history. Down below in the basement was his shop where he'd fashioned Felix many years before, and more recently the hand guillotine. He'd designed it thinking he'd use it in the act. It was to be a trick, to make people scream and spill their drinks as the hands came tumbling down toward the audience, but as he fashioned it, he'd come to another conclusion. All along his unconscious mind had been working on another use for the guillotine, and its first use was with the help of good Mr. Rhodes. While it was satisfactory, he knew he could do better with Heather. With Heather's hands, it would end. He'd be satisfied, and all the wild night dreams and visions of a roomful of hands upon which he'd sleep in comfort and cushion would come to an abrupt end, and he and Felix would go on from there as before.

Heather came to him, actually followed him about like a puppy or cat. She made him put Felix aside, and she began kissing him. She wasn't acting like a virgin. Maybe it'd been a lie. Or perhaps Heather was no virgin, while Sarah was. Of course. That made sense.

"In my room," he said, lifting her off her feet and

carrying her into the bedroom at the foot of the stairs. He didn't like to go upstairs. Upstairs had been his father's domain. Besides, his old bedroom was closest to the work benches in the basement and the guillotine.

Felix's case fell over where he'd stood it, and Felix said, "Ouch," and began to grumble and curse unkindly.

"Please, Morgan," she said, her eyes telling him to continue on his present course.

He glanced back at Felix, steeled his resolve, and closed the door on Felix. As if from far away, he heard Felix say, "Don't do it, Morbid Morgan." But she didn't hear him, and she was kissing him passionately as Heather, who'd been locked away in a cell from the touch of a man for centuries.

She pulled him down over her and they undid one another's clothing, giggling, laughing like children, and she kept saying, "You're wonderful, Morgan Sayer, wonderful."

He had had a similar effect on Rhodes, except with Rhodes it was not sexual so much as a feeling that they had known one another their entire lives and should have beer after beer and story after story to share. Morgan had that effect on people. They looked into his intense eyes, saw and felt the energy all around him and in his large hands, which somehow "healed" wounds in their inner psyches. No, they didn't ever want to leave him ever again.

He knew he could keep Sarah/Heather for as long as he wished, but he mustn't let that erode his resolve. He had lured her here for her hands, and that was all.

Still, he could afford to give her her moment of passion and pleasure before he suggested she die.

Lanark removed most of his bag-lady clothes and the wig at the car, tossing them in the trunk of the old dust-buster he used on such outings as this. As he drove home he saw the life on the streets at this hour was made up primarily of night crawlers: people who could not abide the light of day, who slept with the sun like vampires awaiting the next moon. Some were homeless, but the majority were "working stiffs" of the sort that moved illegal goods of one type or another. If he wanted a collar he could have rousted six such people before reaching home. If Shannon weren't home, he might have run down one of these men in particular, a Joey Riccoleti, whom he suspected of having dealings with Loomis and some other pushers. But he had to let it go this time, had to get back to Shannon. If she should awake . . .

He quietly entered through the back after parking his old rattletrap. He had been smart enough to coast in with lights doused. He made the stairs silently enough, but the door needed oiling and it squeaked like a banshee that'd been cut. At least, in the silent of the predawn, that was how it sounded in Ryne's ears.

Still, Shannon seemed asleep. She hadn't even sensed his having gone. Some detective, he thought, when she rolled over and pointed a gun at him.

"Hooooooold on! It's me!"

"Damn you, Ryne! On another of your nightly prowls? Couldn't you forgo the night-patrol crap while I'm with you?" She was furious and up in an instant, dressing.

"Hey, Shan, I had to make contact with my snitch, that's all. Tony Dinetto—it was prearranged."

"Why don't you go sleep with this Dinetto character! Damn, I wake up, you're nowhere in sight, then I hear somebody creeping up the stairs and the door's jiggled. Christ, I could've killed you."

"But you didn't—"

"And maybe I should have!" She moved about the room in a furor. "Where're my damned panties. You keep away from me! Ryne, Ryne!"

He tried to take her in his arms.

"You look and smell like sewage, damnit. I thought you were the Swamp Thing returned. Get off, get away," she said, pummeling his chest until he let go.

"Easy, easy, babe."

She was in tears. "I just ask for one night, one damned night, but no . . . you can't put it away, can you? You're a

79

cop every hour, every minute."

"Where're you going?" he demanded, stopping her at the door.

Tebo was banging a wall somewhere to tell them to keep it down. Both of them cooled a bit.

"I'm going to my place. I'll see you at headquarters, Lieutenant."

Ryne dropped his gaze and let her go, shaking his head. She was right to be angry. He had no way to stop her from storming out. He knew he'd have to make it up to her somehow, if he could. He'd been a fool to do this to her.

Sarah/Heather extended her hands, placing them through the holes created for them in the guillotine. She was under his control, and once more he felt the surge of titillating excitement shooting through his veins as he watched her obey his commands.

"You will feel nothing, Heather, not even when the block falls and your hands are dismembered," he said in a calming voice.

"I will feel nothing."

"You will not bleed either."

"No . . . no bleeding."

"Through the power of your mind, Heather, you will hold back the blood to retain it within your body. You can do it, Heather. You will re-route the flow of your own blood, and you will feel no pain. You will remain in a deep trance until I give you the signal, Heather."

"I will . . . I will."

"Good, use your will, Heather. You have a powerful will. Use it to neutralize the nerves and the blood. Will you do it, Heather?"

"Yes . . . yes . . ."

He had her where he wanted her. He took a deep breath and released the weight that held the blade over her wrists. It came down with a magical swish and the hands flew into the little tub in the basin of the sink where she stood. She remained unfeeling, unthinking, bleeding at the two gaping ends of her arms, which remained pressed against the outside of the blade that had slashed them. She did not see that the "trick" was no ordinary magic trick, that the trick was that she remained absolutely calm and standing and out of shock by virtue of his hypnotic suggestion to her that, as far as she could see, there were hands at the ends of her wrists.

"You're not bleeding," he told her several times, and soon the blood was staunched by virtue of the power of her own mind, the suggestion taking firm hold.

Anxious to take up the hands and claim them as his own, he took them each from the tub and went through the old house with them, giddy and excited at his treasure, popping open Felix's case to show him.

"Ugghhhh!" said Felix. "You bastard, you did it."

"For you."

"Not me, you."

"To make you better. Look at these," he said, holding high Heather's two hands, the blood dripping from them onto Felix's face.

"*Pa-pugh! pugh!*" Felix spat. "You're sick, Morgan, very sick."

"No, Felix, you wooden-head, you don't understand what this means."

"Power trip, that's all."

"Power, yes, but not just for me, Felix, for all humanity."

"Bull, Morgan. Bullshit, you eat. I don't have to."

Morgan ripped Rhodes's hands from the dummy where he'd stitched them to the fabric of his little coat, angry with Felix. "Little bastard! Ungrateful little bastard."

"Getting more like the old man every day, Morg—"

Heather screamed from the other room. She'd come out of it. Her scream was piercing and awful.

He raced to her. Felix caught onto his hand somehow and was flung head over heel, squealing in a crescendo of pain as Morgan got to Heather, whose bloody wrists were in her eyes where horror now resided completely. She'd lost the concentration, lost the suggestion somehow.

81

Felix's fault. *Somehow Felix always managed to screw everything up!*

He leaped at Heather to get her mouth covered as the blood splattered about, discoloring his nightshirt, the kitchen linoleum, the table, the oven, the fridge. She fell over in a dead faint, her screams dying with her.

But she wasn't dead. In a kind of shock, but not dead. Her body quivered and shook like that of an epileptic in a fit. Her eyes had rolled back in their sockets. He'd been unprepared for this.

Rhodes had been a better subject after all, despite his initial reluctance to go under. He laid her down on the floor and tied her wrists together with an old apron snatched from nearby. He put her wrists over her nude form and tied them tightly, cutting off some of the blood flow. Shakily, looking all about, he saw Felix peeping at him from the doorway where he lay on his stomach, grinning as if to say, "I told you so." He threw a pot at the dummy, but missed. Morgan got to his feet, rushed in for his pants and car keys and a coat. He wrapped her in the coat, and being careful that no one was looking down from any windows outside, he carried her to his waiting car.

Once inside, he saw she'd gotten blood on the upholstery, and he cursed her for this. He had truly thought her a capable subject for the experiment, and all had been going so well until Felix had somehow jinxed it. Damned Felix. Next time, he'd leave the little bastard at the club if this was the way it had to be.

He started up the car and drove. He found himself soon going in circles for a place to dump Heather's body. Her breathing had become so shallow, he was certain she'd be dead within the hour. Then he saw an alley where the vapor light had been busted—by rocks thrown at it by neighborhood children, he supposed. There was Heather's resting place.

He drove into the alley, quickly got out, and snatched what was left of Heather from his car. Below her she'd left a dark purple splotch of blood. He'd have to worry about that later. For now, he dumped the remains amid the trash cans lining a broken-down old wood garage. A dog behind a nearby fence began barking and a light went on over there. He rushed back to the car and got in, and when he drove off, he saw someone amble up to the very spot where he'd left Heather. From the look of the nosey person, it was a homeless street person.

Morgan Sayer told himself it would be all right, that he would think positive thoughts, and that it would be all right. At the moment, he had to get back to the house, clean it from top to bottom, clean his prizes, and refit them onto Felix. He didn't give another thought to Heather.

SEVEN

At 8:10 the following morning Lanark's undercover unit got the call: The nude body of a woman had been discovered dumped in an alleyway not five miles from Lanark's own house and pub. What made this corpse of particular interest to Lanark's unit was the fact the victim was without her hands.

The crime scene was a nightmarish walk-through of the Rhodes killing, except that the victim was a young female, perhaps early twenties, not spectacular in either shape or face, weighing 115 or 120, measuring five-nine. She had disturbed a pleasant walk an elderly gentleman by the name of Winthrop and his dog, Fergie, were taking. Winthrop was taking oxygen at the back of a medic unit when Lanark found him. The man was aghast at his discovery. His dog, allowed off the leash, had run ahead of him, and had begun sniffing around the wounded woman before Winthrop had had any notion of the problem. He had had to go to six different doors before anyone in the damned block would listen to his story and telephone for emergency services.

"First house I went to, the woman was as nasty as could be, chased me from it," he was saying now, catching his breath. Shannon stood nearby, taking notes. "Second place, they said they didn't want to get involved."

"Well, they're involved now," said Shannon. "Point them out to me, Mr. Winthrop . . . that is, if you're

84

through with your questioning, Lieutenant Lanark."

She was still being icy toward him. "He's all yours," he said simply, unable to meet her eyes.

"Looks like we've got a psycho on our hands," she said before taking Winthrop on the walk-through of the neighbors who had turned him away when he begged for assistance. Shannon knew that among those who routinely turned away do-gooders like Winthrop, quite often a witness of sorts could be located: a person who'd seen something but was afraid to come forward, usually out of a sense of overwhelming guilt brought on by the fact that he or she might have helped the victim, but had failed to do so. Some were paralyzed by fear; others, simply anti-social.

Lanark fended off reporters who were anxious for any remarks at all from the police. When he shouted a no-comment, they returned jeers. Among them, he saw his friend Jeff Sandler, and for a moment their eyes met. There was something in Sandler's gaze, an immeasurably deep sadness that seemed to have everything to do with the dead woman.

Lanark filed it away and continued to try to do his job. He returned to Dr. Black, who was already tired of seeing handless corpses, and didn't mind shouting it to the world. "Hell of a thing . . . hell of a way for this unfinished life to finish," he was saying again.

Lanark kneeled down beside him and said, "I noticed a distinct absence of blood. What about you, Doc? Same MO as with Rhodes? Cut elsewhere, dumped here?"

Black's usually blank countenance beamed. "So you came to your senses. Good. Yes, she was mutilated elsewhere. A simple deduction from the amount of blood loss. Where're the stains?"

"What about Rhodes? Anything come of the autopsy?"

"Something always comes of an autopsy, lad."

They stared into one another's eyes over the body of the unidentified woman. Something impish flickered across Black's eyes. It made Lanark ask, "What is it?"

"Rhodes's heart killed him."

"Heart attack?"

"Massive signs of it, yes."

"Brought on by . . ."

"Shock. A very great shock."

"You mean like having your hands chopped off?"

"Yes."

Black was sometimes in a mood, and this seemed one of those times. He wanted to play games with the ignorant cop who needed him.

"Black, Dr. Black, can you just tell me what you're getting at? Save me the trouble of—"

"You police don't want trouble, do you? You live off it, but you don't want any of it. All right, try this out. Rhodes's hands were not taken off with an ax, or a hacksaw."

"You know that for a fact?"

"I'd stake my reputation on it, yes."

"What then?"

"No weapon I can identify. Something like . . . like a meat cleaver, but not quite. Strange striations at the wound, and the weight of the weapon is so . . . so uniform."

"Uniform?"

"When a man stabs with a knife, or wields an ax or cleaver, one part of the blade will strike with a stronger force than another, thus leaving telltale signs, albeit microscopic—"

"Doc, doc—"

"—and the jagged nicks and edges can be made to fit the pattern of a type of weapon, but Lanark, this one's got us stumped."

Lanark shook his head in confusion. "Then you don't know? Why didn't you just say you don't know? Why can't you do that, Black? Hell, this isn't sixth grade."

Black stared a hole through Lanark before saying, "I don't need a third-rate police lieutenant telling me what to do, kiddo, so back off, or do you propose to take a swing at me?"

Lanark frowned and threw up his hands in a gesture of

defeat. "What is it, the full moon or something?"

"I'll know more when I look her over closely," he told Lanark. "See she gets to my lab, will you?"

Maybe Black had just seen too much; maybe he was in a burnout, or a life crisis. Lanark wasn't sure, but the older man had certainly had his hackles up lately. Then it occurred to Lanark that Black had a theory of the crime, at least a guesstimate on the weapon used, but was withholding it because he'd been shy about such things lately. He followed the coroner to his official car, where the man tossed his black valise with all the hair and fibre and skin samples he'd collected from the body.

"Do you have a theory on the weapon, Dr. Black?"

"Nothing, no."

"But it cuts clean, neat."

"Yes."

"Electrical saw?"

"No, that we'd be able to detect. I've seen that before."

"Rotary saw?"

"Ditto."

"Machine of some sort, though?"

"My guess."

Lanark nodded. "Maybe a machine press."

"Press, yes."

"Like with a power ignition; flash, it presses down and off comes the hands."

"*Poof,* yes."

"Well, that tells us something."

"Does it?"

"We'll start to look at machines capable of making such cuts, and men who use them."

"Needle in a haystack in a city like Chicago."

Lanark nodded. "So it is."

"Could also lead your astray. Could be one man with one such machine in his basement."

"I'll get some men working on it. And thanks."

"Sure."

"Don't suppose you have any other bones to toss my way?"

"Nothing concrete yet. Too early to tell."

Lanark thanked him again and watched him pull away. Ames hadn't come, although Lanark had sent word to him of the latest tragedy. He must've been tied up; couldn't get away.

Shannon was making the rounds of the nearby flats with back windows overlooking the alleyway. Mark Robeson and Stokes were working the crowd, on the lookout for that strange breed of witness who came back only to gawk and hide amid the crowd. Sometimes, even the killer did this. They kept note of anyone who appeared particularly peculiar. Now the body was being lifted into what the cops lately referred to as a "Black" bag, a body bag labeled with large letters proclaiming the contents as "belonging" to the coroner's office. It was amazing how many bodies picked up on the city streets never found their way to Black's offices. Where they went was anyone's guess, but most were located in local hospitals if someone cared enough to initiate a search.

Lanark went for his car, telling Robeson he was going back to HQ. "We're all to convene there this P.M., say two, got that? We've got to put something together on this guy quick."

"Put our heads together, huh, Lieutenant?"

"You got any better ideas at the moment?"

"No, no, not complaining."

"Sorry, Mark."

"No problem, Lieutenant. See you at two."

Just then Wood's car pulled up, screeching tires, and from it Wood escorted a frantic woman and a man whose eyes darted in every direction from his thin, drawn face. The couple looked as if they'd been forced to remain awake all night during a grueling session of interrogation. Captain Paul Wood hailed Lanark, waving to him to join them.

They were headed for the ambulance and the body bag.

Lanark caught up. "Captain?"

"Missing persons put Mr. and Mrs. Chambers in touch with us. Seems they've been searching for their runaway daughter for several weeks—"

"Six," said the father.

"God," the mother moaned on seeing the body bag, her hand going to her mouth.

"Maybe this isn't such a good idea, Captain."

"We insisted," said Mr. Chambers. He then took firm hold of his wife and said in the manner of a preacher, "Dear, if it is God's will. If our little Sarah is lying there a few feet from us, it is part of God's plan, and not ours to question."

Her jaw was firmly set, and Lanark thought she was about to agree with him when she suddenly began striking out at him with her balled fists, tears streaming from her eyes as she shouted, "You, you get away from me! You're the reason she ran away, David, you! Not God, you!"

She fell and got up, clawing at the back of the ambulance where the confused attendants looked to Captain Wood for a signal as to what to do. Chambers stood behind his wife. Wood gave the nod. The large zipper sounded like a crackling fire, as a hush had fallen over the entire area, photographers snapping shots of the fear-filled visage of the mother before the corpse that was revealed to her.

She stood stolid, frozen at first. Lanark could not tell if it was their daughter or not until Mrs. Chambers fell into her husband's arms in a dead faint. Chambers moaned inwardly and repeated the name. "Sarah, oh, Sarah."

"Shit," said Wood into Lanark's ear.

Lanark quietly agreed with Wood.

At 2:00 P.M. they were all assembled, including Myra Lane and Wil Cassidy, who'd been on lend-lease to another precinct, working on a prostitution sting. Myra was small, petite, and beneath the sweetness and blonde-bombshell exterior, as tough a cop as Lanark had ever worked with. She was married to Wil, who was two heads taller than she. Both of them enjoyed theater, and were working actors on their own time at The Bridge and other

Chicago playhouses. On occasion, they'd tried to woo Lanark into a production, but he'd finally made it clear to them that the only theater for him these days was the theater of the street.

Stokes and Robeson shared a corner of the squad room. Shannon was drinking a soda, working keenly over a report she'd wanted to finish before they got started, something to do with the results of her and Winthrop's return to the apartments and flats where people had turned Winthrop away in the predawn hours. On the wall a photograph of two men who had died in the early stages of the development of Lanark's special undercover unit looked on—Jeff Blum and Max Yoshikane. They were constant reminders of the inherent danger of the work, as well as the importance of caution and quickness in undercover work. Every new member of the team was introduced to Blum and Yoshikane, as if they were still in the unit—at least in spirit. Stokes had recently been told that Blum was as fast with a gun, and as deadly a shot, as any policeman in the department, but that he'd died when he hesitated shooting a man who fired on him first. He was told that Yoshikane, a master of martial arts with keen senses, had died from a wound inflicted in his back by the infamous Subway Killer—last month's headlines.

Lanark had just started the meeting when suddenly Captain Wood opened the door and stepped in, followed by Commissioner Lawrence and a reluctant-looking Dr. Richard Ames.

"Thought we'd join you on this one, Lieutenant Lanark," said Wood in his official voice. "I think everyone here knows everyone else."

Stokes stood up as if he might salute the commissioner, but otherwise, everyone remained calm. They had all worked cases which had caught the attention, or imagination, of the commissioner before. Usually, as with the Subway Killer, it simply meant that the burners were being turned up, and what they would ordinarily have done, they had to pretend to do faster, for appearance's sake. It looked as if the commissioner knew something, but with Lawrence, this was impossible to tell.

Where Wood was straightforward and barrel-chested, the commissioner was roundabout and flat-chested.

"Please," said Lawrence with a wave of his political fingers, "carry on."

"We were about to put our heads together on the . . . the peculiarity of the missing hands."

"Cause of death, yes," said Lawrence.

"Not so far, as established, no, sir," replied Lanark, who filled them in on what Black would soon be putting into an official report on the condition of Rhodes's heart. "He might have died of loss of blood, but his heart gave out first."

"Interesting," Lawrence replied.

"Doesn't that tie in with the old bum's story, that he was, you know, alive, when he was in that alley?" Robeson asked.

"Certainly adds a ripple," added Wil Cassidy, scratching his head.

"Loss of a hand, if quickly treated, doesn't necessarily have to mean death," Shannon said.

"But when too much time is allowed to go by, the victim loses an inordinate amount of blood, goes into shock," Lanark continued, "then death ensues. Seems to be what happened with the Chambers girl."

The news of the ID on the girl was now common knowledge. Myra piped in, saying, "There's no way the man's death could have been some sort of, you know, bizarre accident . . . someone trying to cover it over? Then the girl's death is some creep picking up on news stories, sees his way to get rid of her?"

"We won't rule any possibility out at the moment," said Lanark, "which also means we won't rule out the possibility we have a serial killer here."

"One who collects hands," said Robeson glumly.

"The coroner has reason to believe the hands came off with some sort of specialized equipment—neatness of the cuts, something to do with pressure all across the field of impact. So Mark, and you, Stokes, are going to canvass the

91

Yellow Pages; get a fix on factories in the area that do metal sheet-cutting, that sort of thing."

"In the area?" asked Stokes.

"Ten-mile radius narrowing to a five-mile radius of where the bodies were located. On the map, you see, they weren't so far apart." Lanark indicated two pins he'd placed on a map of the city pressed against a corkboard in the squad room. Beside it were police shots of the two victims. It was shaping up as a serial search.

Lanark went on with his assignments. "Wil, Myra, I want you two to get as much as you can from Sarah Chambers's parents. Anything might help. Work up a profile on the young woman. Maybe something Dr. Ames can deduce from, okay?"

"Understood," said Myra with a glance at her husband, who nodded in return.

"Meantime, Shannon and I'll continue on with what we can learn about Rhodes." Lanark saw Lawrence visibly flinch and wipe his chin, and Ryne knew now why Lawrence was in on it. Senator Rhodes wielded a lot of power, all the way from DC. "We have a lead we'll pursue. Aim here, people, is to attempt to place Rhodes and Sarah Chambers at some bisecting moment in either time or place. On the surface, they seem to have absolutely nothing in common, but we don't know that, do we? Okay, you've got your assignments—unless there's something you'd like to add, Dr. Ames?"

Ames had not said a word and seemed far away. Neither habit was normal for Ames. His eyes darted to Lanark before he stood and said, "At this point, there's little anyone might say about this supposed killer. Hands, of course, carry great symbolic power. Monkey's Paw, remember? People still destroy apes for their hands." His remarks and his delivery were anemic for those who knew Ames well. He'd normally be well prepared, a firebrand, puffing forth information, ideas, thoughts, ruminations, and psycho-babble along with historical fact. But he was cut off, short-circuited. Perhaps it was due to the fact Lawrence was in the room. Ames didn't like Lawrence and the commissioner knew it. At one time the commissioner had put together an attempt to move Ames out of the department, but it had failed.

"There is a man you might speak to who knows a little about . . . oddities," said Ames. "A Dr. Ito Colucci, Museum of Natural History."

"We don't need a damned historian, Doctor," said Lawrence.

Ames ignored this. "Colucci is also a scatologist, and anthroprologist."

"Scat-what?" asked Lawrence. Lanark too was confused.

"Scatologist—expert on man's more mundane bodily functions and rituals; into the occult, the esoteric, and the supernatural, Commissioner."

"Christ, just what we need, Ames, a goddamned witch doctor."

Ames turned and, with a quivering jaw, the enormous black man looked about to spit fire. He also seemed in some sort of feverish condition, beads forming on his forehead. Lanark grabbed him by the arm and forced him into his office, saying, "Excuse us, gentlemen."

Inside Lanark's office, his old friend Ames accepted a tumbler of Jack Daniels, and he drank it down neat at one clip.

"What's troubling you, Richard?"

"Fucking Lawrence is troubling me."

"No, it's more than that."

"Reference to witch doctor, you heard it!"

"That's just Lawrence. We all expect that crap out of the bigoted—"

"How long before we get men like him out of the department, Ryne? Never?"

"You're not going to talk to me about your problem, are you?"

"What do you think I'm talking about here?"

"I know you too well for this, Richard. You don't let men like Lawrence get under your skin this way. There's something else troubling you."

He stared across at Lanark, his rigid posture relaxing only a moment. He took in a deep, long, sucking breath of air before he said, "You smart-ass white boys all think you know how it is being black; think you can feel what a black man feels, step in his shoes; but you always can step right back out. Hell." He laughed after this, got up, and made for the door.

"Ames!"

"Got any idea how hard it was for me to get where I am? The pressures coming down on me? My mother . . . God . . . and this, this curse!"

He tore open the door and barged through the squad room, almost knocking Shannon over. She entered, asking Lanark what that had all been for.

"Don't know. Just know he's hurting . . . hurting bad."

"Certainly not for himself."

"Tell me about it."

"Checked on this guy he mentioned, this Dr. Colucci."

"Oh?"

"He's with Natural History, all right. Maybe we ought to see him?"

"If Ames says so, we should. But first, we have to see Rhodes's girlfriend, Green. You make the appointment?"

"Yeah, we can go right over. Place is on Harrison near Racine."

"Not the swankiest of neighborhoods."

"Flooded with old factory buildings of one kind or another. Lot of garment industry down there."

"Well, let's see if the lady is a lady."

"Got to be more of a lady than the senator was."

"About last night, Shan—"

"Forget it."

"I was wrong to leave you like that."

"I said forget it."

"But—"

He was cut off by the intercom. It was Captain Wood. "You're going to pursue the girlfriend?"

"That is our intention, yes, sir."

Wood cleared his throat and said, "Lawrence had some

94

flack earlier today."

"The lawyer from DC?"

"Seems he has a few friends in high places."

"How high?"

"Remember the run-in you had with the Feds 'bout a month ago?"

"Who forgets such sterling characters?"

"Apparently, they didn't forget you."

"We cut a deal!"

"That deal's old news."

"Captain, what the hell do they want from us? We have a serial killer on our hands. Are we supposed to sweep Rhodes's connection under the rug, hope for more victims?"

Wood sighed into the phone. "Do your job, Lanark; just go lightly with the results of interviews, and keep the hell away from the press. Pass the word to Keyes and the others. That's all."

"Thanks, Captain."

"For what?"

"Running interference."

Wood grumbled something unintelligible into the phone and hung up.

"What was that all about?" asked Shannon.

"Captain just wants us to watch protocol on the Rhodes affair."

"Still smarting about my having called the bitch a dyke, huh?"

Lanark let it pass. He rang the unit's secretary, Samantha, and told her how long they planned to be out and where they could be reached. They passed her on the way out, and she stopped them for an incoming call.

"Says it's urgent, Lieutenant," Samantha said.

Lanark took it where he stood. He listened attentively to whoever was on the other end for a long time. Shannon found a seat, waiting and watching.

"Is that certain, or are you just blowing smoke, Dinetto."

Shannon recognized the name as one of Lanark's

snitches. She saw his eyes light up with that old fire he reserved for those he truly despised. He jotted down a few notes, folded the paper, and stuffed it into his coat pocket before he hung up. Their eyes met momentarily but he pulled them away.

"Let's get over to this garment place."

"Right, Lieutenant."

The frost had returned to her voice, and her eyes acted as ice picks, plunging into him. "On the way, you can tell me what's going on with Dinetto."

"Not much . . . thinks he may have something for me."

She knew he was lying.

He knew she knew he was lying.

He hoped she'd leave it at that.

She wondered if she should drop it.

Together, they made for the Jaguar.

EIGHT

Green Garments was housed in a large, expansive red brick factory amid a row of similar buildings off the downtown thoroughfares, nestled in an area bounded by Ogden Avenue, the railway tracks, and the Kennedy and the Eisenhower Expressways. They pulled off the "Ike" and ramped down to Racine, drove into the heart of the factory district, and began looking for numbers. Soon, they were before the large exterior sign that proclaimed one of the buildings as that of the Green Garment people.

Inside, the place was much more spectacular, with modern lighting and offices, and even a huge showroom for buyers and customers who appeared to come from all over. It was a thriving place, quite busy. Salespeople and buyers were everywhere. Lanark and Shannon were mistaken for new customers before they frightened a receptionist with who they were. The phones rang incessantly.

The receptionist asked the police people to please have a seat, telling them that she would contact someone in public relations.

"No, no!" said Shannon, correcting her. "Ms. Green. We're here to speak to the boss, no one else."

The receptionist was torn. She knew her job was in a sudden crack and she was hanging by her manicured nails. She was a thin, pretty girl with wispy brown hair and a practiced smile.

"We called earlier," said Shannon. "That is, I did. It's just routine, a few questions about an acquaintance. She's expecting us."

"Uh, I see."

She rang for the president of the company. It was difficult getting through, but finally, it seemed she reached someone close to Muriel Green. She then looked at Lanark and spoke to him as if Shannon were not in the room. "Take the elevator to three and someone will meet you there and take you into Ms. Green."

The woman who met them at the elevator, a middle-aged secretary whose matronly appearance was more reassuring than that of the receptionist's, ushered them into an inner office where a tall, broad-shouldered, extremely well-dressed Muriel Green sat behind an enormous desk staring sternly up at them. "You have ten minutes," she said.

"Very kind of you," said Shannon, "but if it takes all damned day—"

"Lieutenant," said Lanark, slowing her. "It should not take much time, Ms. Green."

"Thank you," she replied.

Shannon bit her lower lip, her anger piqued once more today.

Muriel Green was older than Lanark expected, and he sensed that Shannon too was taken aback. She hadn't wanted to see them, she told them. She was much too busy to be doling out her time freely to two Chicago cops looking into an affair that was over years ago.

"Besides, I didn't even know Rhodes was in the city until . . . until I read about the awful . . . horrible news."

"*Senator* Rhodes seems to think otherwise," said Shannon. "She had no trouble whatsoever in discussing you."

"I'm sure she didn't. She hates me thoroughly. We were close once, but . . . so much has happened."

"You knew her?" asked Shannon. "Socially?"

"We're half sisters," Green said with a twisted smile.

"Of course, she got the better half . . . all our lives she did."

The web was thick and tangled, Lanark thought. Lanark sensed a bitter, tired woman beneath the Fifth Avenue clothes and makeup—applied too thickly to be flattering.

"Has either Senator Rhodes or someone representing the senator been in contact with you recently?" He saw an eyebrow rise and freeze and lower slowly before she replied negatively.

"You haven't lied to us yet, Ms. Green," said Lanark. "Don't start now."

She frowned, reached for a pack of Old Golds lying before her, lit up, and calmly blew smoke across at them. She sat behind a huge desk, in a huge office filled with drawings in pen and ink of various undergarments, some very revealing, others more conservative.

"We know that Rhodes set you up in business," said Shannon.

She laughed and shook her head. "Poor bastard. He thought he was in love with me. I seduced him from her, which wasn't at all difficult. Yes, he helped me get started, but he kept siphoning off funds from the business. When we grew large enough, and when I was strong enough, he was cut off without a cent and sent packing."

"When was this?"

"In '89. We became a wholly owned subsidiary of AcTech Industries. Believe me, he had no place in the new structure. He was a pitiful man, really. Heavy drinker."

"And you're telling us you haven't seen him since 1989."

"Oh, he came round again and again, but I had him thrown out the last time, and no, I never saw him after that."

She had a sophisticated manner about her that seemed practiced. Lanark got the impression she had indeed worked hard to reach her present status.

"You expect us to believe that?" asked Shannon.

"Believe what you want, dear."

"Do you know whom he may have been seeing?"

She leaned forward and stretched her long neck toward them. "I told you, I severed ties with him. I know no one who would have done such a horrid thing to him."

"Ms. Green, do you know of anyone he was seeing?" Lanark pressed.

"Call girls, most likely . . . I don't know. He had a weakness for booze, girls, fun."

Shannon began to ask, "He did not contact you during his last visit to the—"

"We've taken up enough of Ms. Green's valuable time, Lieutenant Keyes," said Lanark, interrupting her and giving her a sign that said get up and go.

Shannon gave him a cold stare, but she did what he wanted. Green seemed surprised at the abrupt end to the interview as well. Now she was almost hospitable, saying, "I'm sorry I could not be of more help, officers. I hope you have a chance to see our showroom before you leave."

"Came through it," said Lanark with a smile. "In fact, can't remember when I've enjoyed myself in ladies underwear so much."

Shannon hurried ahead, frowning. Soon they were passing along the aisles of the factory's "Green Room," the showroom to which Green had referred. "Be careful not to get lost," she told him nastily.

"It's a dead end, Shannon. No sense beating down her door."

"Looks to me like it's been beaten on plenty."

"Come off it, will you?"

They were outside in the lot amid the debris of the various factories sharing that side of the street. "I don't believe you. You let that . . . that former hooker off with a pat on the wrist when—"

"Hey, she was telling the truth."

"Oh, now you're a mind reader."

"No, just a good cop, like you when you're not so head-up over your emotions."

"What's that supposed to mean?"

"Means, Keyes, that you're not thinking clearly. You see her giving us dates like that if she couldn't back her statement? And that crack about call girls, don't you get it?"

"No, Mr. Wonderful, I don't get it. She was brassy, and could easily have been lying through her teeth."

"She was, but not about seeing Rhodes. She may have heard from him, yes, but she doesn't see anybody anymore."

"Meaning?"

"You got it." He could see her mind coming round to his point.

"Green Garment's a front? For prostitution?"

"At least that's how it began."

"That's what she's hiding."

"Wouldn't surprise me if she began in DC, moved her operation here with Rhodes's help, outgrew her need for him, and the rest is garment history."

"Jesus, you think she's still pimping for DC officials on holiday to Chicago?"

"Maybe, maybe not. Tuck it away for another visit, once she's relaxed and thinking she has nothing to fear from us."

"Meantime, we can collect a little history on Ms. Green," she offered.

"How about we go see this witch doctor, Ito? At the museum."

"If you buy me lunch on the way, all right."

The Field Museum of Natural History, situated on a concrete island sanctuary between converging lanes of South Lake Shore Drive, always caught the imagination along with the refreshing lake breeze; and despite the never-ending quicksilver flash of cars darting by on each side of the great structure it seemed held and rooted in time, unchanged from the day of its birth at the World's Fair at the turn of the century. From its Grecian front

101

steps Lanark and Shannon could look out over the expanse of blue that was Lake Michigan and see cub planes flying in and out of Meigs Airport. In the near distance stood Adler Planetarium at the end of Solidarity Drive. Lanark had come here as a child on field trips from school, and in the company of his parents and sister. He thought he knew every inch of the place, and boasted now that he could take Shannon straight up to the greatest and most loved ape in Chicago, Bushman, long since stuffed and mounted here.

"Some other time maybe," she said.

They'd had a pleasant if low-keyed talk over lunch; still, an undercurrent of anger flowed in her.

They had telephoned and were expected. In fact, a uniformed guard came directly up to them on entering, and he escorted them to a pleasant public-relations lady who explained that she would take them down to Dr. Colucci's office.

Lanark twirled about as they passed exhibits of mastodons and dinosaurs and great elephants in the main hall. He had to be called and told "this way" twice before they stepped through a door marked Employees Only.

Beyond this door, they found an elevator that took them down two flights.

From there, the lady guided them through a thicket of closetlike rooms lined with shelves which opened onto a main hall of shelving. The rooms were filled with the archaeological dust and debris of what must have been hundreds, perhaps thousands of "digs" and collections from those digs—ivory, onyx, and wood carvings, and objects of every imaginable size, shape, and texture. Lanark saw that Shannon too marveled at the dense forest of boxes stuffed full with objects collected from the world at large and brought there. Lanark saw one carved ivory boat filled to capacity with a crew of laboring, straining fishermen of an African or Caribbean village, some rowing, some casting nets, all carved out of what appeared to be one piece of ivory. It was amazing, and on the shelf below it the label read, "Ghana, 1931." He stopped the lady leading them through the maze with a question. "Has any of this ever been exhibited?"

"There's too much, really . . . not enough display space, you see."

They continued on. "Strange," said Lanark when they passed another unusual sight there in the bowels of the place. "Strange what we call *natural* history." He lifted a set of attached shrunken heads on a cord that looked like something he didn't wish to verify. The ugly little bead eyes, disfigured nostrils, and crinkled skin of the heads were enough to take in.

Shannon told him to put it down and keep up as they went through doors marked No Admittance, passing along dank corridors of stone, and between more shelves filled again with dust-laden boxes to a fourteen-foot-high ceiling. The boxes, labeled and unlabeled, were filled to overflowing with objects of every imaginable sort—and some not so easily imagined.

They saw light at the end of the tunnel, and their noise must have aroused Dr. Ito Colucci, whose name did not appear on the door that stood ajar. Inside, they heard him shouting.

"It's not possible. The practice goes back to the cultured Greeks? Are you sure?"

All the dust had Lanark covering his face with a handkerchief. Shannon had begun to sneeze. They'd both been hoping that once inside Colucci's office they'd have safe refuge from the irritating paste that the years of dust down there had become. But they were disappointed. The dimly lit office was surrounded with shelves filled with such items as human bones, utensils and pots, stonelike mounds, spearheads, and ornamental objects from jade to quartz.

Colucci looked up from his computer, with which he had been carrying on the argument.

The computer sputtered and printed out something which Colucci took in stride, ripping the paper from the printer when it was complete. "Bizarre," he muttered to himself. Then he looked up at his guests and said, "But then, that's what we're here for, correct? The bizarre oddities? They are fascinating. Now, you are with the CPD, and Dr. Richard Ames advises you to speak with me?"

Colucci was a short man with thin wisps of hair over the forehead, wearing a white lab coat that needed a laundering. His manner was quick and urgent, his features not unlike that of a cherub—or a shrunken head, Lanark thought.

Lanark introduced himself and then Shannon. "We're working on the killings in which two victims have been relieved of their hands."

"Yes, I concluded as much from Lieutenant Keyes's phone call. I took the liberty to see what was on file, got a bit sidetracked, but I do have a bibliography of pertinent reference materials."

"We came to you for help, not reading material," said Lanark after the PR person excused herself, leaving Lanark to wonder how they would ever find their way back.

"God helps those who help themselves, Lieutenant. I do have my hands full here, you know."

"What exactly is it you do for the museum, Dr. Colucci?"

Colucci's skin tone and the shape of his eyes bespoke a mysterious, Oriental strain mingled with Italian stock. It appeared his true "nationality" was that of scientist, at any rate.

He ignored Lanark's question. "So far, I have very little I could tell you. Hands, while interesting in and of themselves, have not been what you might call a specialty with me. Otto, my computer, tells me the Greeks and Romans would extend their long, middle fingers at someone to denote unnatural vice, masturbation or homosexuality, and that it meant then what it does now, 'Go fornicate with yourself,' or 'Stick it up your ass.' You know, *up yours.*"

"Dr. Colucci, if you don't care to help us, just say so," Lanark told him.

"No, no, I didn't say that," he retorted, moving about his confined area like a caged animal. "Perhaps I offended you and the young woman, but to fully appreciate anything I might have to say on the thumb, the forefinger, the ball of the fist, or palm, you must have done some homework. It is as simple as that. If I go about the business of suggesting this or that is true of your killer, or mention a strange, forgotten cult of 'hand-snatchers,' then you will go off with wild notions that your killer must be a surviving member of this ancient cult—"

"Was there such a cult?"

"There have been through the ages many kinds of mutilations and tortures using the hands, and people who felt great power could be had by taking a powerful enemy's hand, just as others believed the power resided in the enemy's heart, or brain, or liver. It's what we call cannibalism today."

"Cannibalism?"

"That is what I said, yes, but that is not to be applied to some faceless killer you are after. I cannot make that assertion, and you cannot work on that assumption."

Lanark imagined Rhodes's hands, and those of Sarah, this moment undergoing ingestion by some deranged fiend.

"I see you are already thinking you have answers to a problem you have not the least knowledge of," said Colucci. "Dr. Ames, I'm sure, had the best of intentions. He will often meet with me, ask for guidance, get me to point him in a direction, but he does his work too. He does not expect miraculous answers from me."

"Nor do we," said Shannon.

"If we understand this, then perhaps I can help you . . . perhaps not. Here is the list Otto has prepared for you." He handed it to Shannon, who took it with a smile. She found the strange, little man a lot like Yoda in *The Empire Strikes Back*, peculiar yet lovable.

"Is there any information concerning when and where hand-snatching occurs today, Dr. Colucci?" Shannon asked thoughtfully.

He frowned, disappointed at her for asking, yet he took a stab at it, in a backhanded way. "My dear, Aristotle called it the 'organ of organs.' Science has always considered it the active agent of the human system. More nerves run from the brain to the hand than any other part of the body, including the sex organs—believe it or not. As officers of the law, you know instinctively that the sweaty palm is the first indicator of stress and anxiety. You still use the galvanic response in your lie-detector tests, do you not?"

Shannon nodded.

"A measure of the electrical resistance of the skin. Fingertips are equipped with an incredibly delicate sensory apparatus—not only in man, but in all primates and most animals—raccoons or otters, for instance." He went to Shannon and took her hand in his, spreading the fingers before her eyes. "Very nice," he muttered with Lanark looking on. "Each tip contains several million nerve cells. On this one surface, like the others, are the tiny ridges dotted with pores. These ridges develop in the fetus by about the eighteenth week of pregnancy. Do you know what is remarkable about this fact?"

"Fingerprinting is made possible," said Shannon.

He dropped her hand and raised his shoulders. "Yes, but these rugae, as they are called, remain without undergoing change whatsoever, until the skin disintegrates after death. Now, if you speak of the larger creases on the fingers and on the palm, these are constantly changing.

"Certain curious labyrinthine carvings found in ancient temples and burial tombs are duplicates of the fingerprint patterns of the man or woman buried there, a kind of magical identification preserved there forever. Science will one day show that the vortices of concentric lines bear a relationship to the convolutions of the brain."

As with the Green Garment Madame, Lanark was feeling they had come up a dead-end alley here, with the eccentric Dr. Colucci talking about fingertips being some kind of duplication of thought patterns in the brain. He saw no way to connect a madman freaking out on hands he chopped from his victims to Colucci's ramblings. The doctor had been right from the beginning. They had truly nothing to talk about.

"You have not located a single hand?" asked Colucci.

"No," Shannon admitted.

"He must be hoarding them, using them in some fixed way, or eating them."

She grimaced. "I thought you didn't want us talking cannibalism."

"I am not now talking about cannabalism. I am saying if he has not discarded them, then the hands are being used for something. Food is one possibility. I am saying there are many possibilities."

"Like cult possibilities?" asked Shannon. "Some sort of ritual? Is that what you mean by using them in a fixed way?"

"Collecting for the sake of collecting is one kind of madness. In a sense, a stamp collector, or even a museum curator, is acting out a mad passion. This is by degree, of course, and some of us recognize the parameters of our various obsessions and the depth of our compulsions, while others are oblivious to these limits because they have none. This is a pure fanatic."

"I'm beginning to see why Dr. Ames and you get along so well," said Lanark.

"Do not be confused by the jargon. You have no doubt arrested 'collectors' of one sort or another. Another mad behavior can come about via a fixed ritual in which the ritual-walker undergoes a powerful transformation that makes the step-by-step of the ritual more important than anything else on the face of the Earth, even himself. This ritual-walker may be a Catholic priest who cannot break tradition to save a human life, as in the case of abortion foes who believe they are right at all costs, even the cost of the mother's life. In true criminal terms, this is when an entire sect is blinded by its own rituals so that one man might lead an entire religious order into mass suicide, for instance, or one man might lead an entire nation into war and genocide. An individual ritual-walker might be a skinhead who decides his views are not simply half-baked beliefs picked up from an arrogant or ignorant father, but God's word; so he picks out an automatic weapon and walks into a McDonald's restaurant and opens fire. He no longer is going through ritual; he is a living symbol of that ritual.

"Cannibalism," continued Colucci, "is just another fixed ritual, albeit repugnant to modern man."

Lanark tried to interrupt. "Doctor—"

But Colucci just barreled on. "In a future time, when a spaceship is adrift beyond the help of others and food is scarce, who do you believe will be the cannibals? Modern, educated engineers and geologists marooned on a planet will be no different than the Donner Party in the late 1800's, or those athletes trapped in the Andes Mountains back in the seventies, was it? You can be certain you have a madman at work here. Whether you can understand his purpose or motives or not is not at the root of the problem. He likely doesn't understand himself or his motives anymore than you do, you see? That does not matter so much as that you understand his *method* and *use* of the prize he seeks. Does he hang them? Does he toy with them? Does he eat them?"

Lanark said, "Let's say he eats the damned things."

"Who gives a damn if he does, or if he doesn't? The thrill-seeker, perhaps, cares; even the extremely squeamish, perhaps, will care to know of this lurid detail if it is put in newsprint. But what is important is *to know* what he does with the evidence. Imagine catching him with even one of the four hands he had made off with. To what use is he putting them?"

"Caught red-handed, you mean," said Lanark, finally finding a place to get in a dig of his own in. "Well, look, Dr. Colucci. It's been informative, but our time is limited."

"I understand this. So is my own. That is why, if you are to ask intelligent questions that could lead to something useful, you must do some homework. That is what the list is for."

"Yes, of course," said Shannon, easing the tension as

best she could.

"I'll be happy to help in the future if there are any further questions," said Colucci, who turned back to his computer and began pecking at the keyboard. Above him and his computer, a skull with enormous sockets for eyes stared back at Lanark and Shannon. They turned and exited the way they had come in, working their way from the maze back to the corridor with the elevator.

When they returned to the afternoon light outside the building, each was glad to be out of Colucci's dungeon.

"Like a visit to the goddamned morgue," said Shannon, mirroring Lanark's thoughts.

"Yeah, except with Black, usually, you get some useful answers."

She shrugged, folding the computer list of books Ito Colucci had given them and placing it in her purse. "Useful, he didn't promise."

"Understandable then? How about understandable?"

"Ames must have believed he'd have something to contribute, else why—"

"I don't know. Lately, I don't understand Ames. It's as if . . . I don't know."

"Go ahead, say it."

"He seems on the verge of a crack-up."

"Do you really think it's that bad?"

"I think it's bad enough."

"Then you should go to him, talk to him."

Lanark shook his head. "I sense that he wants space."

"He's your friend."

"I know that, but—"

"To hell with the buts! To hell with giving him space. Space for what? To take a gun to himself? Christ, Lanark."

"Back off it, Shannon."

They were halfway down the stairs in front of the museum when a bullet whistled by Lanark's temple and struck the enormous column of concrete behind them. The noise of the exploding concrete and bullet sent children and tour groups to the ground or running. Shannon and Lanark were exposed, in the middle of the concrete steps, no cover, scanning from kneeling positions for the bullet's source, when a second explosion rang out from overhead and Lanark fired back at the cub plane that was out of his range.

"Come on!" He took her by the hand and they ran for the car, shots from the small aircraft trailing them.

The plane was coming in lower. They could hear it at their backs. Lanark left Shannon between some cars in the lot as the plane barreled headlong for him. He knew its occupants wanted him. He raced for a grassy field where the trees might afford some cover. More shots rang out behind him. This time from an automatic, the bullets chipping away at the concrete on all sides of him until he dove into the grassy area where the earth was sent exploding into his eyes from the impact of the bullets.

The plane had had to come in low. Shannon was behind it now, firing away, trying desperately to hit some vital component, perhaps the fuel line, anything to slow the plane. Lanark rolled over twice, coming up with his own weapon blazing at the aircraft, but like Shannon's, his bullets seemed ineffective against the soaring machine.

As it passed, he tried to get the call numbers, but was only able to see Ak-2 before it dipped and turned back toward the lake.

Shannon raced to where Lanark was pulling himself up. "Meigs," he shouted. "We've got to get out there."

"Are you hit?"

"No, missed me clean."

"Your luck continues to hold. Who is it?" They talked as they raced for the car. As they rushed for the airstrip that was on the lake, Shannon started to call it in, ask for additional backup.

"Hold off," he told her, putting a hand over hers.

"What the hell for?"

"These guys are mine."

"This is crazy. There were hundreds of witnesses to the attack just now." She pulled the radio in her hand from him. "I'm calling it in. We do it by the book."

He didn't try to stop her, but he doubled his efforts at

speeding through traffic, tossing the strobe light onto the top of the Jaguar and turning in for Meigs.

When they arrived they saw a black plume of smoke rising from the mutilated aircraft, which had crash-landed into the harbor and was going quickly from sight. "We must have hit something after all," said Lanark to Shannon where they stood at the end of the runway they'd driven down. A few local pilots who flew in and out of Meigs regularly, mostly lake fliers who enjoyed it for the sport, stood about talking over the crash and what they'd seen. Lanark and Shannon got a picture of a disabled pilot, unable to control the plane, which was spitting fire from somewhere below the fuselage.

Lanark walked around to the car and radioed in further instructions. "We need a diving team out at Meigs, and a boat. Yeah, got some fishing to do."

Shannon listened in and asked, "You want to see who was in that plane? I don't blame you."

"Yeah, I like to know who's trying to kill me. Maybe figure out how they knew I'd be here. How long they've been hatching this. Sure . . . not likely to find many answers, but—"

"Is it that, or just that you wouldn't want Whitey or that Loomis to die so easily, without your having had a hand in it?"

He stared across the top of the car into her angry eyes. "What do you want from me, Shannon? You want me to show pity, compassion for men who have less inside their hearts than your average hyena? Sorry, kid, but I can't do that."

NINE

Shannon Keyes had to get away from Lanark for awhile, and so she hopped a ride with one of the units that came as backup to Meigs. Lanark remained to oversee an operation to raise the plane from the lake. He was most anxious to learn what he could about the men inside it.

Questions put to the other pilots and the airfield people revealed that the plane was a charter, and the pilot a middle-aged man by the name of Bonner. Bonner routinely took people over the city and the lake for twenty-five dollars. Everyone seemed to think he was out on a fare. More questions revealed the fact he was a high roller, a very well-liked man, and a fine pilot, but that he was down on his luck.

Lanark wondered if the plane had been hijacked, or if Bonner was part of the plot to kill him. It seemed obvious to Lanark that the attempt was financed by Loomis, or another of the drug leeches in the city. Lanark's crusade to find those who'd killed his parents had earned him a dangerous reputation.

However, he didn't have time to wait for hours upon hours to fish out the answers from the big lake. He had "promises" to keep tonight. He intended on keeping them, and in taking Loomis into custody, a very special and up-close custody.

He mentally played back his conversation with Dinetto over the phone earlier:

112

"Remember that re-location effort I tol' you about?"

"Yeah, what of it?"

"It's going down, tonight, and I know where."

"When and where?"

"This one's goin' to cost you mucho bucks, pal. You see me at the church at seven."

Lanark didn't plan to miss "confession" tonight. He had arranged dropoff points in various churches for various snitches. He would go into the confessional booth as a Catholic priest, and his contact would step into the other side to confess his sins; thus, information and money were exchanged. It had worked well for Lanark over the years, although he occasionally had to hear "true" confessions when the snitch didn't show up but someone else happened into the booth. His success in the confessional almost convinced Lanark that he was in the wrong business.

Lanark phoned Wil Cassidy, the tall, calm, and handsome "rock" of his undercover unit, and asked if he would get down to Meigs and see that everything was carried out by the book. He stressed getting ID on any passengers who'd died in the plane crash.

Wil listened attentively, and asked after Lanark's and Shannon's health. News of the shooting at the museum, where bullets had sprayed from a small plane, had run like wildfire throughout the city. "Thank God no citizens were hurt."

"Tell Robeson and Stokes, on the QT, to remain open tonight for a possible job."

"What's up, Lieutenant?"

"Maybe nothing. Just tell them to be close to their phones."

"Anything I can do?"

"Hey, helping out with this plane business, that'll do it for me, pal. Thanks."

Lanark knew he was not fooling anyone. Wil, even through the wires, seemed to be onto him. Everyone in the unit knew that there was one controlling force in Lanark's life when all was said and done. No amount of loyalty to the department, or even to the unit, could supersede his prime objective. No amount of love from Shannon, or help from his friends, or professional help from Ames had been enough to dissuade him from what everyone else saw as self-destructive behavior.

Lanark saw the police boat as it arrived. There was a winch at one end, and it was equipped with the latest in salvage equipment. On the side of the boat was blazoned the name the department had given the boat, "Diver Dan," along with a square-jawed decal of a diver in an ancient underwater outfit, holding an enormous helmet aloft.

Soon after these men received directions via radio, Lanark was relieved by Wil Cassidy. Lanark was about to rush off when Wil said flatly, "Are you the least bit interested in what Myra and I found on the girl, Sarah?"

Lanark turned and gave him a look that asked, "Did you file a report?" But instead of saying so, he replied, "Anything unusual? Anything you think might help us find this guy?"

Wil nodded and leaned against his Camaro. "Yeah, a couple of things. Seems she was ripe bait."

"Ripe how?"

"Recently spent some time in a hospital for the not-too-sane. Something to do with a morbid preoccupation with death and dying."

"Maybe she had a premonition," Lanark said dryly.

"Talked about a past life all the time. Said she was imprisoned in a past life. Parents said she'd had a try at drugs, but that it had only been experimental. Anyway, they'd had her committed—"

"Committed?"

"Kind of for psychiatric evaluations, and all that."

"I see."

"Anyway, she gets out with a clean bill of health, goes home, and promptly runs away at the first opportunity."

Lanark nodded and muttered, "Troubled kid."

Wil agreed, and said, "But she looked to be getting her act together. A friend came out of the woodwork. Seems he knew where she'd been staying all along and hadn't told the parents because she'd made him promise. Anyway, she'd gotten a job."

"What kind of job? Where?"

"Nothing too exciting or exotic. She worked front desk at a dry cleaner's, storefront on Ashland Avenue, few blocks down from Milwaukee."

"Next step?"

He raised his shoulders in a gesture of not knowing, but he said, "Myra's going to talk to some of her other friends, try to establish her whereabouts the other night. I'm going to talk to her boss, people she worked with."

Lanark frowned, but said in his most official voice, "Carry on. You're doing well. Give my best to Myra."

He stopped Lanark with a word. "Whitey, isn't it?"

"No, not exactly."

"Loomis?"

"Right. May have a lead on him."

"Hey, Lieutenant."

"Yeah?"

"Suppose we pull up Loomis with the plane? How do I reach you?"

This made Lanark stop and think. If Loomis were in the plane, Dinetto's information was wrong; possibly spoon-fed wrong, dead wrong. It was even possible that Lanark could be walking into a trap. But then, that went with the territory, went with being an undercover cop.

"Leave word with Tebo at the bar, O'Hurley or his replacement at the desk, or our nighttime girl in the unit."

"If I do, will you take the time to check in?"

"I'll check in *later!* I'm out of here."

Wil Cassidy watched him go, a skin-crawly feeling tickling his neck. Every time he saw Ryne Lanark's darker side, he wondered if he'd ever see him again—alive. Wil knew of no other cop who took as many godawful chances. It was as if Lanark wanted someone to put him out of his misery.

Wil turned to stare at "Diver Dan" on hearing the groan of the winch, the cogs screaming against the weight of the plane the divers had attached the huge grappling hooks to.

Lanark had been ambushed before, but this was the first time it had come in such kamikaze fashion. Already, the lights were going on all round the city and here at the terminus of Roosevelt Road overlooking Burnham Park Harbor, from which the plane was being hauled. Shadows were deep and full.

One man standing in the crowd, an ancient flyer with more time in the air than all the others combined, was saying in all conviction, "Bonner could've brought that plane in; he overshot the field on purpose, like as if he wanted to go down."

Wil wondered how much truth was in the statement. He asked the old man with white stubble and a spindly body if he had seen the plane go down.

"Absolutely, damn shame . . . shame . . ." He was shaken at what he'd seen. He knew the pilot.

"Tell me about it," asked Wil.

"He looked . . . it looked like he was coming in for a normal landing."

"Engine failure," said a second man, listening in. "Fire shut down his engine."

"Fire was spittin' out the underbelly, fuselage area," the first man said. "But Bonner looked to be in control of his plane. Tom, he wouldn't've let a little fire keep him from getting her grounded. But on approach, I heard the engine *pick up speed!*"

"Somebody told me the engine quit on him," said Wil.

"Bull!" The first pilot remained adamant about what he'd seen and heard, making Will more readily believe him.

"The plane stalled out!" said the second pilot.

"Not before he was over the harbor, where he intentionally stalled the plane! I tell you, Bonner pulled the nose up, increased speed, and went on out over the harbor. Swear it! Come right down over the field and up again like a touch-and-go. He could've set her down, but he didn't."

"What'd he do next?" asked Wil.

"Stalled out."

"Stalled?"

"Engine cut out when he pulled up too fast. But he knew it'd happen! Any pilot knows. He didn't have a chance then. Straight down like a lead ton into the harbor."

It sounded as if the pilot had been an unwilling participant in the attack on Lanark, and he'd tried to salvage the situation, but it had cost him his life in the bargain. "Witnesses say there were two men in the plane."

"Yeah, saw 'em on takeoff. Bonner had a fare."

Wil stared out at the water where the tip of one wing of the plane was exposed in the harbor. He was anxious now to see who the passenger was. If he had forced Bonner into the sky at gunpoint, it could possibly by Tyrrell Loomis, or one of his thugs. Then again, Lanark had so many enemies that the dead man might be anyone. It was conceivable that it might even be another cop. There were a number of people at the 13th who still believed Lanark's carelessness and bravado had caused the death of a number of his partners over the years. There were guys who were out to impress the IAD Chief, Morris Fabia, and Fabia himself was *bent* when it came to Lanark, bent with his own hatred and dreams of revenge.

Wil Cassidy got aboard a small boat which would take him out to "Diver Dan." He came alongside as the work of hauling up the plane, filled now with water that cascaded from every opening, continued. Once aboard the police salvage boat, he talked with one of the divers who'd gone below with a searchlight.

"Both men dead," said the diver. "Always wonder what you're diving for—a rescue or a corpse. Never know until you get there. They were both still strapped to their seats."

The cockpit of the plane came above the surface and whorling lights strobed about the faces of the dead. Wil did not recognize either man as Loomis. He could only hope the man had ID on him, and that the weapon which had discharged so many rounds was in the cockpit.

Felix's new hands now looked more in proportion to his

size and weight. Sarah/Heather's hands did much better by Felix. Morgan Lefay Sayer was happy. With his knowledge of curing and drying and stuffing, the outer appearance and skin of the hands would retain their original suppleness, down to the concentric circles on the fingertips. This now was "worry-wart" Felix's new, constant concern.

"Friggin' idiot," he'd said to Morgan. "At least, at the very least, destroy the incriminating evidence with acid or sandpaper." He was referring again to the fingertips.

But so far as Morgan was concerned, they—meaning anyone in a position of authority—could look forever and ever. "Nobody's going to ever make any connection between a flophouse magician's dummy and the deaths of two fools who gave up life to bring you and me closer together."

"How damned close do you want to get? How about you sleep in the box? I'll take the bed."

One part of Morgan's mind replayed the scene even as he conducted his act before an audience at the club. It seemed sometimes that Felix was unnecessarily argumentative, brassy, and uncouth, as well as unfeeling toward Morgan. It seemed at times that Morgan was the one who should be afraid, not Felix. Morgan had had nightmares in which Felix walked into the kitchen, picked out a carving knife, and found Morgan asleep in his bed. Morgan would awake from the nightmare without his hands, blood dripping and gushing from the stems that were left. Then he would really awaken and find himself intact and Felix asleep on the floor in his box beside the bed as usual, the lid leaned back. Felix looked like a child during sleep, a child in a coffin.

Sometimes, he even looked like Morgan at the age of thirteen, maybe fourteen. More and more, Morgan saw it. He knew it was happening—as time went on. Felix knew it, perhaps more than Morgan himself: that their personalities were at a crossroads and like two old cats that'd lived too long together, oddly and mysteriously, they'd crossed and *exchanged personalities*. Certainly, they were in much less conflict with one another. Even the jokes for the show tonight were falling flat because Felix's sarcasm and bite wasn't quite as sharp-edged as before, because in his grudging way Felix was gaining more respect for (and maybe a little healthy fear of) Morgan and what he was capable of.

Someone in the crowd guffawed and threw a beer bottle across the room, and the bouncer went for him. The commotion shook not only Morgan, but the three people on stage with him. One was on all fours, and a second one was riding her. The one on all fours was a wild bronco, and the rider a cowgirl. Danny had said to let out all the stops tonight, to see how far he could go with the animal mimicking and hypnosis; so he did. It bored him, but it pleased the crowd. The noise and fighting that broke out made Morgan tense, and he quickly brought back the two people who were horsing around on stage. The third one, a woman of some beauty, was still deep under. During the confusion, he suggested she return to him by arriving directly at his apartment. He implanted the notion that she was in love with him as well, and would be unable to keep her hands off him when once again they met.

Then he brought her out of it, thanked the audience loudly and profusely, called for a hand for the volunteers, and quickly grabbed up Felix's case and disappeared. It was Monday, the short night, no midnight show. He rushed to his dressing rom and there set Felix up alongside him, and they began removing their makeup and discussing how the show went.

"Same ol' shit, huh?" Felix said.

"Not a bad crowd if you exclude the—"

"What's the idea, Morgan?"

"What? What idea?"

"Look at me!"

Morgan did so.

Felix's dead man's hands, Sarah's hands, lay across his front. "Why'd you tell Elena to come to you tonight? I've got ears, you know. I hear everything you say."

"Oh, that."

"I thought we agreed . . . no more chopping off people's hands."

"I'm not going to chop off her hands. It's just going to be a nice, a nice—"

"A nice clean murder?"

"No, just a nice get-together."

"Bullshit."

"Felix!"

"Hey!" A knock preceded Danny, who burst in with a big smile and a laugh. "You had 'em rollin' out there, kiddo! Finally loosened up a bit!" He glanced over at Felix and gave him an uncomfortable look. "Talking to your pal again, huh? Already rehearsing for tomorrow night. I like that. You know, I had you figured all wrong. You're a go-getter, aren't you, kiddo? And you take suggestions well, like—like the hands! I see you cut down the size of the hands."

Danny tentatively reached toward Felix, but the dummy pulled away, falling over to one side just as Morgan grabbed him and lifted him and put him quickly away.

Danny went on. "Well, anyway, just wanted to say, you keep bringin' 'em in so good and maybe then we can talk about more money."

Danny was gone as quickly as he came. From inside his case, Felix said, "You know how close he came to touching my hands? Christ."

Sometimes Felix's whiny voice grated on Morgan's nerves. Danny always got on Morgan's nerves. He could use a little time to relax away from Felix, and away from all the constraints, pressures, and stresses of his life. He could use some time alone with Elena. She was pretty and her voice was angelic, and her eyes were large and deep and blue. But Morgan wasn't sure he could do it, just get up and walk out of here and leave Felix all night alone. Felix had never been left alone before, not since the day he was created. For that matter, Morgan had never been without Felix in all this time—what, thirteen years now? Elena's hands were thin-fingered, smooth.

He wanted to be alone with Elena. He didn't want Felix

to butt in, second-guess him, or get in the way. He didn't want Felix stealing his thunder, or making decisions for him.

Felix was back in the case, and it was closed, and all he had to do was shove it below the settee and pick it up tomorrow—a thing he hadn't done in all these years.

He feared for Felix.

He feared for himself.

Fear of being alone was a very real anguish he was not sure he could endure. Suppose Elena didn't show up.

But Elena would be there, and she'd be unable to keep her hands off him.

And he had one of his chopping guillotines there, should the urge become overwhelming.

He slowly pushed Felix, case and all, with the end of his toe below the settee. Felix began to tremble and shiver and plead, "Don't . . . don't do this, Morgan."

TEN

Getting into the neighborhood without being seen was difficult. It was one of those Spanish Harlem-type areas that had been something of a center of activity in Chicago for years now, and deep within the confines of its one-way lanes fronted by cottage-type homes, flats, and brick fortresses of three and four stories, all manner of business was transacted. Even on the street here, beneath the soft lines of light radiating from the vapor lamps, people conducted business, usually in their own tongue.

The infiltrator had made a special effort to look—at least from a distance—as if he too belonged here and posed no threat. He carried his weapon, the most deadly one, in a guitar case. With it, he moved along the alleyway that had taken him from nearby Elizabeth Street, where he'd left his car. As he made for his destination he thought of the killing he intended tonight. But first he had to get up high, over the top of the street, where he could do his best work. Then he'd open fire.

But not before all the proper steps were taken. He had a ritual, and he had a plan, and he had to synchronize everything for the exact, right moment; and should he have the right man at the end of his sight, he'd blow his head away.

He was a sniper with orders, orders given him in phantom proceedings.

No one had seen him, or if they had, they'd paid no

mind. The Spanish dress, black with gold chains about the neck, dark sport coat over black shirt and thin tie, made him look somewhat Iranian, he thought. He'd darkened his facial skin several shades. The guitar case was likely the most "attractive" item about him.

But he stuck to the back ways and found the building he wanted, and scaled the back stairs until he came to a door that opened on a hallway, and from there he located the roof. The only one in the building who'd seen him was an infant and his big sister playing in the smelly urinal of a hallway.

Atop the building, he inhaled great whiffs of air. He could smell the cooking of the entire area. He'd been in Puerto Rico once, and there were places in Puerto Rico that smelled like this.

He stood now atop a red-brick facade, a four-story flat in the predominantly Spanish neighborhood. He looked like a Duncan Renaldo, he thought, stroking the mustache. He spent the better part of fifteen or twenty minutes deciding from where he would open fire on the people he intended to spray with lead pellets smaller than most pocket change, deadly and crippling nonetheless.

Suddenly, the sniper heard a noise behind him, soft and nearly indistinct. He wheeled and pointed a gun he whipped from a shoulder holster and cocked it, as his eyes registered the fact that the threat was the little girl in a smeared little smock who'd abandoned the game she'd played with her baby brother to investigate him.

"Si gusta? Si gusta?"

She held no fear of the gun; had probably seen them all her life. She was likely nine, maybe ten.

"Vamonos, decender! Iba, acostarse!" he returned, using all the Spanish words he knew to send her packing. *"Bruho grande!"*

None of it worked. *"Dinero, y billete? Golondrina?"*

This kid had learned the first lesson of the street for girls without a future. Lanark realized only now that she was propositioning him for any bills he might wish to give her in return. This so angered him he wanted to throw her from the roof, but instead he snatched off his shoe and sternly said, *"Astorse o zapato!"*

She scampered from him in fright, and he returned to the business at hand, a good bit perturbed by the angelic face and the suggestion coming from her mouth. The streets and tenements like this bred a "children of the damned" from the beginning, he thought.

But at the moment his full concentration must be on the operation. He fought to regain his all-important concentration. The move was on to get Loomis at any cost. Lanark had pushed word onto the two men he thought he could trust to do as he said, when he said. The meeting at the church had gone smoothly, and Dinetto's information looked to be accurate.

Infiltration had been optimal, if you discounted the child whore. Lanark was now "maintaining" at the rooftop location during the stakeout. Mark Robeson and Jake Stokes were both at separate alleys in appropriate vehicles, making their way closer and closer to the target area. The whole operation depended upon the correct manipulation of their vehicles and the way in which they conducted themselves.

Lanark knew he could count on them both, but *things have a way of falling apart . . . best-laid plans . . . all that.*

Robeson and Stokes kept in contact by radio, but soon would be able to maintain visual contact as well. It was dark, and even the orange glow of the vapor lights along Troop Street were useless. What light they cast only made the dark around the outer edges of light blacker. But Lanark had a night-scanning pair of infrared binoculars, so he could see into the darkness better than the others, including those who knew every inch of the concrete terrain.

He'd had no trouble seeing the comings and goings of people in and out of one building in particular, at the address given them by Dinetto.

Lanark had listened specifically for any sign in Dinetto's voice that he was either lying or knowingly passing poor information. All during his "confession," however, the snitch was calm and positively proud of having learned the time and place for Loomis to be moved out of the city.

Lanark had asked who was behind Loomis's relocation. But Dinetto's information ended where it ended.

Tonight, Lanark could smell rain coming on. He could smell the warmth of the day rising off the tar on the roof where he stood, staring through his binoculars at the activity below. But he did not smell a setup. He watched the way the sentinels outside the drug den looked about and walked up and down, and he saw no evidence of nervous energy. Rather, he saw complacency and ease, even from those going inside and walking away.

Then things began to happen.

It looked as if it would go down on time, as per Dinetto's information.

All night, cars came and went along Troop, horns honking, girls running out to meet their fellows, booze containers being tossed, people shouting out windows. But now the size and nature of the processional of cars that entered the small, cramped street was of special importance. All dark sedans, they appeared to be Mafia types. The street had become silent, windows closed and locked.

Such cars didn't belong to the neighborhood—maybe on nearby Noble or Chicago Avenue, but not here, stopping like this.

Lanark radioed Robeson and Stokes. "It's happening. We go with Plan A."

Strategy had called for determining exactly which vehicle Loomis would board. Lanark would leave this to no one else. As the party of cars moved out, the number of guns would be determined as well. From the look of it—six cars, almost four men to a car—there was a small arsenal on the street, likely including any number of full-powered automatics. Lanark's intention was to lift Loomis from their grasp without anyone's getting hurt, especially his unit men. The decision to keep it down to Robeson and Stokes was partially to minimize mistakes, but it was also to minimize the fight he expected from his own ranks once he got his hands on Loomis.

He had arranged for special accommodations for Loomis. A lot of police involvement and gunplay, and Loomis would be taken into "real" police custody. Lanark intended something else: a place without lawyers or civil rights, a place where interrogation would net him results.

At the moment, neither Robeson nor Stokes knew this. He'd deal with them when the time came. At the moment, the successful manipulation of the bad guys was the thing to concentrate upon.

Lanark stared down at the weapon he'd brought to the job site. It was a sharpshooter's weapon, long and sleek, with a powerful scope, also equipped with infrared. It was a sniper's weapon, and tonight he was a sniper.

The very Spanish neighborhood made Stokes and Robeson stick out like a couple of sore thumbs, or cops. But there were a few "services" and jobs seen by such a neighborhood as "belonging" to black men. Robeson was driving a trash truck around the neighborhood, and Stokes was a cabbie. Pity the poor fool who tried to rob him, Lanark thought now.

Still, they had remained pretty much out of sight, even if they were in undercover garb. A little street nestled deep within the confines of a tough network of Spanish-speaking people didn't miss much, and was not easily lulled into accepting strangers, or changes in habit.

"Red alert," said Lanark into his radio transmitter. "Things are happening down there."

"Ready . . . give the word," said Robeson's rich, familiar voice. It gave Lanark heart to hear him. Behind his voice he heard the grinding noise of the truck.

Stokes checked in, also prepared.

Lanark saw Loomis's protectors coming out, getting into their cars; he was using the telescopic lens on the rifle now, following each man as he exited. He didn't see Loomis, or anyone like a Marty Jenkins, or an "Andy Warhol" type called Whitey. These were men he'd fantasized about torturing before he allowed them to die.

Tired of lugging the weight of remorse, anger, hatred,

and revenge about these many years, he'd have liked nothing better than to finish it tonight. For years he had vowed to make them each suffer long and torturous deaths for what they'd done to him and his, but the bitterness had robbed him of a life, a life he would like to recover and reclaim someday. Perhaps, with them dead, he could begin to do so.

But still no sign, and the cars were practically loaded.

Then it dawned on Lanark. Loomis had been disguised in anticipation of such an attempt as he was making. Of course. He was already inside one of the cars and well surrounded, but which one? It was a high-stakes shell game suddenly, with Lanark looking down on five cars below him, where men and machines were getting comfortable with one another, readying to depart. No one else was coming out.

He had to strike now!

One of the peons went to one of the cars and rapped on its roof after a brief talk with those in the backseat, and somehow Lanark knew it was the middle car, third from the front.

He radioed this information to Robeson, who immediately began to align his enormous machine perpendicular to the point where, from the alley, he'd let the first and second cars go by. Then he'd go into action.

"Stokes, you got that? Third car?" asked Lanark.

"How do you know that? I didn't see Loomis come out."

"Dammit, just do it. They're taking off."

"But Lieutenant—"

"Third car!"

"Yes, sir!"

Stokes was at the alley intersection also, but in a position to see fairly well. His battered cab looked to be abandoned. It sat with its backside to the street and out his rearview mirror, Stokes saw the garbage truck come up from across the street. The plan was bold—bodacious, as they say—and Stokes liked that part, but he wasn't sure it'd work. They'd bag somebody, sure, but Loomis? Not likely. If they did, the man wouldn't be taken alive.

The first car sped by, followed by the second. The huge garbage truck barreled from the alley across from Stokes and rammed the third car with a direct hit so hard it toppled the car, making of it a barricade before the alleyway on Stokes's side. Inside the car, occupants toppled and screamed when Robeson set off a firebomb at the front that blazed before the upturned dash and windshield. Each occupant was knocked senseless by Robeson and pulled out of the way as they scampered from the broken windows. Cars four and five careened into one another trying to avoid a crash; at the same time Lanark opened fire on the men climbing from the doors of cars four through six.

At the same time, Stokes put a gun to the temple of a man who came out with thick blood oozing through makeup. Padding had made him look heavier and older. It was Loomis. Stokes recognized him now. He rushed him down the barricaded alley at gunpoint to the waiting taxi, the trunk popped and yawning like an animal ready to devour Loomis. Stokes didn't need to subdue Loomis, whose wounds were severe enough to make him woozy, but he did snatch a gun from a holster on Loomis's shoulder before dumping him unceremoniously into the trunk and closing its lid over him.

While Stokes was so engaged, Robeson regained his position behind the garbage truck, bullets raining around him, but most of it friendly, insistent fire directed at Loomis's men, pinning them down. An occasional shot exploded into the side of the trash truck, however, and some narrowly missed Robeson. Still, he managed to get back into the protected cab, where bullets bounced off the glass.

With Lanark holding them down, Robeson directed the truck at the cars in his way, smashed into them and backed down hastily again to topple the cars behind him. This tank maneuver sent most of them scurrying like rats as radiators exploded, sending up fumes of water. The little street looked like a war zone now, and not feeling right about it, yet following Lanark's orders, Mark turned the truck back down the alley from which he'd come, crossed over at Elizabeth, raced for Racine where it continued on the other side of the Kennedy Expressway, and barreled into the waiting mouth of an enormous factory door that had been opened by Stokes, ready to receive him. He didn't like it because he'd had to leave Lanark up on that rooftop with no telling how many guys going after him.

Meanwhile, the cab with its contents sat in the middle of the factory floor. The building was an old structure, long since abandoned and out of use. Lanark had put down a month's salary to "lease" it for the night.

"Wow! *Sheeeeessss!* Was that something, or what? Goll' darn, man! We did it! We did it!"

"Lanark's still out there."

Stokes bridled it in, but he was bouncing inside. "What next?" he asked as calmly as he could.

"Get that damned door down."

Stokes did so, and they watched the blackness outside disappear, both wondering where Lanark might be, how much trouble he might be in at this instant, wondering why he was not calling in. The door screamed as the huge wheels that hadn't seen service in some time lowered the huge electric apparatus. It sufficiently hid the garbage truck.

"We wait for Lanark. Do just as he said."

"But if he's in trouble, man."

"Let's get Loomis up," said Robeson.

Mark knew he'd have to keep Stokes busy. Stokes popped the trunk, and a sudden blinding pain struck him in the neck and he fell over, bleeding profusely from a nasty wound inflicted by a derringer that Mark Robeson tore from Loomis's hands, pelting the weakened man into near-unconsciousness. He then fell to his knees over Stokes's bleeding form. Stokes was fully awake and conscious, in a kind of shock, still unaware of just what had happened to him.

"What . . . what happened?"

"You're hit, that's what happened."

"Never thought it'd be like this."

"Shut up . . . save your breath . . . damn . . ." Blood was everywhere. He was losing too much, too fast. Robeson had to stop the flow now. At the same time he could hear Lanark's voice coming in over the radio, asking them to pick up, saying *he* was in trouble.

Robeson raced to the cab, remembering the kid had been munching on sandwiches earlier. He found the discarded paper bag filled with plastic Baggies. He raced back to Stokes and pressed one of the discarded Baggies against his bleeding throat. "You got to help me, Stokes! Stokes!" He lifted Stokes's basketball player's hand and said, "Hold this here, hold it tight, kid! Tight."

The kid tried, but touching the open wound through the plastic made him moan with pain.

"Just a second, kid . . . easy . . . easy . . ." Robeson knew what to do. He just didn't know if he could do it in time. He had ripped off his shirt and torn it into shreds, which he now began to wrap several times round and round the wound, the bandage pressing the plastic deep into the ugly gash. The plastic would speed coagulation at the site of impact and more quickly reduce the blood loss.

He finished tying it off, knowing he had to rush Stokes now to Ravenswood Hospital, the closest in the area. He was well known there, but he wasn't so sure they could keep their little operation against Loomis "off the record" for another hour, much less the night, as Lanark had intended.

He helped Stokes to his feet. "Now, sucker!" shouted Robeson, when Stokes flagged a bit. "Else you're dog meat!"

Stokes emulated the murderous rage with which Mark made himself understood, but all his damaged throat could muster was a gurgle. Somehow he was still smiling over some thought. Robeson placed him in his car, and then rushed back to where Loomis lay only half conscious in the trunk of the cab. To Loomis's cry, Robeson dropped the lid again, locking him up tight to await Lanark's return.

Robeson opened the factory door once more, using a remote. He tore out for the hospital, praying he'd get there in time. Stokes had passed out.

Lanark was on his hands and knees in among some trash bins below street level, trapped and staring out at the enemy. Problem was, the "enemy" was the cops. They had poured like water into the neighborhood moments after the car exploded and the truck Robeson drove took off on its appointed route. Lanark had to be cautious about getting out, not stumbling onto some of Loomis's men as they sought safety and shelter, and now he had the added problem of not being seen by other cops. The way he was dressed, carrying the long-range sniper's weapon, IAD would have him up on charges. He'd likely lose his freedom.

As Lanark thought about him, the ferret-eyed face of IAD chief Morris Fabia came into view. He could hear the little weasel's big mouth even from this distance.

"Check with motor pool at the Thirteenth," Fabia tersely told an associate whom Lanark didn't know, a young guy with ordinary features. "Ask 'em if they've got any trash trucks connected with that undercover operation over there. Looks like the kinda stunt Lanark would pull."

Lanark tried to reach Robeson via radio, but it was out of range, he surmised, and he couldn't shout. Mark was not responding.

Lanark knew he had to do something fast, but he wasn't sure what that might be. The place was crawling with cops, in uniform and otherwise.

Lanark reached for the door behind him, which led into a basement room with laundry facilities. It was completely black inside, and he stumbled about with the guitar case in hand, until someone suddenly stuck a pistol in his ribs and said, "Don't make a move! You're under arrest."

"No comprendo, no comprendo," he said, but the cop wasn't buying it. The cop spun him around and flashed a light into his eyes. Lanark saw the corona of the light and the barrel of the man's gun pointed at him. The man's partner, standing at the other side of the room, moved in and said, in a kidding fashion, *"Arrest-team-mo, comprende* that?"

Lanark heard the cuffs jingle, felt the light boring into him, the arresting officer's eyes behind the light steady on him, as was his gun.

In the dark, neither of them had seen the black guitar case, which Lanark suddenly brought up, crashing into gun and light and grazing the first officer's jaw, sending him reeling back. Lanark circled and dropped the other man with a knee to his groin, doubling him over. A swift kick put this one completely and mercifully out. The first one was back on his feet, diving into Lanark, his gun lost. Lanark went down with the wild officer over him, pummeling him until he heard the click of Lanark's gun, which he had whipped from his shoulder holster.

"Now, get up, slow and easy," Lanark told him.

The cop did so.

"Strip."

"What?"

"I want your uniform, now!"

"You're not Spanish."

"The uniform!"

"All right, all right." As he dressed down, he asked, "What're you goin' to do? Kill us both?"

"Not if you shut up and listen."

He was silent. Lanark directed him to the laundry area to locate rope. "Tie your partner, now!"

He did so, and then Lanark tied him up, putting a gag in each man's mouth. Then Lanark stripped from the clothes he wore, making certain to empty the pockets of anything that might link the costume with him or his unit. He tore away the markings on the linings and any laundry marks that could be traced. He then dressed in the

132

uniform. He hadn't worn blues for a number of years; it brought back memories, good and bad. The fit was pretty near perfect.

He went to the conscious one, pulled off the gag, and said, "What's your unit number?"

"Twenty-six."

"Where is it?"

"On the street, out front, but if you take—"

Lanark shoved the gag back into his mouth and tied it off again.

He couldn't leave the rifle. It could be traced back to him in hours. He took a deep breath, hefted the guitar case, and started out the front. There were detectives and cops everywhere. One of the blue suits, an older man, stared at him a bit and asked what he had.

"Evidence, Fabia told me to see it gets to the lab."

"Hmmmmm," the other man offered. "Fabia's some piece of work. How he sees IAD has any juice on this one, I dunno."

"Ferret-face? Haven't you heard? If he can't find wrongdoing within the department, he's going after Mother Goose."

Mother Goose was street-cop talk for the Mayor's Office.

The other man laughed his hearty agreement and went about his business. Lanark found Unit 26, got in casually, gave it a bit of time, started her up, and cruised off slowly and evenly, backing down the street, which was still littered with car wrecks and damaged parked cars. Down at the other end, fire trucks had put out the flames in the car Loomis had been in.

Lanark drove over toward Elizabeth Street, where he'd left his rattletrap of a car. He parked in front of it, hopped from the squad car, leaving the keys in it, and tossed the guitar case into the trunk of his car. As he did so, he saw another cruiser coming in behind him. They stopped short, and he waved to indicate all was well there. He had left 26's strobe light circling, and in its glow the other cops watched him shove the lid of the old car down, step over to the curb, inspect the car a bit further, then walk away from it, going down the street in a bravado step, checking doorways and alleyways in regular John Wayne fashion.

The other cruiser pulled around 26 and continued on slowly. Lanark thought they'd never disappear around that final corner.

Lanark waited for the other squad car to cruise down the street and turn off before he dared return to his waiting car. Once inside, his keys fished out, he backed the car to an alley, turned it full tilt, and rushed from Elizabeth Street. He was extremely glad he hadn't driven the Jag to this spot and left it. The cops would've been swarming over it like flies by now, and Fabia would have had it impounded. But the car he drove fit in with the scenery so well that when he turned out onto Chicago Avenue and slowly pounded his way across the Kennedy Expressway bridge, no one paid him the least mind. He was soon out of the crime-scene area altogether.

He reached below his dash for the radio there and tried again to hail Mark Robeson or young Stokes. But it was no good. He then had a call patched through to Sergeant O'Hurley at headquarters. The sarge often pulled a double shift, and Lanark hoped this was such a night.

"O'Hurley here," came the brawny man's powerful voice.

"I need a favor, O'Hurley."

"Lieutenant Lanark, is it?"

"That's right."

"Well, sure, anything I can do, you know that, lad."

O'Hurley hadn't ever forgotten the time Lanark had saved his life during a hostage situation.

"What is it I can do for you, Lieutenant? Just name it."

"Robeson earlier requisitioned the undercover unit's trash truck—"

"One you used in catching the Subway Killer, yeah?"

"Yeah, that's it. Anyway, someone from IAD's on his way to see if that truck is in the garage there."

"What's this got to do with—whoa, a minute, son . . . you wouldn't happen to know anything about a shootout off Chicago at Troop, would you?"

"No, and neither do you. Listen!"

"Go on, Lieutenant."

"You know a lot of guys with the city with access to such trucks. Hell, you were the guy that saw to the purchase of ours—"

"And you want me to get another one on a moment's notice and have it parked in the garage?"

"Anyone ever tell you you're psychic, Sarge?"

"Psychotic, maybe . . . got to be psychotic to work with you, Lanark."

"Can you do it?"

"I'll do what I can. No promises."

"All I ask . . . all I ask."

"If I pull this off—"

"Steak dinner on the house at my bar."

"I was going to ask for cash."

"Can you do it, Sarge?"

"Give it my best try, be assured of it."

"No time to waste." He started to hang up, but O'Hurley stopped him.

"Lieutenant, I've got a message from Cassidy for you."

"The plane crash?"

"One guy pulled from the wreckage has been ID'd as one of Loomis's thugs. Other poor bastard just got caught in the middle."

"The pilot, huh?"

"Right."

Lanark's hatred for Loomis had risen another notch. He hung up. He cruised down side streets so narrow as to almost be touching parked cars on both sides of him, ran along a railway bed for the Ravenswood El, and was within blocks of the warehouse. Again, he tried to raise Mark Robeson on the radio.

Nothing.

Now he was beginning to wonder and to worry. This

wasn't like Mark. Being unable to reach Mark was now twitching badly at his nerves. Loomis was deadly. He'd proven that by the bodies he'd left strewn in his wake. Was it possible he had gotten the better of Mark and Stokes? Was it possible that Loomis's men had somehow trailed the trash truck? Were they lying in wait for Lanark at this moment?

ELEVEN

She had a glazed look of confusion on her face when Morgan Lefay Sayer, "The Soothsayer," opened the door. Moments before she had pressed his downstairs buzzer, announcing herself as Elena Jorovich. She'd said that she mustn't be turned away, that she must see him, that it was urgent. But now, standing before him, invited into his living room, with him in a bathrobe, she was not sure why she was here. He told her she had nothing to fear. He told her to relax, and asked if she would like a drink. He was at his cordial best, although inside he was quaking. Without Felix, he felt a creeping fear eroding his resolve to be independent and to do what he damned well pleased with Elena Jorovich.

She said that maybe she should go.

"Go? Nonsense, stay awhile. We can talk. I sense we have much in common."

"I don't know. No, I don't think so. You're . . . well, so sure of yourself. The way you do your magic tricks, and the way you take control on the stage—"

"That's just a *persona*, someone I portray while on stage. Actually, I have a number of problems of my own, Elena."

"No."

"Like anyone, I have my fears, phobia, neuroses."

"I know what you mean."

"Do you?"

137

"I think so, yes."

"Could I see your hands, Elena?"

Her hands went instinctively inward and to her sides, as if to hide, as she asked, "Why?"

"I read palms, you know."

"Really? And you want to read mine?"

"It's a useful occupation, a way to break the ice and hold hands," he said with an impish smile.

"I don't know."

"Why not?"

"I don't even know why I'm here."

"You came seeking help."

She dropped her gaze, a tear welling up from deep within.

"You're crying."

"I'm sorry. This is wrong. I shouldn't be bothering you."

"Oh, no, really. Bother me. You're much too pretty to be crying."

She looked at him, her lower lip in a cupped pout, catching her tears. He handed her a handkerchief and she dabbed at her eyes. "My makeup must be running," she complained. "Could I use your lavatory?"

Delicate word for it, he thought. "Sure, go right ahead, it's in there. And when you come out, we'll have a drink and I'll read your palm."

"Only if it's good fortune."

"Oh, I'm sure it will be."

She smiled at him. He was so reassuring. His voice was so dominating and soothing, a true soothsayer all right. She got up and went out of the room.

Morgan rubbed his hands together and went to prepare a few things.

In a few minutes she exited the bathroom, and was startled by the touch of something cold and clammy on her bare leg. She let out with a small scream and snatched her leg away from the doorway leading into Sayer's bedroom, just off the lavatory. When she looked down to ascertain what had touched her, it was a pair of hands poking from the crack in the door, and then out stepped Morgan's dummy, Felix, saying, "Never could keep my hands off the babes."

Morgan instantly yanked Felix from sight, and had a father-son talk with him that instantly had Felix tearful and apologetic, and from the other room Felix shouted his sad apology to her.

"Where'd you come from? You weren't even supposed to be here!" Morgan shouted at the dummy.

"How do you think I got here?" Felix asked in sudden anger.

"Get in, get in your case and stay the hell there."

Suddenly he rushed back to her, but the door was standing open and she was gone.

"Damn, damn you Felix," Morgan muttered, racing for a pair of pants, tearing on a shirt, and going after her.

She was long gone from the building, but it was a couple of blocks to the train station. If she had driven herself, it might be a lost cause. But he had to try.

He saw his neighbor, Mary Burroughs from 11C. She said hello and gave a little wave, but he got into the elevator and rushed down to the parking garage, where he raced from the building, looking both ways before selecting a direction. He scanned the streets, both sides. Then he saw her sitting in a well-lit restaurant window having a cup of coffee.

He pulled up to the curb, got out, and went for his . . . his what? What was she to him? Another pair of hands? A possession? That was what he had been thinking when Felix botched everything. How the hell had Felix gotten to the apartment on his own?

He entered the restaurant wearing a London Fog over his casual dress. He saw that she went rigid and her eyes went wide with trepidation. She looked for a way out, her gestures like those of a trapped animal. A waitress at the counter seemed to sense there might be trouble, and she stared from her position and then plunked a telephone onto the counter in a threatening gesture, banging it so that the bell inside rang.

Morgan Sayer stopped Elena from getting up, his eyes riveting her in place. "I'm so sorry, Elena. Felix . . . you see, Felix is my problem. You said you were attracted to me because I had no problems. I simply wanted you to know that I too am human. I shouldn't have frightened you that way. Foolish, very foolish and childish of me." *And Felix,* he thought but did not add. "Please accept our—*my* apology."

She swallowed hard and dropped her gaze. It seemed the only way she could regain her strength with this man. If she looked into his eyes, she would do anything he said, *anything,* and perhaps that was what she wanted, someone to make all of her decisions for her, take care of her, keep her. Life had not been easy for her; she spent much of her days and nights fantasizing about a man like Morgan Sayer coming into her life, sweeping her off her feet, becoming her confessor, her conscience, her will, and her lover all in one. She fantasized about a man who didn't exist, a man without hesitation, a man who knew his heart and mind and had no fear of anything or anyone, a man like Morgan—except now he was sitting here admitting to fears and hangups, something to do with that dummy with the frighteningly real hands that had touched her. Something about that touch, like the touch of—

"Come back with me, now. I don't want to sleep alone, and neither do you."

She looked up into his eyes. They held her there as if everything else melted from the world, certainly from her consciousness. "You want me. . . ."

"You're tired. You've been seeking happiness and it has eluded you for oh-so-many years." It was information he had snatched from her mind while she was in a trance, and now it entranced her to think that he could know her so well. Still, the touch of that dummy . . .

"Gentle love . . . nothing kinky," she said. "No more of Felix."

"I swear on my father's grave."

She thought it odd he should say father's instead of mother's grave.

"I knew my father . . . but never knew my mother," he said, as if reading her mind.

He was powerful. He was no ordinary nightclub magician with a hatful of tricks. There was something almost superhuman about him. She liked that. She needed and wanted that. Perhaps he could give meaning to her life.

"All right," she said, unable to resist. "So romantic of you to chase after me this way."

"You're very important to me, Elena." He took her hands in his, studying them, tracing each line and contour. "According to your lifeline, you will find the peace and serenity you seek. In fact, you will find it soon."

"Maybe . . . maybe I already have."

He nodded. "Yes, I think so. Are you ready?"

She got up while he was still holding her hands. The waitress saw him place a fiver on the table and she thought how romantic it had been, the way he had come in and swept this nice-looking woman from her gloom of a moment before. She was radiant now. The waitress wondered if it'd ever happen to her this way. Not likely, she told herself as the loving couple exited the door.

Sometime in the middle of the night, after they'd made gentle and fulfilling love, Morgan lay on his back struggling with his inner drives and urges. He reached below the bed and lifted out Rhodes's severed hands and caressed himself with them. He saw snapshots in his head of hands, hands that filled the room and covered the bed and him, and Elena there beside him. Sarah too was in the bed, as was Rhodes. All of them together.

Elena was a better lover than Sarah had been. Morgan had enjoyed her hands on him, the light touch roving and exploring. He wanted to keep her, but he knew he couldn't; he knew she'd soon leave him. Everyone left him in the end. And when she left, her hands would go with her.

He lay there thinking about it for a long time. Then he

saw that Felix was sitting upright in the chair beside the bed.

"Don't do it, Morgan," Felix told him.

"It's none of your business."

"None of my—none of my—no? What happens to me when they catch you? Lock you in a looney bin, or electrocute you?"

"*Shhhh*, you'll wake her."

"What's the difference?"

"*Shhhh!*"

"You're going to wake her anyway, and chop off her goddamned hands! Fucking crazy asshole, you know that?"

"Felix! Please."

She was roused by the noise they'd made. He quickly took hold of Felix and stuffed him below the bed, his dead man's hands lingering at the edge. "Don't, don't do this, Morbid!"

"Shut up! I'm the boss here."

"Who? What? What is it?" She was pulling herself up and as she did so, he held up a beautiful heart-shaped crystal to her eyes and said, "Look deeply into the facets of the crystal, Elena. Deeper, deeper—"

"Morgan?"

"Do as I say." The command came in so sharp and threatening a voice that she responded. It was what she wanted, after all, a commanding, dominating person to take her into his hands, to turn herself completely over to him, trusting him completely.

He added to the images with words: "You're now mine, and you will only see and feel what I tell you to see and feel. You will only hear the sounds of my voice, and you will believe in me, for I am your power and your guide and your strength."

"Yes, yes, Morgan."

"I am yours and you are mine."

"Yes."

"All mine."

"I am yours."

142

"To do with as I wish."

"To do with as you wish."

It was like a marriage vow.

"You will feel nothing when you are touched."

"Nothing."

"You will not bleed when you are cut."

She hesitated a moment, but went on. "Nothing."

"Your mind and my mind working in tandem will relieve you of any unpleasant sensations, panic, fear, or phobia. You may imagine harm, you may dream of harm, yet you will never know harm again. You will block pain and discomfort completely from your mind. You will staunch the flow of blood in any wound you might encounter."

"It sounds wonderful . . ." *Too good to be true*, she thought from deep within.

"Heavenly," he added.

"Yes, heavenly."

"Imagine, never experiencing pain or illness or sadness or grief ever again, Elena. Isn't that what you came to me for? Isn't it?"

"Yes, yes!"

She was sitting upright in bed, her legs crossed in the lotus position, nude, when Felix crawled up from below the bed and straddled her. Morgan smiled at the immature little prick; he didn't know what to do with a woman. He laughed inwardly as Felix's hands went round about her breasts and played for a time over the flat of her tummy, and then began to explore lower.

"Do you feel any discomfort, Elena?"

"No . . . no."

"Good." She was blocking all feeling under the hypnotic spell.

Felix's right hand was rammed into her as a test. Only her body reacted, the muscles contracting.

"Anything, Elena? Do you feel anything?"

"Nothing."

"Good, very good."

"I want to play with her," said Felix.

"Felix, you're not even supposed to be here, and your angel's heart is not going to . . . to save her."

"You're going to do her, aren't you?"

"Not open for discussion."

"Bastard. She's been good to you, for you."

"How damned long've you been under the bed?"

"Since you came back with her."

"Bastard."

"Bastard."

"Elena, come with me."

"Elena, don't do it."

She responded only to Morgan's voice.

"We're going to go into the kitchen now."

"Angel in the kitchen, devil in the bed," said Felix, "just the opposite around here."

"Shut up, Felix."

"Why don't you shut me up? Why don't you chop off my head? It'd fit in the hole. Go on."

"I'm not arguing with you, Felix."

11C was banging on the wall again, that Burroughs woman. She had the ears of a bloodhound.

"Suppose this one comes out of it like the last and starts screaming? What're you going to do with 11C? Cut her hands off too?"

"If I have to."

"You're crazy, you know that?"

He marched Elena out and closed the door on Felix and his confounded reasoning. His every nerve was titillated and extended like live wires. It was no longer a rational event; nothing of cause-effect, nor conditioning, nor upbringing could explain why he was taking Elena's hands. It was no longer something he could explain away as need, not even to himself. He didn't know *why* anymore; he only knew he had to see it again to believe it possible, and to feel the power of it all.

From beneath the sink he pulled the guillotine and propped it up over the sink on its baseboard. The thing was the size of a large blender. What made it work so efficiently was the well-oiled bearings and the powerful weights held by a hair trigger that shot down on the little pulley. As they were released so was the razor's-edge blade that came down with a *chomp!*

"Elena, you will now see in your mind's eye that you have lost the use of your hands, and next your feet and legs, arms, your entire body. You no longer need a body because you're becoming spirit energy. If this is so, nothing done to your body can harm you. When you see parts of your body destroyed, you will feel nothing for those parts. You will not shout, scream, faint. You will not bleed. Even if your hands were cut away, you would not feel it, nor would you bleed, for you are now spirit energy. Do you fully understand?"

"Yes, I do."

"Good."

He lifted her hands to the guillotine's two holes and closed the top over them.

Felix was shouting through the door in his irritating voice, "Please, Elena, don't listen to him."

Morgan went to Felix, tying his hands and gagging him. He then forced him back into his case, closing and snapping the lid. When he returned to Elena Jorovich, she was exactly as he had left her.

"Time now," he told her. "Are you prepared?"

"Yes."

"Your journey will be pleasant."

"I know. . . . I know. . . ."

He pulled the chain that held the weights and her hands were lobbed off, and he marveled at the way they flew and slid about the sink, and how little blood was let, and how Elena maintained her calm under his spell.

She was the best so far.

"You shouldn't've done it, Morgan."

Morgan looked from his victim to Felix. Felix sat alongside him on the kitchen cabinet, bug-eyed, staring at what Morgan had done to Elena's hands as if he'd never seen it done before. Morgan wanted to shake him and throw him from the room, but instead he said, "You know I had no choice."

145

"Shouldn't've and you know it."

"No, I don't know it."

"Yes, you do. Pretend not to know, but you do know it's wrong . . . wrong, Morgan."

"It's going to prove beneficial to all of mankind—"

"Bullshit."

"—some day!"

"Crapolo-corola!"

"You just wait and see."

Felix jumped, or was pushed from the cabinet top— Morgan was unsure which. His mind was filled with a matrix of conflicting emotions. "It had-ta be done," he pronounced.

"Sure," said Felix, "couldn't help but be done . . . can't help yourself. You're pathetic, Morgan."

Morgan lashed out at Felix with a vicious kick, sending him screaming across the room and disappearing into the living room somewhere, licking his wounds, cursing under his breath.

"Bastard dummy," mumbled Morgan to himself. "Won't spoil my experiment, not tonight. It's not all just fun and games, you know!" he howled at the dummy.

Next door Mrs. Burroughs began banging on the wall and threatening to call the cops because of all the racket. He looked up at the clock to see that most of the night had gone! He'd lost a lot of time, and was unable to fill in certain gaps, as when Felix had disappeared into the living room and had later returned.

"Go ahead, call the fucking cops! I dare ya!" he replied, and refocused on Elena Jorovich and what he must do next with her.

"She's gonna do it one a these days!" It was Felix again, coming back for more, half in and half out of the kitchen, lying on his stomach at the entranceway. "Cops come in here and they'll smell the goddamned blood, Morgan, and you'll piss in your pants and mine!"

"Leave me alone! Why don't you all just leave me the fuck alone!"

"Temper, temper! You'll awaken the *hand* maiden, and

146

then there'll be blood from one end—"

"Get outa here, Felix. Please, just leave."

"*Hmmmmph,* and I thought all this was for me."

"It *was* for you, but you . . . you ridicule and you mock the importance of it."

"Go on, masturbate with your fantasies and your fetishes and her hands and be done with it. Just don't expect me to be happy about it, Morgan, okay?"

Lanark was involved—the same moment that Elena Jorovich was losing her hands to Morgan Sayer's madness—in his own madness. He had hung Tyrrell Loomis up on a pulley in the middle of the ancient factory, lifting him higher and higher. Loomis was conscious and certain he was about to die.

"You know what I want, Loomis."

"I tell you, I don't know."

Loomis's face was bloody from the beating Lanark had given him. He remained stubborn. Lanark was out of patience and running out of time. He had promised that by daylight he'd turn Loomis over to Robeson and he'd be booked properly on charges of murder in connection with the death of Willie Floyd, along with an array of narcotics charges.

Lanark had found the abandoned factory empty save for the garbage truck and the cab. Neither Stokes nor Robeson had hung around. He'd seen each man make it away from the storm of fire they'd created, and it did not occur to him that either man had been hit. But on entering the silent, empty old warehouse and factory he had wondered aloud, "Where are they? And where's Loomis?"

His first impulse was anger at Robeson. Mark had surely rushed Loomis to the safety of a holding cell at Precinct 13, probably with Stokes's blessings. Damn them, he had thought. They'd decided when he was delayed to take their own action. He could hardly blame them, given the circumstances.

But then he heard a slight moan in the darkness. He

heard light noises coming from the trunk of the cab, and then he saw the blood discoloring the concrete and dust at the back of the cab. Lanark knew instantly that something had gone wrong. Something terrible had happened.

Inside the cab's trunk Tyrrell Loomis was both kicking and cursing. Lanark went into a rage, locating a crowbar and prying open the locked trunk, dragging Loomis out by his lapels, knocking him senseless, tearing off his coat until it fell away in shreds.

Using his belt, he attached him to an enormous hook at the end of a universal joint and pulley. He hit a button and sent the man skyward. With Loomis dangling overhead like a rag doll, he radioed in for a location check on Robeson. No one had any word. Then a message came through from Mark. He was at Ravenswood, and Stokes had been "injured" in an "incident."

"Is he going to be okay?"

"Yeah, he's resting quiet now."

"Anything I can do?"

"Don't trouble yourself, Lieutenant. Off-duty cop tried to foil a burglary and gets wounded doing so."

Lanark was aware that Mark was aware they were on an open line. "File a report and I'll have a look-see tomorrow," said Lanark.

"You got it, Lieutenant."

"And thanks for . . . letting me know right away, Mark."

"Tomorrow, Lieutenant."

"Right, see you then."

Lanark hadn't been disturbed since. He'd let the worry with the trash truck go to O'Hurley; let the worry with Stokes go to Robeson; let the worry with Shannon simply go, at least for now. Loomis was his ticket to a man with no last name, a man that two dead men had fingered only as Whitey, and another man named Marty Jenkins who seemed not to exist. Lanark had checked out every Marty Jenkins and aka's for them that could be found in the police computers. Whoever these two remaining bastards were, they were either dead, or extremely well placed. And since Loomis was reluctant to talk, it would appear that the two men who remained on Lanark's personal hit list were living-agenda items after all.

"Willie Floyd died for your sins, Tyrrell, and so did your woman. That didn't bother me so much, but now you've shot a close friend of mine, and he's fighting for his life in the hospital as we speak."

Loomis only groaned in response.

"Know what I can do with this contraption, Loomis?"

Another groan, and Loomis tried to lift his head.

Lanark continued his unofficial interrogation, saying, "I can drop you straight into the floor with the press of a goddamned button. Be like riding an elevator to your death, unless I chose to stop it just before you hit bottom, maybe snap every bone in your filthy body, but that way you'd still be alive."

The torment with words wasn't working fast enough. It would soon be light, and Lanark would have to turn him over to Mark to fulfill the terms of their agreement.

"Not interested, huh? No understand, huh? You don't know anybody named Whitey? No one named Marty Jenkins?"

No response.

"All right, but you remember, *compadre*, I gave you a chance to talk. You remember that when they find you with a broken back."

Lanark punched the button and then punched it to stop. Loomis's body darted down with the falling pulley and suddenly snapped. Lanark hadn't allowed him to fall more than eight feet, but the effect was one of whiplash and multiple pain. Loomis screamed for mercy.

"No mercy, drug man . . . not until you tell me what I want to hear."

The door began to rise and Lanark hit the up button, sending Loomis back toward the ceiling. Through the door drove Mark Robeson, a grim look on his face. Lanark feared that Stokes had taken a turn for the worse. He went to Robeson, who got out of the car and aimed at Loomis, preparing to dispatch his soul at once.

"No!" Lanark pushed aside his weapon. "Mark, what's happened?"

"I'm goin' to kill that bastard."

"Mark! Is Stokes dead?"

"No, but could've been. Damnit, Ryne, we take this grease-scum into the station in his condition and what'll you think's going to happen? He'll scream police brutality. The DA'll take it to court, and it'll be tossed out, or he'll be given a light sentence and—"

"Mark, settle down. I don't want the mother killed until I get some answers from him."

Robeson looked into Lanark's eyes to see if he was sure. All he saw there was a fiery determination to get the answers he sought from Loomis.

"Go home, Mark. Get some sleep."

"What about him?"

"He'll keep. He's not going anywhere."

Robeson looked up at the dangling man and nodded, and then he laughed. "For once he's hooked instead of getting others hooked. Good show, Lanark. You always put on a good show. Some kinda tactician. What we did over on Troop, they'll be talking about that for years. Word's circulating it's a gang war. Loomis's people with the black dealers. Guess somebody saw Stokes or me, or both."

"We did take 'em out, didn't we?"

Robeson smiled wide and pointed at Loomis. "And we got the prize. Stokes . . . he was jumping like a chicken on a griddle and he got careless."

"When he frisked Loomis, he overlooked a weapon?"

"Yeah, that's about it."

"Go home, Mark, get some sleep."

"No, too keyed up, I guess. Came back to see you do him. Go ahead, Lieutenant. I want to see him beg and squirm."

"I do my best work alone."

Robeson had heard this line before. He had also helped Lanark out on unofficial casework before. He didn't like the way he was being shunted out the door.

"You didn't do tonight alone, Lanark; you just remember that when you see Stokes next."

Mark went for his car. Lanark followed, putting a hand on his shoulder and saying, "I'm sorry about Stokes—"

Robeson came around with a powerful fist into Lanark's jaw, sending him reeling back. The two had boxed together at the gym for years as partners, but this was the first time Lanark had ever been struck by Mark's powerful, naked fist. Lanark went straight down and sat amid Stokes's blood and the dirt of the floor, staring up at Robeson, who hit the remote for the door and tossed it at Lanark without another word. Just before peeling out, Mark said, "You'll get what you want someday, Lanark. You'll see every one of them killed, I know that now. But you know what?"

"Mark—"

"You'll be alone in the end, Lanark, completely and totally. Nobody'll want to be near you."

Robeson burned rubber backing out, and he disappeared into the distance as Lanark closed the door behind him.

"Damn," he muttered before turning his attention back to Tyrrell Loomis.

TWELVE

Shannon Keyes's dream was of faraway lands and peoples, travel and adventure with Lanark at her side. At least, that's how her comfortable dream had begun, but it quickly deteriorated into a dream about an enormous hole in the earth in some forgotten desert of Asia. A full-scale archaeological site filled with bones and artifacts, and directing the organized mayhem of the dig was Dr. Ito Colucci and Dr. Richard Ames. Ames and Colucci argued fervently on the "meaning" of things in a language that was English, yet it was a vague and indecipherable dialect spoken only by these two men, an extinct language. But one item filtered through the verbal hieroglyphics: Someone in the pit below had discovered the ancient remains of a human buried there, followed by another and another, male, female, child. But in all of the bones there were no fingers, no metacarpals, nothing of the hands.

Colucci's dream form burst forth with a shout. "We've located them!"

Ames replied by lifting up his own arms, severed at the wrists, saying calmly, "But you'll never find the hands."

In her dream, she looked down into the open pit and inside it, looking back at her, was Lanark, but then his features coalesced into her own countenance.

A shrill bell rang out and everyone began clawing their way from the pit, hurrying as if the earth meant to swallow them up. Some slipped and fell down and from the bowels of the pit reached a giant hand into which they disappeared. She heard the bell, and she too was climbing, climbing, almost at the edge, slipping, pulling. Again the bell, and this time the sound snapped her from the deep pit of her confusing dream as suddenly as if she'd been awakened from a hypnotic smile by the snap of a finger.

Alongside her bed the phone continued to ring. She shook involuntarily with the memory of the hand reaching up to snatch her down, but there was no time to analyze the dream, and since it made no sense to her conscious mind, she grabbed for the phone as if grabbing onto a life preserver thrown her from a phantom ship that'd passed by her dark room.

"Keyes? Is that you?"

"Yes, sir?" It was Captain Paul Wood's voice at its most irritated.

"Lanark with you?"

"No, Captain, he is not."

"Don't lie to me, Keyes."

"Captain, he is not with me! What's this all about?"

There was a pause. "Another victim of The Handyman, alive this time. Could be an eyewitness if they can save her."

"Alive?"

"Thanks to fast police and medical assistance, yes."

"Where?"

"Maywood."

She puzzled over this. "Getting further afield in his gory games, isn't he?"

"Chance of a copycat job, perhaps, but who knows? Maywood cops have it at the moment. They almost got the bastard—"

"Almost," she groaned. Almost didn't count.

"They get a license plate?"

"Partial. Cop that saved the woman has to be interviewed by you. Want to get out there like an hour ago?"

"You tried reaching Lanark at—"

"Everywhere! He's incognito, out on one of his

goddamned prowls, and this time it erupted into a gun battle—"

"What?"

"—that's had repercussions all the way to Lawrence, who's all over me with some cock—shit—that Lanark attacked an entourage of drug dealers—one of which was an undercover guy for Broadway—and kidnapped! Get this, kidnapped Tyrrell Loomis—"

"Lanark could be hurt!"

"—to beat information out of him."

She tried to piece what he was saying to her together with how Lanark had been acting lately, and the so-called tips he'd been taking from Tony Dinetto. She wished that she had time to locate and shake Dinetto down; she wished that she had guts enough to tell Captain Wood to see to it. But if she brought Wood into direct confrontation with Ryne in such a manner, it could end everything between them.

"Have you tried Mark Robeson? Wil Cassidy?"

"Everyone connected with the unit."

"Why'd you call me last?"

He hesitated. "Your partner better be clean, better sure harness himself in, Keyes, or—"

"Why'd you call me *last?*"

He hemmed and hawed.

"Giving him the benefit of a doubt, huh? Trying to piece it together so you could put the best light on it for his poor stooge partner?"

"Let's just say I had my reasons." It was a cop-out by a tough cop. "Now, get yourself out to Maywood, Precinct Four."

He hung up before she could say what she thought of his "protective" tactics. As far as she was concerned, all men were bastards. For all she knew Ryne Lanark was lying in a back alley somewhere, his blood running into the gutter. The image frightened her and recalled her recent night-mare so vividly she re-lived it as she dressed hurriedly to race to Maywood and the most recent crime scene in the case that Lanark seemed to be letting others "handle."

All the way to Maywood she radioed people she thought might know of Lanark's whereabouts. She particularly grilled Jack Tebo, who answered the phone when she was patched through from central. There was a police-band radio running twenty-four hours a day in Lanark's apartment and in the bar. Tebo was groggy and didn't appreciate Maria's sleep and his own being disturbed, but she was desperate and worried. This soon filtered through to Tebo's sleepy mind when he rushed upstairs, checked on the fact his often-foolish nephew was out, his bed unused, and returned to the phone. He tried to reassure her that Ryne knew his way around, that he wasn't nearly so reckless as he'd been a year before, and that he'd turn up.

She couldn't get hold of Robeson any more than she could Lanark. He'd only deny for Lanark, even if he knew, his sense of allegiance to Lanark was so strong. In fact, he very likely was with Ryne. Stokes too was suspiciously unavailable. Captain Wood hadn't spoken to the entire team. He too had been unable to raise either Robeson or Stokes. Neither Wil Cassidy nor Myra Lane had any idea of the whereabouts of the others. They were speeding toward Maywood just as she was.

"They'll show up," Wil tried to assure her over the radio.

She wasn't so sure. Lanark was notorious for two things: his temper and his reckless acts. There had been hour-long sessions at The Lucky 13th during which all of Ryne Lanark's exploits and exploitation of others had become legend.

Captain Paul Wood, Wil, and Myra made it to the scene of the crime ahead of Shannon. It had been a mistake to run by the precinct. Everyone was at the crime scene, everyone except the young woman whose life hung by the "threads" of modern machinery that stabilized her as doctors worked to repair the awful damage done to her. She'd gone into a catatonic state, doctors told Shannon at Heinze VA Hospital, *in order to cope with the loss of her*

155

hands—what the doctors called "the situation." When she might be able to testify was secondary to the question of her ever opening her mind again.

Shannon had caught the tail end of the operation and ministrations heaped upon Elena Jorovich in the mad rush to save her, but it appeared she might be saved for a life of self-induced imprisonment. She was in such a state of shock that the doctors had argued over the wisdom of operating. An older doctor named Wells, with white hair and a bent back from years of operations, had gone ahead with the procedures to save the young woman from bleeding to death. The stitching was done without anesthetic. It was considered bad form to put any type of medication into a catatonic patient, and the state of her condition was a form of anesthesia stronger than any produced artificially.

Shannon spent some moments just staring at the pale features of the woman fighting for her life. But was she fighting? Or had she given up the battle? Was that her response to the vulgar attack that had ended her evening with the killer? Shannon felt wave upon wave of sadness for the tall, frail-looking woman as they wheeled her out to recovery, life-sustaining tubes and gray metal boxes moving in tandem with her bed. Keyes was then hit with a tidal wave of helplessness and anger that threatened to engulf her. It had all begun with Rhodes, then the Chambers girl, and now this one. Outwardly, they had nothing in common. Even ignoring the fact that one victim was a man, the two women were very different in appearance as well. Physically, they were near opposites. One was medium in height with sandy blond hair and blue-gray eyes, the other statuesquely tall and model-thin with brown hair and eyes like Audrey Hepburn despite her gangliness.

What linked them besides the obvious fact that they all had hands all wanted by the killer? There was some definite reason the killer selected these people as his victim; the appearance of randomness was too neat, almost staged. She pondered these thoughts as she left the operating theater, outside of which she half heard the report from the doctor who had been dispatched to talk to her and other cops who were on hand representing various precincts in the area.

Then she caught sight of the reporter Jeff Sandler lurking about a waiting area, no doubt fantasizing about being the first to talk to the only eyewitness that could tell them anything about The Handyman. She imagined his imaginings. He planned to tell the hospital staff, if he hadn't already done so, that his name was Jeff Jorovich, husband or brother, next of kin. He'd gotten the name of Elena Jorovich by listening in on the police band, same as she, when information on the woman had come over.

Sandler saw her staring at him, gave a small smile of recognition, and dropped his gaze, his mind reaching for something to say to her, before he waltzed into her path with his questions.

"Anything new break?"

"Isn't this new enough?"

He frowned. "She's not talking, or haven't you heard."

"I heard."

"Where to now?"

"Crime scene."

"Is that where your partner is?"

"Yeah," she lied casually.

"Funny, I heard different."

"Jeff, you're in my way."

"Any new leads? Come on, give me a break. This is front page."

"I've got nothing new to give you. Now, please!" She stormed by him and rushed for her car.

From the hospital, in her rearview mirror, Lieutenant Second Grade Shannon Keyes saw that she was being followed. Jeff Sandler followed. His intrusive shadow didn't subside until she reached the police barricade at the scene. There she was allowed to drive through while Sandler had to back up and find a parking area along the

157

highway out on the roadway. It appeared the locals were doing a fair job of keeping the press in check.

Driving on, dawn now lighting the area where birds chased in frantic darts and squirrels squealed at the intrusion of the policemen who came too near their nests, Shannon saw that it was going to be a cloudless, clear blue day filled with sunlight and warmth. The morning woods' serenity was at great odds with what she felt in the pit of her stomach and the images of Elena Jorovich on her back in an operating room. Then she spotted Captain Paul Wood, and the married police team of Wil Cassidy, a former Navy Seal, and his partner, Myra Lane. Together, they'd already organized searchers. Policemen in uniform were scavenging the area for any sign of clues. Centralized in the weed-infested parking lot, deep in the forest preserve area, was an evidence-technician van on lend-lease from Maywood Central. She thought she saw Dr. Black, puttering inside the van, but it turned out to be the Maywood coroner instead. She'd wanted Black to be there, and she repeated this to Wood the moment she came up to him.

"He's on his way, maybe."

"Maybe?"

"Hey, the man's got a busy schedule, Lieutenant. Besides, when the investigating team's honcho is too busy to be on scene, then why should the coroner bother, huh?"

She didn't want to get into it with Wood, not here and not about Lanark. She too was angry with the man. "Just came from the hospital," she told them. She pictured the near-vegetable person that she had viewed from the deck of an operating theater as the doctors worked to clean and cauterize the massive wounds. "Girl's on respirator, heart-lung, condition's stable but—"

"Then it's true?" Wil asked. "This one's alive?"

"She is alive, but in a comatose state. No one knows if she'll regain consciousness, or check out altogether." She turned to Paul Wood. "How was she found, Captain?"

"Talk to Officer Dale Norris, the tall one, over there."

Shannon was immediately struck by the officer's size

and build and good looks. He was wearing a skin-tight blue uniform. She gave Wil Cassidy and Myra operational instructions. Neither Stokes nor Mark Robeson could be located. Suspicions about a bombardier raid of sorts on a group of cars in another part of the city were beginning to focus on Ryne Lanark. It didn't help his case that he could not be found. Further, the absence of two vital members of the 13th Undercover Unit exacerbated rumors and talk. But now Wil was answering a call from HQ, and he was shouting the news that young Stokes was in hospital at Ravenswood, something to do with having stumbled onto a burglar and having been shot through the throat. He was expected to recover.

Wood heard this news and frowned. No doubt it explained where Robeson and Ryne had spent the night.

Still, there seemed something skewed about the information, and Shannon decided to reserve judgment.

Shannon carried on, going to Officer Dale Norris for the information she could glean from him. She introduced herself as Detective Lieutenant Keyes.

Norris was cordial if a little upset. He was also tired. As he explained, "It all came about right at the end of my shift."

"You riding alone?"

"That's right. Partner replacement is very slow. You know how it is."

"Lost your partner?"

"Yeah."

"The good way, or the bad way?"

"Took a knife in the rib cage when we were called into a disturbance. Couldn't do nothing for him."

She could see he was still shaken from his experience. "So last night you were cruising in and around the woods here, alone, and you saw the victim?"

They were standing in the middle of Thatcher Woods, a Maywood municipality forest preserve which, from time to time, required cleaning out, as it would become infested with bikers who happened to also be druggies. Norris was with the Maywood Police Department. Maywood authorities in the past had said in the papers that they would not long endure the insult of being a "dumping ground for Chicago murderers." It looked as if they needed to beef up their efforts.

"Not exactly, not right off, no," replied Norris in a slow, deliberate manner.

"Where you from, Norris?"

The question caught him by surprise. She smiled at him. "I detect an accent."

"You're the detective."

"Quite a few rummaging around here. You've probably told this story six times already."

"Got our guys out in force. Riverside's here, and so's Brookfield, and now Chicago. Guess when you get one like this . . . God, she didn't have any hands . . . it's just natural everybody wants to get into the act. Lord knows why."

"Just trying to cover all the bases. You know we've had two similar cases in the city."

"Yes'm, I know."

"So, where you from, Officer Norris?"

"Originally? North Carolina, up around Raleigh."

She sensed military and Old South all over him. "Did a stint in the Army?"

"Navy. Thought I'd like to be a Navy Pilot."

"Got it out of your system?"

He shook his head. "Had it knocked out of my system, you might say. Accident. Everything kinda went bad for me after that. They didn't trust me. Could've happened to any one of them, but . . . it's like everybody's wired up in the Navy and one string on the old guitar snaps and they scrap the whole damned thing. Know what I mean?"

"So you sought a discharge?"

"Yes'm, but sometimes sure wish now I'd stayed."

"You look like you could use some coffee, maybe some ham and eggs?"

He half-smiled at this. "You sure are a good detective."

She smiled at this. "Come on. You can explain what happened sitting down over coffee as well as standing

160

here." It was beginning to crowd up, and reporters were appearing. "Come on. Anybody squawks, and you're with me."

"What about Gilley?"

"Gilley?"

"He gave chase to the man that did it. Got a partial plate number too."

She became instantly excited. "You're sure of this?"

"Gilley and his partner, Screw—ah, Mike Scroon. We call him Screw." He pointed them out. They were surrounded by men from other districts, all taking depositions.

"Do you know the plate numbers?"

"Gilley saw the car speed outa here. So he got on the box and called me for backup, said for me to check out parking area three in the Thatch. When I drove in, I saw her, running, falling, flailing her—her arms. Hands were pumping blood. It was awful. I caught her, put her in the back of my unit. She's bleeding all over me and the car, but I just pretended it was tea or something, and just kept going. Raced her to VA at a hundred miles an hour, almost got killed doing it, but got her there and they stopped the bleeding, but not before she'd gone into what they call a catatonic state. Doctor over there said it was likely the only way her mind could deal with the loss of her hands."

A search, she'd been told, revealed nothing of the missing appendages. "What were the license-plate numbers?"

"BKT-41 was all Gilley could get before he lost 'em."

"Where did he lose them?"

"Series of underpasses. Just outfoxed him and his partner. But they're pretty sure of the numbers."

"Did the getaway car fire at them?"

"No, no, ma'am."

"You ready for that breakfast?"

"Uh-ooh," he said as a small army of reporters began to descend on them. "They got the word it was me found her."

"Run for it, come on!" she said, dashing for her car.

Norris did the same, and they peeled out ahead of the flashing cameras.

"I don't know if I should thank you or not," he said. "They want to make me a big hero over this thing. All I did is what anybody'd have done."

"Not quite anybody," she said, recalling all the people who'd turned their backs on Rhodes and the girl Sarah.

Shannon got on the radio in an attempt to find Lanark. He came right on. He was beating his way toward the crime scene now. She told him what she had, about Norris and the plate numbers. She'd meet him at the Holiday Inn at the Hillside exit where she intended on buying Norris a hearty breakfast.

"Sounds good," said Lanark in a tired voice. "I'll join you there."

"By the way, Wood's after your ass."

"Talked to him already. I know."

"Smoothed it over with him, did you?"

"Was up all night with Stokes."

"Want to hear all about that one. You wouldn't happen to know anything about a commando-style raid on a drug caravan the other night, would you? Millions of bucks in contraband seized, but no one on hand to take the bows."

"Think I did hear something about that."

She frowned and cut him off as they arrived at the Breakfast Nook at the Holiday Inn, Hillside.

"One more call," she told Norris inside, going to a phone and making the request of DMV for a computer rundown on an address to accompany the first few digits of the plates they had.

"Roger," said the female voice at the other end. "Could be a number of these."

"Zero in on any in Maywood. Call me back at this number." Shannon gave them the phone number at the Nook, crossed her fingers, and returned to Dale Norris.

THIRTEEN

When Ryne Lanark had finally shown up at the Nook, Norris had already downed several eggs and some bacon slices, and Shannon had finished a second cup of coffee. When Shannon saw him approaching from across the room, it occurred to her that she was sitting alongside a man who was just as handsome and who seemed far more interested in her, and was indeed a great deal more stable. And as she watched Lanark's powerful body move toward them, she saw that it lacked some of its former drive, and that in his eyes there was a deep hurt—or was it a racing sign of jealousy that she'd missed there. In any event, he looked like death at lukewarm temperature. He'd been up all night.

"You look terrible," she told him when he sat down and introductions were over.

"Thanks, I need that."

"She's right," said Norris in his tight-fitting uniform. "You sure don't look very . . . official."

"Up all night with Stokes. He took a bullet in the throat."

"Last night?"

"Freak accident with his weapon when he was cleaning it." Lanark and Robeson had agreed on this story after discussing the alternatives.

"Freak accident, huh?"

"He's doing well, and will be all right."

163

She thought of how poorly this news would be received by Wood, and other cops in the department who already viewed Lanark with suspicion and contempt for the number of partners he'd had who had fallen in the line of duty.

"Tell me about this Jorovich woman," Lanark said.

She asked Norris to recount his story to Lanark. The waiter called Shannon away halfway through the tale, saying she had a phone call at the bar.

When Shannon returned, she announced that they might have the suspect's address. Dale Norris was gung ho, wanting to be the first to get there, but Lanark put up a hand to him and put him down quickly. "The task force in charge of this case, kid, you're looking at them. We handle it from here. Come on, Shannon."

She pulled away from Lanark. "Just a minute. I drove Dale here, and he's got no ride back."

"He can call. Come on."

"Ryne, you're being rude and bullying."

Lanark had been rude and bullying for the entire night toward one Tyrrell Loomis. It wasn't easy to turn it off. He turned back to Norris and said, "Come on, we'll get you back to your unit, and some of your guys can back us up."

Norris sullenly said, "Sure, if we can find the time."

It seemed lately that everything Ryne Lanark did was to intentionally hurt her, Shannon thought as they arrived at the street where the suspect's house was, at the end of the block. She'd been right about the day. It had come in perfectly: too bright, too clean, and too breezy, making her wish she were at the beach, listening to the lake waves lap in and out, feeling the play of the air over her midriff. Such fantasies were for another time, however. She realized this the moment Mark Robeson, Wil Cassidy, and Myra Lane all joined them at the rendezvous point.

They had all donned various disguises according to a hastily concocted plan they'd had little time to study or prepare for. They feared losing The Handyman before

164

they had him, if they allowed any time to pass. It was the consensus that, if a police car chase ensued, the killer could easily bolt and run from here to Washington State.

Robeson's loose-fitting, baggy trousers with moth-eaten holes, his lumberjack shirt, and shoddy Wellington boots made him look like a sharecropper. Wil Cassidy had on the uniform of a meter-reader, compliments of the nearby Commonwealth Edison power plant. Myra Lane was dressed in the clean-as-a-pin, tightly buttoned-up clothes of a Jehovah's Witness, just as Shannon was. They'd gotten their attire from the mobile custom unit which had been called out to Maywood. Lanark wore a blue denim jacket and jeans, desperately trying to look as if he might fit into the neighborhood, which ran primarily to black families and a sprinkling of Chicanos, a handful of whites.

Shannon had narrowed the possibilities from the license plate numbers and addresses given them down to this two-story frame house which had seen better days in the late fifties and early sixties. DMV had given her several ways to go, but this place was the nearest in proximity to both the woods and the highway. Whoever had run ahead of the police from Thatcher Woods knew the frontage road system and the underpasses and loops here well enough to confuse the cops, who presumably knew their territory.

Given Lanark's condition, Shannon assumed command of the overall plan, and Lanark didn't stand in her way. He knew better; he also knew that she was a good cop, and that she had proven herself many times over in undercover operations. The members of the team sensed the tension between them, but they were smart enough or tactful enough to ignore it.

The members of the team responded well to Shannon, and they now descended on the house with customary assertive behavior, creating the decoy offensive necessary for successful penetration. Shannon had all the paperwork necessary in hand before moving in. She'd gotten the complete cooperation of the Maywood authorities, and the warrant had been handled through them in ten-speed fashion. It was the kind of cooperation which Lanark, increasingly, could not get from others. The other team members didn't say a word about this, but they all felt secure in the outcome of the operation, knowing there was a warrant to enter.

The purpose of decoying in tandem with a warrant was due the fact that observers at the scene had noted that the place housing the suspect was filled with people, many of whom were children and teens. A ruse, getting them inside, would allow for the detectives to determine who needed a gun pointed to his head immediately, before a hostage situation evolved.

Shannon, neatly and primly dressed in a pale blue skirt and white blouse buttoned to the neck, a pair of fake glasses at the end of her nose, her hair tied in a bun, walked briskly alongside Myra, who wore a print dress. Myra's hands clutched tightly to a bible. Shannon carried a small briefcase filled with copies of *The Watch Tower*. They'd come to spread the word as two Jehovah's Witnesses.

Meanwhile, Mark Robeson wandered about the trash cans across the street and to the rear of the women, appearing to be aimlessly guided but in fact making his way to the suspect's house as well. He did a drunk's tap dance in the middle of the street to slow himself down. He shouted at the proper ladies to lend him a quarter. It wasn't a question but a command.

The two Jehovah's Witnesses chose to ignore the begging man, save for a word about his seeking Christ's redemption at his very next opportunity.

The surly beggar just laughed at them and spat. "You're lookin' at Jesus, sister! I *am* Jesus. I *am* Jesus in the Second Coming." He began to dig through the considerable trash around the house in question, mumbling to himself. "Didn't even see me coming! Me, Jesus. Gots to work a miracle for your kind to believe. Me, alls he gots *to do* is pro-viiiide . . . provide!"

The house looked like the sort of place that might be holding secrets, housing a serial killer. It was filthy. The porch was littered with throwaway furniture that had soaked up rain and sun and snow over the years. The yard was littered with papers, bottles, cans, chunks of discarded plastic containers, wood, and metal objects. An ancient rusted car seat sat out back amid weeds. The houses on either side, with the same construction and age, appeared to be palaces by comparison to this run-down eyesore. Some of the windows were covered with cardboard and newspapers where they'd been broken and never replaced.

The secured warrant from a Maywood court was inside one of the bibles. In dealing with killers, you didn't knock on a door and serve them with warrants. It could end up bloody. Halfway down the street, in a parked car, Wil and Lanark hung back. They were the most threatening in appearance, and most likely the easiest to spot as cops since they were not disguised. But their eyes were riveted to the action around the door.

"Let's make our way around back, Lanark," Wil suggested.

"Slow and easy."

They got out of the car and went separate ways to reach the same point. The windows under which Lanark walked held curious eyes. It was a mostly black neighborhood of Maywood. It was the first time he had considered the possibility that the killer could be a black man. Maybe one of those voodoo cultists on the South Side had moved west. And yet he knew that statistics suggested that the serial killer was a white man.

He made his way through the causeway and out into an alley. The windows of the suspect's house on the second story were staring right at him on this side. They either saw him or they didn't. Impossible to tell. On the opposite end, somehow Wil had made it to the alleyway there. His approach was more tentative than Lanark's had become.

The net was closing.

Shannon rang the bell again.

There was still a wait.

She rang again, and abruptly the door swung open. She was staring at a young woman perhaps eighteen who looked as if she were two feet off the ground, she was so high. Myra went into her bible and began reading from Revelations and asking the girl if she knew what that meant.

"Sure, sure . . . but whataya' want? We ain't got nothing here you want."

A guy pushed her aside and stepped into the doorway. "Well, looky here, a couple of white girls working our neighborhood for pocket change. You sweeties want some candy?"

Robeson pushed through the gate, asking for work.

"What the hell is this, a convention? Hey, you, nigger! Get off my property!" said the man at the door. He was white, tall and thin, with a Sonny Bono appearance, the long hair braided at the back, the mustache too long even for a handlebar mustache. "But you two, come on in and we'll talk about the Bible. I know a lot about the Bible."

"You're inviting us in?" asked Shannon.

"A looker like you, hon, I'm no fool, sweet thing!"

Robeson made his way to the porch, weaving, saying, "Can't no man! Can't no man talk to me thata way."

The white man in the doorway shouted for someone named Billy to come and get rid of the nigger. "Meanwhile, you two honeys, just come on in and we'll pray together."

Myra pretended fear, particularly when she saw Billy, an enormous ox of a man who looked semi-retarded.

"You gotta' go, mister," Billy was telling Robeson when the women stepped inside.

The instant they were on the inside, someone grabbed Myra from behind. It was another man. "Let her go!" shouted Shannon, who suddenly found the first man had his hands draped all over her as he offered her his tongue in her ear.

"Sonofabitch!" she shouted, and brought him suddenly to his knees, his arm twisted up pretzel fashion against his back.

Myra had her spiked heel in the other one's face as he lay sullenly against the wood floor. All around them, women of various ages were shouting and pelting them with objects, saying, "Let'em go! Let'em alone!"

"Police!" shouted Shannon, whipping out the warrant. "And everything in this damned place is confiscated!"

Robeson burst through the front door, pushing Billy ahead of him. Billy was in tears and he went to one of the older women, who nestled him against her bosom, telling him it was all right.

Just as she did, Lanark and Wil burst in through the back, pushing several near-escapees of the commune into the room.

"Whose car is the green sedan outside, license number BKT—"

"Mine, it's mine," said one of the young women, her eyes wide with fright.

"Were you driving it last night?"

"No, I don't ever hardly drive it."

"Somebody was driving it last night out of Thatcher Woods, honey. You want to tell me who?"

The man Shannon held down was released now. He groaned with the pain. The young woman's eyes alone told Shannon it had been him with the car the night before.

"Anybody else in the house, upstairs?" asked Lanark of the cowering women. They were all dressed in ragged clothing, most stoned even at that early hour.

"Carol, Sue, and Bobby," said the sober one who owned the car.

"You going to arrest all of these children?" asked the older woman who held big Billy. "They didn't do nothing bad, officer." She spoke her plea to Lanark.

"Whoever was in that car last night, lady," replied Shannon sharply, going to her, "you point them out and we'll see to it the rest of you can stay put."

There was a long moment of hesitation. It was apparent the men ruled with fists here. Several of the women had old bruises and scars about the jaw and cheekbones.

"But they didn't do anything."

"Who are *they?*" pressed Shannon.

"They murdered a young woman," said Myra point-blank, "and crippled another."

"That's a lie," shouted the one still on the floor.

The other one turned and begged Shannon to listen to him. "Sure, we were in the woods, but it was just a buy. We didn't do that to the girl."

"Which of you were in the car?" Shannon shouted.

"It was John and Daryl and me," said the sober girl. "I told them we shouldn't've left that woman. It was horrible. She was cryin' for help! Somebody ordered her out of a car and drove off."

Shannon and Lanark exchanged a look. Both recalled the old drunk's tale of how Rhodes was alive when he first saw him, that he had appeared as if from nowhere in that alley. They recalled how the second victim appeared to have been dumped, and Black's absolute conviction that they'd sustained their wounds elsewhere and were dumped.

"You three that were in the car, you'll have to come with us. Meanwhile, Wil, Myra, Mark, search the house for— well, you know what for."

"We didn't do it," pleaded the leader, the one called John who had the sixties radical look down pat.

"Outside," said Lanark, shoving him and his partner. The girl who'd sacrificed herself along with John and Daryl was kissed all round by the others. She seemed to be looked upon as a leader of some sort. "It'll be all right," she kept telling the others, who called her Keri.

"I think we ought to take them all the hell into custody," said Shannon suddenly, making Keri wheel and plead for Billy, for Carrie Sue, for Marty, who was too stoned to speak for herself.

Lanark agreed. "Call Maywood for backup, Wil."

"Looks like Charles Manson all over again in here," said Robeson when he saw the red paint against the off-white wall that spelled out "Megadeth."

FOURTEEN

The team was still in Maywood and it was nearing dusk. They called in a Maywood search unit complete with coke-sniffing dogs and dogs trained to ferret out dead bodies, some of them fully expecting to find severed hands hidden in cubbyholes, beneath floorboards, or back of joists, in little shoe boxes, but nothing came of the extensive search in this regard. Several kilos of hashish, cocaine, and marijuana and the attendant paraphernalia were found, along with several weapons. The weapons were hunting rifles and small-caliber handguns, no semi-automatics. But nothing of the hands which would tag the mutilation of Elena Jorovich and the dead victims to this house and these people.

The search was taken up outdoors for any freshly dug earth, the dogs sniffing madly for some scent. Again, nothing came of it, and the detectives were worn out from the disappointing raid before they even began interrogating Keri and the two young men who were with her the previous night in Thatcher Wood.

Regardless of the fact that they knew they did not have The Handyman in custody, Lanark and the others knew there could be some clue that Keri and her friends might offer. The process of interrogation had taken up the hours as the search units had gone over and over the house and its grounds without result.

Still, some information was gleaned. The killer's car

kept coming up either beige or white, both from the young men as well as from Keri. It was a late-model BMW, maybe, and certainly not at all like the green sedan parked beside Keri's house. The plates were too far away for them to make them out; they weren't even sure if the plates were Illinois plates. The car was a sporty little BMW to one of the "witnesses," while the other two thought it was more like a late-model Mercedes. They'd only got a fleeting glimpse of the driver, a shadow who'd ordered the woman out and simply driven off.

Lanark and Shannon had been questioning the girl named Keri when this information surfaced. Lanark stopped her, saying, "Wait a minute. He got out of the car?"

"Yes, sir."

"The others said she was shoved from the car."

"They weren't watching."

"Keri, tell us in exact detail what you saw, every step," said Shannon.

She was tired of the questioning sessions. "What's in it for me?"

"I'll do what I can for you."

She frowned. "We're all of us in a lot of trouble, aren't we?"

"'Fraid so."

"I tol' them." She began to cry.

Lanark groaned, extremely tired himself. "Oh, shit."

Shannon looked around at him where he was pacing. "Go out and get us some burgers and drinks, will you, Lieutenant Lanark?"

Lanark stared in response before deciding it was a good idea. Let the women talk privately. When he returned, Shannon had gotten what she wanted from Keri.

One of Shannon's strongly improved abilities of late was getting people to open up in a stressful situation, getting them to trust her, whether they ought to or not. She had watched and learned from experts in interrogation techniques. A few concessions, a few promises, a bit of barter between women, and she'd had Keri opening up, and doing so on tape.

Shannon was saying, "You've done the right thing, Keri," when Lanark re-entered with food and drink.

Keri gobbled hers, looking at the Big Macs and Cokes as if they were a gift of a million dollars. She had relaxed considerably in Lanark's absence, and for the first time, Lanark realized that she'd been afraid of him right along, and that in large part, her withholding of information could be traced back to his steely-eyed stare.

Shannon had picked up on this, but Lanark hadn't, not until now. In so many ways, he'd become as mean-seeming as the lice he chased daily on the streets. He'd become exactly what he hated. The thought put him off his food, and Keri grabbed up what was left of his fries when he indicated they were for the taking, a kind of "truce."

After finishing the meal, Keri was led away by the guard, Shannon saying good-bye at the door as if they were sisters.

"Think we can get the hell outa Maywood now?" he asked.

She lifted the tape, saying, "I got what I wanted."

They took the tape with them downtown, leaving Keri and her boyfriends to the Maywood cops. Downtown, the stationhouse was abuzz with the latest news. Reporters were sitting on the doorstep, waiting for Lanark and Shannon. They were hungry for information, any crumb. Even Sandler was among them and getting obnoxious. It seemed that the entire city had gone bananas with the latest news of the awful work of The Handyman. Everybody wanted to know what the creep wanted with the hands, *what he did with them*. Everyone was like that Dr. Ito Colucci down in his basement at the bottom of the museum. They had a morbid fascination with the details of the crimes, just as they had with the Son of Sam killings in New York, and the Hillside Strangler case in California. They wanted to know everything down to what breakfast cereal the killer liked to eat. The newspapers were conducting a contest of sorts, a weird request for the killer to get in touch with such columnists as Bob Greene and Jeff Sandler.

"You guys make me a little sick, Sandler," said Lanark, driving through them and into the restricted parking area.

"You cops don't do shit!" shouted one man in the crowd.

"What do we pay you for?" shouted another.

Lanark heard Sandler shout, "You're no better than anybody else!"

The Handyman was screwing up a lot of people and relationships, Lanark thought.

Once they were inside the squad room, all of Lanark's unit's members present, Shannon played the tape of Keri's story.

Keri's voice was shaky: "I heard the car come up. The others, John and Daryl, were out of it. I told them there was another car. Our connection'd just left. I said we should get going. John said hold on."

Shannon's voice: "Then what happened, Keri?"

"The car come to a stop, and he got out."

"Who?"

"The driver."

"Was it very dark?"

"No lights, no moon . . . yeah."

"How far away were you?"

"I'd stepped closer. Told the others to shush. Maybe sixty yards, the other side of the parking area. Our car couldn't be seen . . . behind some bushes and trees."

"Go on," said Shannon.

She cleared her throat. "He come around, opened the door . . . like a gentleman, I remember thinking. Can't remember the last time a man did that for me. Anyway, he said . . . I don't know . . . can't recall exactly . . ."

"How did his voice sound? Squeaky, irritated, how?"

"Pretty."

"Pretty?"

"Well, not pretty . . . strong, you know, masterful, in control."

"You said earlier that he ordered her out of the car. Did

174

he shout at her?"

"No, not like that, not like John'd do . . . no, more like it was time and she was to do exactly as he said because . . . he knew best and she just had to. For a time, I thought it was like love, beautiful . . . like that TV program, *Beauty and the Beast*, the way he talked and the way it kinda got to you."

"He had a nice voice?"

"Rich, mellow . . . yeah."

"What did he say to her?"

"'Elena.' Yeah, he called her by name but he stretched it out. 'Eee-lay-na, come to me now.'"

"And she got out of the car?"

"Yes."

"Then what?"

"He, like, told her she wanted to go for a walk in the woods alone. I thought that was odd. She just started to walk off from the car. He rushed back around, got inside, and drove off. I couldn't believe it."

"When did you see her hands?"

"She started suddenly screaming, waving them—not—well, waving her arms, like this . . . when she realized he was running out on her. It was then, I saw it . . . her hands, I mean, and I screamed, and she came running at me."

"What did you do then?"

"I raced back to John and Daryl, and by now, hearing the noise, they were for racing out of there. John peeled out, not listening to me. But we caught her in our headlights and it was . . . it was awful, like being in a horror movie. I'll never forget the sight of it. Is she, is she dead? I told John, I told him to go back for her, I swear. But then the police started in after us, and he . . . he just freaked."

She clicked the tape off. "What do you think?" she asked Lanark and the others.

"Bizarre . . . real bizarre," said Wil Cassidy.

"Did you ask her if she saw a weapon?" asked Myra. "I mean, when did he take her hands off?"

Shannon nodded. "Went over and over it with her. She

swears, the whole time her eyes were on them, she saw nothing, not so much as a penknife, and no assault on Elena.''

Lanark joined with the others in shaking his head over this. But he added. ''The other two victims, reportedly, were mutilated at a different site, and only dumped where we found them. If that's the case, there's something going on here not readily apparent to Black's microscopes anymore than it is to us.''

''I don't see we have any more than we had before all this happened,'' said Mark Robeson in frustration. ''Fact is, with the killer going so far as Maywood to dispose of the victim . . . it's just that much harder to understand.'' He went to the map on the wall with the concentric circles highlighting where The Handyman's other two victims had been found. Thatcher Woods was miles distant from the other two.

''With all the news coverage, he could be getting jumpy,'' said Wil.

''Wising up,'' added Myra. ''Can't keep dumping them so close to home. Someone'll pick up on his geography.''

''Geography of murder,'' said Lanark thoughtfully, staring at the city map.

''George Evans's oldest girl rode a pig home yesterday,'' said Shannon.

''What?'' asked Lanark.

''Oh, just something I remember from elementary school: how to spell geography. First letter of each word.''

''All I remember is the principal imports and exports of Uruguay and Paraguay,'' said Robeson with a slight chuckle.

''Oh?'' asked Myra. ''And what are they, Mark?''

''Hmmmmmm, guess I don't remember. I only remember we had to memorize them, and I hated geography for it.''

''I don't think we have time for reminiscing about geography lessons, people!'' shouted Commissioner Lawrence, who had opened the door on their conversation. He was followed by Captain Paul Wood and a somewhat somber Coroner Black.

Lanark didn't care for the intrusion. The earlier one had been announced. This one hadn't been. He said sharply, "Captain Wood'll tell you geography has a hell of a lot to do with solving crimes, Commissioner."

Wood agreed instantly. "One thing every good cop knows, Commissioner. A serial killer has a certain terrain he keeps pace with, just like a tomcat on the prowl. He doesn't like to break with that routine he has. Soon as Lanark and his team discover some connecting thread in the geographical interweaving of the three victims and the killer, we'll have our man."

"Geographical interweaving? Wood, this bull isn't going to fly downtown. The press and the public's all over us. Three victims now, count them, three!"

"We're doing all we can, sir," said Shannon firmly.

"Well, maybe all you can, Lieutenant, isn't good enough anymore."

"What's that supposed to mean?"

"It means that the Twenty-sixth is taking over the handling of this case if you don't show me more than talk, and I mean soon!"

"That's why I asked Dr. Black here this morning," said Wood. "Now, please, Commissioner, if you will have a seat."

"No, I'm not having a seat, Wood. I'm leaving this matter in your hands. I just wanted to make it clear to your hotshots here that this takes priority, and that any goddamned moonlighting that might turn a city block into a war zone isn't going to be tolerated!"

Lanark and the others started to react, but Lawrence stormed out. All the while that he'd been speaking, Dr. Howard Black had been methodically setting up a series of slides in the back of the room. He was about ready when he said, "Guess all our butts are on the line once more, Wood. Ought to be used to it by now. Even if we solved this case tomorrow, it wouldn't be fast enough; and even so, the brass'd come down again and treat us like dogs in waiting come the next horror from the streets."

Lanark saw a tiredness in Black that was far more

unsettling than the fatigue he himself was feeling at the moment.

"What've you got for us, Dr. Black?" asked Wood while Wil pulled the shades and the screen. Shannon hit the light and sat down beside Lanark.

The slides began with closeups of the victims' wrist wounds, and a discussion as to the uniformity of impact by the weapon all around. "The two victims examined," said Black, "appear to have sustained both wrist wounds at or about the same instant. We can tell this by the amount of blood, amount of coagulation at the site of—"

Lanark interrupted. "Are you saying the hands were lobbed off simultaneously?"

"We believe so, yes."

"Makes a difference in the weapon used, doesn't it?" said Wil Cassidy, mouthing everyone's thought. "Not even a circular saw could take them both off at exactly the same moment."

"Well, we're pretty sure the cuts, as they stack up under analysis, occurred at the same instant," said Black. "What that suggests—"

"Something like a guillotine," said Lanark.

"Yes, or a paper cutter of the more modern kind," added Wood.

"I've seen a couple of those since we been looking," said Mark. "Clean as a whistle . . . very effective."

"This slide means nothing to you, I'm sure, but in scientific terms, if you follow the angle of the cut, you will see the blade left unusual striations. Two conclusions cannot be argued here. One, there is a definite bevel to the blade that did this. Two, the blades conform in most respects, same particles and angle seen at the microscopic level, but they differ enough in the striations to tell us there were two separate instruments of murder used here."

"Two?"

"Maybe he's the kind of nut that discards his weapon as he uses it," suggested Lanark. "A different, but similar

178

weapon each time."

"This finding has not been the most troubling," Black announced cryptically.

When no one asked for further clarification, he snapped on another slide. "This is a photo of a cross section of tissue taken at the end of the bleeding stub, what was left of Rhodes's forearm, looking straight on. This can't be duplicated because the tissue is destroyed in the process, but I can guarantee you this is not science fiction, although the results seem so, even to me."

"Science fiction?" asked Myra.

"*Not* science fiction," he corrected her. He pointed to a series of dots. "Ends of arteries which have healed themselves, coagulation. Quite a bit of the blood was slowed, even staunched in some remarkable way here. No sign of outside interference, no drug used, not even iodine, and yet the process of healing over had begun."

"But that's . . ."

"How is that possible?" asked Shannon.

"When I have no answers, Lieutenant Keyes, why do you persist in asking for them? Some of our findings," continued Black as he went through the slides, clicking them on and off the screen more quickly now, showing every conceivable angle of the wounds, "some of it seems unimaginable, like . . . like . . ."

"Go on, Doctor," said Wood.

"Like *science fiction*, for Christ's sake."

No wonder he'd been reluctant to come over, Wood thought to himself now.

"What precisely do you mean, Doctor?" asked Shannon when no one else did.

"For instance, the wounds had begun . . . at some point while the victim was still very much alive . . . to heal."

"How do you mean?"

"The blood flow was not right from day one. You know that, Lanark. The first scene—some question as to the amount of blood loss at the scene, remember? We assumed

179

then that the greater blood loss was at a remote area, and the body was dumped at the scene. This only seemed logical."

"Yeah, so we discussed."

"But the blood flow was partially . . . I don't know how else to say it . . . *staunched* somehow."

"Drugs?" asked Robeson.

"No, nothing like that. Rhodes's blood had a fairly high alcohol content, but nothing else. Even so, we know that alcohol is of no use to a bleeding man; he somehow managed to . . . well, that's where I get lost."

"Transfusion?" asked Cassidy. "Suppose somebody was trying to keep him alive via transfusion."

"No, no trace of it, no catheter marks on the body . . . no, something quite unknown to my kith and kin, I'm afraid; perhaps something a priest or a voodooist might better help you with."

"Voodooist?" said Cassidy.

"Voodooist?" echoed the others.

"You mean like blood freaks?" asked Robeson.

"Vampires?" asked Wil.

"I mean perhaps, just perhaps, we're dealing with a tort four."

"Tort four?" asked Robeson. "What's that?"

"FBI lingo," said Lanark, "for a guy who kills and drinks his victim's blood. Fourth level of torture."

"*Jeeeeeze*, what's . . . what's the fifth," Robeson asked.

"Never mind," said Lanark. "I don't think Dr. Black really believes this is a case of blood and silver chalices, do you, Doc?"

Black shook his head to indicate that he did not. "Still, there's something here that we may never understand. And perhaps we're going to have to live—and work—with that fact firmly in our grasp."

Myra said a kind of litany for them all. "If the killer suddenly stops, then we'll never catch him, will we?"

"That's my assessment, yes," said Black.

"Kinda ironic. He goes free if he doesn't kill anymore. We catch him only if he does kill again, and yet the only reason we're here is to put an end to him.''

"Voodooists?" repeated Wil.

Lanark thought for a moment of Ames. He'd made some remark about witch doctors the day before. Had it been queer concidence, or was Ames being "psychic" with regards to The Handyman.

"This is crazy," said Black. "I know it, and you know it. Makes no sense, but somehow both Rhodes and the young woman showed definite signs of healing. This evidence is indisputable, except that no court in the land would believe it."

Lights went on. Black went about the business of gathering his materials. No one spoke. No one knew what to say to his "science fiction." Some were wondering if Black had not gone off the deep end. Black was wondering what everyone was wondering. When he went to the door, Lanark thanked him for coming down.

He replied directly to Wood. "Command performance, hey, Captain? I can only say I'm glad Lawrence didn't stick around, and I'd appreciate it if all that's been said in this room remains in this room. I'm on my way to Heinze VA."

"The last victim?" asked Shannon. "Did she . . . is she dead?"

"Not quite, no, and I'm not going for last rites. They've agreed to let me do a few samples at the site of her wounds. Sedated as she is, she won't feel a thing."

"Going for a matchup?" asked Lanark.

"All we've got right now to work with, crazy or not."

Black disappeared, leaving them all more befuddled than before.

"What do you suppose that was all about?" Mark wondered aloud.

"Black's no amateur," countered Wood. "If he says it's unusual, then it's unusual. He's seen every kind of wound a thousand times."

"Maybe once too often," replied Wil.

Wood let it pass. "I think our best bet is to center our attention on the weapon, and I like that geography idea.

I've seen it crack cases before. These three people have some person, place, or thing in common. A relative, a friend, an associate, a church, a school, a bar, a house, a hobby, an interest, something that connects them. Your questioning of relatives and friends should center on this."

"Sarah had hangups, spent time in a mental facility," said Myra, thinking of the young woman that'd been assigned to Wil and her.

Robeson piped in, adding, "Rhodes had the drinking habit, and the womanizing."

"Anything on the new victim?" asked Wood.

Lanark turned to look in Shannon's direction. She'd followed up on Elena Jorovich, the woman identified through her purse, which had been found flung into the woods near where she had been rescued by Officer Norris.

Shannon had amassed some information from the hospital and relatives located by them. "Elena Jorovich, twenty-six, lives alone; characterized as shy, retiring, fearful of meeting men, but working out of that. She'd started going regularly to an aerobics class and had begun to see men. She wanted marriage, according to her parents, but hadn't found Mr. Right."

"Whatever it takes . . . more footwork, more snooping, more questions, we've got to find a common denominator between these victims. We aren't likely to see that girl come out of her coma to point a finger at her attacker." Wood apologized for the unintentional slip. "We can't afford to wake up tomorrow to another handless woman lying in some alley in our city."

"Standing assignments," said Lanark as the meeting was breaking up. "Except for you, Mark."

Robeson looked up. "Yes, sir?"

"Check out some of the area musuems—you know, the weapons ones, and the Wax Works. Get somebody in the know to give you a lesson on Old World weapons that might take off a man's hands."

"See what I can do, after I check on Stokes."

"Sure, and tell him we're all rooting for him."

Wood and the others had left. "Sorry about last night, Ryne," Mark told him.

Lanark rubbed his sore jaw. "Don't mention it. I had it coming."

"Get anything out of that weasel?"

"Lost him."

"What?"

"He lost consciousness."

"Where is he now?"

"Still there, waiting for me to come home."

Robeson's eyes flicked on and off with the painful thought. "You're not careful, you'll kill him, you know that?"

"I'll be careful."

"He dies and you're implicated. It means me and Stokes'll go down too. You still want me to tell him you're rooting for him?"

Robeson rushed out, and Lanark was alone in the squad room.

FIFTEEN

"What do you hope to get from Ms. Green Garments?" asked Shannon when they pulled into the parking lot of the factory.

"Just do me a favor. Stand outside with this camera," he said, handing her a Nikon, "and snap pictures of people coming and going."

"Out in the open, full view?"

"The more open and full-viewed, the better, yes."

"Blackmail?"

"You might call it that."

Lanark went inside and demanded to see the boss lady once again. He was sent up after a moment of indecision at the other end. This time, at the other end of the elevator, he was met by Ms. Green herself rather than her flunky.

"Detective Lanark, so surprised to see you again. I thought I made myself clear during your last visit."

"Clearer than you think, Ms. Green. Now I want some answers."

She saw by his determined stare that he knew all about her front and the sham performance of her hookers.

"Inside my office," she said, turned, and walked ahead of him. He saw from her slim waistline and walk that she had kept in shape, and had probably either taken modeling lessons or had studied via the television as a teenager.

When the door closed on them, she turned like an angry

cat. "What the hell do you want from me? Damnit, it's never over, is it? Once in your life you begin to make something of yourself and everybody wants to tear you down! Damn you, damn you all!"

"Ms. Green, I don't want to tear down anything."

"Then what's she doing downstairs in front of my place frightening off my customers?"

"You can keep your lousy customers and your lousy operation if—"

"If. There's always a goddamned if, isn't there."

"—If you cooperate with us regarding Rhodes."

"I tell you I did not see him."

"But one of your girls did."

She leaned over her desk, baring her teeth, her breasts heaving. "How goddamned much do you want?"

"Just a few answers, Ms. Green, from the woman who was seen with Rhodes the night of his death!"

"No one here knows anything about his bloody death!"

"Someone here damned well knows something, and I want to speak to her, or else you'll have Vice down here like you have lice now!"

This stopped her, and she began fidgeting with a button before composing herself and sitting down behind her large, modern Scandinavian desk. "You don't understand. Rhodes and some of his friends in DC set me up in business here long after . . . long after it was over between us. But they had stipulations too. I didn't at first own Green Garments—not entirely, anyway."

"I surmised as much."

"And so you also surmise that Green Garments is a—"

"Prostitution front."

"Was, but no more," she replied. "It isn't. Not anymore. I gained controlling interest and I ended that . . . that feature of the business. My control of the company is public information, which I can prove. Now, do I call my attorney and have your ass hauled into court?"

"Don't try to bully me, lady. Just tell me about Rhodes."

"Rhodes." She repeated the name as if it brought bile into her throat to say it. "He was a leech, a curse, a part of

185

the past that wouldn't go away."

"At the moment, Ms. Green, you're the only suspect in his murder, the only one we know of who'd gain by his death."

She laughed at this. "I said he was a leech, a bloody thorn. Kept coming back and saying I owed him, and he kept threatening."

"Threatened to disclose the facts about Green Garments?"

"I needed more time to build product recognition to the point where no one could touch me, to the point where even if a bastard like Rhodes blew the whistle on how the company got its start-up funds, it wouldn't matter. In fact, I foresee a time when such a scandal could only help the company."

"But that time is not now."

She shook her head.

"Are you going to risk it all on my good nature?"

"I might bribe you if I thought you'd take it, but no . . . you strike me as a fool, one of those Keystone variety of cops who thinks what he does actually makes a difference."

"Then cooperate with me, or I'll see to it you're front-page news tomorrow, along with Senator Rhodes and her late husband."

"You are also a bastard."

"Believe it."

She looked suddenly very old, her makeup gruesome. "Well, one of the girls who works for me who was also a call girl . . . agreed to take William off my hands this one last time. Now, you want me to reveal her to you and jeopardize my company?"

It was either the truth or she was very smooth, he thought. "Ms. Green, I'm not interested in harming anyone's reputation or livelihood," he said calmly, watching her assess him. "I'm after the man who murdered Rhodes and has left two other victims, with a fourth very likely to be discovered tomorrow morning in some back alley. You help me, and I'll help you."

She saw that she had no choice. She got on the intercom, buzzed someone named Joyce, and asked Joyce to come to her office. She looked up at Lanark and said, "Joyce is head of Personnel, and we're *close*."

Lanark understood the innuendo, that they were two women who'd found solace in one another in a male world.

In a moment, Joyce knocked and entered. Green introduced him as Captain Lanark. Lanark didn't bother to correct the error, instead simply nodding and saying, "I'm here to ask you a few question about the evening you spent—"

Green interrupted him, saying, "The officer's investigating William Rhodes's death, Joyce, and we . . . we must cooperate fully. I told him you were dating Rhodes infrequently, and that you had seen him that night."

Joyce at first looked stricken, and she sat down as if a great weight had been placed on her. "I . . . I was so shocked to hear about his death, but he left me at my place and I swear, I never saw him after that."

"What time was that?"

"Maybe eleven or so. He was just sobering up a bit. He was acting strange."

"Strange? How?"

"Like his mind was a million miles away."

"I see."

"I was sure he wasn't going to leave until he had my clothes off, but he wasn't interested. He just got up suddenly and said he had someplace he had to be, and he left. I was relieved, actually, and then the next day . . . God. I swear, I'm telling the truth."

"Where had you gone that evening with Rhodes?"

She let out a long expulsion of air as if it might help her to think. "He dragged me through several bars after dinner at the Marriott."

"Can you recall exactly where you went?"

"*A Chorus Line* was playing at the theater across the street—Old Town Theater, yeah. One place we went to was the Rusty Nail, but after that, it was all kind of a blur. I had to keep pace with his drinking in order to put up with him. He was obnoxious and rude and he had his hands all over me."

"But he didn't sleep with you?"

"Had a room booked at the Marriott and everything. We were supposed to wind up there, but somehow we wound up at my place and he was saying good night."

"Can you recall the names of any of the other bars he took you to? It could be important."

She tried, scrunching up her green eyes, squinting to recall, running a hand through her long, blond hair. Her features were rather plain and simple. There was nothing one might refer to as character in her face, unless you counted the hardened look in her eyes. Lanark felt as if he knew her. He'd met hundreds like her on the street in the course of his work, but here was a hooker who had found a safe harbor with Green Garments, who only did the occasional trick to please her boss and lover, the powerful Ms. Green.

"She's told you everything she can remember," said Green, going to Joyce and putting her hands on her shoulders. "Now, please, Captain Lanark, won't you leave her alone? She's been through enough."

Like a protective tigress over her young, Lanark thought. Lanark read off the list of nightclubs and bars given him by Myra Lane. "Any of these ring a bell with you?"

She didn't readily answer, but then gave out with a pitiful, "I'm sorry, no. I was pretty far gone."

"All right, we've cooperated with you. Now please leave us alone," Green demanded.

"Thank you, ladies. I know my way out."

"Good," he heard Green say as he closed the door. "Keep going."

Outside, waiting for Lanark, Shannon continued to take snapshots of the Garment Factory's front door as people came and went, unnerving not a few people. Maybe Lanark's suspicions about the place were on target, maybe not. It certainly looked legit enough, but these days, she mused, nothing was certain.

She'd brought a copy of Keri's tape with them at Lanark's request. He didn't say why, but he wasn't using it here. It remained in the Jaguar.

Some things about Lanark were beginning to drive her wild. The disappearing act, the way he'd bullied Officer Dale Norris, his rudeness and moodiness and secretiveness. Maybe it had all been part of the allure, that mystery that hung over Lanark which had attracted her to him like a moth to the flame at the outset of their relationship, but much of the luster was worn thin now. Perhaps because he had now begun to be rude, moody, and secretive with her, even to the point of keeping her uninformed. He'd been sketchy at best on what had happened to Stokes, and he had denied any part in a commando-type raid in which Tyrrell Loomis was presumably attacked by several men and machines. And now Lanark was keeping her in the dark about his movements with regard to a case she had spent more time on than he, The Handyman case. She might be able to accept his mood swings, even his temper and rudeness, even his secretiveness, but she drew the line now at what he was thinking about the case they worked together. They were, after all, police partners here, on the street.

What were his plans for the tape?

When he exited the Green Garment door she snapped a picture of him.

"Cute," he said. "Let's go."

"Get what you came for, Lieutenant?"

He looked at her across the top of the Jaguar into her questioning gaze. He knew he'd been abrupt with her all day, even shitty toward her, and it was time to bring her in on his plans. "Rhodes was in the Old Town vicinity doing the bar scene the night of his death. Strike any chords with you?"

"Myra had placed Chambers there." The geography of

murder was taking shape in their minds firmly now. "But how do we know this?"

"A friend of Green's was with him."

They got into the car, Shannon nodding, saying, "A green-eyed blonde, Green Garment hooker?"

"Let's just say she wears green eye shadow. Important thing is, Rhodes and the Chambers girl've both now been placed in Old Town on the night they died. We should concentrate on the bars Myra Lane's come up with."

"You think the killer's roaming the bars?"

"Mr. Goodbar, yeah, a real possibility. Seems that Rhodes left the blonde untouched that night, according to her. Had someplace else he had to be. Left her in her green jammies."

"Good work," she said as he pulled from the lot and they headed downtown. "Where to now?"

"Twenty-sixth Precinct."

"What's at the Twenty-sixth?"

"Ames."

"You're going to see Ames? With the tape?"

Lanark nodded to this. "Something about her story and Joyce's—"

"Joyce's?"

"Joyce Little, the woman who spent the evening with Rhodes—something about the story, like Keri's, struck me as odd."

"Odd? Like how odd?"

"Remember when Black said something about the case was science fiction?"

"Yeah."

"That odd."

"That odd?"

"I want Ames to hear the tape."

"You think he can shed some light on this?"

"More so than Ito, let's say."

"Hey, I checked out a couple of books Dr. Colucci told us to look over. That's what I was doing last night when you were playing tag with Loomis."

"Everybody in the whole damned department has me doing things last night I—"

"Hey, I know you like a book, and I also read some of the reports flying around. Like two cops were overpowered by an assailant who was disguised as Spanish-speaking, but was actually a WASP who carried a guitar case from the scene. Don't you keep a guitar case in your closet for that nasty, high-powered—"

"Speaking of books, what'd you learn from Ito's books?"

"There're some weird people in the world."

"Oh, good for you! You just learned that, huh?"

"Some people believe that the hands of certain people send out powerful, healing, radiant waves, Lanark. Now maybe—just maybe—this guy, this nut, is trying to find just the right pair of hands, you see, to heal himself?"

"Oh, I get it. Murderer heal thyself?"

She didn't appreciate his sarcasm or humor. "Laying on of hands," she continued, acting unperturbed by his manner, "to transmit blessings, grace, touch-healing. Hell, in ancient Greece men with such hands were called *cheirourgos*."

"Cher-what?"

"Hand-workers. What we today call surgeons."

"Gotcha. Does it say anything about head-workers? Shrinks?"

"The Jews say that the hands of a holy man at prayer give off a radiance, and the early Christians believed that the saints could send flames out their fingertips." She had begun recounting points from her reading.

"Is that right? What's that to do with our case?"

She sighed. "Don't you see?"

"No, frankly, I don't."

"Open your mind! Modern high-frequency photography has confirmed that the human hand does send out strong, bio—bioluminescent rays, and that the fingertips of natural healers do emit them with greater force. Bioflux, it's called."

191

"Where does that information lead you?"

"Hell, the city's been filling up with this New Age stuff since the sixties—bookstores, occult shops, bio-groups."

"Yeah, and every damned university and college has its own group. We're talking hundreds, maybe thousands of leads that could all be dead end."

"All right, so it might. But I think I got a lot from the books Colucci pointed us to."

"Any practical help?"

"As a matter of fact, yes."

"Lay it on me."

"The thumb—"

"Yeah?"

"Hiding the thumb in the closed fist is a defensive, introverted, disturbed gesture—"

"Is that fact, or someone's opinion?"

"—of a person seeking protection, or feeling persecuted."

"We already know all that, Shan. The guy with the fidgety mind doesn't know where in hell to put his hands; he toys with a handkerchief, button, cigarette, or drums on a table."

She knew all the lessons as well as he. "I know all that."

"Limp hands show lack of purpose—"

"I know!"

"A guy with his hands constantly in his pockets—"

"Ryne, I've taken the course."

"Just reminding you."

"If we had any damned suspects to question, we might put it to use. We ought to be questioning Elena's friends and relatives, not—"

"I've got to talk to Ames."

"Then we go to meet the Joroviches?"

"Right."

They had trouble finding Ames at first. He was in a group session with cops who'd recently been under fire, most of whom had *dropped* a man and were in need of ardent counseling to get them over it. Lanark wanted to

192

wait the half hour, Shannon didn't. "What do you hope to get from Ames?"

"I don't know. He's been strange about this entire case. Usually, he's all over us for information. This time, we can't give it away."

"What're you driving at?"

"Like I said, I don't know."

"Something's on your mind."

"Here he is," said Lanark, seeing Ames emerge from the session.

Ames, his handsome, black features drawn tight on seeing them, feigned enthusiasm. "What a pleasant surprise."

"We've got something we'd like your opinion on, Dr. Ames," said Lanark. "Shouldn't take but a half hour. A tape. I'd like you to assess the credibility of the witness, and tell me if you find anything strange in her story."

"Witness?"

"The most recent work of The Handyman," said Shannon.

Ames stiffened. "I see. In my office. Come along."

Lanark and Shannon exchanged a look and then followed. Shannon recalled how Keri had fixated on the killer's baritone, hypnotic voice. She imagined the killer's voice not unlike Ames's own. Then it occurred to her that Lanark was thinking odd thoughts too; thoughts he'd had difficulty expressing earlier to her, and perhaps to himself. Since the first killing, Ames had acted oddly. At the scene of Rhodes's death, and at the second scene. He had flatly refused to join them in Maywood at the bedside of the comatose, handless woman named Elena Jorovich.

Now Lanark had come full circle back to his old friend, the man who had helped Lanark deal with his internal warfare all these years. For what reason, to accuse him? Shannon was both shaken by the notion and feeling foolish for the very thought.

Yet it had been Ames who had led them to Ito Colucci, and the book Shannon had read on phobias and fixations made it clear that anyone with a human brain in his head was subject to irrational fears, compulsions, and urges, some of which seemed to ride the eons of time via genetic codes lost and found from generation to generation. Ames had professed a weakness and an illness in the face of the corpses without hands, a downright fear of them. Why?

Shannon's mind raced back to her reading as they entered Ames's semi-dark office, where he indicated a chair for each of them before his desk.

Ames looked across at his two friends and said simply, "Sometimes even the simplest of things becomes rough, like trying to get to work, to a meeting on time, finding dinner, or a sock that matches . . . sleep."

"You haven't been getting any lately?"

"Looks like you're having the same problem, Lanark. You look as if a truck has hit you."

"Never mind me. What's going on, Richard? What gives?"

He glanced at Shannon and bit his lip. She saw that his hands busily played over the back of his neck and his fingers scratched at his hair while his eyes blinked in near-uncontrollable fashion. He then balled his fists up and looked as if he might sit on them. He was most uncomfortable. "In the old days, you know how they got rid of a zombie, Lanark?"

"What?"

"Zombie, damn it. You know, like the movies, *Living Dead*."

"What about zombies, Dr. Ames?" asked Shannon.

He opened a drawer and pulled out a bottle of rich, brown brandy. He grabbed two other glasses. "Drink?"

"On duty . . . you know that."

He frowned and poured himself a tumbler. Again Lanark exchanged a concerned look with Shannon. He'd never seen the unflappable Ames in such a state. Ames downed the brandy and said. "Old superstitions have it that the only way to end the career of a zombie is to remove its hands."

Lanark nodded slowly.

Shannon caught her breath. "Do you know something

194

about these deaths, Dr. Ames, that you're not telling us?"

"One might . . . say so."

"What the shit is this, Ames? You're not into voodoo. You're not Haitian or from Bimini or Barbados. You grew up here, in Chicago, Illinois, U.S.A. Now what's this crap about zombies?"

"Some of my family, a brother included, is heavily into the dark sciences."

"You don't for a moment—wait a minute. You think this guy that's going around slashing off hands, that it's some ritual act, something doing with these relatives of yours?"

"I didn't say that."

"You don't have to."

"I've seen the killings, Lanark. I close my eyes and I see the hands and I feel the pain, and my ears fill with the screams. I wake up in a cold sweat and I feel like if I look at my hands they won't be there. I had the first dream the night several nights before you found Rhodes, and then when I saw the condition of the body . . . it . . . I couldn't deal with it."

"This is weird," said Lanark.

Shannon shushed him. "Dr. Ames, did you see Rhodes's execution?"

"I saw a man's hands chopped off and I was that man."

"Is the dream a recurring one?"

"It is."

"And the details?"

"The same, except for the hands . . ."

"They were different?"

"Yes, smaller . . . still *my* hands. Twice now."

"When was the last one?"

"The last time I slept, night before last. Now, I doze, I rest, I fall off, but I don't sleep." He seemed a jumble of nerves, on the edge.

"Perhaps you ought to seek professional help," suggested Shannon.

He stared at her for a moment and quietly said, "I am a professional."

"A doctor who treats himself is a fool," said Lanark. "Shannon's right, Richard, you need help."

"Help? Do you really believe anyone can help me? I am clairvoyant at times, Lanark. I see into the future. I see what will happen. I've already seen your fourth victim, or at least felt her."

"Then you must help us," said Shannon. "Tell us everything you've seen, felt, imagined."

"Imagined." He snickered. "I've imagined the worst. I've imagined horror. I've imagined that I'm the killer. That I somehow cause it. If I dream it, it happens."

"But that's nonsense, Dr. Ames, and you know it."

He downed another tumbler of brandy. "I know nothing of the kind."

"Dr. Ames," said Lanark, "you have friends, people who want to help, and perhaps, in the bargain, you can help us. You have a Rolodex filled with colleagues who admire and care for you. Now, I want you to call Rogers, or Corby, or one of those hypnotist specialists, and let's get down to cases. If you can relate any remote item about our killer, you have to. You have to take it a step further in order to deal with it. Your words, remember?"

Ames stared across his desk at his longtime white friend. "The student teaching the teacher . . . very well. You're both right, of course. Nothing to fear, right, except fear itself." He lifted his two large hands. "Heard the story of the zombies all my life, and how they'd come in the night and take the hands of living people to replace their own. Silly, but most phobias are. One woman I met in an asylum was deathly afraid of three-legged stools. Figure that one. Another patient feared anything that was in the shape of a square. Couldn't be in a square room, couldn't sleep on a bed. Fears he'd fall through a 'door' in time. Phobias may seem irrational, my friends, but fear is a very real and powerful force."

"Then you'll call Corby or—"

"I've been aware for sometime of the killer's presence, even before his first victim."

"Yes, so you said."

"Strange, it was like watching my fear peel itself off my mind and go to a mirror in the room and stare at itself. I find myself protecting my hands all day long." Brooding and alternately laughing, he held his hands to his eyes again. "Silly to be so . . . so self-absorbed. Silly and dangerous, not unlike *him*."

"Him?" asked Shannon.

"The Handyman, you mean," said Lanark.

"Exactly. He's completely alone, in the primitive region of his own mind where his ego broods in solitude. His phobia draws its strength and energy from the bottomless well of self-protection. He's afraid of the zombies too."

"What about an interview with Corby?"

Ames looked as if he had just come out of a self-induced trance. "Yes, of course. You're right." He began to put a call through. Then he said to Lanark, "You don't understand what I'm saying, do you?"

"No, not entirely, I don't."

"And you, Lieutenant Keyes? Shannon? Lanark's anchor? Do you understand?"

"I . . . I'm trying to."

"I'm saying that it requires an unhealthy, enormous self-absorption to travel to work through crowds while obsessed with the possibility that a madman will destroy hundreds of others in order to get to me just so he can have my hands to add to his collection. The killer, *he thinks the same damned way*."

The call was put through and Ames told Dr. Frank Corby that he needed his help, and that it was an emergency.

A few words were exchanged.

"He's coming right over," Ames told them.

"He makes house calls?"

"I've been leaking bits and pieces of my . . . my breakup to him. He's . . . he believes I'll be more relaxed in my own environment."

"We'll give you your privacy back, then," said Shannon.

197

"No, you must stay," Ames said quickly, getting to his feet. "Please. The only reason I'm agreeing to this is the remote possibility it may help to solve this horrible case."

"We're not going anywhere," said Lanark. "We're remaining as your friends, Ames, you understand that?"

Ames nodded and breathed deeply. "I thought for a time it'd all go away." He laughed but there was no joy in it.

SIXTEEN

Dr. Frank Corby was efficient and quick. He was at Ames's office in forty minutes, and in ten minutes he had Ames under hypnosis. He had introduced himself to Lanark and Shannon. Lanark had told him what Ames had confided in them, and while Ames was under, lying on his own couch, Corby told them what he knew about Ames's symptoms.

"Richard is gifted with ESP, and it gets the better of him at times. It's very difficult to control normal fears. Imagine one brought on by an ESP episode," said Corby. "His going phobic on us, it's very disturbing for a man like him to admit."

"Phobic?" asked Lanark.

"Phobics are people with unnecessary fears, such as a fear of water going down a drain that causes a man to race from a bathroom in a nervous sweat. A phobic is as egocentric as a bloody cat. People who spend a lifetime trudging up and down stairs, deathly afraid of elevators. Why, hell, they don't mind if their children ride in them."

"What's this got to do with Ames?"

"Some people faint at the sight of blood. Some phobics only faint at the sight of their own blood. See what I mean? The untreated phobia can become the controlling force in a person's life, and is certainly one of the most powerful forces in the psyche."

"What exactly is Ames's phobia all about?"

"Hands . . . something to do with hands. When's the last time you shook hands with Dr. Ames?"

Lanark blinked and thought. "I can't remember."

"That's because he has become adept at not taking or giving with his hands. Tracing this phobia back to its origin, even if we could do it, is pointless."

"Pointless?" asked Shannon. "But if we knew the cause . . ."

"Knowing the cause doesn't alter the force of the fear. Hell, if you're into Freud and psychoanalysis, you can explain the fear of urinating in a public restroom with castration anxiety, or fear of not measuring up, but even if you could prove this shit, it doesn't make the fear go away."

"What's the answer then?"

Frank Corby was a heavyset man with a smoker's rasp and a bright, broad face. Most of his hair was gone, the rest thinning. He was Lanark's senior by a good fifteen years. But he seemed filled with energy.

"Some jokers would tell you that just telling the patient that his fears are absurd is of use, but it isn't. Hell, Ames knows better than anybody that it's ridiculous. He's probably told you as much, hasn't he?"

"As a matter of fact, yes."

"Phobics aren't anything like paranoids. Paranoids really do believe there is a basis for their fear. Paranoids *know* they are being persecuted. Still, the fear that phobics experience is just as real, irrational or not. They do not imagine they are afraid, they are afraid! Their palms go sweaty, hearts race, dizziness threatens, and they get weak-kneed and short of breath. They go through a full range of panic. Doesn't matter that this panic attack is brought on by statues, doorknobs, or crickets instead of the threat of the Bomb, because in the end what they really fear is the panic attack itself—or more accurately, having one in a public place, far from the security of home and family."

"I'm beginning to see the depth of the problem," said Shannon with a shake of her head.

"This anticipatory anxiety is only heightened by his

200

extrasensory perception. A typical short-lived fear you and I have is multiplied tenfold by the phobic; with Richard it's multiplied further, and it may take quite a number of sessions to convince him to come in out of the neurological storm he's become trapped in."

Corby was told of the connection that Ames had made between himself and the killer. Corby took it in stride. "Given his line of work, the pressures . . . not surprising he should identify himself so closely with the killing mind."

"Commissioner ever gets wind of this . . ." Lanark said, then let it go.

"Okay, here goes," said Dr. Corby, who began talking to Ames. "Echoes, Ames, your mind is filled with echoes of events in the past."

"Shadows," said Ames. "Shadows without faces . . . a number of them. Bodies without mind, without hands that work, or mouths that speak . . . like zombies . . . lying in coffins."

"Where are you, Richard?"

"Small case . . . locked away . . . no air . . . trapped."

"Are you afraid, Richard?"

"Paralyzed . . . death lying in wait . . . around every corner . . ."

"Who is there with you, Richard?"

"Larger shadow."

"Shadow?"

"Reaching for me . . . dead hands! Hands! Hands! Get them away! Get them away!"

"Richard, they can't touch you! Look closely at them! Go on! They can't hurt you! Reach out and touch them! Touch them!"

Ames was visibly terrified. Lanark had never seen this strong, powerful ally demonstrate the least fear. At the moment, he was perhaps seven years old. "No, no!"

"Doctor," said Shannon.

"Shhhhhh! Richard, they're not real!"

"They're real, all right. Big shadow chopped them off and gave them to me."

"Who? Who gave them to you?"

"Other me."

"Your other self?"

"Yes. Told him not to, but he did it anyway."

Corby's eyes met Lanark's and then Shannon's. It almost sounded like a hypnotically induced confession of guilt. Corby's raspy voice said angrily into Ames's ear, "You are Richard Ames, Dr. Richard Ames, Chicago Police Department Psychiatrist, Ames . . . Ames . . . you are not a killer. Now, tell me who is it you see before you?"

"Dum . . . dum . . ."

"What?"

"Dummy."

Corby frowned, taking it personally. "Who do you see forcing the hands at you, Richard? Richard, is there a face with the shadow?"

"No . . . dummy. Hands *are* wrong. Hands are real. Consumed by death. If Jesus tells me I'm not going to die, he's a liar too."

"This is getting us nowhere," said Corby. "I'm going to bring him around, and we're going to try a hands-on experiment."

Lanark raised his shoulders, unsure; Shannon bit her lower lip. Corby was slowly bring Ames around. He was glistening with sweat, and had shown signs of unrestrained fear of the shadows he'd visited.

"When I give you the signal, I want six hands on this man. Will you do it?" asked Dr. Corby.

"If you're sure," said Lanark.

"It's the only way."

They stood all around Ames's prostrate form, and at the instant he was snapped from his hypnosis, they all laid hands on him. He panicked, shouting, trying to fend off the hands, making Lanark and Shannon back off, but Corby kept shouting too, "Keep on him! Press your hands into him!"

"He's panicking!" Shannon said, having seen and heard enough.

"It's the only way! He must see he can live through the

panic; that there's another side he can reach!"

Lanark grabbed onto Ames, who pushed Dr. Corby onto the floor, where he grabbed at Ames's legs. Shannon rejoined the attempt and in an instant, Ames went to his knees, breathing like an exhausted basketball player, his skin glistening in the dark.

"Oh, I'm okay . . . okay," he told them. "Fine now . . . fine." But he was shaking.

Lanark knew how difficult it was for him to expose his inner feelings this way. Shannon found a cloth from his office john, put some cool water on it, and placed it across his forehead. "Are you all right, Dr. Ames?"

The others echoed her concern.

"I saw some things . . . things I'd blotted out before."

"You don't have to talk about that now," said Corby.

He shook his head. "Could be useful. Saw a sink . . . sink kept changing. Some kind of mechanical device held over the sink. He . . . he uses it to cut off the hands. Not afraid anymore . . ."

"The panic ends, Richard, and you can survive it."

"I know that now." He went on with his visions. "Rooms, inside. He does it inside, a house or an apartment. Maybe a basement . . . unsure. He's not alone. Has family. Forces the hands on them."

"What do they do with the hands?" asked Shannon, recalling Ito Colucci's question.

"Don't know . . . play with them, maybe."

"Play with them?" asked Lanark.

"Sickness . . . very real . . . can't see anything else except somewhere there is a hidden hole or box—"

"Where he keeps the hands?"

"No, where he keeps the boy."

"The boy?"

"His boy . . . one of his boys . . . I think . . . uncertain. Get this overwhelming sense of being shut away inside a coffin. It's the boy, the killer has a boy."

"You're sure of that?"

"No, I'm not sure, but . . . feels right."

"But you think he has more than one child?"

"Yes . . . but, can't be any more specific than that."

"Any numbers, names?"

"Danny . . . Danny . . . maybe the boy. No numbers, no addresses or license plates."

"Perhaps next time," suggested Corby. "When we go back—"

Ames's face flashed a look of concern.

"—together, Richard. We'll do it together. You, me, Lieutenants Lanark and Keyes."

"I don't think so. I think I'm done with this now," he said. "I'd like my office back." They knew he wanted his life and his dignity back, to prepare the real Dr. Richard Ames for the rest of the world to see.

"No problem," said Corby. "We'll talk about it later. Meanwhile, you know how to get in touch, day or night."

Dr. Corby shook Lanark's hand and gave a little nod to Shannon as he exited. "We'll be on our way too, Dr. Ames," said Shannon.

"Richard," said Lanark, going to him, extending his hand. "Shake. You did a hell of brave thing just now."

Ames wet his lip and stared down at the extended hand. He tentatively reached out for it at first, then his hand leaped at it like a lizard going for a fly. Lanark's strong grip seemed to give him sustenance, and when their hands parted, he breathed deeply and relaxed in his chair.

"We're out of here. We'll see what we can do with your insights into the crime scene, my friend."

"Been a long time coming, any help from me."

"Hey, pal, you're doing just fine."

When the door closed on him, Dr. Richard Ames allowed a tear to well up, climb over the crest of his eye, and trickle slowly down. He hadn't cried since his thirteenth birthday, not for anyone anywhere. He now cried for himself.

Before Lanark and Shannon allowed Dr. Frank Corby to escape Precinct 26, they had found an empty room and played the taped confession Keri had given Shannon.

Once it played out, Lanark put to Corby what he'd come to put to Ames.

"I know it's hard to tell, but when the victim was ordered from the car, the way Keri describes it, would you say that the victim might have been—"

"Under his control, yes."

"I sensed that too," said Shannon.

"As in hypnosis?" asked Lanark.

Corby shrugged. "There is a whole range of control people wield over others. You don't have to hypnotize people to get them to do your bidding—for instance a parent over a child, a man over a wife, vice versa in some cases. Then you've got peer pressure, gang and mob mentality, all the way up to a Jonestown kind of control, so it's not necessarily hypnosis, no."

"We're trying to understand one other facet of these killings, Dr. Corby, and it too might point to hypnosis."

"Oh, and what's that?"

Lanark thought he might be a bit eager for the information, and he cautioned Dr. Corby first. "Remember, what we say here is strictly confidential, Doctor."

Corby looked a bit hurt, but said, "Absolutely."

"I mean, you're in private practice. A good reporter, like say Sandler of the *Times*, he could play on your sense of civic duty to the public and have you spilling your—"

"Manipulation I'm familiar with. Trust me. Go on."

"All right, according to our coroner—"

Ames entered. Someone had pointed the fact out to him that Lanark, Shannon, and Corby hadn't left the building. He looked angry, as if he thought they were conspiring against him. "What is all this?"

"Richard," said Corby.

"Getting professional advice on our killer," said Lanark.

"I see. And no time to wait around for the cripple to get better."

"It's urgent, Ames," said Lanark. "This guy's freaking. Doing a victim a night now!"

"Maybe Dr. Ames can contribute," said Shannon.

Lanark agreed. "Yeah, I should think so. You know something of hypnosis."

"A recent alumnus," he said grimly.

Lanark put it to the two men. "Is it possible that a person under hypnosis can refrain from bleeding?"

"What?" They were confused.

"Can an hypnotic suggestion be so entrenched and so well implanted as to stop the flow of blood from a wound, like . . . like say a psychic placebo?"

"Interesting question," said Corby. "Must remember it for our next convention, hey, Dr. Ames?"

But Ames's pinched features played over the notion hard. "Hypnosis can be a powerful drug."

"True, but to stop blood flow from a wound? I'm not so sure."

"I read of cases of war wounded who went into trancelike states during which time they would have otherwise bled to death, and yet the mind took over, slowed the heart rate, controlled the fear; men were saved who by all accounts ought to have bled to death," countered Ames.

"Yes, interesting point."

"Suggestibility ranges from induced political psychosis and menticide to healing by laying on of hands," Ames went on.

"Menticide?" asked Shannon.

"Brainwashing," explained Corby. "But to overwhelm the physics of the body, the very blood flow? First of all, even as a hypnotist, it wouldn't occur to me to attempt it."

"Every true hypnosis overwhelms the body. It is mind over matter, mind over body, mind over physics. Almost any person, save an imbecile or an insane man, can be hypnotized. Suggestibility is also increased by fatigue, strong emotion, drugs, or hysteria. Willing subjects, of course, are far more easy to hypnotize," Ames explained.

Corby agreed with all that he said, adding for Lanark and Shannon, "Those susceptible to hypnosis are not necessarily of lower intelligence—"

"Thank you, Doctor," said Ames.

"—nor are they more gullible, submissive, or feeble of will. In fact, to do the miraculous thing you suggest, I should think the victims would have had to have strong willpower."

"Then you accept the possibility of staunching a wound while under hypnosis?"

"We can be made to feel pain that is not there while under hypnosis," said Ames. "Suggest an ordinary ruler is a burning-hot piece of metal, apply it to a hypnotized man's arm, and he screams in pain. Afterwards the scar will heal as normal, but there will be one."

"Hell," said Corby, "James Esdaile, the Scottish surgeon, performed countless major and minor operations in the 1800's without anesthetics. He used suggestion."

"Any cheap nightclub act using hypnosis'll show you people who are made drunk on water—"

"Or cataleptic, a condition impossible to assume in wakefulness." The two shrinks were on a roll now.

"Menstruation, lactation, micturition, bowel movements can all be affected by suggestion," said Ames. "Loss of pain, euphoria."

"It can also account for stigmata, automatism, shaman feats, and other so-called supernormal activities," added Corby.

"Body temperature can be raised or lowered at the suggestion of the hypnotist." Ames held up his two large hands like griddles at the ends of their handles. "The temperature of the two hands can be made to differ, one being turned to ice, the other to fire."

"Then you don't think it's science fiction to say that a person under the control of a powerful hypnosis could, if given the suggestion, retard the flow of blood from a wound?"

"Yes," said Ames firmly. "That's how he does it. I got a copy of the coroner's report too. I found it hard to read, made me nauseous, but I also found it confusing."

"Dr. Corby?" asked Lanark.

"Men and women can do extraordinary things under

207

hypnosis. I would have to agree, although I don't see the killer's purpose."

"That's because you're not a cop," said Shannon. "If he's using his home, he doesn't want to fill his closets or his backyard with bodies; nor does he want to get blood all over."

"He's squeamish to a large degree," suggested Lanark. "He doesn't hang around to hear the screams of his victims. He dumps them alive. Lets others deal with the results, or fail to deal with them."

"Far cry from Richard Speck, a rampage killer," said Shannon. "He's working out some bizzarre ritual. I think Dr. Colucci is right about that."

"Then you found Colucci of help?" asked Ames.

"Some," said Shannon.

Lanark only frowned and said, "Someone out there, by night, hypnotizing people—"

"Suggesting they feel no pain," said Corby.

"That they please hold back on their bleeding," added Ames.

"While he chops off their hands," said Shannon. "What kind of bastard are we looking for?"

"You're beat, Lanark. Admit it and go for some rest. I'll cover for you," she told him on the way back to the 13th Precinct.

"No time!" He rode passenger, and sat adjusting his speed-loader and gun where it bulged beneath his sport coat. The bulge was quite noticeable when slumping, not so bad when sitting upright. Lanark wore no tie and a pair of designer jeans with the casual coat. He looked like he might be a grad student at the University of Chicago, or a first-year intructor there.

"You'll be no good to anyone if you fall over," she was saying while the police squawk box announced a 10-22 in progress at an address not a block from their position. Ryne responded by telling her to turn the car around.

"What?"

"Robbery in progress!" He called into dispatch, "Unit Eleven, Lanark and Keyes, ten-seventeen! ETA two minutes! On it!"

She tore onto the street where the robbery was occurring just as Dispatch said, "Change that ten-seventeen to ten-thirty, Eleven proceed with caution."

"Armed and dangerous," said Lanark.

He was pumped up by the action. Needed it, the same as he had needed air, she thought. Then they saw the scene of trouble, screeching to a stop outside Kenyon Savings and Loan, the location Dispatch had given them. Response time was under one minute. Lanark flashed on that fact, comparing it with the ten that it had taken for cops to get to his parents' bar one night. But he had to focus every thought on the here and now.

He and Shannon flew from the car and took up positions outside the bank, either side of the door. Shannon crouched, crawling below the window frame when it was exploded from inside by gunshots. The bank alarm began to blare in response, until gunshots from inside exploded the mechanism controlling the alarm.

There was an ominous silence that followed as police cars from all around encircled the entire block. Lanark had no intention of remaining there for hours negotiating with the gunmen. He had neither the time nor the patience for that. He shouted to Shannon that they should back out of the line of fire, leave it to the tacticians. "These guys are too well entrenched. We don't know anything about them. Could go off like a bomb in there—"

But one of the bank robbers, hearing Lanark's voice, began shouting threats and demands. Shannon lay completely still, and for a moment, Lanark feared she'd been hit. He saw blood trickling from a wound caused by flying glass.

Lanark motioned to her to get back, but she stubbornly held. She was an excellent marksman, and Ryne knew this. She didn't wish to give up the position she'd

209

established. She could pick off a man from where she was with her .38 as well as any SWAT team man with a Remington.

"I want safe conduct!" shouted the man inside. "A car fully gassed—"

"Hell man, didn't you see *Dog Day Afternoon?* Even if we gave into your demands—" Lanark began, but he was cut off.

"Don't fuck with me, man! I'll kill one of these people in here, I swear it!" He sounded as if he might be high on drugs. He sounded like the loudmouthed comedian Sam Kinison. Then he got into an argument with his partner.

The partner was shouting, "Just let us go, or else somebody's going to get hurt."

"Tell you what," shouted Lanark. "I'll give myself up to you. Give you my gun and everything."

"No deal!"

But Lanark's .38 was tossed in through the broken window. Then he shouted, "I'm coming in! Just remember, so far, you haven't killed anyone!"

"How the hell do you know if we've killed anyone or not?"

"Let's just say I'm psychic. Let's just say I know you boys don't want to kill anybody here. And I know you don't want to die." He then simply disappeared into the bank, despite the cries of a captain in the department who was waving and ranting at both him and Shannon to get the hell back.

Shannon knew that Ryne carried a second gun, his enormous .45. What was he up to? She gave him a few moments. Inside, she could hear the Kinison-voiced character ranting, "You're crazy! You know that? Crazy! Now, what the hell're we going to do with you?"

"Bargain with me. I'm a lieutenant in the department," said Ryne coolly. "Fact is, I've got awards and honors for bravery, all that. The department values me a lot more'n they will a bank teller, or a housewife."

The two robbers were young, and it was likely their first job. Lanark told them this as if he could read their minds.

"You botched it, badly. Now, if you go and kill someone—"

"Shut up! Shut up! Got to think! Can't think!"

Lanark worked his way closer to the high-strung one with the irritating voice. Both young men were dirty, looking like they carried head lice. Both were white, and between the ages of twenty-two and twenty-six, he guessed. "Either one of you got any priors? Anything big?"

"Derek there does," said the second one.

"Shut up! Don't say nothing to him! He's just trying to confuse us!"

"Confuse you? Hell, you're doing a fine job of that yourself!" Lanark had taken in the situation at a glance: a couple of punks in over their heads, guns pointed at two whimpering female hostages who were shaking; along the length of the floor people who'd been ordered to kiss the well-worn tiles pretended to be mannequins. Other than the broken glass, the place was amazingly clean of debris.

"Are you crazy, Lanark!" shouted Shannon from her prone position.

This so frightened one of the robbers that he turned and fired on Shannon, who ducked. Lanark's hands went up more in a gesture to slow the hotheads down than in a show of surrender. "Easy! Hold your fire! Damn! So far, you haven't killed anyone! You take that step, and your lives are worthless! May as well put your guns to your own heads!"

"He's right, Derek, Derek!" shouted one of them to his partner.

"Throw down your weapons. The street outside is filled with cops, Derek." He turned to the other one and asked, "What's your name, kid?"

"Myles."

Derek screamed for silence, and clicked back the hammer of the gun he held at the middle-aged woman's ear, making her swoon and go limp. Lanark reached for the woman, saying, "Damnit, now look what you've done."

211

But Lanark let the woman down fairly hard as he dove into Derek's legs, sending him flat on his back, Derek's gun going off, chipping a marble column nearby, and ricocheting into a wall, making everyone scream. The second one stood over the struggling pair, unsure what to do while Lanark's fists knocked Derek into unconsciousness.

At the same instant, Shannon shouted at the one named Myles, her gun pointed so the bullet would go through his brain. "Drop it! Now, sucker!"

SEVENTEEN

When he arrived, driving in through the garage, his nostrils filled with the smell of grease and hard steel. The garbage truck had been returned, along with the cab, which also belonged to Undercover Operations at the 13th. When Lanark pulled in, it was into a large, open room, the floor covered with a thick layer of sawdust and over this, particle dust. Lights were out, save for the one that went on automatically when the door rose. Lanark could see out the corner of his windshield that Loomis's limp form remained toward the top of the arena—a real circus performer, sonofabitch.

Lanark had dropped Shannon at HQ, saying he was beat and planned on doing exactly as she prescribed: go home and crawl into bed. Although invited to join him, she'd declined, saying he needed *sleep*.

But he didn't go to his place. He had to get back to Loomis, see if he was ready to talk. He imagined that by now, he'd be most willing. It had become dark, and Lanark's drive had been eased only by the sound of easy music coming from the radio. The factory in which Loomis remained a dangling prisoner to Ryne Lanark's darker side had once manufactured heating and cooling systems. The place was filled with archaic lifting and moving machinery, filled with hooks, pulleys, cogs, and wheels. There were rotors and belts, all left in working order when the place simply closed down. The real-estate people called it a fully functional factory. Perhaps it was. It was certainly functioning for Lanark.

But Lanark was indeed tired. He laid his head back into the cushion of the Jaguar, resting his eyes. He had no idea how long his eyes were closed when something woke him. A pair of enormous, demonic eyes—no, *headlights*—coming straight at the Jaguar's right side—right for him! He instinctively tore open the door and rolled out just as two huge cold steel claws smashed through the windows and rammed into the seat where he'd been sitting, the powerful claws rising, lifting the car skyward. In the dark, it was as if a mad robot had stormed in from nowhere, programmed to kill. Lanark saw the forklift's wheels outlined in the dark now, and he saw the operator's next move just in time, rolling away and away from the impact when the car was dropped over him.

He rolled into some barrels and boxes, knocking them over and scrambling to get behind them as the forklift, shunting around the demolished Jaguar, came straight for him. Lanark raised his weapon and fired and fired and fired as the forklift operator slumped over the controls and the machine smashed into the debris before Lanark. Ryne dived free of the collision moments before the monster machine came to a halt, its occupant falling from the cab.

Lanark went to the man, whose Spanish features proclaimed him one of Loomis's friends.

A shot pinged off metal beside Lanark's head, and he realized the entire place had been infiltrated by Loomis's people. He dove and wheeled and came up shooting, hearing one man's painful cry in response. Semi-automatic weapons opened up on him, and he could not remain in the poor cover of barrels and boxes.

Lanark heard Loomis's voice, shouting for someone to get him down. He was still hooked!

More bullets convinced Lanark to back off. He found a duct in a wall and kicked it out, climbed in, and traveled the length of the duct, estimating where in the building he was. His attempt was to get behind them, and closer to the controls that kept Loomis in the air.

Outside, he heard men swearing and shouting in Spanish. He waited for another volley of cursing and gunfire before he kicked out another screen and jumped from the wall. He was still a good distance from the controls. He made a run for it as gunfire erupted all around him. He dove onto a conveyor belt, slapping the button that activated it, flattening himself on it and firing at anything that moved. He brought another and another of his assailants down, and felt a bullet graze his shoulder. He looked up and saw a gunman on a turret above him, readying to fire again. He rolled from the belt and onto the filthy floor, where, on his back, he brought down the man on the turret. The body flew like a bird beside Loomis, who remained helpless and screaming.

All fell silent as adversaries tried to determine one another's location and strength. Lanark heard the garage door open, and it made him wonder if they'd had enough, if they were on the run. But they hadn't entered that way. They'd entered silently through some hole somewhere in the facade. Lanark raced the several yards to the controls, and he slammed every button he could find. Lights went up, flickering, some blowing with the spray of bullets. Belts all around began moving like so many trains. Large universal joints with pulleys began to move about in robotic fashion, along with Loomis's dangling, complaining form. Pressers and punchers started up with grating sounds of metal on metal.

And Lanark saw Mark Robeson's car plunge into the garage, bullets riddling it on all sides, but Robeson was nowhere to be seen. It looked as though he must be dead or dying on the front seat where the bullets had reached him. His car exploded into flame, igniting the sawdust about it, the chemicals that'd been spilled in the drums earlier, the forklift, everything.

Shadows of men—ten, fifteen—a small army raced in all directions, Lanark bringing down some until someone shouted, "Hey, it's me! Watch your damned cross fire!" It was Mark. He'd sent his car in empty to create a diversion, and it had worked.

Robeson made his way to Lanark, his hair singed, his skin glistening with sweat, his eyes wide and his smile intact. "They found your location, how?"

"I haven't a clue. Got to get Loomis down before he fries."

Lanark used the descend lever for the pulley, bringing the raging Loomis down slowly. The man was a pitiful wreck, blubbering now that he'd talk, when one of the assailants, hanging back, opened fire with a semiautomatic and sprayed Loomis with enough bullets to cut him nearly in half. He was instantly out of his misery.

Both Robeson and Lanark fired at the spot from which the gunfire had come. Their shots resulted in a small explosion, the bullets hitting some chemicals stored there.

The factory, with all its contents, including a number of bodies and the department's Jaguar, was going up in smoke fast.

Lanark quickly detached what was left of Loomis from the telltale hook, dumping him. He rushed about from one disabled man to another as Robeson tried to pull him out of the place, the fire now roaring around them. "I want one of them alive! I need one alive!"

Mark pulled, tugged, struck Lanark, and Lanark returned the blows, pulling away, continuing his search, until he saw that it was useless. The factory was a death trap for him and Robeson now, so they found a stairwell deep in the back which took them out through a basement area, where they heard rather than saw cars disappearing into the darkness. On the other side of the building, fire trucks and emergency vehicles were pouring in.

"What the hell're we going to do now?" asked Robeson. "We . . . they'll know it was us by the cars."

Another explosion rocked the place, sending them

to the ground. "I don't think they're going to be able to identify a damned thing," Lanark suggested, "unless we hang around here."

"Risky, you know that . . . life's goddamned risky around you for a mile radius, know that?"

They got up and ran the length of the alley, climbing over a fence, skulking down causeways, putting the distance of blocks between themselves and the destruction. For Lanark, it was a sad end to a promising beginning. He didn't know any more about Marty Jenkins or his killer companion called Whitey than he had before. All the time spent, all the careful hunting. How had the others learned of Loomis's whereabouts?

They stopped to catch their breath, leaning and then sitting against a wall. "Thanks, Mark. Saved me in there."

"Saved you, hell. Lanark, you're like a drowning man. Anyone grabs onto you to help you, and you drag 'em down wid' you, man."

Robeson had blood on his lip where Lanark had struck him. Lanark's eye was cut. "Guess I'm kind of crazy."

"Six kinda ways you're crazy."

Lanark stared at him for a moment before laughing. His friend joined him. Someone in a window above them told them to move along, and they slowly did so.

"I've got so used to it now, I almost feel your hatred is my hatred," said Mark.

Lanark slapped him on the back. "Guess you've earned it over the years."

"How in the hell're you planning to explain the Jaguar to Wood?"

Lanark frowned and raised his shoulders. "I'll have to work on that one."

"And what about my old Ford?"

"Was it paid for?"

"I got it at police auction. Yeah, it was paid for."

"Insurance?"

"Up to my eyeballs."

"Collect."

"On what? What do I show them?"

"Say it was stolen, used in a crime."

"Lanark, you're beginning to think like a criminal."

"Takes one to catch one."

Robeson fell silent. "Stokes has been asking after you. You ought to find time to go over and see the kid."

"Will do. Promise."

"How about right now?"

Lanark was beat, but he nodded. "Right. Ought to be a cab or two over on Chicago." They made their way to the bustling street, sirens in the distance. There they found a cab at Ekhardt Park near a hot-dog stand. They were in the same neighborhood where they'd successfully snatched Loomis who was now dead, and Lanark silently asked himself, "For what?"

Dr. Richard Ames slept. He slept for the first time in a long time, but then, refreshed, he was up and going again. It didn't matter that he couldn't hear or see clearly, or even feel anything. He could see the hands hovering above his line of vision, directing him, and he knew they'd direct him to wherever they wanted him to be.

He saw a sign in the far, far distance of his mind. Neon, in need of some repair, somewhere in the city, crowded around by other buildings, busy street. The sign loomed closer. It read Danny, Danny something. The hands opened a door to him and he was inside watching a floor show of some sort, a bizarre nightclub act using pigs, cows, chickens all hooting and clucking and grunting at once and pawing about the stage, and in the middle of the stage there were a pair of white-gloved hands, magician's hands, disembodied due to a display of lights combined with black clothing and backdrop.

Ames began to choke on the smoke and the closeness of the room. He smelled perspiration. It was so strong and odorous he began to gag on it. He smelled something else also, something sticky sweet and pungent, near-metallic. It was something coming down along the walls beyond the magician's hands, something cascading down like oozing pus, except that it was red, rich red. It was blood, and dancing on stage alongside the barnyard animals now came a parade of hands of all sizes, shapes, colors.

Ames saw his father on the stage. His father had been a preacher in the neighborhood where he grew up in Chicago. He'd been a good man and gentle, but Ames had learned as he grew older that much of his father's ministerial "magic" was practiced and rehearsed over many years. After learning of this facet of the "business," he grew to feel both guilty and ashamed of his father.

His father, in retaliation, took him to visit some not-so-distant relatives who practiced a different sort of religion, voodoo. As a boy, Ames had felt the power and the pull of such beliefs, but he had fought them and the images his young mind had been introduced to. He knew of the "hypnosis" involved in religion and magic that began with the acceptance of the tenets of a faith.

His father, for many years, had used young Richard in his church, used him like a prop.

Ames now saw the face of the man on the stage with the hands dancing about, waving in jubilation. It was the face of his father behind those white-gloved hands.

He woke with a start, sweating, shaken. Somehow, he felt close to the taker of hands, the man who was destroying people in his heinous fashion, but he didn't know why.

Like a werewolf undergoing lycanthropy, he wondered

at such times if he might not *be* the killer, or in some bizarre, telepathic communique telling the creature what to do!

He got up and rushed into the bathroom, glad for the first time in years that he lived alone. He felt ill, and spent some time leaning over the sink, prepared to vomit. He stared at himself in the mirror for ten minutes, looking for any signs of the madness which had, in the end, taken his father. He then climbed into the shower again and prayed this time he could wash all the tainted flesh from himself along with the guilt and the harsh memories.

In the shower, the man-made rain beating rhythmically against his brain, relaxing him completely, he began to sing an old song, one of his father's favorites, "Amazing Grace, how sweet thy name," but he switched in midstream to, "Oh, Danny Boy . . . the lights . . . the lights are dimming. . . ."

Then like a flashbulb going off in his brain, he saw the neon sign in his dream and it read, *Danny Boy's.*

Felix was misbehaving again, and the crowd loved it. But it was a different crowd, easier to play to, Morgan knew, giddy on good brandy, quality vermouth and martinis, not Danny's piss-weak whiskey. Tonight, Felix was entertaining at the home of Harold Stover Davis II, the same Davis whose name graced the peanut cartons which had made him rich. It wasn't that Davis's peanuts were any better, only that they were packaged so uniquely and advertised so ingeniously. One of his relatives, a hanger-on from all appearances, had caught Morgan's act at Danny Boy's, loved it, and hired him for this special gig. It was good money, the best Morgan and Felix had seen in many years. It could also mean more such jobs as news got around to Davis's crowd. And the air and the booze and the lake here in Northshore heaven couldn't be beat.

Morgan had selected his volunteers from among the

large crowd around the pool. The fact that he chose three young ladies in bikinis delighted his male hosts. He had the young women in animal poses in no time, their minds easily manipulated. Some of the mothers were taking exception, so Morgan made Felix stop his wisecracking, off-color remarks, and he got right into the animal mimicry which so delighted everyone that nothing could be done but to carry on with the show.

Morgan had a surefire, quick method of hypnosis which had really very little to do with either his command, his tone of voice, his words, or the lovely crystalline heart he dangled before the eyes. Morgan simply used sleight-of-hand, as taught him by his father so many years before. He'd grasp the neck in what appeared a kindly gesture, but which was really a very old technique of producing a state of trance in untold occult rites. It was the same method fakirs who practiced suspended animation used when they pressed firmly on their own carotid arteries. Gentle pressure on the carotid of little miss Penelope Hogath, Carolyn Wamouth, and Gloria Sue Davis made each in turn responsive to suggestion. It was a speedy method, and fast hypnosis made a crowd go *ohhhh* and *ahhhh*. In the wrong hands, the technique itself was dangerous. In Morgan Lefay Sayer's hands, it was often lethal, but like so many of his illusions, only he knew this—except for Felix. More and more, Felix seemed to know all his secrets.

Felix had been put away in his dark box for now, but he suddenly shouted from his hidden quarters, making everyone except the hypnotized young women and Morgan laugh. "You got enough, Morgan! Leave the girls alone!"

Everyone roared, thinking it was a part of the act.

Morgan had thought not to place any post-hypnotic suggestions in the ear of any of these sweet, young things, but Felix's remark made him defiant. Now he'd do it just to spite Felix. Damned if Felix was going to run him, or ruin his evening for that matter.

As Morgan worked the crowd, moving from young lady

to young lady, continuing on with the demonstration of hypnosis, he thought he saw himself standing on the edge of the crowd with a look of approval on his face. He thought for a moment that he looked a lot like his father standing there, but his father had never shown him any approval.

His showman father, master hypnotist, magician, had been a fraud. He'd used his son in his act the way Morgan used Felix! Used him for years, cutting off the use of his hands, tying them to his back, covering them over with a loose, black coat, the boy straightjacketed beneath! Outfitted with an invisible bit in his mouth that nearly strangled him while his father threw his voice into the boy's silent throat. His father had perfected the act when he'd fashioned a kind of straitjacket with arms and hands, the jacket wrapping around Morgan's front, pinning his own hands and arms back. His father had painted his face in greasepaint, laid on the makeup and lashes as if he were a doll to be dressed up; he'd turned him into a dummy, a Felix! Beneath the makeup was a living, breathing, thinking boy, but this didn't stop Morgan Sayer Senior from stuffing him routinely into a chest at the end of each show.

He'd turned his son into something between flesh and wood, and the goddamned freak-show mentality of the audiences he worked loved it.

In the meantime, between shows and on the road with his father, Morgan the Dummy learned fast, especially about the hypnosis. His father had used it on him for years. He picked up the magic tricks as well, and one day he became so good at diversion and misdirection he almost escaped his father by running away. When this failed, he caught his father while he slept and using what he now knew of hypnosis, he convinced him that he was having one of his seizures. He'd already seen to it that his father's cyanide pills had been flushed down the toilet, blaming it on Felix, his stage persona! He had a good laugh at that.

His father didn't laugh, though; he was too busy grasping out at Morgan in an attempt to strangle him. The hands got round Morgan's neck and tried choking the life from him, but with the old man gasping for breath, his heart pumping down, down, *down* until it stopped—just as he *suggested* it would—made the hands go slack and lifeless. By the time police arrived, the pill bottle was returned to his bedside, empty. And Morgan was free of his curse, or so he thought.

At the funeral, after everyone had gone, Felix and the boy, in his early teens at the time, went back to the grave site. He paid off the men there to allow him a few moments alone with the casket. He'd had a morbid nightmare on the eve of the funeral that somehow Felix held the spirit of his deceased father, and that the dummmy was imbued with a supernatural life. He'd awakened to find Felix at his throat, attempting to strangle him. Somehow, his magician father was reaching out from the grave with both hands to strangle him in his sleep. He'd watched how the old man died, gulping like a fish out of water for air, and turning blue. It had been horrible.

He took the one remaining dummy the old man had fashioned himself from wood, brought it to the casket, and dropped it inside.

Now he wished that instead he had cut off the corpse's hands, because they came to Morgan in his sleep again and again, choking off his air; the cold, vampire hands reached across time and dimension to Morgan's throat, just as on the day when he had killed his father.

The nightmares never fully left him, but lately the intensity and the sightings of his father standing nearby, ever watchful, had increased tenfold. One night, before he had taken Rhodes's hands, he'd awakened to find his Felix, the Felix that he had himself made, atop him there in the bed, his wooden hands around his neck tightening like a vise until he threw Felix from him.

Ever since, he had been trying to regain control over Felix. Now, he sensed that he had accomplished that much. But out of the corner of his eye he saw the shadow man walking, and in his ear Felix's uncontrolled remarks were buzzing again.

"Why don't you have that one come back to your place after the show, Morgan?"

The crowd laughed, some nervously.

"Shut up, Felix! This isn't a roadhouse! We're guests here! Guests of Mr. Davis and his lovely family!"

"Too many eyewitnesses for you, huh, Morgan?" said Felix with a laugh all his own, bordering on hysteria.

Morgan apologized to the crowd for his behavior.

"Me? *Me?* Don't apologize for me, you poor slug!"

"That's enough, Felix!"

The crowd watched as Morgan went to the box, kicked out viciously at it, and laughed when Felix groaned and said, *"Uhhhh,* right'n'da'nuts! Good night, Mrs. McGillicutty, wherever you are! *"Ohhhhhh."*

Vicious little bastard, he thought, but turned to the crowd with as large a grin as his showman's sense knew was warranted. Then he went to work, *stroking* his new victim with the melodious words she'd be unable to refuse later, depositing the post-hypnotic suggestion as succinctly and as magically as he did with all his sleight-of-hand. Felix had actually done him a favor, turning the attention of the crowd on himself and away from Morgan just for that brief moment he needed. He found himself strangely enough looking forward to their rendezvous. To hell with Felix and his paranoia.

But even Morgan was paranoid enough about the police and his "handiwork" to know *not* to select Davis's daughter. He took the homelier one next to her instead, Carolyn Wamouth, now on her knees acting like a jackal.

The crowd, well-to-do people, refined in manner and dress, had at first been cool toward the Sooth-

224

sayer's control over members of their company. But now, like all humans, they'd succumbed to the hilarity and sheer tribal fun of the games Morgan played. All but the shadow man far to the back now, disappearing toward the lake just as Morgan announced an end to the show.

EIGHTEEN

When Lanark and Robeson arrived at Lanark's bar, the Lucky 13th, they were filthy, their faces grimy and sooty. They had burns on their wrists and arms, as well as singed hair. They tried to quietly enter the back way, get to Lanark's place, clean up, and get into a change of clothes. But they were met by Jack Tebo, who had a stricken look on his face, and he was followed by Shannon, who raced into Lanark's arms, crying tearfully but calling him a bastard.

"What's going on?" asked Lanark.

"What's going on? He's asking? You nuts or something?" replied a tongue-tied Tebo.

Shannon sobbed, "They said you were killed in a factory fire. Your car went up in flames, some sort of gun battle."

"Well, we survived," said Robeson, "but how we're going to survive the upshot is anybody's guess."

Lanark laughed over a thought, making Robeson stare at him in puzzlement. "What do you find so damned funny?"

"Just thinking about Morris Fabia, and how long this'll keep him busy. We'll tell them we were working an undercover operation, making it look like a buy."

"We didn't requisition nothing, man! No money, no extra frills."

"Hey, a forty-thousand-dollar car is frills enough for some people."

"What the hell went down?" Shannon demanded to know.

"You don't want to know," said Mark.

"I know I don't," said Tebo.

Lanark and Shannon kept eyeballs locked, and he said, *"The less you know—"*

"Is our relationship back to this? Bullshit, Lanark! I'm on a need-to-know basis with you, emotionally, you got that?"

Lanark turned to Tebo. "Jack, take Mark upstairs. See to those burns, get him a change of clothes."

"Sure, sure, Ryne."

The others were gone, leaving Ryne and Shannon in the dimly lit hallway back of the bar. She began to cry again. "I don't know how much of this I can take. We were told you were dead. They took out seven bodies from that place, all burned beyond recognition."

"Good excuse to take a few days off."

"It's not funny!"

"Sorry . . . it's just that I don't know what to say. Maybe being dead, or *thought* dead, isn't such a bad cover for an undercover cop . . . that's what I meant."

"Why? So you can go after Jenkins and that invisible man you think may be named Whitey?"

"Maybe."

"And get yourself killed in the bargain?"

"Maybe . . . hey, either one of us could've been killed stopping that holdup today. It comes with the territory, remember?"

"Your territory ranges too damned far outside the law, Lanark," she said sternly. "If you aren't soon killed, you will be put behind bars for . . . for . . ."

"For murder, go on, say it."

"Or some other excess!"

They both fell silent and he took her in his arms. "I know what you're saying is true, Shan . . . believe me, I know. But do you remember what Dr. Corby said about phobias and phobics? Huh? Maybe a person knows something is foolish, but that doesn't stop him from being foolish, or reckless in my case."

They heard a noise at the end of the hall, and suddenly realized that someone was standing in the shadows and had been listening to them the entire time.

"Who's there? Who the hell's there?" shouted Lanark.

Someone in the dark cleared his throat and stepped into the light. It was Jeff Sandler, the reporter, trying to stretch a smile, saying, "Just me . . . needed to use the john."

"John's on the other side," said Lanark. "You were snooping, eavesdropping, weren't you?"

"Pretty mean fire not far from here. Word is you were involved, but word also has it one of the bodies pulled from there was you."

"That's how we learned the news, Tebo and me," she said. "Jeff brought it to us."

"What now, Mr. Reporter? Story's juicy enough for you, isn't it?"

"Some pieces missing," he replied. "Care to fill me in?"

"No," Ryne said adamantly.

"Wouldn't have anything to do with the kidnapping of a certain drug czar by the name of Loomis, would it? Lot of fire involved in that story as well, and that wasn't too far from where the factory went up."

"Just keep putting two and two together, Sandler, see where it gets you."

"Hey, we've never had cause for an adversarial relationship, Lieutenant. I'm sure we can find some mutual ground here, exchange ideas over a beer. Just tell me, why'd you run from the scene?"

"Out of my head, I guess."

"And Robeson? Was he also out of his—"

"Keep Mark outa this."

"But he was there. I saw the condition he was in."

Lanark moved on the reporter in a threatening manner, Shannon grabbing hold of him, trying to calm him. When she got his attention, she turned to Sandler and said, "Jeff, this story's small potatoes compared to what we've got on The Handyman."

"Is that right?"

"Shannon, Lieutenant!" Lanark said to her.

"That's right."

"No way, Shannon," shouted Lanark.

"They're going to find out one way or another anyway, Ryne. Bribe a lab tech, a secretary in the DA's office, or run a decoy operation of their own, get into an office where files are kept. Everything we know they'll have in a few days. Look what happened in Maywood." A cop was up on charges for having released unauthorized information to the press there over the latest in The Handyman mutilations.

"Goddamn it, Shannon, I won't let you do this!"

"Is it a deal, Jeff?"

"Yeah," Jeff replied, latching onto it.

Shannon turned to Lanark, and said, "Let's do it officially, through Captain Wood. We use the papers this time, instead of them using us."

"Use away," said Sandler.

"It could flush the killer out, or ring a bell with a witness who may not know he was a witness, something, anything. It beats what we're doing."

The idea had its appeal, even to Lanark now. "Okay. Then what you saw and heard here, Sandler, stays buried, forever."

"My word on it."

"And I'm supposed to believe that that is any good?"

"Best I can offer. Best in the business. I've gone to jail for not revealing my sources on other stories."

Lanark considered this. He reached out his hand to the reporter a bit reluctantly, and Sandler took it. "Deal then."

"We can handle Wood," Shannon assured Sandler.

"High hopes," said Lanark, who went up the stairs to his place to get cleaned up.

Carolyn Wamouth was like clay in his hands. He molded and sculpted her mind to fit whatever scenario he wished, and he wished to have her hands. This time, he'd locked Felix outside, in the trunk of his car, and it'd then

229

be impossible for the increasingly creepy personality of the dummy to intrude with his objections, snide remarks, or uncouth behavior during the preparations for Carolyn.

Like the others befor her, Carolyn had told no one where she was going. She'd just broken off from her group at the party, complaining of a migraine, and she'd met him out in the parking lot where entertainers were shunted off through the back gates of the mansion. There had been no one around and no one to see her go. The noisiest bit of commotion in the lot had been Felix, who'd objected strenuously to being placed in the trunk, doubly locked away, a coffin inside a coffin there in his case in the trunk. All the way to Morgan's house, the little pisser had kept shouting and fighting with his case there in the back. It had seemed to delight Carolyn, but it had made Morgan frantic and angry; angrier than he'd ever felt toward Felix before.

"He can be such a devil," he'd told Carolyn.

"Oh . . . I can see that," she'd replied and laughed, asking, "How do you *dooooooooo* that?"

"Do what?" He hadn't been aware he was doing anything. "It's not me. It's him."

"Where're we going?"

"My place . . . you want to go to my place, don't you?"

"Yes, of course."

"Don't you?"

"Yes."

"You like me, don't you?"

"Yes, I do. I like you and Felix."

"Forget Felix."

"What?"

"Concentrate on me."

She smiled a coy smile. He'd suggested to her that she would *like* to make passionate, unbridled love to him. She'd acquiesced like melting butter to his touch; he'd squeezed firmly at the neck, and his voice, and his appearance, had conspired against her will. She now saw him as a star, as handsome as any in Hollywood. All these suggestions her mind had absorbed hungrily and greedily.

230

She was a bored young rich person no more. Nor would she ever be bored again.

The ritual was going as planned.

The ritual had taken on meaning and a power of its own, necessary for its own sake.

They were soon at the old Victorian house that rambled up and back and around itself like a tortured animal. It sat squat and belligerent, back from the street, nestled in among other houses more modern and sleek. It was of another era, built when big was beautiful, and labor and materials cheap. By day it was gray and in need of paint, peeling as if diseased. By night it was a dark, eerie blue that seemed to invite city bats to its spire and gables. By night the diseased and bubbled paint and scaly exterior didn't look half so bad. His mother had lived here once—a woman he had no memory of. She had died giving him birth. All that Morgan knew of her was a single, faded photograph in which she seemed to be reaching out to the photographer with her expression and her eyes, a queer smile and a mysterious pair of wide eyes that offset some of the incredible beauty she possessed. Besides the picture, he had memories of what his father had had to say about her, that she had died because of Morgan. And Felix had memories of her, happier memories which he would sit up nights speaking into Morgan's ear sometimes. But not lately, not since Rhodes.

Carolyn was not allowed out of the car until he pulled far back into the driveway and against the back door where he routinely came and went. He looked all about them for anyone looking out windows, walking dogs, carrying bundles, or pushing carts. The neighborhood there on Chase was quiet by night. By day, the noise of nearby high-rise buildings going up was a constant. He knew he'd awaken to the construction in the morning, like the noise of an army of garbage trucks attacking the houses.

Carolyn offered no resistance. She didn't wish to resist. She wanted him. He had convinced her of that. And there was nobody else there.

"What about me?" asked Felix *from the backseat* as

Morgan began to help Carolyn out on the side buttressed to the back door of the house. "You're not going to leave me out here all night, are you?"

He stared for some time at Felix, trying to recall when he'd unlocked the trunk, pulled him from his case, and set him there. He did not remember any of it. "You'll be fine here, Felix. Better off, really."

"Easy for you to say. You get to sleep with Carolyn and then—"

"Felix, I'm old enough to make my own decisions now."

"Oh, Mr. High and Mighty!"

"Screw off, Felix."

Felix's one eye fell closed as if in a wink. "Suppose you think Carolyn fell for you instead of me. Want to ask her who she fell for first? I dare ya."

Morgan closed the door on Felix's pitiful protests, walked Carolyn inside, and once the door was closed, she couldn't keep her hands off him. As always, Morgan was an ineffective lover, clumsy and unable to come, but this seemed not to matter to Carolyn, whose fantasy was complete.

He guided her from the bed and toward the waiting instrument in the kitchen. He knew the house so well he needed no lights. He guided her steps, talking in soothing tones to her, asking her how much willpower she possessed. "You'll need it all tonight," he said when suddenly saw something ratlike, a baby opossum-type creature dart across the floor in front of him, waddling in armadillo fashion before streaking away. This befuddled him, and then he tripped over something that yelled and swore at him and groaned in the dark.

He sat up and came face to face with Felix. "Bastard! How'd you get in here?"

"I'm everywhere, Morgan. You ought to know that by now. I'm here, and I'm there, and I'm everywhere. . . ."

Morgan grabbed Felix by the throat and began ripping at him, strangling him. Felix's voice let out with a bubbling and a gurgling which disturbed and frightened

Carolyn, who at first giggled to see Morgan choking his own dummy. Then she began to beat on Morgan, saying, "No, stop it! Stop it, now! You'll break it, and then what?"

"I'm . . . in the car . . . at the apartment . . ." Felix choked out each word. "In the grave," he finished when Morgan's grip loosened.

Carolyn was astonished. "What happened? I don't remember . . . how'd we get in here? Where're my clothes?"

"Take her home, Morgan," said Felix. "Do the right thing."

Morgan glared at Felix.

"Do it . . . do it for me."

Morgan scratched his temple. "Bedroom that way," he told Carolyn Wamouth. "Get dressed and I'll get you back safely."

He watched her go, wondering why he was listening to Felix. Maybe it had something to do with the fact he'd locked Felix up doubly tight tonight and still here he was. If it meant that much to Felix . . . okay. He'd control his urge . . . but he wouldn't lift the suggestion placed in the girl's mind. Someday soon she might just pop up on his doorstep again, and then he'd show Felix who was boss and who was not.

Carolyn dressed rapidly and acted differently now. She was silent all the way back to her place. *She knew* . . . if not the entire truth, the truth of the fact that he'd seduced her via hypnotic suggestion. She wasn't sure how she felt about it now, he thought.

"I don't remember much," she said when they arrived at her parents' posh four-story place by the lake. "Did you . . . did you enjoy it?"

"I loved it," he said. "You were magnificent, Carolyn. Wonderful."

"Really?"

"Really."

"You just saying that?"

"I never lie about such things. Would you like to see me again?"

233

"Yes . . . I . . . I think so."

"Tomorrow night, midnight, after my last show at the club. Be there at my house. I'll meet you there."

"All right," she replied, getting from the car and staring at Felix, who was sitting upright in the back seat, his scant body buckled in, one eyelid down as if half asleep —or was he winking? She wasn't so sure she liked the dummy anymore. She wasn't in the least certain she wanted to see Morgan Sayer ever again. She'd just lied to him to let him down easy, and to keep from having any confrontation. He and his dummy were just too weird for her. Someone else maybe would find it fun, as she had at first, hadn't she? But not her, not now, after seeing the way he was fighting with the thing.

"You're not going to give me a good-bye kiss?" he asked her.

"What about me?" asked Felix.

"No," she said, feeling a shiver come racing up from the spine to her brain. "I'll save up my kisses and passion for when we meet again."

She wasn't sure where that had come from—romance novels read over a lifetime, she supposed.

"See you then," he replied. "Until then, I'll be thinking of you."

"And I'll be thinking of you . . . you and Felix." She bounded off toward the house.

Behind her she heard him holding conversation with the dummy. "Now, aren't you pleased with yourself?" said the dummy voice.

"Not really," he said in his own voice.

"Trust me on this one, dummy."

"You think you're so smart."

Morgan drove away with the chatter.

"Just cautious," said Felix.

"Sawdust for nuts."

"Sawdust for brains."

"Shut up."

"Make me."

Morgan took the dare. He drove down a dead-end street

234

toward Lake Michigan.

"Morgan?" said Felix. "What're you doing?"

Morgan said nothing.

"Where're we going?" Felix asked when Morgan stopped the car, unfastened Felix's seat belt, and helped him out. "Morgan? Oh, *Morrr-gannnn?* More-again-Morgan . . ."

"Felix," said Morgan, as he approached Lake Michigan. "I think a lot of my problem is you."

"Hey, partner, who keeps you going? Huh? Who helps you up when you're down? Who tells you right from left?"

They stood before the great, vast lake atop mammoth square stones placed there as a barrier.

"Morgan . . . please."

Morgan said no more.

"I'll behave."

Morgan lifted Felix high over his head.

"How're you going to do the show tomorrow night?"

Morgan let fly with Felix. He could hear Felix's cry far out over the water, "I'll *beeeeeee-gooooooooooood.*"

"Too late, Felix. Too damned late."

As for tomorrow night, he'd do the act without Felix. Danny might complain, but it wasn't Danny's decision. It was Morgan's Sayer's act, his decision.

He returned to his BMW and drove quickly from the site because in his ears he continued to hear Felix's voice coming up from the water.

Felix's voice haunted him all the way back to his house, where he put away the guillotine and put himself to bed, all without benefit of lights. Felix was whispering something unintelligible, just on the tip of his understanding. Something Felix was trying to tell him, but he couldn't get it, and he fell asleep trying.

He awoke later in the middle of the night, however, to a terrible pain in his forearm, and even in the dark he could see the gash. He'd been scratched horribly. Somehow he knew it was Felix. When he'd held Felix overhead, just before plunging him into the water, Felix had torn at him with his dead man's hands, the nails digging into him. But he was so keyed up that he'd not felt a thing until now.

Nails, like hair, had a life of their own, confirmed by the fact that both continued to grow on a dead person. They also contained mana—personal emanations of the individual to whom they belonged. Little wonder they were used in magical rituals and sabbats. The night before he'd even clipped Felix's new nails, and so how did they dig so deeply into his flesh unless . . .

He'd had to use nail-polish remover on Felix's newfound nails. When he got them back to their natural state he could see his reflection in them. So could Felix. In ancient times, with light reflecting off her nails, a scryer stared at her reflection on a thumbnail and did her scrying, foretelling of disaster.

That was the feeling weighing on his mind and chest when he tried to go back to sleep, the pain in his arm throbbing.

NINETEEN

One way in which Lieutenant Ryne Lanark dealt with pressure from above, either in the form of Fabia, Lawrence, or even Captain Paul Wood—whom he regarded as a good friend as well as a good commander—was to shut them out even as they yelled into his face.

Ryne was doing this now at two A.M.

Lanark's method, suggested initially by Ames many moons ago, and perfected by Lanark over months of practice, was to replay the old police-band messages in his head and thus tune out what his superiors were barking about. A certain amount of barking was necessary, part of the arm-twisting and abuse every cop took for the heat caused outside the precinct, either on the streets with citizens or downtown with the uppity-mucks.

Wood continued berating him for his being too secretive. "This isn't the goddamned SS! And you're not Adolf Eichmann, mister! Despite what you may think . . ." And on it went.

Lanark replayed the night's complaints and calls in his head instead: A 10-30, violent assault in progress, handled by Pete Glass and Mike Boyle, two uniforms. Turned out a guy had pushed his wife through a window and she'd fallen two stories, very much alive and in pain. Rushed to County, husband arrested and booked.

There'd been a 10-59, fire alarm, but the fire had turned out to be another alarm prank. The summer would see literally hundreds of these.

A theft-in-progress report had come over and cars were on the scene, but the 10-22 had turned out to be another family squabble, a man removing what he perceived to be his property from her apartment.

There had been the usual vehicular accidents in the rush of night traffic that compounded police problems.

A strange story was making the rounds about a possible dumping of a body in Lake Michigan, but this was in Winnetka, a long way off, and being investigated by Coast Guard officials from Evanston. Report had it that a witness had seen a man throw a child into the lake at a dead-end location. However, no body had been recovered. Searchers would be joined by CPD boats at the first light.

There'd been several narcotics apprehensions as well as the usual number of prostitution busts, and a few runaways taken into custody on missing persons reports.

"Are you listening to me, Lieutenant?" shouted Wood. "Look, I'm not happy being placed in this position, having to stand here and tear you down, Lanark. We've been through a lot together, you and I, and we've build something impressive and important in the Thirteenth for the first time in the history of this cursed precinct. I just don't want to see our undercover operation shut down because its commanding officer has turned into Rambo."

Captain Paul Wood was furious at Lanark, so furious, in fact, others in the building at Precinct 13 could hear the commotion on the other floors. Outside the captain's office, waiting patiently, was Jeff Sandler with Shannon Keyes. Sandler had said some fifteen or twenty times that Wood wasn't going to buy into the deal, that it was obvious he was too upset with Lanark to buy into anything Lanark wanted. It was nearing dawn. Wood's sleep had been disturbed.

Inside the office, Wood was banging and shouting. "Are you completely out of your skull? Here, take this damned office apart, set the fucking building on fire, do what the hell you wish; you are, after all, super-cop, and nobody but nobody'd dare get in your way! Well, I'm here to tell you, Lieutenant, you've got people crawling up and down you now. Everything you ever touched, every move you ever made is being reviewed by people in the department—"

"Fabia!"

"Fabia and Lawrence and any number of others. You're no longer considered just armed and danger-ous! You're now armed and demented! Fabia's shitting green over this matter, taking it to the top. He's bringing up ancient history, earlier incidents, all manner of hog swill and—"

"And people are swallowing it?"

"He's quoting from your old files with the shrink, Ames, trying to get old business revived and opened! Lawrence has called Ames for your file! Ames has called me!"

"The file was burned when we got it back from the Feds."

"I'm aware of how it was disposed of. I'm also aware that Ames was smart enough to create a new one, one that's more . . . favorable, better light on things, he says. Says he has no choice but to boot it up."

"All games, Captain . . . playing bullshit games."

"Political games can eat you alive, Lanark."

Lanark paced the room tiger fashion before stopping at the window and looking down over an alleyway. Not much of a view, but the 13th wasn't much of a neighborhood either. "Look, Captain, neither you nor Ames has to cover for me. I've done nothing wrong."

"You don't worry about Ames or me, Lanark. Right now the flack is falling straight overhead, your head. That warehouse, all the equipment damaged, the department has to make restitution, not to mention a damned expensive vehicle! Unless we prove you were *personally* responsible and not working a case, which I know damned well you weren't. I covered for you anyway!"

"Captain—"

"I know what you were working on."

"Loomis, sir . . . you'll find his body among the dead."

"Dammit, Lanark, your interest in Loomis was nil, and we both know that! You were working one of your *special cases,* pro bono to the ego! I'm not blind or stupid, despite what you may sometimes think—"

Lanark recalled the time that an irate Captain Paul Wood had flown to California under an assumed name to hunt down a murderer who'd been given his freedom in an FBI relocation plan when he'd testified. Wood had blown the man's brains out. Some people in the department still believed it was the work of Ryne Lanark because the *signature* was the same.

"Captain, we were operating a sting."

"Don't screw around with me, Lanark. We've worked cases together in the past, and I've brought you along. I got you the undercover unit, remember? I know that you're on some vendetta. Christ, everybody in the department knows you've got problems—"

Shannon knocked and came through the door all at once, saying. "Captain, we've put together a plan to help catch The Handyman." Behind her, a reluctant Jeff Sandler stepped tentatively in.

"What the hell's this? Keyes to the rescue? What is it? Good news, I could use."

Lanark sat down. At this very moment Mark was writing up a set of bogus reports for the file on the "sting" they'd been carefully putting together which involved Loomis. If carefully worded, using the "kidnapping" operation properly, along with just the right terminology, they might pull it off.

Wood listened to Shannon and Jeff Sandler as they pitched the plan. Most of what the police knew about the killer had remained tightly sealed. The reporters knew only slightly more about The Handyman, and the way he worked, than did the man on the street. Security on this one had been extremely tight, all offices working overtime to keep it that way. Jeff told Wood that if they hit the stands with a story that catalogued the excesses of the killer, holding back some special information for later use in ID'ing the suspect, as was custom, then the "shock" value of it to the killer himself could send him into making mistakes, such as trying to rid himself of evidence.

"That's assuming he reads," said Wood dryly. "Jeff, we've always had good relations with you. I know you have the best of intentions, but some of the details of these killings will only serve to shock old ladies and children, women living alone. Do we want that?"

"Who knows whether or not the information might keep some kid alive? Hell, I've seen the results of this guy's work. I think it's time we warned people in no uncertain terms."

"Maybe you're right. Who knows . . . and what else have we? Not much. Just do me a favor, and don't turn this into a head-hunting piece, like what the crap is the commissioner doing, and where's the mayor in all this, and that kind of stuff. You got any negatives to fire at the department, fire away at this level, okay?"

"You got it, and you won't regret it."

"Keyes, open the file to Mr. Sandler."

She nodded and gave a glance at Lanark. Once more his behind was pulled from the flames rising to pull him down. How many lives did he have left? And all he could do was sit there, feeling bitter over the fact he'd lost the scent of his prey. With Loomis's death, a very thick and large door was slammed in his face.

"Oh, by the way, Lanark . . . one other item you should know," said Wood, who stopped them at the door.

"Report came in of a homicide, turns out he's one of your snitches, kid named Tony Dinetto."

Lanark thought of the kid for a moment, and the last time he'd paid him for the information he'd gotten from him. Another of Lanark's street friends, more reliable in the long run, had warned Lanark not to use the kid, that he was bad news. When pressed to explain this, the friend said, "He'd just as soon stab you in the back as anyone else, for the right price." Lanark had let it pass at the time, thinking little of it until now. The kid's information had netted Loomis. But no one was supposed to know of the factory setup, and yet they had found out; maybe the kid had died with the fact on his lips, leading Loomis's people right to Lanark. If so, Tony Dinetto had become an unsuccessful mole, a double agent in the war on drugs. He'd become a real mercenary, informing on Lanark as well as on men like Loomis. Maybe he just hadn't seen a difference.

Shannon was talking quietly with Sandler outside when Lanark rejoined them. She'd arranged to have the files he needed spread out in a nearby room. He could not take them with him. A police guard was placed on Sandler. "Go to it," she told him. "Remember, what we'd like to hold back is the fact the killer may be using a form of hypnosis to overpower his victims."

"Hypnosis?" Sandler was intrigued.

"We've got to hold this back."

Sandler nodded, shook her hand and then Lanark's. "You know, despite all the ranting, Wood's got to know that without guys like you two, this precinct would still be known as Wood's Hole."

"Come on, cowboy," Shannon told Lanark when they were out of range of Wood's ire. "You can take me home."

"Now that sounds inviting."

Morgan Lefay Sayer stood at the threshold to his apartment bedroom, staring in at the unreal sight before him, shaken. In the darkened interior where the drapes were pulled closed against the light from outside, he could see that someone, or some thing, was lying in his bed. The profile in the dim light told the story, but it was impossible . . . *impossible!*

He took a step inside not knowing he was moving. He'd lost all track of time and place. He didn't recall driving back to his apartment; didn't recall riding up from the parking garage, the elevator, or opening his door. He'd blacked out all of it.

He heard Felix's familiar snore and moan, the sound of contented sleep, coming up off the bed. But Felix was gone. He remembered throwing him into the lake. Or had that been all a dream?

Felix turned over and faced him, his eyes open, when Morgan put out a hand to him. It made Morgan flinch and back away.

"Morgan," it said to him.

"You . . . but how?"

"I saved your ass, Morgan."

"What?"

Felix who lay there like a ghost, grinning, had come back to haunt him. *Was it a dream, or was it real?* Was it possible that the beastly little dummy could actually come back from its watery grave? Could it come back from the dead? No, it was not possible . . . yet here Felix was. *How?*

"Took care of the ol' nosey Burroughs bitch for you, Morgan. Did just what you would've done."

"What?"

"While you were away."

"What're you talking about, Felix?"

"Dammit, you getting dense? I killed her, look!"

Felix was sitting up against the headboard now and his human hands, Ms. Burroughs's hands, were displayed with open pulpy palms at the end of each of Felix's wrists. "Whatya think? Think we got it right this time?"

Morgan's eyes went wide with amazement. He raced from the bedroom and out the door, banged several times

243

on Ms. Burroughs's door, but got no answer. Somewhere in the knocking he twisted the knob and her apartment door swung open. Inside he saw a trail of purple splotches along the cream-colored carpeting that led to her bedroom.

"She won't be pounding on the fuckin' walls anymore," said Felix in the doorway behind him, leaning against the jamb as if resting.

Morgan could still not believe it: that Felix, alone, was capable of such actions. As if reading his mind, Felix said, "Learned it all from you, Morgan."

"No, not happening," he said, trying desperately to remember when he had himself done Ms. Burroughs.

Shaken to his core, Morgan tried to recall what had occurred here between himself and Ms. Burroughs, but he simply could not. As if following him and reading his mind, Felix, his feet up against the doorjamb, looking jaunty, said, "Hell, Morgan buddy, you didn't do it."

"What?"

"Me. I did."

"That's crazy."

"So what's new? Come on, they find you here like this, who're they going to believe, you? Or me?"

Maybe it all had something to do with his blackouts, Morgan thought. He must've done it during such a spell.

"I did it," insisted Felix. "I cannot tell a lie."

"Shut up! Shut up!"

"Sure, pal, if you say so."

He tried desperately to think, but his mind was a jumble of confusion and anxiety. He didn't know what to do. He tried to understand how Felix had gotten there, but hell, he couldn't this moment explain how he himself had gotten there.

He inched toward the bedroom where the door stood ajar. Even from the hallway he could see overturned furniture, the sheets and pillows vivid with rivulets of blood, tossed and lying in disarray. As he drew near he saw her too, lying on the far side of the room, just her feet in view. He didn't want to see anymore.

How could Felix have been such a fool? Killing the next-door neighbor? Inviting trouble to come crashing down their door?

Felix shouted from the other room, still reading his mind, replying, "Hey, pal, you know she was onto you! She knew! And she came to the door snooping. What was I supposed to do? She was going straight to the cops next."

Morgan's own weight seemed too heavy for him to carry as he ponderously made his way back to the door. Just down the hall, outside, he heard someone exiting a door and heading their way. He snatched Felix inside and shut Ms. Burroughs's door, the acrid smell of blood teasing his nostrils where he and Felix stood with their backs against the door praying the passerby would just keep going.

But there was a knock at the door, loud and thunderous, almost making them jump. They fought back fear together and tried to remain in control. Another knock, and a female voice called out, "Jean? Jean?"

A third knock and a lilting, "Jean, are you home?"

Morgan held his breath. Felix did likewise. Their eyes met in the darkness.

The intruder's footsteps moved off, and soon became faint and indistinct. Morgan took his time, his heart racing. He then inched out, taking Felix with him, and returned to his own apartment.

Felix sighed heavily when they got back to the safety of their place. "I'm really bushed," he said.

Morgan carried him in and laid him down on his bed, tucking covers under his chin, telling him to get some sleep and that he would take care of things.

"You're sure?"

"Yes."

"You've been acting very strange lately."

"I'm sure."

"Very forgetful."

"Don't worry."

245

"Be happy, huh? With you blacking out half the time and dreaming bad dreams the rest?"

Morgan flinched, for again Felix seemed to be reading his mind. It was exactly what he was thinking. He'd decided this was all just a bad dream: Felix's coming back this way, Felix's uncharacteristic action against Jean Burroughs, all of it just a nightmare from which he'd soon awake.

Or would he?

Sometime later, he found himself in his car, driving aimlessly and realizing it was getting late and that he'd be missed at Danny's. He was usually in rehearsal by now. He had to explain to Danny that he intended on cutting Felix from the act, that it was necessary for the survival of the act—to keep it fresh and with the times. Danny wouldn't understand it if he told him it was necessary for the survival of Morgan Sayer.

With these pressing thoughts he drove for the club in Old Town. As he did so, he realized that he'd been right all along about Felix and Jean Burroughs, that in fact it had all been a gruesome nightmare, a hoax created by his own fatigued mind.

The fact of the matter was that Ms. Jean Burroughs was having late afternoon tea with a friend at the Book Nook where she worked, and Felix was at the bottom of Lake Michigan being picked over by fish.

Morgan felt instantly better for having decided the truth of the matter.

The following day Shannon telephoned Dr. Ito Colucci, determined to see him again. Lanark, ever skeptical of the help Dr. Colucci could provide for the investigation, told her not to waste her time.

"Is that an order?"

"No, just a suggestion."

"I see," she said, and left for the museum alone, promising to be back in time for a departmental meeting

246

in which all the facts gathered to date on the various victims would once again be sorted through and sifted for clues.

For now, she was retracing the strange, curious route to Dr. Ito's "office" and was quite lost. She ran into people who worked amid the collections behind the closed doors and who seemed like busy mice: not in the least interested in her or her problems. She had to beg directions before she regained the thread of the maze and finally located Colucci's office. But he was not in it.

She stared at the items about his shelves. Bones, stones, amulets, pottery—all with markings, including some on the bones. She reached out to a collection of skeletal materials, lifting a box beside it. The box was made of wood, hollowed with sound-makers inside. It was something like an ancient castanet, a musical instrument perhaps. She was playing and toying with it when suddenly she jumped at the sound of a human voice behind her.

"Lieutenant Keyes! I didn't think you would be quite so early—oh, sorry, didn't mean to startle you. Lovely, isn't it? The sound it makes, I mean."

He pointed to the sound box in her grasp, not larger than one of the modern containers that held wristwatches.

"Yes, different anyway." It had made an odd, rattling dice sound against the soft wood.

"Talk about a use for hands!"

"Playing instruments, you mean?" She was confused.

He took the box from her and carefully opened it with a tiny awl. "All wood, including the pegs that hold it together. Remarkable find, really." He tipped it to one side for her to glance inside at the contents. It looked like an assortment of jumping jacks, but it wasn't.

"What is that?"

"Knucklebones."

She gasped, "Oh."

As he put it away, he said, "So, you've come with more questions?"

"Yes, I have."

"Please, have a seat," he said, then quickly looked around for one that was not filled to brimming with papers, books, boxes, and other items. "Never mind, stand. You haven't much time for sitting anyway, I wager."

"In one of the books you suggested, there's a half page or so that touches on a people who more or less worshipped the human hand, the . . . the . . ."

"The Xeniads, yes—some believe they never existed, but more proof of their existence is being unearthed daily. A largely forgotten people, a subculture, in a way the lepers of their world—"

"Far East?"

"Asia, right. Funny, I've given your . . . the city's current problem with this killer some thought, and I confess I too thought of the Xeniads. They had an absolute worship of the form and function of the human hand as if all else in the universe resided there." Ito's features were half hidden in the poor lighting there and she could not make out his facial expressions. For all she knew, he could be putting her on.

"Please, tell me more about them."

He did so, explaining that the ancient cult was wiped out as early as the Ming Dynasty. As he spoke, she realized that much of his appeal was that of the eerie storyteller of old, humped before a fire, spinning his tale, weaving in detail with knit-one, purl-two, explaining the unexplainable in a round and round attempt. Maybe Lanark was right about Colucci.

"The hand was the symbol they used for everything, the way Christians use the cross. It was revered, and in battle they didn't take scalps or trinkets like teeth, no . . . they took their victims' hands."

"Did they cannibalize the hands?"

"They did. But that was the end result of an entire worldview. The sun to them was God's fingertip, the brightness his corona. In their eyes, they could look up daily and see God's hand stretched down from the heavens, his index finger pointing straight at them. At night they were shown the end of his small finger, the moon. Of course they weren't the only race to commit human sacrifice through bloodletting, but they did perfect a peculiarly "handy" method, replete with instruments to lob off the hands, and other instruments you are—for all your worldly wisdom and profession—too delicate to hear spoken of. History, my dear, teaches us one thing: Man possesses the finest and the cruelest mind working on the planet."

She wondered momentarily what he meant by instruments he simply refused to discuss with a woman, but she didn't press the point with the doctor.

She began to think of him as a strange, modern-day Buddha himself. He was rotund and tawny in skin color, and his smile was enigmatic. His manner was as calm as any statue she'd ever seen.

"The Xeniad beliefs did not remain in Asia. They spread, as with any idea, along trade routes. There is no known existing cult of them today, but given southern California's attraction for bizarre cults, who can say? The Xeniads went underground, and eventually fell through the manifold cracks in history and archaeology. They were a race, coincidentally, of large-handed people. They had an absolute obsession with the form, filling their art with it. To them, the hand was seen as a star, each finger a point in the star."

"But you don't really believe there's a stray Xeniad

living in underground Chicago in 1990?"

He shook his head from side to side. "No, but my dear, what I am saying is this: If an entire community of people could obsess over the sign of the hand to the point of human sacrifice and warfare for its capture ... it is easy to conjecture about one man's morose behavior in regard to the hands."

"Is there anything, anything, you can tell me about the killer that might help me immediately?"

He thought for an intolerably long time before saying, "Perhaps this. Your killer will be a man who uses his own hands a great deal; finds pleasure in his own hands; uses them in his work; spends much time staring at them, I should think."

"That's what I was thinking."

"Then we are on the ... how do they say it, same wave?"

Ito Colucci promised to give some additional time to the puzzle once he finished a project that was facing a deadline. "There is much fascination about your work, Lieutenant Keyes."

She shook his hand and found it was smaller than her own. "Thank you, for your time and your insights."

"Your friend ..."

"Lieutenant Lanark."

"He has no patience."

She smiled and nodded. "Yes, none whatever."

"Then he is lucky to have you as his partner."

"Thank you. I think so too."

"I wish you luck in finding this madman. I saw the papers this morning. I had no idea he used hypnosis. You said nothing about hypnosis before. Did you know that people once painted their nails in order to fend off evil spirits and ghosts when they waved their hands about? I often think of hypnotists in the same light."

She was only half listening, her anger rising to the surface with the sudden jolt. Sandler had used the

250

information on hypnosis—pure conjecture for one thing, and also a betayal. Damn him, she thought.

"Are you all right, my dear?"

"Yes, yes, thank you. Do you have a copy of the story you mentioned?"

"Take it, I'm finished with it," he said, handing her a copy of the *Sun Times*.

They parted with another round of thank-yous. Once above, in the main hall of the museum, she opened the newspaper to the story, reading it. Sandler played up the hypnosis, to the hilt, choosing to leave other incidentals from the story instead. That had not been their bargain, and it certainly wasn't up to him. She rushed from the museum for the *Sun-Times* offices.

When she got there and she saw Sandler talking in a small circle of colleagues and friends, laughing and waving his hands, she said firmly, "You bastard!"

He threw up his hands and gave her a sheepish shrug. "Story was rewritten, I swear! My editor did it. Paul Schroder.

"You damned fools just threw the case into jeopardy, and for what? Paper's ailing, needs a boost, and you're promised a bonus? All comes down to cash, doesn't it?"

"This story's going to flush this sicko!"

"Goddamned cash, and meanwhile the killer's alerted to our every move. You just sold guns to the goddamned Iranians, Jeff!" She threw the paper in his face and stormed out, leaving people all about staring. Sandler said to an associate who patted him on the back, "Hey, it was just too good'n angle to kill. Besides, it'll work! It'll draw the bastard out! Got to . . . got to . . ."

Sandler had already made plans to see that the second installment of the story would be ready by midnight. He envisioned the killer being caught "red-handed" as it were, as a direct result of having read his own profile in the series of articles Sandler would continue, maybe a series that would get attention in New York and LA and other important places. Maybe it'd be good enough to get results: bag a killer, yes, but also a Pulitzer. Money—hell, it wasn't the money, Sandler told himself as he slumped into his desk chair. It was more than money.

TWENTY

The papers had it.

Felix had been right all along.

Everyone knew.

They even knew that he was some sort of hypnotist.

They knew he used a "guillotine"-type instrument to relieve people of their hands.

They theorized that he ate the flesh off the hands, and he thought that was really sick. Who ever thought that one up ought to be put away.

The papers named the victims and ran photographs, but old photos, no one being depicted in their "handless" state.

He ought to have listened to Felix. Because now, they were onto him.

He'd just lay low ... no more giving in to the urge again. That was the ticket. Go about his normal routine.

Don't upset the applecart. He wished that Felix was here, but then he thought of Felix's hands. Maybe it wasn't such a bad idea, throwing him into the lake that way, ridding him of the very evidence that could convict him.

Then he thought of the other hands he'd taken. He ran down the list of victims. It hadn't seemed to him there had been so many, but if the newspapers said so, then it must be true. He wondered what he'd done with the other hands. He wondered how he was going to get through the day without Felix.

He wondered again about the strange nightmare he'd had which had resurrected Felix and had Felix somehow killing that Burroughs bitch in the apartment next to his.

Danny'd left a copy of the *Sun-Times* lying on the cramped little stage where he'd be working in a few hours, working without Felix. Danny had finished with the sports section and the funnies and had discarded the rest, ignoring the story on page one altogether. Morgan wished that he could ignore it, but he knew he mustn't. He knew he must curtail his actions, and with Felix truly gone, it seemed there was no reason not to. Maybe if the handless victims just stopped showing up, police would just give up their pursuit of The Handyman, him.

Some of the strippers were coming in, saying hello. They saw him reading the paper. If they thought he was reading about the killings, they'd know . . . everybody would know. He shivered at the thought.

The phones in every precinct in the city were ringing, every line abuzz with calls related in one manner or another to Sandler's news story and The Handyman case. Sergeant O'Hurley had collared Lanark when he entered the precinct, his Irish dander up over the story and its results. Lanark had heard nothing about it until he walked into it. Captain Paul Wood was supposedly on his way to allegedly murder Keyes and Lanark.

"The idea is to stir the pot," Lanark told O'Hurley.

"Well, lad, you've done that much, but I'm not sure you're going to like the stew."

"One good bit of news," said Wil Cassidy, who came in on Lanark's heel, tossing him a morning paper that'd been read by Wil and his wife, Myra.

"What's that?" asked Lanark.

"Nothing in the papers about an overnight victim."

"That, gentlemen," said O'Hurley, "remains to be seen."

They both looked at the big sergeant, puzzled expressions asking him to continue.

"A call came in last night. I only heard secondhand,

you know, but it sounds like a murder. Old man was looking out a window, lakeshore area; swears he saw a man lift a child, or a small woman, over his head and throw the victim into the lake. Coast Guard and police cutters're searching the area now."

"Doesn't sound like our man. Doesn't sound like his MO," said Wil.

"Keep us posted if any bodies are found without hands, though, Sarge."

"Oh, you can count on it, Lieutenant."

"And thanks, for the other night."

"Ahh, no mention of it would be fine."

"So, what about the newspaper account?" asked Wil.

"What about it?"

"You trying to tell me we released all this information to Sandler only? It was only in the *Times*."

"We thought . . . we believed Sandler would handle it with the respect it deserved. Guess we were wrong."

"He's told the creep exactly what we have."

They'd remained at the front desk and O'Hurley had one ear cocked.

"Part of our plan to show the guy our cards," said Lanark, leafing through for Sandler's story. Which, while page-one news, was buried due to Wil's having gotten the paper completely screwed up. "Part of our plan was that he'd back off, ease up, give us a chance to find some answers. Wasn't part of our plan to show the SOB all our cards, particularly the hypnotism theory. Damn, we told that newspaperman to not use one word about the hypnotism."

"Then he goes and does it anyway, so we've gained nothing that we know of," replied Wil, "and lost points by showing our hand."

"He'll be showin' his *hands*, soon! Huh, Lanark? If we know our boy, Lieutenant Lanark," said O'Hurley, listening in. He went away laughing at his own lame joke.

"I got some interesting items on Sarah Chambers," said Myra, who came in now from outside.

They went to the squad room and were joined by Mark Robeson.

"Let's take it out of the hallway. Too many ears," said Lanark. "Upstairs, the unit squad room. Sergeant O'Hurley, keep up the good work."

O'Hurley frowned. "We'll be having crank calls all day and night over this one. I've got several confessed Handymen in holding again, as of this morning."

"Anyone look good?"

"Not a one of 'em."

"Any of then know hypnotism?"

"All of them, *according* to them."

In the squad room they were joined by Robeson and a shaky Stokes whose bandages were still on. Stokes got applause on entering. With a croak of thanks, as his voice box was still mending, he took a bow. Lanark looked for Shannon, but she'd not made it back yet. He started without her, summarizing for those who did not know that Loomis was no longer a consideration for their concern. "Robeson and I had a gun battle with him and his men last night that resulted in his death, along with six of his henchmen."

Stokes said something unintelligible. Robeson, who'd spent the most time with Stokes, translated. "Says he wishes he could've been there."

"No, you don't," said Lanark.

"Why weren't we apprised of this operation?" asked Myra.

Wil gave his wife a look of disapproval, but she went on, speaking her mind. "This is supposed to be a unit, but half the time, most of us aren't aware of half the things that're going down."

"That's past history," said Lanark. "We were testing the waters and everything exploded in our faces, right, Mark?" said Lanark. "Anyway, we're here to cross-check one another on the Handyman business. What've you got on Sarah Chambers?"

"Had changed her name to Heather Allen—not officially, but she was going under the new name.

256

Searching for some sort of independent identity, friends say."

"She have many friends?"

"Few, select few. One she was living with."

"A guy?"

"Female, shared the rent."

"Go on."

Myra pulled open a hand-held notebook and read a list of relatives' and friends' names, stating that none of them so far were stacking up as good prospects. "Father, the preacher, is the weirdest one of her acquaintances, so far as I can tell. Something underneath, hidden between them. Something that drove her out."

"Abuse?"

"Not so's you'd notice, not physical abuse," she said. "Certainly no evidence of it."

"Myra's got damned good antennae," said Wil. "She picked up on something there."

"Can you be more specific?"

"He wanted her to be the perfect minister's daughter, same as his wife was the perfect minister's wife . . . but she couldn't live up to that."

"So she ran away?"

"Looks that way," said Wil.

"Right into the hands of our killer."

"Sarah was distant, aloof, always held herself in check, according to those who tried to get to know her. Even her parents didn't always understand her, or how her introversion had come about, although they in effect had a hell of a lot to do with it. She was repressed, in *every* sense of the word. Roommate claims she was still a virgin."

"Not according to Black's report. She'd recently had sex," said Lanark.

"Possibly with her killer," said Wil.

"As a child, she'd been outgoing and as loud as any child in the neighborhood. Puberty, junior high, high school changed her, they—the parents told me.

"Sarah Chambers was hospitalized once for attempted suicide."

"How? What method?" asked Lanark.

Wil answered, "Slashed her wrists."

"She never fully recovered from the experience. Ran away a couple of days after release from the hospital," said Myra, whose sympathetic voice made it clear that she'd "lived" in Sarah's shoes for the time that she'd spent investigating her. "Talked a lot about former souls, reincarnation . . ."

"No one knows where she'd been the night she disappeared?" asked Robeson.

"She spent the evening with friends, bar-hopping. Her roommate got lucky, spent the night out. Another of her friends saw her to her door, and it was the last anyone saw of her alive."

"Have you got a list of the bars they went to?"

"Sure, right here." She flipped to it and read the names which meant little to anyone in the room. "Fidos, Men's Room, Danny Boy's, Bullys."

"Got the address of each?" asked Lanark.

"Yes, of course."

"Read 'em out. You others on Rhodes, Jorovich, take note of the geography. Mark'll stab the map for us."

Mark Robeson located each address as Myra read it off, sticking a green pin into the map at each location.

"Now, do you know the order in which she went to each establishment?" he asked Myra.

"Just as I gave them to you."

"Time for each stop?"

She read these off.

"Out pretty late for an introvert."

"She was making progress," countered Myra.

He nodded and dropped his gaze, understanding how easy it was for a detective to get caught up in a victim's life.

"The friend who dropped her at the door," began Mark, who was promptly shut off by Wil.

"Story checks. He's not a lady's man; more like one of the girls on an evening's bash. He's been devastated by the attack on Sarah, so much so he was hospitalized a day ago for an overdose. Says it was accidental, but who knows."

"You sure about this guy?" asked Mark. "Sounds like a possible to me."

"You haven't seen him. No way he could overpower the girl, much less talk her into anything."

"So, without Shannon's input on Jorovich, we're back to Rhodes. We know that Rhodes was partying the night he died. Slim thread, but so far, only one we've got. We need to know exactly where Rhodes went that night. Interestingly enough, we know he was in the Old Town area. Got to shake some trees."

"Where's Lieutenant Keyes at?" asked Myra.

"Researching something at the museum."

"Spending a lot of time lately on culture, isn't she?"

Lanark laughed lightly, and the others joined suit. "I don't know that it'll do any good. I honestly expected her back by—"

The phone interrupted him. "Hey, you all know your assignments and how to proceed. Stay in touch, and Myra, please tack up a copy of those clubs and bars on the board, thanks."

Samantha Curtis had taken the call, but she was waving to him, saying it was Lieutenant Keyes, and it was urgent.

Lanark, going for the phone, continued to spew forth orders. "Everyone's to commit the list to memory. I want to know if Rhodes went to any of these bars, if Elena Jorovich made the same rounds."

He took the receiver from Sam and said curtly, "Where've you been?"

"We got a pair of hands!"

"What?"

"White, Caucasian, set of identical hands; one right, one left. Black is on his way down to take charge of them. Says he'll match them with Sarah Chambers."

"Where? When'd this happen? Where are you?"

"Washed up with some other interesting debris at Oak Street Beach. Report came in that there was a dead little boy on the beach, drowned."

"Little boy, drowned?"

"Turned out the little boy was made of wood but—"

"Wood?"

"Will you shut up and listen!"

"All right."

"I heard the call. Know it was far from where I was, but the radio car that got there first called in the report on the hands. You haven't gotten it yet?"

"You're the first."

"Ryne, the dead girl's hands . . ."

"Yeah?"

"They were . . . stitched onto the sleeves of a dummy."

"A dummy, as in a mannequin?"

"No, an entertainer's dummy. You know, like Jerry Mahoney and Howdy Doody and Edgar Bergan's Charlie Mac—"

"Jesus, Shan . . ."

"Flesh on the hands has turned fish-belly, parts torn away. You coming down here with a photographer?"

"On my way."

"At least now we know," she suddenly said.

"Know what?"

"What he does with the hands."

In all his years of investigation, police work, gun battles, and fights, Lanark had never seen the likes of what lay at his feet on the beach at the terminus of Oak Street. Robeson, Myra, and Wil joined him for the viewing. As they had driven for the scene, they'd informed Dr. Richard Ames, who'd said that he would be there despite the fact that Lanark had said it would not be necessary.

The police barricade held bathers and curiosity-seekers back. The coroner's evidence-gathering team arrived with a van equipped for remote work, a fully equipped computer behind its doors. Police photographers completed their work over the "part" body, remarking on the peculiarity of the situation. No sign of Ames. And the more Lanark thought about Ames, the more it troubled him.

"Shan," he said to her, taking her aside, "do you recall what Ames said in his office the other day?"

"Yes, of course."

"Every word?"

"I think so. Something about *real hands*, remember?

"He called out the word *dummy* not once, but twice. At the time, Corby thought he was calling him names, remember?"

"Oh, God, yes . . . now that you mention it." She stared down at the soaked black coat and pants that wrapped the wooden form. When it was turned over by Black, who dispensed with hellos by a mere wave of his hand, it stared up at them with a grotesquely human appearance: a wide-mouthed, wide-eyed expression of shock and horror. The features were as close to human as its creator could have possibly made them—particularly the hands.

Black slit the stitches holding the skin and fabric at the wrists together. The hands were stiff and hard to the touch, the nails sharp and intact but loose from the time spent in the water. Still, the fingerprints were intact as well, telling him the tissue hadn't had time to decay. But there was more to it than that. He looked up at the anxious faces of the police and said, "The hands have been preserved artificially."

He detached one of the hands, and it was so stiff it could sit upright atop the sand of its own accord. Black studied its interior. Then he pronounced that the hand he was gazing at had been "stuffed" in taxidermy fashion.

261

"Now we know what he does with them," said Lanark.

It left a chilling thought to hang in the air. "You think," said Myra, holding onto one of her wrists with the other, unconsciously turning and squeezing it, "that this madman manufactures these things for retail shops or something?"

Ames came suddenly from nowhere, straight for the horrid sight. Lanark wondered if he shouldn't cut him off, tell him the better part of valor was to get straight the hell out of there. But when Lanark tried, Ames pushed past him.

He stood staring for a moment, and then his huge form began to tremble. Robeson asked what was wrong with the man. "Just couldn't get it right . . . can't get it right," Ames was saying uncontrollably when Sandler from the *Times* broke through the police barricade with a half-assed story about working undercover with Lieutenant Ryne Lanark. Sandler had brought a camera with him and he was snapping shots all over the place, including shots of the shaking, quaking Dr. Richard Ames.

"Did it again," Ames was saying. "Going to do it tonight! Danny's . . . Danny's boy . . . Danny Boy's."

Lanark stared at Ames, stunned at this sudden revelation from Ames. It wasn't lost on the others, either, except for Shannon, who'd not heard the name of the nightclub before. If Lanark didn't know any better, he'd have had Ames hauled in and put behind bars, proclaimed as the murdering Handyman. But it couldn't be, not Richard.

Sandler's camera continued to flash and snap, and inside Lanark felt something snap also. He rushed at the newspaperman and sent him flying into the sand, lifted the camera and threw it fifty yards. It landed in the lake and disappeared. Sandler, no match for Lanark, was furious and he was shouting about police brutality and the power of the press, the First Amendment, and a few other things before Lanark turned and decked him. It felt good. It felt like a thing that needed doing.

"That's for lying to Shannon and me. As for today's

discovery, it stays here on the beach. You print one word of it before we're ready to release it, and you'll have more broken teeth."

Sandler staggered to his feet, his Fifth Avenue appearance shot to hell, his London Fog pockets filled with sand. "You'll regret this, Lanark, you sonofabitch. I've got a lot of influence in this city, and I'm going to use it. Going to dig up every piece of dog shit you ever stepped in!" He tore off, urged along by two uniformed cops.

Lanark saw Morris Fabia had been looking on, and now the Internal Affairs chief went looking for Sandler to cut a deal with him. Meanwhile, Richard Ames was being led off for paramedic attention by Shannon and Myra. He was hyperventilating, and looked on the verge of a heart attack. Damned if he didn't look as if he felt guilty as sin, and maybe he did.

The entire time, through all the commotion, the coroner calmly completed his work over the hands.

"You're going to let that hot head of yours bring you down one of these days, Lanark," warned Black.

Lanark ignored the remark. "So, whataya think, Doc?"

"About what? You? Ames? Sandler?"

"The goddamned hands."

"I think we will find they belonged to Sarah Chambers."

"That was my guess. Small hands, girlish. Elena Jorovich was taller, bonier. Her hands'll be longer."

"And where are Rhodes's hands?"

"God knows."

"God and the man who did this," said Black, and then he stared the distance to where Ames was being helped away. "And maybe that poor bastard."

"This is . . . has been very rough on Doctor Ames."

"So I gather."

"Don't let it get around, will you, Doc?"

"Shit, Lanark, it is around, all around. Every crime scene he's come to involving this hands-killer, he's gone away a basket case. Why? No one's blind. Why? everyone asks. It's no secret."

"Lawrence gets wind of it, well, it's all he needs. Ames is

a good man—"

"Was a good man. Look at him. He's no use to anyone in his state."

"The number of victims goes a notch up then, if we give up on Ames, if he loses his job."

"To hell with his job. What if he loses his mind?"

Lanark dropped his gaze, rubbed his chin, and shook from somewhere deep within. This kind of thing wasn't supposed to be able to touch a man like Ames. If it could happen to Ames, it could happen to any man. The thought made Lanark suddenly weak and in need of a drink.

TWENTY-ONE

Jeff Sandler poked about his desk with an unlit cigarette. He'd given up the bad habit, but still toyed with the damned paper-and-plant tubes like a child with a favorite bottle to suck on. He stared at the flashing red light on his phone which indicated the caller was still holding. He'd had calls all day, from as far away as Tempe, Arizona, from confessing killers, escaped victims of The Handyman, and people who thought they knew who The Handyman was. His story had tweaked every bug in every piece of dead wood in the city, and they were all crawling out as a result, plunking down a quarter to talk to the man who'd written the most revealing article on the killer to date. Some had come into the newsroom, and a guard had had to be posted. One such person, an extremely well-groomed and expensively dressed young woman, was trying desperately to get his attention now from the other side of the huge guard who was trying to contain her. She'd gotten a message through to Sandler that she was Carolyn Wamouth, daughter of the prominent banking financier who had also produced a number of stage plays and films. She claimed to know the name of The Handyman, and where he could be found.

Where had he heard that one before? The stuttering old woman on hold had had a bead on the killer too.

Sandler had spent the day this way, and between the idiots and losers and low-lifes he had interviewed, he had pondered the possibilities of the news story of his career, and the hip-deep shit it had placed him in. Still, it was potentially a story that gave him a running start at a Pulitzer—if he could follow it up. But he'd also burned important bridges to get it this far. He didn't have an in with Lanark or Keyes any longer—nor anyone at the 13th for that matter. In fact, cops all over were turned off by what he'd done, all except one.

Was a shot at the Pulitzer worth a lifetime of courting and creating and massaging good contacts in Chicago? It was, if you then moved on to, say, New York or LA. But such considerations hadn't seemed before to matter so much to him; as things had begun to unfold, as in many a profession, however, the brass ring had become too alluring to simply turn away from. And why should he? He'd worked hard for years to arrive at this juncture. And now, with the help of a Chief of Detectives on the force named Morris Fabia, he could go all the way with the story.

He didn't particularly like Fabia or his cliché-ridden mind: "You wash my back, I wash yours . . . one hand washes the other, and since this case is about hands . . ." But Fabia had connections and access to important information and people. Hell, he was the head of IAD for a quadrant of the city.

Fabia had approached him with a deal which in essence meant they work in consort against Ryne Lanark. Fabia had some long-standing hatred for Lanark which he'd summed up in a simple statement: "Lanark's no good for the department." Sandler, a good investigative reporter, hadn't left it at that. He'd done his homework on Fabia, learning that he and Lanark went back quite a few years. Lanark had burned Fabia on more than one occasion, but hostilities seemed to have become heated recently when Fabia had put a great deal of effort into an investigation his Internal Affairs Division had initiated on Lanark with the cooperation of several agents of the FBI. Sandler knew that with a few broad strokes of the pen he could easily have everyone in the city wondering why Lieutenant Ryne

Lanark appeared always to be under investigation, and why the list of his major busts read like a who's who at the morgue.

But Lanark was not Sandler's objective, regardless of what Morris Fabia wished to believe. As for Lanark's roughing the reporter up, Sandler knew he had had it coming. He had used Lanark and Shannon Keyes and could not have expected any better treatment. It came with the territory. Now, he had to cultivate new and better police sources, and perhaps Fabia was just what the doctor ordered.

At the moment, the reporter had a terrified old lady on hold on the line, and he wondered if she was just another crackpot whose next-door neighbor—beyond any doubt—was The Handyman. He'd had literally fifty calls that claimed a neighbor fit the proclivities of the killer. To most of these, he had suggested they telephone the police. Some had said they had, but that the police didn't understand or believe them.

The girl just outside the newsroom suddenly threw one of her shoes against the glass in an attempt to break it, but the shoe slid off the pane instead. The guard took this as his cue to heave her out or call the police to come and take her away. The poor man was exhausted.

Sandler saw her eyes lock on him. Something in her appearance, and perhaps the fact she was so well connected, made him get up and rush out, leaving the old woman on hold indefinitely. Outside now, he said to the guard, "Ralph, I'll talk to her now."

"Sure, Mr. Sandler, be my guest."

"How about some coffee?" he asked Carolyn Wamouth, studying her features as he did so. Plain, yet pretty in a straightforward, no-makeup way. Her clothes were very fashionable, the best money could buy. He guessed the deep blue of her eyes was due to contacts more than nature, but something in the way she held herself told him she had the makings of a strong character in time. He guessed her age at eighteen, maybe nineteen, dressing to mid-twenty. Yet there was nothing on her face, not even fake eyelashes.

"Sorry for my appearance," she suddenly said, making him realize he was staring too long and too hard. "I just raced over here without putting on any makeup when I saw your story. I've been trying to see you for an hour!"

"Here I am."

"I know who he is."

"The Handyman, I know. I've had sixteen confessions and about fifty eyewitnesses and relatives who swear they know who the—who he is."

She shook her head. "But I was with him. He hypnotized me."

"I've heard that one before too."

"His name is Morgan Sayer, and he has a dummy and a magic act, and he really knows how to hypnotize people."

He got a little excited over the word dummy. "Dummy? What sort of dummy?"

"Ventriloquist's dummy."

"What'd the dummy look like?"

"How should I know? What's that got to do with—"

"Describe the dummy!"

She tried to think. "Large eyes, wide mouth, big grin, plastered-down black hair . . ."

"What kind of clothes?"

"Kinda like a tux, you know, black coat and pants, like he was a little copy of his owner."

"What about the dummy's hands?"

"What about them?"

"Anything unusual about them?"

She shook her head. "Large, pale hands. In his act he's touching himself all the time with the dummy, you know, for laughs."

For the first time all day Sandler believed he had something useful. "Why didn't you go to the police department with this information?"

"I tried but they didn't believe me. Then I saw your story after I got back home. I tried calling you, but your line was busy."

"I want you to talk with a friend of mine in the police department."

"But—"

"He'll listen if I bring you to him."

"All right, but you don't understand."

"What? What don't I understand?"

"I have this urge to, to . . ."

"Yes?"

"See him again, this man, tonight."

"Urge?"

"Like, like a compulsion, like I can't wait. I don't know why, and I don't know why he . . . he didn't kill me . . . but he didn't. But there was some time lost when I was with him. I just know he had hypnotized me. I'm . . . I was planning to see him tonight."

Sandler said, "If this is true, how'd you get away from him?"

"I think . . . I think he's crazy . . . and somehow he . . . he talked himself out of killing me, but I can't be sure. He talked the whole time."

"Talked the whole time about what?"

"Nothing, really, just little everyday things to the dummy. They . . . he argued with it."

"The dummy?"

"Yeah."

"Schizoid, huh?"

She didn't answer.

This was better than he could have dreamed. "When? When are you supposed to meet him?"

"Midnight, his place, but I'm afraid and I won't go. If I have to ask my mother to lock me in my room, I won't go."

"It's okay, it's all right. You don't have to go. But if you could tell us where."

"Sure. I couldn't tell you the exact address, but I could take you there."

"Perfect. Come along."

He rushed back to his desk, lost the old woman on hold, and had started to dial for Morris Fabia when he thought of Lanark and Keyes, who'd put in so much time on the case and had handed him the story to begin with. But the hesitation was short-lived. Sandler was smart enough to know that if you could court a police chief or a detective lieutenant, you chose the higher-level man. Fabia's influence was such that Sandler must go with him. He finished dialing and was soon put through to Fabia.

"What've you got, Sandler?" asked Fabia.

"Something that'll knock your socks off."

"That's fine, but will it hurt Lanark in the bargain?"

"What would you say to making the collar on The Handyman?"

Fabia was silent at his end until he said, "Give me the particulars." In his voice, Sandler heard the nervous desire, the silent prayer that they had something Lanark did not have.

So bad was the attack on Dr. Richard Ames's psyche that he had had to be hospitalized, leaving men in police circles to wonder about his competence. The news of the doctor's mental collapse at the bizarre sight of the severed hands stitched to the sleeves of a dummy had traveled like wildfire to all sectors of the Chicago Police Department. Already room was being made in the department for Ames's successor, and so far as Commissioner Lawrence was concerned, the sooner the better. The news boys were making hay over Ames's unfortunate "demise" in the department. Cops throughout the various precincts were taking bets on what mental institution Ames would be shipped to.

Meanwhile, Lieutenant Ryne Lanark stood vigil outside Ames's room, haunting the halls for information, nailing doctors to the wall who were unwilling to confide in him. Shannon stuck too, spending most of her time on Lanark's arm, trying to get him to remain calm.

When several hours had passed this way, Lanark suggested she go home, get some rest. The coffee had turned rancid and the waiting room furniture tiresome. Every picutre on every wall was put to memory.

Dr. Frank Corby had arrived earlier; he'd been difficult to get, involved in some conference at the U. of C. Finally located, he was in with his "patient" and friend now.

When Corby emerged, he looked drained.

"How is he?" asked Lanark, on him like a bull dog.

"Holding up, under the circumstances."

"Meaning?"

"Prideful man in there. Pride's been hurt badly, sees his image as shattered, but in time, he'll gain complete control again. For the time being, he needs plenty of rest, and, oh, I . . . for the sake of Ames's sanity . . . I'd suggest he simply have nothing further to do with this case involving the hands."

"I thought he'd overcome his fears," said Shannon.

Lanark asked Corby, "What do you think happened to him, on the beach out there? A relapse of the fear?"

"Richard's a hell of an actor. I don't believe he truly and completely faced his fears, and this may be one phobia he can't overcome, no matter what method we use."

"Then he was faking it before?" asked Shannon.

"Not entirely. I think he had convinced himself that he was okay, strong enough to take it."

"Had me convinced too," replied Lanark. "Undercover material," Ryne finished with a sigh.

"Then what hit him on the beach wasn't—strictly speaking—a relapse?" asked Shannon.

"As good a word for it as any, yes. He was confronted with the hands. He'd had images of a dummy with severed hands. Seeing what you had to offer this morning, well . . . it was just too much for him to take in all at once. He might've been prepared a bit better had I been called in, but hindsight's a wonderful thing."

"I'll go see him," said Lanark, thinking of all the sessions he'd had with Ames. Ames, always in control, always a step ahead of him, always strong, someone to lean on, tell your troubles to. Now, it was Lanark's turn to show a little compassion. He wondered if he remembered how. Being a cop all these years, having the compassion cut from him when his parents and sister were murdered . . . he wasn't so sure if he could help Ames.

Ames was sitting up in bed when he entered. "Hey, you

look like you're ready for a game of poker."

"I'm fine," Ames lied.

"Look good," Lanark lied in return.

"Freaked , freaked bad . . ."

"Nobody's blaming you, Ames."

"In front of the men . . . no good. They look to me for help."

"Time they gave a little. Hell, Richard, you've bailed every damned one of 'em out at one time or another."

He scratched, pulled away his hand from his ear as if it were an alien thing, and stared at it. Lanark tried to ignore the gesture.

"I want you to get me outa here, Ryne."

"Sure, first thing tomorrow—"

"No! Tonight."

"Tonight?"

"*Shhhhhhh!* I know where the killer is. I don't know who he is . . . but I know where."

"A place called Danny Boy's?"

"You know about it? Have you caught him?" There was a desperate hope in the question.

"I heard you mention the place, and coincidentally—or maybe not so coincidentally, Myra Lane came up with it in connection with her background check of Sarah Chambers. The girl had gone there the night she died."

"I knew it!"

"But how, Richard? How'd you know about the place?"

Ames swallowed hard, looked for and found a pitcher of water, and shakily poured a glass. He drained it before he answered Lanark. "Saw it . . . saw it in a moment's flash, just . . . just after a nightmare."

"A nightmare about the killer?"

"Yes."

Lanark nodded and sat down before the bed.

"I know it sounds crazy, but—"

"Everything about this case is crazy. Hell, you want to hear crazy, talk to your friend Ito what's-his-name about the case. Ought to hear what he's telling Shannon."

"Don't underestimate Colucci's information or advice, Ryne."

"No, no . . . we won't."

"Will you do it?"

"What, break you out of here?"

Ames gave him a lopsided grin. "You've pulled much worse stunts. What do you say? I have to see this thing through, re—"

"Yeah, I'll help any way I can."

"—regain myself."

"Shannon's okay. She'll help us. What about Corby?"

"You crazy? Corby wants me under observation for the rest of the week. He's finding this all very fascinating. He's being very clinical, of course. Suppose that if I were in his position . . ."

"We'll find a way past him."

Shannon put her head through the door and said a friendly, "Hello, Dr. Ames. How're you feeling?"

"A little woozy. I didn't swallow any of their damned pills, but wasn't anything I could do about the hypodermic."

"Come in and close the door," Ryne told her. There was a conspiratorial twinge to the tone of his voice that made her ask, "What's up?"

They did indeed find a way past Corby and the other doctors and nurses. Shannon hadn't been sure of the plan, and still didn't like it. Suppose something happened to Richard Ames. The shock reaction he'd gone into at the beach had frightened her, and Corby had called it a relatively mild reaction. She feared seeing Ames display a strong reaction to his phobia. She herself was allergic to penicillin, and had had a bad reaction to the drug once when it had been administered before anyone knew. Ames's near-convulsive state at the Oak Street Beach had reminded her of that horrid occasion. She had not given in easily to Lanark, but had known right along that regardless of her objections, he was determined to help Ames in his bad decision. Lanark told her, however, of the link between Myra's nightclub and Ames's remarks about a neon sign in his extrasensory dreams that had the same name. Furthermore, Ames had not seen or heard the name from Myra or anyone in the unit.

For this reason, Shannon had relented, pushing back her doubts. She'd also been determined to show Lanark that he needed her.

She'd brought the car around back to an exit used primarily by employees of the hospital. Lanark and a weak Ames passed the area where a corkboard filled with internal communications and personal items hung alongside the time cards and clock for the hourly employees. They wasted no time in getting outside. Ames said it was wonderful to feel the air on his skin.

"Shut up and get into the car," replied Lanark.

It was an ordinary, unmarked police car. It would be a long time before Lanark's unit would get a replacement for the Jaguar, if ever.

"Now, exactly where is this place called Danny Boy's?" asked Shannon.

"700 block of Rush, Old Town area, just off the main drag," said Lanark, "on Erie."

"Got it."

The entire way to the nightclub, Lanark and Ames were silent. The silence made Shannon edgy. Somewhere in that silence was the question on her mind, and it seemed lodged too in Lanark's mind: How was Ames connected to the killer? Was he a "brother"? Had he some special connection to the mutilation deaths? A relationship with a voodoo priestess of some sort? Was that why he'd sent them to Ito Colucci?

As if to answer their unspoken question, Ames began to talk freely. "I feel him nearby."

"The killer?"

"I don't know that he is the killer, only that he knows . . . knows about the killings, and can tell us. He wants us to catch him so that he can tell us."

"You know this through feelings?" asked Lanark.

"Feelings, images, glimpses . . . hard to put into words."

They'd had to park in a garage a block away, and now they had returned to Danny Boy's. It had once been a fancier place, a restaurant, now refurbished as a nightclub with as many tables as the building inspectors would allow. It had a sleazy appearance both inside and out, and when they opened the door, they stepped into a black hole of a doorway and this opened onto the bar. On stage, full-frontal nudity was being whipped up and down and about in the faces of the patrons, as a stripper was just finishing up her act.

They found a table near the back that was empty. A look around the place told them that most of the audience was male, but there were a number of women with male escorts. Very soon a waitress found them there and asked after their needs.

"I'm buying," said Lanark. "Just won a big contract today, honey, and we're going to celebrate, right?"

"Ohhhhh," cooed the waitress, who'd seen better days and the makeup didn't hide the fact. "What kinda business you in?"

"Retail construction."

"Sounds . . . like you make boo-coo bucks."

"I do, sugar, now about those drinks."

They ordered all round.

"When's the main entertainment come on?" asked Ames.

The waitress laughed. "Honey, you just missed her."

"No, I mean . . . the magician. Marquee outside says you've got a magician?"

"Oh, Morgan . . . sure . . . midnight show's his last. Told me he wasn't comin' back, but the boss, he don't know that and I'm not—well, about midnight."

She rushed away, realizing she'd already said too much. Shannon glanced at her watch. It was close to show time already. "You really think we're going to learn anything here?" she wondered aloud.

275

"He's here," Ames said.

The drinks came quickly. Lanark boisterously said to the waitress, "Keep 'em coming till we either say stop or we drop."

"You got it, handsome."

"What do we do now?" asked Shannon.

"We wait."

Shannon remained doubtful of the course they'd taken, at having helped Ames out of the safety of the hospital. It was obvious, staring across at him as he searched the dark interior of the club for boogies and demons, that there was something definitely and deeply disturbed about him.

TWENTY-TWO

Backstage, in the cramped dressing room, Morgan Lefay Sayer was having a business disagreement with Danny, the owner and manager. It had been a running argument since Morgan had come off his last show, which he'd done successfully without Felix. Morgan had been patting himself on the back heartily, congratulating himself on performing so well without the dummy, when Danny had stormed in. Danny had been enraged, wanting to know where the damned dummy was.

"You just see he's in the act, or you can pack it in and get the hell outa here now!" Danny had shouted. Everyone in the place had been able to hear him. The two waitresses, the strippers—they'd been all on Danny's side at first, saying Felix was so cute and funny, but when they saw Morgan stand up to Danny, they'd begun to take him more seriously, and realized he had a right to change his act how he saw fit.

The stalemate had lasted until now. Now it was coming on show time again. He confessed to Danny.

"I threw Felix away." Morgan's memory of Felix's having returned and having killed Ms. Burroughs was now only the memory of a bad dream. It'd been a sick dream.

"What?"

"Threw him in the goddamned lake, last night. He . . . he was driving me crazy, Danny, don't you understand?"

"You been drinking, or what?"

"I'm stone sober, and I tell you—"

Danny tore back a curtain and said, "Look, damn you! Get the dummy back in the act!"

Felix was sitting upright in a corner of the closet behind the curtain, atop his case, staring out at Morgan. His one eye was closed in a wink, and his damnable grin was one of satisfaction. "Tol' ya' I'd never leave you, Morgan," said Felix.

"Cut that out!" shouted Danny at Morgan. "And cut the bullshit! People come to Danny's to see Felix, not you, Morgan! They come to laugh at the dummy, and the shit you do to people's heads, making them crawl around on all fours like chickens, pluckin' at the floor. They come to laugh, not to see you, damnit! You got that? The dummy, back on stage, or you're out!"

"To hell with you, Danny!" shouted Morgan. "I'm not doing the act with Felix anymore."

"The hell you're not!" shouted Felix. "Whataya think I came back for?"

"Two minutes! You got two minutes," shouted Danny, "and either you're on stage, or . . . or I'll sue you six ways to Sunday! Remember that contract you signed?"

"What contract?" Morgan replied, befuddled. "I never—"

"Yes, *youuuuuuu didddddddd*," cooed Felix. "Well, technically speaking you did, but I put you up to it. Always thinking of *our* future."

Danny had disappeared for the front. Others going by Morgan's dressing room heard him talking to Felix and felt glad that things were back to normal.

"How . . . how did you come back?"

"Your father, Morgan . . . he saw to it."

"My . . . my father?"

"Look . . . he even gave me his hands!"

Morgan lifted Felix's hands to his eyes. They were large, flat dead weights with stubby nails; most assuredly the hands of a dead man.

Felix chuckled. "Helped me claw my way back to you, babe . . ."

Morgan heard the fanfare for his act, struggling with himself right up to the moment he stepped onto the stage. He felt an ominous end would come of this night, instead of the delightful new life he'd planned for himself, a life without Felix. He'd see Carolyn Wamouth tonight. She'd be there at his house after the show, just as he'd told her to be. He'd make love to her again and once more take her home, and he wouldn't do anything bad to her because he didn't have to, because he wasn't saddled with Felix anymore. He could do it if he liked—cut off her hands—or not do it if he liked. It would be totally and absolutely his decision and he could make it without any undue pressure or stress. And he swore to himself he'd do what was right. He believed Carolyn liked him, and that there was a chance for a normal, pleasant, even happy life ahead of him without Felix or shadows of his father following him about everywhere he went.

But now he was on stage, and he opened after the introduction with several rope tricks to warm up the crowd. So they'd come to see Felix and laugh at his antics, and to laugh at fellow human beings turned into groveling barnyard animals. Fine, Morgan Sayer would deliver to their primitive brains what they thirsted after.

A heckler in the crowd called for better tricks.

A voice shouted back, "All the tricks you could handle're at Lincoln Park Zoo; building four, the ape house!"

Everyone roared in response when Morgan, his eyes going up with his shoulders, searched for the source of the voice. He went back to the case at the rear of the stage as if he had no idea how it got there. From inside he heard knocking and, "Get me the fuck outa here! Trying to suffocate me?"

"Ladies and gentlemen," said Morgan, "I apologize for

279

this interruption and for my friend's foul tongue."

"Ha! That's a laugh," said Felix as he rose from the case. "See, folks, I know where Morgan's tongue has been, and I love him anyway."

This drew mixed laughs and hoots. Everyone was delighted with the dirty little dummy, who suddenly grabbed for the magician's crotch where he sat on a stool with the dummy on his knee. "Stop that, Felix."

"Said last night you liked it!"

"Felix!" He had to pause for the howls to slow. "I'm sorry, folks."

"I'll drink to that. Anybody got a drink?"

"You're not old enough to drink, Felix."

"Let me get this straight," replied Felix in rapid-fire fashion. "I'm old enough to work, old enough to make a fool out of you and me up here, but I'm not old enough to drink?"

"That's right."

Grumbles from Felix. "Old enough to be drafted?"

"You'd be turned down."

"How do you know?"

"Flat-footed homos aren't wanted in the service."

"You cad!" Felix cackled, enjoying the give-and-take of the moment. "Did we rehearse this?"

"No, you were late getting here, remember?"

"Oh, yeah . . . sorry 'bout that. I was tied up, so to speak. Darlene, the waitress . . ."

"What do you mean?"

"She had tied me to her bed."

"That doesn't sound so bad."

"It is if she's using you for a baseball bat against intruders."

"Oh, is that what she used you for?"

"That's what it felt like when she was done!"

More howls, tearful crying from some of the patrons.

Felix asked Morgan abruptly, "Why don't you ever wanna hypnotize me?"

"Takes a certain amount of, you know, *brains!*"

"Go ahead, I got brains."

"Could be dangerous to an imbecile."

"Are we going to tell handicap jokes now?"

"All our jokes are handicapped."

"Hey, handicapped people, handicapped jokes."

"I'm not *handicapped!*"

"Yes we are, aren't we?"

"You are now!" He tore off the dummy's right hand and tossed it over his shoulder, making some people squeal and others say, "Oh, gross!"

When Felix stopped screaming, he asked, "Why'd you do that, Morgan?"

Morgan didn't know he had. He went on with the show. "What I mean to say is that when I call for volunteers, I want people with imagination and intelligence, not people like you, Felix."

"Go ahead, try me, try me! I dare ya! Can't do it, can ya?"

"All right, watch my hand—"

"The one on my knee, you rag-fag? Or the one stuck on my backside? You know you perspire a lot?"

"Concentrate, Felix. Your eyes are getting—"

Felix's entire body deflated and he fell away in a dead faint at the simplest of gestures and a suggestion from the magician. He was completely limp. Morgan Sayer gave the audience a signal: His index finger to his lips to indicate that he needed silence to keep Felix under.

Whispering conspiratorially to the audience, Morgan said, "We don't want to wake him, please."

Morgan slowly and cautiously returned the bawdy dummy to his case amid some low-level boos, and one man said, "Let the little guy up, why don't ya?"

"Yeah," agreed some others.

"He's too disruptive during the hypnosis," Morgan said, putting the lid over Felix. "Now, I need three courageous, and intelligent volunteers. You, sir . . . yes, you." Morgan went out to the tables to select people, looking for men and women who were willing, half out of their seats. But when he caught sight of Dr. Richard Ames sitting tall and granitelike in a corner, staring a hole through him, he instinctively moved off. Morgan had seen the dark shadow man for years now, and had for a long time believed it was that objective part of his own mind that sat out in the audience and watched his and Felix's performance. Lately, however, the shadow man had mutated, taking on the form and manner of his dead father. The dark skin was that which had become desiccated in the grave over the years.

He fought desperately to fend off the sight of the dead man in the corner. He tried gallantly to go on with the show, welcoming two of his selections onto stage, positioning them there. Beyond the other side of the floodlights he could sense that the dead man was still out there, still watching him, but he had moved from the corner table and was somehow moving about the perimeter of the room. Exactly where, Morgan was not sure for a moment, not until he saw the black silhouette coming closer now from out the corner of his right eye.

He typically found a third volunteer at this point, but he didn't want to go back out "there." He felt if he remained in the glare of the lights, his dead father wouldn't, or couldn't, touch him with those large hands he was now raising like the flats of two iron griddles up at him.

Then Morgan went rigid because the shadow man was speaking, saying, "Take me . . . take me."

Morgan had seen the shadow man walking the perimeter of the room; then he was suddenly closer; now he was very, very close and it was scary. He'd come back for his son, Morgan; he was even threatening to reach across the lights with his hands and take hold of Morgan. He'd come back for him. His father had really come back this time. It was madness to flee, and there was no place to hide, but Morgan didn't know what else he might do.

"It's you! You!" Morgan stumbled back, pushing past his guests and tripping over Felix's case, snatching it up and throwing it—Felix and all—at the man who'd come up on stage after him.

The case hit Dr. Richard Ames full force, and from it fell Felix, his dead man's hand hard and scratchy against Ames's face. Ames fell in a heap with the dummy atop him, gasping for air, in a paroxysm of fear and loathing. At the same instant, a woman picked from the audience and on the stage had picked up the human hand which Morgan had wrenched from the dummy and tossed. Her reaction was a scream. She was joined by Ames and others in the room, some shouting for the lights to be turned up.

Out the back exit, Morgan Sayer fled, caught up in his own horrid fear. He raced to his car and sped away, never looking back. His dead father would have to content himself with strangling Felix.

Lanark and Shannon had watched Ames get up from the table in the midst of Sayer's act, excusing himself. They saw then that he was moving about the room, getting ever closer to the magician and his dummy. Lanark had said the dummy's hands looked unnaturally natural, but heavy and weighted. Shannon had said they looked like the hands of the dummy washed ashore at Oak Street, and that the dummy itself was a replica. Ames had sat in stolid silence, just watching, as if fascinated with the act. But then he began to roam closer and closer to the stage for a better look.

"What're we going to do?" asked Shannon.

"Let him finish the act. Then go backstage for a chat."

"With whom? Morgan or Felix?"

"See us arresting the dummy, taking him in for a lineup, interrogation?"

"Down in front!" someone had shouted at Ames.

"Better go get him," said Lanark when he realized the man on the stage conducting the hypnotism session was himself mesmerized by Ames. He stood in a state of frozen anxiety, visibly quaking.

"Ames," shouted Lanark, but Ames had leaped onto the stage after Morgan Sayer.

"Cut him off around back! Shannon!" Lanark shouted, pulling his weapon to the screams and shouts of others. But when Ames fell with the dummy sliding over him, it sent Ames into a convulsion of fear. Lanark rushed for Ames, and so did Shannon. Lanark wrapped his hands around his huge friend, holding tight, saying into his ear, "It's all right, Ames! Ames, I've got you! I've got you!" As he said this, Lanark lashed out with the heel of his foot and kicked Felix across and off the stage.

Shannon rushed to Ames as well, and she held onto him and spoke soothingly into his ear. "We've got to get him back to the hospital, Ryne! This is crazy."

"Get the dummy."

Lanark helped Ames to his feet. The owner of the place was shouting bloody murder, and that he was going to call the cops.

"We are cops," Shannon informed him, grabbing one of Felix's arms while the owner grabbed the other.

"What's this all about?"

"Look at the damned dummy's hands, mister! Take a good look! Go on!"

One of the hands, limply hanging by a thread or two, now was slapped onto a table between Shannon and Danny Dunbar. The man almost fell over finding a chair to sit in, his face going white.

"Your magician is The Handyman."

"Christ . . . always thought he was kinda nuts but . . . but nothing like this."

"We're taking the dummy in evidence."

"Be my guest." He let go as if the dummy were plagued.

"Do you have an address on Sayer?"

"No . . . nothing . . . he never said."

"Where do you send his checks?"

"Picks 'em up here."

"All right, we may be back with more questions later."

"Sure . . . sure . . ."

Lanark had already gotten Ames out of the smoke-filled club, and Ames was looking much better outside in the air. "Stow that damned thing," Lanark shouted to her as she

284

came out, tossing her the keys. She popped the trunk and placed the wooden dummy and the human hands inside. She came back around to hear Lanark saying to Ames, "We'll get him! We'll get him, but you, you're in no shape, Richard."

"I'm all right! That . . . what just happened in there, that was my nightmare . . . come true, don't you see? All those nights, it was a premonition . . . premonition of this moment . . . some clairvoyance involved, seeing the sign, but now . . . now I remember, I'd been here before once. Long time ago, not the same place now, but the same sign, same name. The dummy coming at me with its hands at my throat in my dreams, it's over . . . it's happened and now it's over."

"Then you're actually feeling better?" asked Shannon.

"Yes, finally, after all this time . . . I feel free of it."

"Well, I don't," announced Lanark.

"Nor I," agreed Shannon. "Not until we put this guy away."

"One fashion or another," agreed Lanark.

"We need an address on him."

"Somebody inside must know," said Lanark, starting back through the door.

"I'll put in a call downtown to see if he's got any priors. If so, they'll have an address on him."

"DMV," he replied, "much faster."

"Right." She got into the car and radioed the Department of Motor Vehicles. She made her request and said it was an emergency. When Lanark emerged with nothing, she had an address.

"Probably a high-rise apartment complex," said Lanark. "I know the area, near Sheridan and Chase. Suggest we get backup, and have Black on standby."

She radioed all this in. Soon they heard from Wil and Myra, who agreed to get a court order for search and seizure as well as a warrant for the arrest of Morgan Lefay Sayer. Mark and Stokes were descending on the position from another location.

"I just hope he hasn't recently moved," said Shannon.

285

"Any ESP tell you about that, Dr. Ames?" asked Lanark.

But Ames was asleep in the back of the unit. He'd finally come down so far and so fast, it was all his body could do to tolerate his mind.

They got Black on the line, telling him of their recent recovery of a pair of male hands, presumably those of Rhodes. They told him where they were going now, and why.

"I want to be there," said Black.

"We still don't have paper," said Shannon to him when they pulled up in front of the apartment complex.

"His car's a BMW, license-plate number we now have from DMV, and it was seen at the scene of a crime, Maywood, remember? That means—"

"Probable cause."

"All we've got to do is ID the car, then we can go in."

They radioed their intentions to Robeson and Stokes, who were still trying to get to the scene. Ames stirred in the back, woke, and asked where they were. Shannon quickly explained while Lanark went to find the superintendent, or gain access to the parking garage the hard way. Shannon and Ames followed.

Their efforts were thwarted, however, when they found no BMW in the parking garage with Sayer's license plate. He wasn't home. He'd chosen some other place to run to.

"Lost probable cause," said Shannon sadly.

The superintendent was aghast at all the excitement over Mr. Sayer, and yet now he began to remember that he kept what the super considered "oddball hours."

"Ms. Burroughs is always saying the same, though she ain't made any complaints lately."

"Who is this woman?" asked Shannon.

"Next door to Sayer."

"Take us to the apartment, to this lady."

The superintendent obliged and together they found the elevator and rode up.

"Ms. Burroughs seen him come and go at weird hours,

and she says he's always talking to himself at night. I told her it was the dummy—"

"The dummy?"

"He does an act—"

"Yeah, we caught it earlier."

"Anyways, he rehearses all the time. I mean all the time. It's his life, I guess."

They arrived and went for the apartment next to Sayer's. The super knocked and knocked again. "Guess she ain't home."

"When's the last time you saw her?" asked Shannon.

"'Bout, I'd say, Tuesday morning."

"Open it," said Lanark.

"What?"

"You got a passkey, open it!"

"But it's against policy to—"

"Here's your damned policy!" Lanark's gun was in the man's face. "Open it, now!"

The man searched through his keys, grumbling, "Damned cops. Think you own everybody."

"We're concerned for the lady's safety," said Ames in that powerful, full voice Lanark hadn't heard in a long time. Maybe he *was* fully back, Lanark thought.

The door swung inward on a darkened room filled with a stomach-wrenching odor. "Find the light switch," said Shannon.

The super drifted back to the hallway, sensing now that the cops had been right. Something wasn't right inside. All of them felt it, as if a spirit had shot past them when the door opened.

The light in the living room area came on, just a single corner lamp. It showed nothing amiss. Lanark led the way into the bedroom, where the odor of blood and decimated flesh was strongest. "Jesus," he moaned, "it's in here." He found a light switch and turned it on. The mellow beige carpet and white bedsheets and bedspread were covered with ruby splatters that made it look as if a wet cat had run through the bedroom, dripping all over. Across the length of the floor, the stains made a trail to the opposite side of the bed where a nightstand had been pulled over. Her feet protruded from the end of the bed.

"It's her," said Lanark. "Get the super in here for an ID, Shan."

"You sure? Look at this place? Maybe we'd best wait till the body's carried out on a stretcher."

"We don't have time for niceties, Keyes! This is our goddamned probable cause now, and we can get into Morgan-the-mother's apartment."

"We don't need to ID the woman this way. Just take him next door and get the place opened. Wil and Myra'll be here soon with the paperwork anyway."

Lanark relented and turned to Ames. "You're right. Want to come with me, Richard?"

"Got to see her hands," said Ames, staring at the place where the Burroughs woman lay.

"Oh, no!" shouted Shannon. "No way, Dr. Ames!"

Lanark stopped him, standing in his way. "It's not necessary, Richard! Richard!"

"Maybe not for you, but I have to deal with this now." Richard Ames, as tall and as strong as Lanark, was prepared to fight for the right.

"Suppose it sends you *back?*"

"Suppose it sends me *forward?*"

"Dr. Ames," Shannon pleaded.

"I have no choice."

Lanark stood aside, and when Ames went to the body, he was close, looking over his shoulder. "Try not to touch her."

It wasn't necessary to touch her. The woman's arms were overhead and both were missing hands. Blood covered the stems. Ames braced himself and fought back the fear that stared back at him. He struggled for some moments, gritting his teeth, perspiring, but never taking his eyes away from the horror. Finally, he said, "We've got to stop this man, Lanark, tonight."

"Come on, let's take a look next door."

Ames allowed Lanark to lead him away. There'd been no noticeable trembling. Nothing resembling his earlier deliriousness. Shannon exchanged a look with Lanark. They both knew now they'd done the right thing helping free their friend and colleague from the hospital.

"You'll meet Black when he arrives?" he asked Shannon.

"I'll wait for him outside," she replied, not wishing to be alone with the corpse.

TWENTY-THREE

Lanark again led the way when they opened Morgan Sayer's apartment. It occurred to him that Sayer could be inside, hiding, having parked his car down some alleyway. Lanark pushed a light switch and a lamp came on and blew out at the same instant, causing him to wheel and almost fire. He stepped further into the darkened interior, Ames at his heels.

"Hang back," he advised Ames.

Ames replied, "He's not here, Ryne."

"I'm not so sure."

"Why was he so careless with the neighbor's body?"

"I don't know."

"When he was so cautious with all the others, painstakingly so. It's as if . . . as if . . ."

"As if what?"

"A *part of him* wants to be stopped."

"Next thing you'll be telling me is that his dummy killed the neighbor in an attempt to implicate him."

"That's not as farfetched as it sounds."

They'd found the kitchen. "Farfetched as my Aunt Harriet's—"

"Don't you see, he's a classic schizophrenic."

Lanark switched on the light in the kitchen, saying, "Dual personality?"

"Multiple."

The kitchen was a pullman. A fridge, stove, sink, and in

the glare of the fluorescent bulb they saw the sink was covered with a strange object. It looked to be a prop for Sayer's magic show, and it also looked like an object of torture. Inside a heavy wooden frame rested a shining blade, a guillotine.

"The murder weapon," said Lanark. "Damned sure wish they'd get here with that warrant. The whole case could be compromised."

But Ames was transfixed by the contraption that sat across the top of the sink. He came closer, staring, his hand reaching out toward it.

"Don't touch it, Richard."

He looked from Lanark to the instrument of death and said, "There, all about the edges of the two hand holes, it's encrusted with blood."

"Let's check the back rooms, come on."

They had to go through the darkened living room area to get to the short hall with a closet, a bath, and a bedroom. The bath and closet were clear of anyone. They went to the doorway of the bedroom, which stood ajar. On the bed someone was lying face up, silhouetted against the floor-length windows where the curtains stood open. Lanark felt the stillness of the other person in the darkened room, and he believed for a moment that it was over, that Sayer had ended his own life, and thereby cheated them all. But Ames found the light and switched on a flood of light over the bed where another *Felix* lay, his head turned in their direction, eyes open, mouth wide.

"It's . . . it has *her* hands," said Ames, pointing.

"Christ! How many of these damnable little things does Sayer have? And where the hell is Sayer?"

The warrant arrived soon after Dr. Black and his assistant. Black was both pleased and amazed with the sudden progress on the case, the fact they had a suspect and were standing in his apartment. Lanark was less pleased. When Robeson arrived earlier, he'd sent him back to Danny Boy's to shake up the place hard for more information on the possible whereabouts of Morgan Lefay Sayer. Meanwhile, an APB had been put out on the man and his vehicle. All bus, train, and air terminals were being watched. A poster at Danny's place was confiscated to be turned into a mug shot of the suspect, top hat notwithstanding.

Black did a thorough job on both apartments, and his office took charge of the ominous tool of destruction atop Sayer's sink. Photographers snapped pictures of everything at Lanark's request.

Outside the building, Lanark was called over to a radio car. Mark Robeson was now trying desperately to get in touch with him.

"Mark?"

"I've got another address on the bastard," Mark said.

"Give it to me!"

"936 Chase."

"Where does this come from?"

"Seems the owner had a contract with the creep, and the perp put it down as his address."

"Could be faked."

"Yeah, could be, except for one thing."

"What's that?"

"One of the waitresses here, a babe named Darlene, says she's been to his house on Chase."

"That's a go. See you there."

Lanark shouted for Shannon and Ames to join him at their car. In a moment, they were speeding away, followed by two squad cars, lights flashing.

"Where're we going?"

Lanark explained, finishing with, "This time, we're going to nail him."

The siren roared as Lanark punched the gas.

Morris Fabia was a family man with three children and a heavyset wife who knew nothing of the true horror of the policeman's day. He had been out to Maywood VA to see the single handless victim who'd lived through her attack, the woman named Elena Jorovich. He'd made the trip on his own time. He had bribed people to get in to see her when he was turned away. They didn't care who he was. And he had gotten in to see her.

From the first, she was terrified of him. The doctors had said that she had blocked out all memory of the horrible experience, and that it might take years for her to accept her condition and to reconstruct the elements of her past which had led up to the heinous attack that had left her so disfigured. She would, in time and if she gave herself the will and opportunity, learn to maneuver in life with the newest in prosthesis equipment, replacement hands, which were being paid for by the incredible number of dollars that were pouring into the hospital for Elena every day. A trust fund had had to be created for her.

But she was not talking. Could not. She shed not a bit of light on the killer. Some nonsense, gibberish about how she had once fallen in love and that her love was destroyed by a man. She professed to hate all men now, and could not abide looking at one.

She was pretty far gone, Fabia decided, and certainly of no more use to him than she had been to Lanark's crew out of Wood's Hole. Fabia had then quietly disappeared from his failed attempt at gaining some nugget of information that Ryne Lanark did not have. Now, perhaps he had it in the form of Carolyn Wamouth, although the kid was a bit spacey and dippy.

There was much Morris had to protect his family from daily: such items as how terrifying the human mind could become, and even his own deep well of murderous rage against Lieutenant Ryne Lanark. Once he had seen his job in quite simple terms: ferret out the dangerous elements in society and put them away, or into gas chambers, or into electric chairs. But now much of the worse elements in society wore badges! Self-absorbed, self-pronounced demigods like Lanark, for instance. Fabia had once had a simple desire in life, but it had all been complicated by Lanark. He'd once believed that there was only one thing important in his life—getting ahead. It didn't matter how a man of his ability got ahead. If that meant cooperating with the Feds and being a *yes* man to the captain and up the ladder to the chief and to the commissioner, then so be it. If it meant over the backs of less ambitious, or less shrewd men, that too did not bother Morris Fabia. Hell, he was known as the man who had climbed over the back of a dead partner to get where he was. At least, that's what every son of a bitch cop in the department believed— thanks to Lanark and, perhaps, to his honest ambition. But what was wrong with ambition?

He intended to retire on an early pension with all his limbs intact. The IAD responsibility put him into close proximity to players at the top, and allowed him to gain control of many at the bottom. IAD cops were treated like lepers; he knew this going in. It was not something he could refuse. It was handed him by high command. And while it had not appealed to him at first, he had grown used to it.

IAD made others squirm. He liked that. IAD might be hated, despised, disdained, but most important, it was feared. He could live with that.

In Internal Affairs, he was seen as the new Provost Marshal, the MPs' MP, watchdog of morals and rules and regs. Damned near top dog. And the more Fabia was in it, the more it came to suit him. He liked dragging down bad cops. Bad cops should be put away, but not before being publicly humiliated, stripped of the colors before the eyes of the world, shown up for what they really were: lice on the body of the force. And the worst parasitic creature living off the blood of the department was Lieutenant Ryne Lanark, so far as Morris Fabia felt.

Fabia didn't give a damn about circumstances, extenuating or otherwise, and he didn't like whining and complaining.

For the past year he had harbored a hatred that had evolved into a desire for blood, for Ryne Lanark's blood. But Fabia would settle for Lanark's head on a platter, and perhaps tonight he would have it. The circumstantial evidence that involved Lanark in the kidnapping and killing of Tyrrell Loomis had been inconclusive. But tonight he planned on taking out The Handyman himself, right out from under Lanark's nose. He'd make the expense of Lanark's unit stick out like a sore thumb in the department if he could show that through his own carefully prescribed plan, operating on a small budget, he had netted the killer before Lanark.

Fabia knew from his moles in the 13th Precinct that Lanark's people were close to cracking the case. It had been a lucky break that the reporter, Sandler, had called when he did. Fabia had asked that the "witness" be brought to him at a secret location. He personally interrogated Carolyn Wamouth, first dispelling his own notion that somehow Dr. Richard Ames might be the killer. He went over the girl's testimony and took down names and numbers, the most important of which she did not have. She just recalled the killer's name as Morgan, his dummy as Felix, and that he lived in a house in a neighborhood she could take them to. She'd know the house if she saw it, she swore.

Fabia wanted more firm information. He asked about how this Morgan had gotten invited to the party. Who was paying him? Carolyn had given them a name, but the man could not be reached. He was out of the country, and no one seemed to know anything about a Mr. Morgan.

Finally, Fabia agreed to patrol the neighborhood and locate the suspect's house. The search was quickly over when she pointed it out, a two-story graystone with a massive stone porch, a light at the back, a small beige or off-white car sitting in a carport alongside. Fabia had his people ready and waiting when he called in the address for the warrant. He radioed in the license-plate number to DMV, asking for any information on the owner of the car.

They had a considerable wait for the warrant. Meantime, information on the suspect was forthcoming. No prior arrests, a couple of parking violations. His name was not Morgan, but then he may well have used a stage name if he was a magician. But his occupation was listed as an accountant. He was married with one child.

"How old's this information?"

"Several years, Chief," said DMV.

"Drops out, takes up his avocation of magician, wife leaves him, taking the kid with her," Fabia mused, sitting in the car alongside Sandler. Carolyn Wamouth wanted to be taken home.

"Not until you ID this guy for us," said Fabia, snapping at her. He then apologized, saying, "You know how important this is."

She just pouted and closed her eyes, resting them. She'd had no idea the night was going to be so tedious and long.

"You willing to go up to the door, ring the bell, honey?" Fabia asked her.

She opened her eyes. "What?"

"We'd be right behind you. Soon as he opens the door men'll be busting through the back door and the front. One look at you'll distract him long enough. He's expecting you, right?"

"Sort of . . . but, like I said, he was acting weird and he didn't tell me exactly how I was supposed to get back. Hell, I had trouble finding the place even with your help."

They were in a residential neighborhood being encroached upon by the high-rise fever that had captured this area west of Sheridan Road, bounded on the north by Calvary Cemetery and the Chicago city limit running along Howard, the west by Pottawatomie Park and Ridge Boulevard, and on the south by Pratt Boulevard. It was part of the 39th Precinct from which Fabia had drafted uniforms who were on standby but were told nothing.

"Okay, it's damned near time," said Fabia. He got on the radio and gave approaches for the radio units as they arrived. He wanted the man inside taken by complete surprise. No sirens, no lights. On foot from a block away. He gave orders that no one make a move until the suspect came to the door.

"You wait here, Sandler," he told the reporter.

"No way, we had a deal."

Fabia frowned, knowing he might need Sandler again some day. "All right, but don't get in the way."

"With this baby?" he lifted a camera with a high-powered zoom. "Not a chance." Sandler then looked over his shoulder at the Wamouth girl. "Kid, be careful. Moment he opens the door, jump clear and let the chief and his guys with guns take over."

She frowned in uncertainty. She hadn't counted on this.

"Where the hell's that warrant?" grumbled Fabia.

"It's several minutes past midnight," said Sandler.

"We wait much longer he'll begin to get suspicious. He's expecting the girl to answer his post-hypnotic suggestion, right? She's late, he'll begin to wonder."

"I'm not sure he didn't you know, take it off—the suggestion, I mean," she said from the rear. "I mean, I don't feel like, you know, drawn to go up to that door and do this, you know?"

"You're not getting cold feet on me now, kid?" asked Fabia.

She did not answer. Sandler gritted his teeth, wondering why he was allowing Fabia to bully her into doing this. If she should get hurt . . .

She opened the car door and got out. Fabia said, "Damn the warrant. It's on its way. We go in." He radioed the signal that told the other units they were putting the operation into effect. Carolyn Wamouth was taking tentative steps up to the stone steps that led into the killer's domain.

At the intersection sign, Sandler made out the street names. They were at Estes and Greenview. Fabia moved in toward the building, low and commandolike, his weapon pulled. Sandler got from the car and looked for a safe place from which to snap shots with the Minolta. He found some bushes below the porch, and he realized that someone was watching the activity from across and down. He also found a child's toy hidden deep in the bushes, Big Wheels, and in the carport there was a shelf with a used plastic hamster habitat amid the gasoline cans and paint thinner and hardware. Whoever this guy was, he didn't mind being ripped off, Sandler thought. Then the significance of the Big Wheels and the hamster cage hit him. There were children inside.

At the same instant he came to this conclusion, he heard the doorbell ring overhead. Across from him, in the bushes on the other side of the porch he saw Fabia backed by two uniformed policemen, readying to charge.

"Something's not right about this," he tried to tell Fabia, but the door swung open and Fabia raced up the steps, his gun pointed at a man in a dago-T and suspenders. Carolyn did exactly as she was warned. She gave the suspect one glance and she jumped clear, hearing the footfalls and shouting of the policemen behind her, but she too was shouting, "It's not him!"

Sandler had the presence of mind to snap off shot after shot of the man who stood aghast, his arms in the air, pleading for them not to fire. They backed him roughly into the house, pushing him to the floor, shouting, "Police, raid, on the floor! On the floor!"

At the same instant, the back door was kicked in and men and guns poured in, finding a terrified woman in a child's bedroom where she hugged her two sons to her breast, begging for mercy.

They'd raided the wrong place. Sandler knew it in his toes. Carolyn Wamouth knew it. But Fabia, shaken at the notion, would not accept this. He dragged Carolyn in to confront the man in front of his wife and children.

"It's not him. It's not the same man."

Sandler kept snapping off shots, now of the wrecked interior and the small army of men standing about the terrified family with their semi-automatics in hand.

"Hell of a job, Fabia . . . hell of a job."

A plainclothes cop rushed in at this point with the warrant Fabia had gotten.

TWENTY-FOUR

Ryne Lanark and Dr. Richard Ames were the first on scene at the house on Chase Street where Morgan Lefay Sayer lived out his disturbed existence. Robeson was closing in and would be there soon. Shannon had remained behind at the apartment with the Burroughs body to oversee the gathering of evidence there. She had since been joined by Wil and Myra.

Looking at the residential street, no one would suspect that inside the old Chicago home at the center of the block a serial killer ate his breakfast each morning and went about straightening and tidying up, doing dishes and watching TV. Yet there was no mistaking it. In the drive, parked near the rear of the house, was the BMW with Sayer's license-plate number.

"Maybe you'd best hang back," said Lanark when Robeson's car pulled onto the street and parked some distance behind them.

"I'm going with you," said Ames firmly.

Lanark took in a deep breath of air and said, "In that case"—he leaned over and drew out a hidden gun from below the seat, a police special—"take this."

Ames stared at the gun a moment before he hefted the .38 in his hand. "All right."

Lanark radioed Robeson's car, telling him they were moving in.

Robeson said, "Did you hear about Morris Fabia?"

"No, what?"

Robeson had heard something of the gaff Fabia had made, explaining to Ryne that it was a mere three, maybe four blocks from their present location, and that Fabia had thought he was onto The Handyman when he managed to terrorize a family of four instead. "I can see the lawyers jockeying for position now," Robeson said.

"Poor Morris. Couldn't've happened to a nicer guy, huh?" They had a laugh together, and Ames, knowing Fabia and his "bent" nature, especially in respect to Lanark, approved the laughter with a sincere nodding of his head. But he was in no mood for laughter, his eyes again pinned on the house.

There seemed no movement inside. Lights were out. Anyone looking at it would say the resident was fast asleep, but that didn't figure, not after what had occurred at the nightclub.

They made their way to the front quietly, Lanark half expecting a shot to ring out any moment. But the killer allowed them easy access to the wrought-iron fence, and then up the stone steps and to the door and windows. Lanark signaled to Robeson to take the back. He intended a full frontal assault, and when he felt Robeson was in position, he backed up and kicked in the door with two quick, successive jabs at the lock. It burst open on a dark interior that was filled with silence.

"Cat and mouse," whispered Lanark to Ames. "He wants to play games."

"He is a magician. This could all be a sucker's bet," replied Ames, who was uselessly flicking light switches on-off, on-off. "He's cut off the lights, for our enjoyment."

"So where is he? On the street, on the run? His car's been left out back to decoy us a little longer, like the body was left at the apartment to get us off his trail?"

Robeson entered from the back, saying, "Nothing out my way."

They found the stairs for the rooms above. It was an old, rambling house with high ceilings and fixtures that one

300

saw only in museums these days. Lanark led the way up the stairs, cautiously followed by Robeson and then Ames. But Ames stopped cold and said, "You hear anything?" The other two were already on the second-story landing.

"*Shhhhhhh!*" said Robeson.

Second-floor bedrooms were assailed, weapons at the ready. Ames heard the doors flying, but nothing else. Lanark discovered another dummy in one of the rooms, and Robeson came out with another in his arms. They did not, however, have human hands attached to them, and for this the men were grateful. "How many of these damned dolls does this guy play with?" asked Robeson, who'd seen another such dummy lying on the kitchen floor. It had so startled him that he'd almost blown its face away.

Again, Ames heard the soft human voice he'd heard before, buzzing and far away like a radio playing in another room.

"Now, do you hear it?" he asked the other men, who came to a stop at the bottom of the stairs. "Kitchen?" he asked Lanark.

"No," said Robeson, "nobody in there." Robeson looked queerly at Ames, and then he exchanged a curious look with Lanark, his shoulder rising in a questioning gesture.

Lanark hadn't heard a thing either. And Ames seemed on the edge; he was perhaps on the verge of another *psychic storm*, as Dr. Corby had called it. Lanark wondered if he should not usher Ames out of this place immediately.

Just the same, Ames determined the noise was coming from the direction of the kitchen, and followed it to that room. There, Lanark and Ames saw another guillotine straddling the sink. Ames went right to it, as if drawn to it—as if the killing weapon had been making the sounds he alone heard in his head. Robeson had gone by the metal and wood contraption but hadn't paid it any heed. So innocuous did it appear in the kitchen, in the dark, it might be just another appliance. Now, with Lanark and

Ames showing so much interest, he realized what it was he had overlooked—the murder weapon.

"There is a door in this room . . . leads to . . . a basement," said Ames as he began to explore the perimeters of the kitchen. "Here, over here."

Lanark went to where Ames had drifted like a dowsing rod, honing in on Morgan Sayer through psychic touch, because in all actuality there hadn't been any sounds made anywhere in the house other than those made by the cops.

"Go out to the car, Mark, and get us some flashlights."

"Sure, be right back."

The sounds in Ames's head seemed to increase. He put his hands up to his ears as if they'd become deafening. "Terrible fear and pain," he muttered. "He's down there in the dark. It's a grave he's dug himself."

"You're sure?"

"I'm certain of it."

Lanark placed his gun to his cheek before slowly pulling back the door.

"You won't need that," said Ames.

"What?"

"The gun . . . you won't need it."

"You telling me he's unarmed?"

"He's unmanned, helpless."

"Helpless enough to kill three people, maim a fourth?"

"He's frightened, I tell you."

Lanark knew that frightened people could be just as dangerous as drunk people, or people brave on PCP. "Just the same, I'll keep this handy."

Mark returned with the lights, panting. "Other units have converged on the house. We've got backup you would not believe. If he is in here, he's got no way out." Mark loudly repeated it down the black hole for Sayer to hear: "No way out, mother!"

"He's freaked out, Lanark," said Ames.

"Freaked-out people kill, Ames."

"You can take him alive."

"I will, if I can."

"Sure, sure you will."

Lanark stared into Ames's eyes. Ames truly believed he'd murder the creep below if he was given the slightest provocation. "All right, Mark . . . you go down for him, and I'll back your play."

"Let me go," said Ames.

"What? No way, Doc."

"He's finished, Lanark."

"You don't know that."

"He'll offer no resistance."

"I'll believe that when I see it."

Some uniforms came through the back door, making Lanark look away. Ames snatched one of the lights from Robeson and rushed down into the depths of the basement. Lanark cursed and called after him, rushing behind, followed by Robeson.

When Lanark got to the bottom of the stairs he was stopped by the force of what he saw at the end of Dr. Ames's flash. The blue corona of the light revealed a workshop filled with tools and a wall lined with little Felixes, all sitting upright, all grinning and staring back at the police, all except one that was centered in the middle, too large and ungainly for the others, but whose face was frozen in a mad grin and a wide-eyed stare that not even the bright light could bring to blink. It was Morgan Sayer, his wrists bloody where he'd taken off his own hands.

Robeson's light picked up a duplicate guillotine on a second workbench, and beside this lay Morgan Sayer's hands.

The voice Ames had heard was low and guttural, but easily that of Felix, and it now said, "The hand is quicker than the eye. Now you see 'em, now you don't."

"Felix," said Ames, "I want to talk to Morgan. I want to help him, get him to a hospital."

"Morgan is dead. You killed him. You finally killed him," Felix said tearfully.

"He's not dead—"

"Yet," Felix finished for Ames.

Ames turned to Lanark and said, "We need paramedics, an ambulance if we're going to save this man."

"Robeson," said Lanark, "do it, will you?"

Robeson rushed back up the stairs, gratified at the opportunity to leave the bizarre musty basement filled with the stench of Sayer's blood. He wondered why the man, a magician, had cut off his own hands. He didn't think Sayer would live long enough for help to be of any use to him.

"He's gone inward in a kind of self-induced catatonia. He cannot move. Nerves and muscles are stiff. And it's slowed the bleeding process," said Ames. "If we hurry, we can save him."

"For what, a life in a prison for the criminally insane?"

"He is why we have such places."

"So he can be studied like a rat, sure."

"Can you think of any worse punishment for him? A slug to the temple would be merciful, I suppose."

"I see, and you're feeling no mercy?"

"I feel he is pathetic, and that maybe we all are, to a degree, pathetic, at the beck and call of inner drives and convulsive urges we ultimately cannot control. Yes, I'd like this man studied, Lanark, in the impossible hope that what we learn from him could conceivably tell us something about the next Morgan Sayer we encounter. Meanwhile, he's bleeding to death."

Lanark went to the wounded man who'd deemed it necessary to inflict the same torture on himself as he had on his victims. He tore off his shirt and tied off the wounds using plastic bags he had called for from the kitchen, brought in by a uniformed officer who stood trembling before the scene.

"Besides," Ames told Lanark, "your bringing in The Handyman, alive, will send a clear message to your superiors, Lanark. And since you pity this poor bastard more than you hate him, why not send that message?"

Lanark said nothing in return, brooding over the thought that even Ames and his closest partners wondered if he were capable of bringing in a killer alive.

"Father," said Felix, startling Lanark, who saw not so much as a vein twitch in Morgan Sayer's throat when he threw his voice to the dummy beside him. "Father, you can't hurt me anymore. I don't feel a thing."

Ames said, "When he's taken into custody, Lanark, the dummy'll have to be taken in as well."

Lanark finished tying off the wounds, and was grateful he might back away from Sayer's limp, rag-doll form. "How does he do that? Sure, yeah, the dummy's evidence, all of this is evidence."

"You don't understand. He'll only talk now through the dummy."

"Who you calling a dummy, nigger? Hell, at least I knew you weren't the old man! I'm smarter'n Morgan ever was."

This made Lanark look anew at all the Felixes lined in a row. There must be eighteen. He wondered if Sayer would have gone on collecting as many pairs of hands as he had constructed dummies here in his private world.

"You mean to say—"

"He's completely taken over by Felix."

"Schizo, huh?"

"Who you calling schizo, Double-O Seven?"

A paramedic team arrived, and to a chorus of insults from Felix, they managed to stabilize Morgan Sayer. He was helped upstairs and placed into an ambulance, where attendants objected strenuously to Felix's coming along, saying they wished to maintain a germ-free environment as much as possible during transportation.

"Germ-free? What am I, riddled with lice? Do I look that bad, Lanark?"

Now Felix was getting on Lanark's nerves. Lanark drew a circle on his nose with his .38 muzzle. "Just go along with Dr. Ames for now, got that?"

"Uhhhhhhh, yes, sir, Mr. Dillon!"

Lanark wanted to blow the dummy's face away, but he lowered his weapon instead, feeling foolish that a piece of wood could elicit so much emotion from him.

When the ambulance pulled away and Felix was silent

for the first time since they'd found Sayer, Lanark asked Ames, "Do you really think he's out of it, or is he faking, Ames?"

"He's really gone, Lanark. Something deep and dark in his brain has sent him into what may be a permanent state of silence. He'll only talk through the dummy, and it's going to be like pulling teeth to get the dummy to relay essential information about Sayer, about his victims, about his motives, his upbringing and early years."

"You shrinks always think there's something in a killer's childhood that triggers this kind of behavior. Don't you?"

"FBI has interviewed more mass murderers than any other law-enforcement agency, and childhood molestation and abuse, both physical and mental, comes up as the most recurrent theme, Ryne. This much we know. Morgan both hated and feared his father."

"How do you know that?"

"Somehow, he equated me with him at the club. When he saw me, he ran. He wasn't running from me, but his father. We may never fully understand, unless he's willing to cooperate via Felix here."

One of Felix's fake eyelids shut down in a mechanical wink at this point, as if to emphasize his part in the play and Ames's theory.

"What about you, Richard? How are you holding up?"

"Are you kidding? This is the first time in weeks I've felt in control, not afraid of my own thoughts. For a time, I felt like . . . like some sort of Wolfman, and that maybe I was the killer."

"Don't be ridiculous."

"Meaning you never gave it a thought?"

"Not once," he lied, and for this Ames was grateful.

Shannon arrived on the scene, and together they started away, leaving the overseeing of evidence-gathering to Dr. Black and Mark Robeson. Already, Black was inside the house, and one of his assistants was crawling all over the car outside, and a third was in the kitchen, and Black himself was in the basement with the last pair of hands the killer would ever take.

Black swept the hands into a plastic bag and told a uniformed cop to see that it got to the hospital where Sayer had been taken. There was a chance the man's hands could be restored to his wrists if it were not too late, and if a specialist were called in, and if Sayer had paid up his premiums.

EPILOGUE

Dr. Howard Black left nothing to chance. What he had seen of The Handyman's work had embittered him and disgusted him. A man who had thought he'd seen it all, the coroner was shocked anew at what he found in the apartments that had been Morgan Sayer's and that of a female neighbor named Burroughs. He had taken two sets of hands into his care for analysis, one pair given him in a plastic bag by officer Shannon Keyes, which had been taken off a nightclub entertainer's dummy, and the second off another dummy lying faceup in Sayer's bed.

He wasn't half finished with stripping the Burroughs apartment and Sayer's place for clues and evidence when Keyes informed him that Sayer had been captured and they were wanted at a house on Chase Street. Black left an assistant in charge at the apartment complex, and went along with Keyes to the end of this grisly trail. The hands in his bag would have to be matched to Sayer's victims at a later time.

Once at the old gray Victorian structure on Chase, Dr. Black and a handful of medical assistants and an evidence-gathering team began work. Black walked through the house, Shannon and Lanark following. Sayer had been taken out and was now in a hospital, all security measures having been taken. His own severed hands had been located by the paramedics and transported to the hospital with him in the off chance some specialist might be made

308

available to do reconstructive surgery on them. Sayer had remained in a state of catatonia, and it wasn't very clear to Black that an operation of any sort could be performed with him in such a condition. On the other hand, it would be too merciful a way for him to go.

Ames had gone to the hospital, taking the one dummy who'd spoken during his exchange with Sayer in the basement. The paramedics had refused to allow the dummy into the ambulance, despite Ames's protests that the man could not communicate without it.

"This man can't communicate period, mister!" one of the paramedics had said.

Ames had looked to Ryne for help, but Lanark had thought he should give it up. He hadn't been so sure Ames should not distance himself from Sayer, and the dummy.

But Ames had stubbornly gone ahead, taking the wooden dummy with him, waiting all night for word on Morgan Sayer, almost like a father, saying he had a professional interest in the man.

Black's professional interest was in the man's furnishings, particularly the guillotines. He took these into custody, along with bedclothes splotched with blood the naked eye could not see. He knew that with the right chemical application, he could lift bloodstains off the linoleum tiles in the kitchen as well, despite how often Sayer had bleached and washed them. He had his team lift and remove in plastic bags a four-foot square of these tiles. He located preserving agents and tools Sayer had used for cleaning out the center of the hands, stuffing to fill them with, and the sort of stitching material used by taxidermists.

"We're going to fry this guy six ways to Sunday," he assured Lanark.

"Ames doesn't see it that way. He sees his chances of getting off as a mental at about ninety-nine percent," said Lanark.

"Hey, look around you . This is all cold, hard evidence of premeditation. Hell, the man built the weapon—weapons."

One of the uniformed cops was going by with yet another dummy they'd found. Many of the dummies were without hands—*unfinished.* It suggested that if Sayer had not been stopped, he would have continued to collect hands for his dummies.

Lanark stopped the officer with the dummy, telling Black, "Look at this, Dr. Black. The man also made these in his workshop. He's not retarded or slow. In fact he's bright and fast. I caught his act. He'll also prove to have more than one personality." Lanark wasn't sure why, but he found himself defending Richard Ames's position on the killer. "And God knows what causes brought about his warped fetish. And at the moment, he can't even speak without that damned dummy to do it for him."

"All well and good, but the evidence against him is overwhelming. It'll bury him. No jury in the country will see it otherwise."

Black went back to his work, as admirable in his way as Ames was in his.

Lanark saw that the police work was over save for the report. Wil Cassidy was taking care of that end of things. He'd interviewed everyone connected with the finale, and all the unit members had had a good laugh over Morris Fabia's misguided raid. It was likely to result in a suit against the department and a black mark on Fabia's record.

"Take me home, will you, copper?" Shannon asked Lanark in her most sultry voice.

"Ten-four."

At Morgan Sayer's hearing the defense attempted to get information from Sayer via his dummy, but the court struck Felix down before he had barely uttered, "Your honor—"

"I won't have this courtroom turned into a circus."

"Why not?" shouted Felix. "We already got a clown!"

Sayer's hands had indeed been restored, and although Felix informed everyone he had little or no feeling in either hand, and they were bandaged thickly about the wrist area, he did work Felix's mouth and arms and eyes in a kind of slow motion. The effect was that Felix was on a high.

"Get that dummy out of here, now!" ordered the judge.

The bailiff approached and Felix said, "Nice uniform, honey. What're you, Salvation Army?"

As the bailiff carried Felix from the room, Sayer threw his voice completely across to where he was, saying, "Pussies, you're all pussies." The bailiff nearly jumped, dropping Felix, who shouted, "Police brutality!"

"Your honor, my client cannot speak without the use of the dummy," said the public defender. "Dr. Ames, who is a psychiatrist, will attest to this."

"No to the dummy," said the judge.

Thereafter Dr. Richard Ames became the central focus of the hearing. He was called to make remarks on the alleged killer and why he was driven to his actions. Ames knew more about Sayer's motivations than anyone in the room, including Sayer himself, who sat through the hearing still locked in a semi-catatonic state.

The judge saw no reason not to bind him over for trial, despite his condition. Ames warned the judge that on appeal, due to the fact Sayer was being denied his civil rights, he'd win and would go free due to the stupidity and rigidity of the court. Ames was fined for contempt of court, and Sayer was remaindered over to a prison for the mentally disturbed until the trial date.

Ames visited Sayer day after day, taking Felix with him to have long conversations with Sayer through Felix, his literal "mouthpiece." Ames taped their conversations, and began to put together a complete profile on Sayer which shed light on his peculiar phobias and fetishes. He saw a story of horror and betrayal perpetrated on a young boy, of abuse both physical and psychological which far and away outstripped anything Ames's father had done to *him*.

It took time and deliberate, stony persistence and tolerance of Felix's personality to dredge up the whole story, but it was coming, and Ames felt he was finally beginning to truly understand Morgan Sayer. He was prepared to pass along this information to the public defender's office. Sayer's lawyer didn't have the time, the desire, or the dedication to the truth that Ames had shown, but he'd be happy to review the tapes and listen to his interpretation and that of an FBI expert.

Ames kept Lanark and Shannon apprised of the Sayer case, and when he revealed some of Sayer's history, Shannon grew increasingly soft on Sayer. Lanark, by comparison, saw the man—whatever the reasons that motivated his actions—in more the harsh light that Dr. Black had shed on his activities through the physical sciences. Black had determined a pattern of willingness on the parts of the victims, which meant hypnotic suggestion, which in turn had reduced the traumatic impact of the brutal cuts, which had then slowed the bleeding process. He'd told a story of sex and acceptance of Sayer as a modern-day "snake-oil salesman" to whom lonely and desperate people went for help and solace—a bill of goods he had somehow sold them. He was a charmer, a magician, and the hand was quicker than the eye, or common sense. An interview with Carolyn Wamouth and Elena Jorovich corroborated this view of the man. And it was certainly easier to understand and deal with than all of Ames's psychological mumbo jumbo.

Still, Ames pounded home his side of the case, and more and more people were listening. Myra and Shannon began taking time out of their busy lives, and between work on additional cases, seeking out points of fact in Felix's story. They learned about Sayer's father and the history of the old house where the boy grew up from lifetime residents of the neighborhood, many in their seventies and eighties, who always knew the boy would come to no good, who always knew the father was a tyrant and a bully and a "beater." They found the report on the senior Sayer's death and began to punch holes in the way it was handled. The boy was under age at the time and had witnessed his father's death, and yet no one had seen to it that he got counseling or aid of any sort. He was shipped off to an aunt in Ohio, but he soon returned to the house that was haunted by his past. Slowly, a case for conditioning, brainwashing, and brutality was coming to light, and it pointed up the fact that while Sayer was a kind of Frankenstein Monster, he had not created himself. His father had used torture, sensory deprivation, and sexual abuse against him, a thing only Felix knew, according to Ames, since Morgan had so totally blocked this from his own mind.

Time passed.

Lanark got an anonymous tip from a "friend" who claimed to have had close ties to the Tyrrell Loomis gang.

"Oh, yeah? You wouldn't have happened to be in a certain warehouse on Ravenswood that caught on fire the night Loomis bought it?" asked Lanark.

"Hey, they said you were sharp."

"Who said?"

"Trying to get me to hang on long enough for a trace, huh? Sure, I was there."

"How did Loomis die?"

"He died dangling from a hook that you put in him when one of our guys plugged him. The guy had orders."

"Orders from whom?"

"Hey, you speak real good English. You're so smart, why don't you see what's under your nose, Detective."

"Don't jerk me around, jerk! What's the purpose of your calling me?"

"Loomis was my mother's son."

"Go on."

"Jenkins . . . you want Jenkins, right?"

"That's right."

"He owns half the cops downtown, man. He's very well placed."

This sounded impossible to Lanark. The man he was after had been a street fighter and punk, high on drugs when he'd killed and mutilated his mother, his sister, and

313

his father along with three others. Two of them, Lanark had run down and put away. Two was halfway, an average, and Lanark always felt that average was as close to the bottom as to the top. He wanted over the top. He wanted Jenkins and the man called Whitey. These two had put contracts on Lanark's head. For the past year or so Lanark had been hearing a recurrent theme, that Jenkins was untouchable and Whitey was invisible, that they were both well placed and well protected. Information on their criminal records had been erased from computer files. Maybe Loomis's brother at the other end of the line could be believed. On the other hand, what he had to say could be a trap. Traps for Lanark had been set before.

"I need more to go on than that, Mr. Loomis."

"Hey, shhhhh, don't use names here."

"What've you got?"

"There's a cop in the 34th, name of Lou Stansaaaaaaa!"

The phone went suddenly dead, and Lanark got the impression that so did brother Loomis.

Lanark had punched the tape on the conversation and for the entire day he had played and re-played it, trying to determine if it was for real, or all an act to sucker him in. In the meantime, he began making quiet inquiries into the life and record of one Sergeant Detective Lou Stansa, 34th Precinct. So far, Stansa was coming up clean, a shining example of a police officer. Lanark would have to stake him out, dig a little deeper, determine if he was on anyone's payroll and pray that it led to Jenkins. It would all take time and energy and sleepless nights. But he swore to himself that he would eventually avenge the deaths that so haunted him.

Meanwhile, the caseload continued to grow before the eyes of the unit members. Vice had called them for backup on a large operation in the Broadway district. They had their own full-scale sting operation working out of a pool hall where drug traffic had become heavy among teens and pre-teens right on Ashland Avenue not far from where Lanark had attended high school. They had a suspected family murder, two rapes, and now some nut was going about the streets at night, baying at the moon and ripping out the throats of young people and women, his only weapon his teeth. The papers were calling him Wolfman Jack.

Lanark's docket was full, and his sleep disturbed, when the phone rang at his place, waking him fully from an already fitful sleep. He grabbed the phone quickly, hoping Shannon might sleep through the blaring noise.

"Yeah, Lanark here."

It was Ames and he said flatly, "Morgan Sayer is dead."

"Dead? How?"

Sayer was in a maximum-security prison for the criminally insane. Meals were eaten with spoons. Every precaution was taken so that the inmate could not harm himself. For a moment Lanark flashed a picture before his eyes of Ames going off his nut and strangling Sayer to death. But that didn't fit.

"It seems Sayer's hands . . . well, he must have had more control and strength in them as time went along . . . anyway, he strangled himself tonight with his own hands."

"Jesus, his own worse nightmare."

"Exactly."

"You okay with this, Ames?" God, Lanark thought, his words sounded lame, clichéd. Ames had continued on for so long with Sayer that no matter one's feelings about the case, you had to admire the doctor.

"I guess you might say it was his time to go. Perhaps in the next life he'll have a better start. For now, his internal storm is over. Maybe all for the best."

Lanark didn't know what to say to his friend Ames; he was unsure if there was anything anyone could say. "Richard, you did everything anyone could do for the man."

"But nothing for the boy."

"Come again?"

"Lanark, he was doomed to his fate as a boy. We just got him as a man."

"Yeah, I understand." Lanark had seen FBI interviews with the likes of Ted Bundy and Manson and Gacey and others. They'd all suffered abuse as children in one way or another.

"Just wanted to let you know the . . . the results."

"Look, Richard, you've got to now begin to think of yourself, man. Protect yourself, okay?"

"Patient telling the doctor what to do?"

"Hell, yes, if it helps. Remember, you've got friends in the department at the Thirteenth. We're all behind you."

"Thanks, I needed to hear that again."

Lanark wondered momentarily about Felix. The damned dummy had gone to the prison in Ames's car, stayed with Ames at his house, and sometimes was sitting in a goddmned chair in the man's office. Some of this was getting to everyone, including Lanark. The collection of other Felix look-alikes had been confiscated for the hearing, and it was planned that they would be either incinerated at the cost of the city in the city incinerators, or donated to needy children's organizations. Either way, Ames's Felix had to go with the others. Lanark broached the subject when Ames cut him off.

"Not to worry, I'm having Felix buried with Morgan."

"They going to allow that?"

"They barred him from court, but they can't bar him from a pine box provided by the State. Look, it's my way of putting an end to the entire episode."

"Catharsis, huh?"

"And thank God. Good night, and thanks for remaining a good friend, Lanark."

"Any time."

Ames was gone. Lanark dropped the phone back onto its carriage. Shannon rolled over and put her arms around him. "You can be so gentle and diplomatic and sensitive, Ryne. I certainly would like to see that side of you more often."

"You heard then?"

"Sayer's dead, yes."

"For the best, perhaps."

"Think anyone'll shed a tear for The Handyman?"

"Ames perhaps . . . you and me, maybe?"

"Think we've learned anything by all this?" she asked.

"I don't know. Ames may shed some light on why such offenses against innocent people are perpetrated, but that won't stop the flood of brutality, no. Something out there called evil perpetuates itself through man throughout history. Began with evolution, the kill-or-be-killed mentality in the genes of apes, caveman, down through the ages, highlighted every so often by a Jack the Ripper, a Vlad the Impaler, de Sade, until we can no longer ignore the fact that we all have a dark past, a dark side to the gene pool. Men like Ames know this and understand the criminal mind better than the rest of us. They empathize and they know."

"Hold me, Lanark . . . hold me close."

He did so, and they fell asleep in one another's arms, Shannon dreaming of a doll she had had as a small girl, a doll that she'd become so attached to that she had for years believed in its ability to communicate and feel, cry and argue with her. She was swept back in time to a place of comfort and love and play. She held tight to these images and they allowed her restful sleep.

Lanark's own mind played over the rocking horse he'd had as a child, and the many hours of play he'd gotten from the wooden animal. He had played at being a cowboy, and in doing so he had blown away hundreds, if not thousands, of villainous souls. But now the rocking horse's head turned in his dream and stared back at him there in his cowboy outfit, and the head was that of Felix, just staring. In his dream, the boy Lanark was had shot and killed Morgan Sayer. The body lay on the floor in front of him.

Perhaps it would have been better in the long run if the grown-up Lanark had done exactly that for Morgan Sayer.

PINNACLE'S FINEST IN SUSPENSE
AND ESPIONAGE

OPIUM   (17-077, $4.50)
by Tony Cohan

Opium! The most alluring and dangerous substance known to man. The ultimate addiction, ensnaring all in its lethal web. A nerve-shattering odyssey into the perilous heart of the international narcotics trade, racing from the beaches of Miami to the treacherous twisting alleyways of the Casbah, from the slums of Paris to the teeming Hong Kong streets to the war-torn jungles of Vietnam.

LAST JUDGMENT   (17-114, $4.50)
by Richard Hugo

Seeking vengeance for the senseless murders of his brother, sister-in-law, and their three children, former S.A.S. agent James Ross plunges into the perilous world of fanatical terrorism to prevent a centuries-old vision of the Apocalypse from becoming reality, as the approaching New Year threatens to usher in mankind's dreaded Last Judgment.

THE JASMINE SLOOP   (17-113, $3.95)
by Frank J. Kenmore

A man of rare and lethal talents, Colin Smallpiece has crammed ten lifetimes into his twenty-seven years. Now, drawn from his peaceful academic life into a perilous web of intrigue and assassination, the ex-intelligence operative has set off to locate a U.S. senator who has vanished mysteriously from the face of the Earth.

ED MCBAIN'S MYSTERIES

JACK AND THE BEANSTALK (17-083, $3.95)
Jack's dead, stabbed fourteen times. And thirty-six thousand's missing in cash. Matthew's questions are turning up some long-buried pasts, a second dead body, and some beautiful suspects. Like Sunny, Jack's sister, a surfer boy's fantasy, a delicious girl with some unsavory secrets.

BEAUTY AND THE BEAST (17-134, $3.95)
She was spectacular—an unforgettable beauty with exquisite features. On Monday, the same woman appeared in Hope's law office to file a complaint. She had been badly beaten—a mass of purple bruises with one eye swollen completely shut. And she wanted her husband put away before something worse happened. Her body was discovered on Tuesday, bound with wire coat hangers and burned to a crisp. But her husband—big, and monstrously ugly—denies the charge.